THEY S[...]

Su[rrou]nded by an e[...] faces, Scaro the Mrem marched his warriors toward the keep. Above his head, he saw the flash of metal. More Liskash guards awaited them on the first level.

"Clawmaster...?"

"Drillmaster, I see," Emoro said mildly. "Don't let it happen."

"Yes, sir," Scaro said.

"Climb," the brass-hat said, as they reached the wall. Scaro put a foot on the rung. "The females first!"

"Sorry, I don't understand your accent," Scaro said. He swung up, signing to his men to follow him.

When they had all reached the first walkway, lizard guards reached out to seize him.

"Lord Tae wants only the females," their commander said to the brass-hat. "Chain them and kill the rest."

Scaro waited just long enough for one of the lumbering fools to come toward him with the chain in its hands. He stepped forward, grabbed the hanging links, and elbowed the guard in the face.

Momentarily stunned, it let go of the hank of chain and clapped its hands to its face. Scaro came around with a roundhouse kick and knocked the guard off the wall. The guards took so long to react that he had time to whip another with the armful of chain.

"Go, Dancers," Scaro gritted, swinging the chain back and forth in a deadly figure-eight. The enemy tried to pass, but he smacked down one after another. Blood lust rose in him as white bones pierced through gray skin and green blood spattered the walls.

EXILED

CLAN OF THE CLAW
BOOK ONE

S.M. Stirling
Harry Turtledove
Jody Lynn Nye
John Ringo
Michael Z. Williamson

Exiled: Clan of the Claw

This is a work of fiction. All the characters and events portrayed in this book are fictional, and any resemblance to real people or incidents is purely coincidental.

A Baen Books Original

Baen Publishing Enterprises
P.O. Box 1403
Riverdale, NY 10471
www.baen.com

ISBN: 978-1-4516-3788-5

Cover art by Stephen Hickman

First paperback printing, July 2012

Library of Congress Control Number: 2011020951

Distributed by Simon & Schuster
1230 Avenue of the Americas
New York, NY 10020

Pages by Joy Freeman (www.pagesbyjoy.com)
Printed in the United States of America

To Midnight, Lila and Cassandra

CONTENTS

INTRODUCTION

THE MREM ARE DESCENDED FROM CATS, JUST AS humans share an ancestor with apes. Which brings up the question as to why would any carnivore need intelligence. Squishy, tasty humans needed to evolve brains in order to find dinner and not be it. But with tooth and claw, why be smart too?

The ancestors of the Mrem faced just as great a challenge as we hairless apes did. It occurred simply because there are few asteroids in their solar system. Asteroids? Huh? Going a bit astray here? Actually it is straightforward. With no asteroid hits, there would be no great extinctions and the age of reptiles would never have really ended. Given tens of millions of extra years one of the descendants of the first reptiles would have reacted to their own fierce competitiveness by very slowly developing both their own kind of intelligence and more. Other creatures, even herd animals, would too have needed to develop better defenses and had time to do so. Mammals would have evolved, too, but always under pressure from the cold-blooded, reptilian Liskash.

The Liskash ruled unchallenged for literally millions

of years. They developed a basically static society based upon local dominance by the mentally most powerful male. Then came the ice ages. In the colder northern plains, useless and ignored by the Liskash, the Mrem evolved from pack hunters to intelligence. At first the Liskash were slow to react. They saw the furry upstarts mostly as a source of slightly more superior slaves, and occasionally food. The Mrem fought back, as pack hunting cats would, forming fiercely independent clans.

At the end of the current ice age there are hundreds of Mrem clans all competing for the same limited grazing lands. The clans rarely cooperated. The population grew much faster than the glaciers retreated. There came a time when there was not enough land to support all the clan's herds. Clans who could not keep or take grazing land starved. The battles between clans were fierce. So vicious that some clans chose to face the Liskash, living demons, and move south.

Then the entire world literally changed. A massive valley—picture our Mediterranean Sea as a dry basin—has sat through the now ending ice age as a warm, lush and Liskash controlled jungle. Some of the valley is hundreds of feet below sea level. Mrem tribes, the most aggressive or those driven out, have begun to also live in this valley. Some have even emerged to the cooler steppes south of it. But as the ice melts the seas are rising and in the east the great ocean finds an opening.

Suddenly a wall of water surges as the small width of land that had been holding the rising ocean out quickly erodes away. Within days the jungle becomes a sea. Tens of thousands of Mrem and hundreds of thousands of Liskash die. Those clans trapped south of the new sea find themselves outnumbered by Liskash lords that have ruled there since beyond memory. The Clan of the Claw begins what was to be known as the Great Trek. Their only hope for survival as other than brain-dazed slaves is to march around this new sea and return to the Mrem-controlled northern steppes. Forced to cooperate, the other clans join them in the march or wait to join and assist in keeping the way open. The Trek and what the Mrem learn from it change their culture forever, starting them on the road to civilization.

This is the story of the Great Trek.

—Bill Fawcett

The Mrem Go West

HARRY TURTLEDOVE

And the demons held fast to the Lowlands. Brother fought brother. Yet He saw their plight and spoke to Her that was the land.

"Give back to the grasping sea that which you have taken," Aedonniss asked. "For from that hot land they will enslave the true people."

"This will lessen me, so you as well," the goddess of the earth protested.

"So it must then," the sky god spoke. "Many will be lost, but more will be saved. Better we are less, than every dame and kit a slave."

And so it was that with a trickle, then torrent, and finally as a great tide Assirra willfully sacrificed much of her domain to the sea.

—*The Book of Mrem*, verse seven

RANTAN TAGGAH STARED NORTH ACROSS THE ARMS of the sea—the New Water, the Clan of the Claw called it. His lips narrowed, so that the tips—well, more than the tips—of his fangs showed. Like the rest of his clansmates, the talonmaster called the New Water other things, too: things as foul as he could think of. An angry growl rumbled, down deep in his throat. The New Water was much too likely to mean death, not only for him but for all the Clan of the Claw, which meant for all the Mrem trapped south of it.

A fly landed on the tuft atop one of his upstanding ears. The ear twitched, but the fly didn't leave. He scratched his ear, shooting just the tips of his claws from their sheaths. The fly buzzed away. His ear twitched again, as if reminding it not to come back.

High above the salt-smelling water, a sea bird circled, hunting. No, not a bird: the long, drooping tail said it was a flying Liskash. The leatherwing folded its wings and plummeted, striking the sea like a spearpoint. A moment later, it flew off again, a fish writhing in its toothy jaws.

Where one hunter had luck, others might hope for more. That was a rule everywhere and for everything and everyone: leatherwings and birds, mammals and meat-eating Liskash, Liskash nobles and Mrem. A second flyer dove at the water, visions of a full belly doubtless dancing in its narrow skull.

Something reared up out of the sea to greet it—something far bigger, far fiercer, far toothier. That enormous mouth opened and closed. Rantan Taggah stood too far away to hear the crunch of breaking bones with his body's ears, but it was sickeningly loud in the ears of his mind. A leatherwing was far from enough to sate something that size, but snacks were always welcome.

"Aedonniss!" Rantan Taggah muttered. "What were you thinking when you made those horrible things?"

The sky god didn't answer. Rantan Taggah hadn't expected him to. Aedonniss looked for his folk to take care of themselves and not waste his time. He was a hard god . . . but then, it was a hard world, and getting harder all the time.

Mrem who'd lived by the Old Water spoke of the savage reptilian monsters in the sea when they came inland to trade or to raid. Like any other inlander, Rantan Taggah listened to the tales. Why not? They were an entertaining way to make time lope by. Just because you listened to a story didn't mean you had to believe it. He'd discounted most of what the seaside Mrem claimed.

Now, though, he'd had the chance to see the ocean monsters for himself. The really alarming thing was how little the talespinners exaggerated.

He snarled. No, the *really* alarming thing was that

he'd had the chance to see the ocean monsters for himself. He hadn't gone traveling. On the contrary— the ocean had come to him.

Some few Mrem priestesses and learned males had always claimed the great depression by whose southern edge the Clan of the Claw dwelt was an ancient seabottom. With a great part of the world's water tied up in sheets of ice, land advanced while the sea retreated. Now the glaciers were melting, shrinking, as if ensorceled; and, as the world warmed, water in the oceans piled higher and deeper.

Piled higher and deeper...and sometimes spilled. For as long as the Mrem could remember (and, surely, for longer than that), the Quaxo Hills to the east had held against the Old Water, held it out of the Hollow Lands. Rantan Taggah, now a male in his prime, had just been coming out of kithood when the Quaxo Hills held no more.

Now the Hollow Lands were vanished from maps and charts. Now the hunting clans and townsMrem who'd lived there were either fugitives from their homes or, most of them, vanished beneath waters Aedonniss only knew how many bowshots deep.

Rantan Taggah snarled again. Few of the Mrem had much use for water or for travel across it under any circumstances. And that said nothing of the reptilian horrors like the one he'd seen, creatures that preyed on anything they could reach. The Clan of the Claw—and the handful of survivors from the drowned Hollow Lands—would not, could not, rejoin their kind by sailing across the New Water.

The only trouble with that was, the Clan of the Claw couldn't stay where it was, either. Rantan Taggah turned away from the New Water and toward the south: toward the Warm Lands, the lands where the Liskash flourished best. The pupils in his emerald eyes widened from slits almost to circles, as if he were confronting his folk's foes in truth, not merely in thought.

His clan was rich, as these things went. Peering south, he saw broad herds of horned bundor and krelprep and shambling hamsticorns. The Clan of the Claw did not lack for meat or milk or leather or hair and wool.

But one clan, alone (or as near as made no difference), could not hope to stand against the Liskash nobles and the weaker but still dangerous reptiles the nobles could gather to fight at their side (or rather, under their feet). Not for nothing did the Mrem picture the demons who opposed Aedonniss as being formed in the image of the Liskash. Maybe it was the other way around: maybe the Liskash looked like demons. Priestesses and savants argued about that, too. Savants, of course, would argue about anything. It was part of what made them savants.

There were times when Rantan Taggah enjoyed arguing as much as anybody else—more than most males. What the Clan of the Claw had to do now, though, was not a matter for argument. He didn't think so, anyhow. But he was only too certain plenty of other males—and females, too—would be ready, even eager, to argue with him about that.

✦   ✦   ✦

Looking at Sassin, you wouldn't think he was a god. By the standards of the Mrem, the Liskash noble was short and spindly. He looked even scrawnier than he was, because he had no hair to fluff out his silhouette.

Not, of course, that he would have cared even a scrap of shed skin's worth about the opinions of a swarm of hairy vermin. Like all Liskash with wits above lizard level, he despised, hated, and feared the Mrem. If they had but a single neck, so he could slaughter them all with one great stroke...

But, worse luck, they didn't. He was a god—if you didn't believe it, you had only to ask him—but he was not so powerful a god as that. No god so powerful as that had arisen among the Liskash for lo these many years.

He thought that was a shame. A Mrem might have thought that their stupid god's failure to destroy the Liskash was a pity. All Sassin knew about pity was what he'd heard from captured Mrem he was tormenting. He understood little of the notion. What he did understand, he thought uncommonly foolish. He had trouble believing even the Mrem really believed in the idea. By the way they often acted, so did they.

His tongue flicked out, tasting the air around him. Change was in the wind. Sprung from an ancient race, Sassin did not think well of change. He was not sorry when the barrier of the Quaxo Hills failed and the sea poured over them into the Hollow Lands. He was sorry it hadn't drowned all the Mrem: *that* was a change he would have approved of.

Now the ones who had survived were all astir. He knew what they would stir up, too. Trouble. It was all they were good for.

Sassin stared out from the tower topping his castle. He could see a long way, and he was lord of all he surveyed. Were that ever to become untrue, he would find himself enslaved or slain. Such was life among the Liskash nobles. Even now, some powerful young wizard might be sneaking around out there, plotting to lay him low. Until the enemy chose to strike, he would hide himself from Sassin, lest he be struck first. Though only distantly related to poisonous serpents, the Liskash were close spiritual kin.

Herds of meat animals ambled over the sun-baked plains. Some were scaled, others hairy; when it came to meat, Sassin liked variety. Liskash herders and enslaved Mrem kept the animals moving and didn't let them eat any one stretch of the countryside bare. Some of the Liskash were hardly more clever than the beasts in their charge. The Mrem . . .

An unhappy hiss escaped from Sassin's throat. If he was a god, he was not divinely cheerful. He had the mental strength to rob Mrem of their surnames and hold them in thralldom. That was part of what being a god entailed. But it wasn't easy, effortless, the way it was with most of his own breed. (The nearest Liskash he could not easily subdue, a noble named Hishash, ruled a domain about the size of his own off to the west, and was a god in his own right there.) If he didn't keep a mental eye on the Mrem he'd enslaved, they were liable to recover some of their own personalities and either try to escape or try to stir up trouble inside his realm.

He hissed again, this time with purpose. "Lorssett!" The summons was mental, not oral.

His steward appeared behind him on the battlement almost at once. Lorssett was a larger, physically stronger Liskash than Sassin. He had bigger jaws, sharper teeth, and longer claws. He was, in his own way, clever—he would have been useless to Sassin if he were not. But his powers of mind were minimal. He would never be anything more than a steward; rising to godhood simply was not in him. Understanding as much (which was part of his cleverness), he made a good steward indeed.

The Mrem had rituals wherein inferiors showed their superiors deference. The Liskash neither had nor needed them. Sassin and Lorssett both knew what their status was. Sassin knew Lorssett knew; he could read it in the steward's mind. Had Lorssett been able to conceal from his god what he knew and what he felt, he would have been a different male, and an altogether more dangerous one.

"What do you require of me?" Lorssett inquired.

"Fetch me the Mrem called Grumm," Sassin told him. "I have a new use for the creature."

"Just as you say, so shall it be," Lorssett replied.

"Well, of course," Sassin said complacently. When he said something, it was supposed to happen the way he said it. What privilege of godhood could be more enjoyable?

❖   ❖   ❖

Enni Chennitats was irked with her fellow priestesses, irked with the Dancing because it hadn't gone well, irked with the Quaxo Hills for not being tall enough to hold out what was now the New Water—irked with the world, in other words.

She tried not to let it show. It wasn't the attitude a priestess of the Mrem should have had. She breathed deeply, trying to calm herself and purify her spirit of the nasty thoughts that stained it. She prayed to Assirra, begging Aedonniss' wife to persuade the sky god himself to bring her peace.

Nothing seemed to help. Too many things had happened to the Clan of the Claw and around it for anyone to go on with an easy spirit: so it seemed to Enni Chennitats, at any rate. Some males and females had no trouble, though. They were so constituted that they could not feel the lash on someone else's skin if it happened not to fall on theirs. Even some savants and priestesses were made that way. It disappointed Enni Chennitats, and infuriated her, too.

She walked away from the Dancing that had produced no meld of minds. One of the other priestesses called after her. With a deliberate effort of will, she kept her ears from turning in the direction of the sound. If she pretended she hadn't heard, she wouldn't have to answer.

"Where are you going in such a hurry, Enni Chennitats?" Rantan Taggah asked.

She couldn't ignore the talonmaster the way she had the priestess. If she'd gone on for another couple of steps, she would have run into him. But she didn't want to unburden herself to him, either. "I don't know," she answered. "Anywhere. Nowhere."

His whiskers twitched. He was too polite to come right out and say he didn't believe her, but he obviously didn't. Since she hadn't been telling more than a quarter of the truth, she couldn't very well blame him. He pointed back toward the Dancing ground. "Things didn't go well?"

"No," she said before she could help herself. Then her eyes narrowed in annoyance—whether at herself or at him she wasn't sure. The Clan of the Claw needed a clever talonmaster. The New Water and all the trouble it had stirred up meant the clan needed a talonmaster of that stripe more than ever before. But did Rantan Taggah have to go and show off his cleverness?

"Why?" he asked bluntly. "Has Assirra turned her countenance away from us? Will she not speak to Aedonniss on our behalf?"

Enni Chennitats's claws shot out. Her finger twisted in a gesture that averted evil. A moment later, Rantan Taggah made the same gesture. But he still stood in front of the priestess, waiting for her reply. "Say not so!" she told him. "No, we have no sign of that. But magic is an uncertain business—for us, anyhow."

He showed his teeth. "Would you rather be a Liskash?"

She made the apotropaic gesture again, more vigorously this time. "You know better than that," she said, and waited till he dipped his proud head to show he did. Then she went on, "They *must* be demons. Otherwise, how could one of them hold as much magic as a whole troupe of Dancers?"

Rantan Taggah shrugged. "I don't know anything about that. I don't much care, either. All I know is, if you shove a spear into one of them, he'll die. That's the only thing I need to know."

"If he doesn't spell you into spearing a clansmate instead, thinking it's him," Enni Chennitats said.

"Yes. If." Rantan Taggah scowled. "Well, we'll have to figure out how to keep that from happening, because we'll be traveling through Liskash country—through a lot of it, I'm afraid."

"We are going to travel, then?" The priestess had known it was likely. Hearing it would actually happen still felt like a punch in the belly, though. "We had a good life here."

"We had one, yes," Rantan Taggah agreed. "No more, not with the New Water at our backs. We're cut off from all the other Mrem in the world. The only reason the Scaly Ones didn't jump on our backs before this is that they're hatched cowards."

It was more complicated than that. Enni Chennitats knew as much, and the talonmaster surely did as well. The Liskash rarely hurried in anything they did. She wondered if their being kin to lizards and snakes and other crawling things accounted for that. Lizards and snakes had no will to overcome their natural deliberation. The Liskash did—if Liskash nobles were anything, they were creatures of overwhelming will—but usually stayed slow all the same.

"Some of our clansfolk won't want to travel into the

unknown," Enni Chennitats said. Liskash nobles weren't the only ones who kept on doing what they'd always done whenever they got the chance. The Mrem also like to curl up and go to sleep in their old, familiar haunts.

"Well," the talonmaster said, "we'll have a clan meeting tomorrow to hash things out. The way I see it, if we don't move when we want to, we'll move when the Liskash force us out of here—if we can move then. Better to go on our own terms. That's how it looks to me, anyhow."

"What if the clan sees things differently?" Enni Chennitats asked.

He shrugged once more. "Then they'll have a new talonmaster tomorrow night, that's all. I won't be sorry, or not very. If there's anything more wearing than doing things for males and females who don't want them done, curse me if I know what it is."

"But you've done a good job," she said. "I can't think of any other male who'd be better. I can't think of anyone else the whole clan would follow, either."

"To tell you the truth, neither can I." Rantan Taggah was not a modest male even by the modest standards of the Mrem. He turned to go, then checked himself. "Oh, and a male just came in from the southwest. A runaway Liskash slave, he says. He'll know more about what's going on with their nobles than we do now."

"He says," the priestess echoed. "How far can you trust him?"

"About as far as I can fling a mammoth," Rantan Taggah answered cheerfully. "But we'll want to hear him out any which way. And we'll want your priestesses somewhere not far off—someplace where you can Dance. If he is under a spell, maybe you can draw him out of it."

"Maybe." Enni Chennitats knew she sounded troubled. If the Dancing today went so poorly with nothing at stake, how could she count on it to beat down whatever magic the Liskash had loaded onto this poor "escaped" Mrem? She couldn't, and neither could Rantan Taggah. Still, it was what they had. Without it, the Liskash would have devoured the Mrem centuries before. With it...

They may devour us yet, she thought miserably. Part of her knew that was a reaction to the failed Dance. The rest knew as much, too, but was not reassured by the knowledge. If the Dances failed, the Scaly Ones triumphed. They might triumph all the same. She had reasons for her misery, sure enough.

As Rantan Taggah had looked out over the New Water, so he stared out at the sea of Mrem faces at the clan meeting. The males of the war band looked back, some at him, some at the scepter he held. It was the length and thickness of a good mace. Instead of being topped by a head of flanged, sharpened bronze, though, it was surmounted by a Liskash noble's skull. Those large eye sockets, the domed braincase so much like a Mrem's, the projecting snout with the sharp teeth all just alike...

Only the male who held the scepter could address the meeting. So said ancient clan custom. Most Mrem wandering clans and city-states had similar rules.

Rantan Taggah's hand tightened on the scepter; the reddish wood was worn smooth by many generations of palm pads.

Off to one side stood males who had joined with the Clan of the Claw but had not joined it. They were refugees from the clans and small towns that had lived down in the Hollow Lands. No more, no more. Some of them had fought alongside the Clan of the Claw's warriors and shown their own courage. Others would, when and if they got the chance. Rantan Taggah thought they would strengthen the clan if they became part of it. Another thing to decide on one of these days...

He lifted the scepter high. The males of the clan had been talking among themselves, arguing unofficially about what they would soon be arguing about officially. They fell silent when the scepter rose: it marked the shift between the one kind of argument and the other.

"Do you hear me, males?" Rantan Taggah shouted. "Do you accept me as talonmaster of the Clan of the Claw?"

If anyone said no to the second question, the argument about what the clan should do next would be preceded by an argument about under whose leadership the clan should do it. That would not be an argument with words. Rantan Taggah had thrust a spear into the ground behind him. An axe lay beside it. He wore a bronze sword and a broad-bladed gutting dagger on his leather belt. He'd taken special care sharpening his claws. He didn't particularly expect a challenge, but he believed in being ready even for things he didn't particularly expect. That was one reason he made a better talonmaster than most.

No one called him out. A few males answered, "We hear you!" Most stood silent, waiting for what would come.

Rantan Taggah raised the scepter again. Eyes and ears not already pointed toward him swung his way. "Warriors!" he said. "Most of you were kits like me when the Old Water finally poured over the Quaxo Hills and started flooding the Hollow Lands. Some of the folk who listen here today fled before the great wave whelmed them. Honor to the memories of the males and females who could not get away."

"Honor," the assembled males echoed.

The talonmaster pointed north. "Now the New Water separates us from our fellow Mrem. The Clan of the Claw was always boldest. We were the ones who came out of the Hollow Lands and drove the Liskash before us, even though these warm southern lands suit the Scaly Ones well. We won broad plains for grazing. We won great glory, too."

He lifted the scepter higher yet. The hollow eye sockets of the Liskash skull that crowned it stared blindly out at the Mrem. The warriors growled approval.

"And we won our own salvation," Rantan Taggah went on. "Had we stayed down in the Hollow Lands, we likely would have been swept away like so many others. But we were bold. We pushed on. And so we lived."

He took a deep breath. Now was the time to get down to business. "I know the Clan of the Claw will never be less than bold. Boldness, though, offers us two trails now. We can stay here where we are, cut off from all cousins and kin, and fight the Liskash who surround us on every side but the north for as long as we can. This we have done, and bravely, since the New Water thundered past us."

"That's right!" a male called. "And we can go right on doing it, too!"

"*I* hold the scepter, Zhanns Bostofa," Rantan Taggah said sharply. "Your turn will come, but it is not here yet."

Zhanns Bostofa glowered but held his peace. No one in the clan denied that he was sly. His bright eyes, his sleek black-and-white coat, and the midsection that was thicker than it might have been all showed he'd done well for himself. That fleshy midsection also said he lacked a certain something as a warrior. Most of the time, he didn't need to fight to get his way. Most of the time, the clan could go on doing what it had always done. Most of the time, but not always.

Seeing he wouldn't be interrupted again for the time being, Rantan Taggah went on, "In the end, I think, staying where we are is a losing play. The Liskash nobles hate us as much as we hate them—they hate us even more than they hate one another, which is saying a great deal. They will hurl monsters at us until we are all dead or enslaved—if we let them.

"If we let them," he repeated. "If we set out to the west, along the shore of the New Water, sooner or later we will come to where it stops. We can go north again then, and join with our own kind once more. The Liskash will not look for this, for they would never think to do it themselves. Like their cousins the serpents, they stay in small spaces and travel little. We will always meet new nobles on our trek—they will not be able to join together against us. It will not be easy, but it can be done. A moving target is harder to hit. I say we should move, as soon as ever we may. Now I have spoken. Who will be next?" He lowered the scepter, showing he had indeed finished.

The prominent males gathered near the front of the assembly all clamored to take hold of it. Rantan Taggah ostentatiously ignored Zhanns Bostofa. It wasn't so much that he disliked the black-and-white male (though he did)—rather that Zhanns Bostofa had talked out of turn while the talonmaster held the upraised scepter. Instead, Rantan Taggah passed the emblem of authority to a blocky warrior named Ramm Passk't, a tough, one-eared fellow whose herds grazed lands the Liskash claimed as their own.

"It's like Rantan Taggah says," Ramm Passk't declared in a raspy, carrying voice. "If we stay where we're at, we sit still so the Liskash can aim whatever they want at us. They always have the edge that way. If we're on the move, we surprise them instead of the other way round. And they're slow—you all know that. They don't like surprises, Aedonniss bedevil their scaly hides with ticks. That's how it smells to me." He lowered the scepter.

More shouts from other males who wanted to sway the assembly. Reluctantly, Rantan Taggah pointed toward Zhanns Bostofa. Both sides needed to be heard.

Better, he hoped, to get it over with and then turn the heavyset male's arguments against him. Ramm Passk't stumped over and handed Zhanns Bostofa the scepter. A greater contrast between two males would have been hard to imagine.

"Thank you," Zhanns Bostofa said sardonically as his clawed hand folded over the staff. He raised it high. "I have my reasons for thinking your plan is foolish, Rantan Taggah. First is a plain fact: we are still here. The New Water poured into the Hollow Lands years ago now, and we are still here. The Liskash have fought us, and we have fought them, but that is so whenever Mrem and Scaly Ones meet. I daresay we have given them as much as they want, and more besides."

Rantan Taggah wanted to shout to the world what an idiot Zhanns Bostofa was. But the other male had the scepter. The talonmaster had to hold his peace... for the moment.

"Leave that out of the argument, though," Zhanns Bostofa said with what he wanted to sound like generosity. "It could be that the Liskash will concentrate more against us as time goes by. I do not believe it, but it could be. What I want to know is, what happens to us if we pack up everything we have and start off on this smerp-brained trek Rantan Taggah is so wild for?"

Of themselves, the talonmaster's claws shot out. Had Zhanns Bostofa said something like that without upholding the scepter, in short order he would be lying on the ground with his throat bitten and his guts torn out. He had to know it, too. But no male could be challenged for what he said with the scepter in his hand. Most of the time, Rantan Taggah thought that was a good rule. Most of the time, but not always.

"Rantan Taggah says we will surprise the Liskash nobles by moving from our longtime grazing grounds. He might be right—they could be surprised to find us so foolish," Zhanns Bostofa said. "He might be, and they could be. But he is not, and neither are they. And I can prove it. Grumm, come forward."

His bulk and the presence of his retainers had concealed the sorry starveling male who now stepped out from behind him. A shudder ran through the assembled warriors as they stared at the runaway slave of the Liskash. When a scaly noble took a male of the Mrem as his own, he sorcerously ate the Mrem's surname. Even if the poor fellow somehow escaped his master, as Grumm had, he was never the same again. Part of him was gone forever.

Making as if to give Grumm the scepter, Zhanns Bostofa asked Rantan Taggah, "May I?"

"Yes, go ahead," Rantan Taggah answered harshly. "If, that is, I may have leave to question him along with you."

The black-and-white male inclined his well-groomed head. "But of course." He handed Grumm the scepter.

Before raising it, Grumm stared into the eye sockets of the Liskash skull. His lips skinned back from his teeth; it was as if he confronted a live noble, not one long dead. Rantan Taggah was far from sure Grumm's twiglike arms *could* lift the scepter. After that anxious moment, though, Grumm did raise the scepter high.

He seemed easier once he was no longer eye-to-eye with the skull.

"I am Grumm," he said in a dusty, defeated voice: the kind of voice no Mrem should ever have used. "I was Sassin's slave. I *am* Sassin's slave, even here among you. Some things do not go away."

Sassin! Well, of course he would come from Sassin, since he'd fled out of the southwest. Sassin held the lands west of those that belonged to the Clan of the Claw: the lands through which the clan would have to pass as it began its journey, in other words. "And so?" the talonmaster asked Grumm. "What do you say about Sassin? Or what does the Scaly One say through you?" His nose twitched. He imagined he could smell the rank reptilian stink that clung to the Liskash. It was only imagination, of course. Grumm would be clean of that reek by now. But the impression did not want to go away.

"He knows your plan," Grumm answered. "He knows it, and he laughs at it. He wants you—he wants the Clan of the Claw—to try to cross his lands. He has been readying himself for the fight for years. All manner of scaly monsters await you: everything from snakes on the ground to crocodiles in the rivers to the terrible hunters of the plains to countless thinking Liskash, all moving under a single controlling will: his."

"There!" Zhanns Bostofa said. "Do you see? Do you hear? Do you smell? Only death and destruction will meet us if we set forth. You said the Scaly Ones would not be ready for us. You said it, but that did not make it true."

He was more careful of his speech when he wasn't holding the scepter. More careful, but maybe not careful enough. At another time, Rantan Taggah might have decided he'd bent the rules and call him out. Not now. Now there were more important things to worry about.

The talonmaster pointed a clawed forefinger at Grumm. For an instant, Rantan Taggah seemed, at least to himself, the literal embodiment of his clan. Whether anyone else felt the same way... Again, he had more important things to worry about. "You have heard what you say from Sassin himself, I gather?"

"I have," Grumm said.

"And you know it is true because...?"

"Talonmaster, he let me—no, he made me—see through his eyes, feel through his hands." Grumm shivered at the memory. Rantan Taggah wanted to shiver with him. Mrem were not made to be subjected to minds like that. The Liskash were too horribly different. Gathering himself, Grumm added, "He showed me the truth. I saw it as he saw it. I felt it as he felt it. If the Clan of the Claw tries to cross Sassin's land, the scavenger birds and leatherwings will gorge themselves on our carcasses."

"There!" Zhanns Bostofa said again. "Who knows more of what this Liskash intends than one who has seen and felt for himself?"

"What the Liskash intends is to put us in fear," Rantan Taggah replied. "Plainly, he has done what he intends with you, at least."

"Sometimes being afraid is sensible," Zhanns Bostofa

said. "We have to teach our kits to be careful, or none of us would live to grow up."

"They don't need to jump in the air at every passing shadow, though," Rantan Taggah said. "That is what you . . . may be doing." He left it there. He could have said something stronger, but he might have been wrong. Sassin might really be as strong as he claimed.

Or, no matter what Grumm had seen or felt, the Scaly One might not.

"Will you risk the clan on the strength of your whim? Will you risk our hangers-on?" Zhanns Bostofa's wave took in the males who'd made it out of the Hollow Lands alive. "Will you risk all the Mrem on this side of the New Water? That is what we are—you said so yourself. Is your whim alone so strong?"

"Not my whim alone, by Aedonniss," Rantan Taggah said. The other male talked too much, and gave him time to think. "Let us test poor Grumm here. Let the Dancers see if they can undo whatever magic Sassin worked against him. If they can, if the Liskash was lying, we go forward as I proposed. If not . . . If not, let it be as you say, Zhanns Bostofa." The words tasted like rotten meat in the talonmaster's mouth.

The plump black-and-white male inclined his head. "Agreed."

Rantan Taggah would have agreed in his place, too. Zhanns Bostofa had by far the better half of the bargain. If Sassin was telling the truth, the plump male would get what he wanted, and the Clan of the Claw would stay where it was. Even if Sassin was lying, if he was a strong enough sorcerer his spell would prevail against everything the clan's Dancers could do to oppose it. Only if he was lying and they had the power to beat down his lies would Rantan Taggah get to do what he was convinced needed doing.

Why Aedonniss had made the world so one Liskash noble had at least as much magic at the tips of his scaly fingers as a clan's Dancers could muster all together, why Assirra hadn't softened her divine mate so he showed the Mrem more mercy... Rantan Taggah shrugged yet again. Wonder why the gods had done what they'd undoubtedly done and you headed straight down the track to madness.

Enni Chennitats eyed Grumm with pained sympathy as the escaped slave took his place in the center of the clan's Dancing ground. The male left with half his name exuded misery just standing there. Even with the Dancers all around him, he looked more alone than anyone else the priestess had ever seen.

He gnawed on a scrap of smoked meat. He seemed to eat all the time. If he kept it up, before too long he wouldn't be skin and bones any more—he'd get as remarkably fat as Zhanns Bostofa. And then... And then he would be fat and miserable instead of scrawny and miserable. Maybe that was better. More likely—or so it seemed to Enni Chennitats—it was only different. Confusing better with different was likely to make a new misery.

She wondered whether Rantan Taggah's plan to set the Clan of the Claw on its great trek was better or only different. She wanted to think it was better. Priestesses traveled from clan to clan, bringing news and sharing knowledge (males called it gossiping, but what did males know?). Like most of her sisters here on the Dancing ground, she felt trapped by being confined to a single clan. She craved the trek in a way most of the clansfolk would never understand.

Even so, it might prove a dreadful mistake. There was Grumm, who'd already spent too long under Liskash bondage. Maybe all the Mrem on this side of the New Water were doomed to slavery or death if they persisted in Rantan Taggah's scheme. Or maybe they were doomed if they clung to these grazing grounds like a snail clinging to its rock.

If the gods were kind, the Clan of the Claw was not doomed at all. If.

The senior priestess was a brindled female named Demm Etter. She raised her hand with the same authority Rantan Taggah used in holding up the clan scepter at a warriors' assembly. "Are we ready?" she asked. She wasn't only brindled; she was grizzled as well. But her voice belied her years.

None of the two dozen other priestesses said no. Enni Chennitats would have been astonished if any of them had. If they weren't prepared for what lay ahead, they would not have come to the Dancing grounds. Still, the question had to be asked. Ritual demanded it, and ritual helped forge in the Dancers the strength the Liskash had straight from Aedonniss.

Demm Etter dipped her head. The priestesses Danced in a circle around Grumm, first sunwise and then, at a signal from Demm Etter, deasil instead. They began slowly; they did not want to—did not dare to—spill out their power before it was fully formed. Grumm watched them circle. His jaws worked as he went on chewing.

At first, Enni Chennitats was aware only of the ground under the pads of her feet, of her rhythmic breathing, of her need to hold her place and to keep in time. This was not magic; this was only motion. But out of motion sprang magic. Sometimes. When magic felt like springing. When the Scaly Ones' hot, nasty sorcery wasn't too strong. You could only try. Trying was a magic of its own—so priestesses often said.

Sunwise. Deasil. Faster. Sunwise. Deasil. Faster yet. The world around Enni Chennitats began to blur into unreality. The Dance was the only thing that mattered. Out beyond the edge of the Dancing ground, warriors would be watching, though none would presume to set even a clawtip on the hallowed earth till the Dance was over. Enni Chennitats knew they were there. They faded from her consciousness, too. She knew how much Rantan Taggah had riding on the Dance, and how much she had herself. She knew, but she stopped caring. The Dance was what it was. It would do what it did. And then the clan would decide where to go from there, or whether to go.

At the center of the circle remained Grumm, like a mountain shrouded in fog. Excitement trickled through some small portion of Enni Chennitats that the dominant Dancing part barely noticed. That was the kind of image priestesses needed to form their spells. Now—was it hers alone, or did her fellows feel it with her?

Sunwise again. That was good. That was as it should have been. The sun burned fog away. "Let us see clearly!" Demm Etter said. "Clearly!" Enni Chennitats's excitement grew. The old priestess sensed what she sensed, too, and pointed the other Dancers towards it.

And it was noon, or near enough. The sun stood high in the southern sky. What better placement for it to burn away fog?

The Dance quickened yet again. "Clearly!" Demm Etter called once more. As she Danced, she focused her gaze on poor Grumm in the same way that a cleverly ground piece of rock crystal brought the sun's rays to a bright, hot point. The other Dancers, Enni Chennitats among them, followed her lead. Again, she might have been a talonmaster and they the band behind her.

Like a band following its talonmaster, they met resistance. No natural fog could have lingered round a mountain with such fierce sunlight turned on it. And no natural fog was this. It was thick and cold and clinging. Noxious vapors floating above a swamp might have had something of the same feel to them, but in lesser degree. This was fog fueled by malice and hate: fueled by a Liskash noble, in other words. As Enni Chennitats fought to break through it and see what it concealed, she felt as if she were squelching through slime.

What would happen if she and the rest of the Dancers could not pierce the foul fog? Would they enslave themselves, as Grumm had been enslaved? Better to die quickly; that, at least, was clean. And better by far not to think of such things. Better to believe Demm Etter would lead them all through to victory.

"Clearly!" the senior priestess cried, her voice rising urgently. The fog writhed and seemed to spring forward to choke her. "Clearly! Clearly!"

How strong *was* this Sassin? Enni Chennitats knew he was dangerous, as any Liskash noble was dangerous. But could a single Scaly One beat back the combined wills of two dozen and one Dancers? She never would have thought so, never till now. But her confidence trembled.

"Once more, friends!" Demm Etter called. "We can do it!" What spurred Enni Chennitats like a pair of krelprep yoked to a chariot was that magical word, *friends,* and the *we* that followed it. She could conceive of an immensely powerful, immensely wily Liskash noble. For the life of her, though, she could not imagine such a noble with friends.

The sorcerous fog surrounding Grumm faltered all at once. It was as if the stuff were faced not with Demm Etter and her two dozen retainers and subordinates, but with twenty-five priestesses all alike, all potent. The fog could not attack every one of them at the same time, and did not know against which of them to concentrate. And so, instead, *they* attacked *it*.

Enni Chennitats yowled in triumph as it broke before their onslaught. Now she saw what Sassin had wanted Grumm to perceive, and how much of it was real, was true. Some, yes. She had hoped none would be, but that was a faint hope, and she knew as much. Sassin *was* a Liskash noble, and had no small store of strength in his domain. As much as he pretended? As much as he wanted the Clan of the Claw to believe? No.

Little by little, guided by Demm Etter, the Dance slowed. Enni Chennitats realized she was panting as hard as she could. Sweat dampened her nose, the palms of her hands, and the soles of her feet. Part of her wished she could sweat all over her body, though wet fur would have left her chilled more often than not.

As things chanced, she came to a stop facing Grumm. The escaped slave gravely nodded to her. "He lied to me," he said. He sounded more . . . certain than he had before the Dance. He was still broken—he would always be broken—but perhaps not so badly now.

"He did," Enni Chennitats agreed gravely.

"I will take vengeance," Grumm declared. "I know not how, but I will."

"May it be so," the priestess replied. Maybe the male without a surname was bragging a little, as if to deny as much as he could of what Sassin had done to him. Maybe, though, the Dance had also given him a moment of the extraordinary clarity the two dozen and one used to pierce the mists darkening his spirit. Enni Chennitats did not know which. The power of the Dance no longer held her. She knew only what she hoped.

Sassin stopped awkwardly, in the middle of a stride. Lorssett almost ran into him from behind, which would

have been a fatal breach of etiquette: literally, odds
were. But the lesser Liskash was able—just barely—to
check himself without touching his god and master.

"What is it?" he asked, doing his best not to sound
surprised. He had to assume Sassin had some good
reason for stopping. He assumed the noble had some
good reason for everything he did. The alternative to
assuming that was turning Mrem. Lorssett might not
have been the tallest hill in the range, but he was
no abomination, either.

As for Sassin, he knew exactly why he'd halted. A
sudden pain transfixed him, as if someone had driven
a spear through his head. He knew what that meant:
knew what it had to mean. One of his spells had just
spectacularly fallen into ruin.

His first thought was to wonder which of his
enemies—which is to say, his neighbors—had dared
to thwart his will. He wouldn't have believed Fykahtin
had the nerve. And Pergossett was hardly stronger
than Sassin's own aide: so it seemed from the Liskash
noble's jaundiced point of view, anyhow.

But the way his magic had failed didn't feel as it
should have if another of his own kind had suppressed
it. Which left... For a moment, the pounding ache
behind his eyes made him doubt it left anything. But
if the Liskash hadn't defeated a sorcery of his, only
the Mrem could have.

His hiss made Lorssett cringe. The idea that those
hairy screechers could do anything that seriously
impeded his own kind disgusted him. Everything about
the Mrem disgusted him, in fact. If only the coming

of the New Water had left them all as prey for the scavengers of the deep!

It hadn't. All he could do about that was deplore it. He'd tried his best to make them think twice about invading his lands. Too much to hope for, no doubt: the Mrem commonly had trouble thinking even once. But if they thought they could despoil what was his, they needed to think again.

And, if he couldn't frighten them out of coming this way, he would have to beat them. He wished he truly were as mighty as he'd made that slave believe. That made him hiss once more, although this time only in ordinary annoyance. He'd lost a slave and got nothing in exchange—one more reason to despise the Clan of the Claw. Well, he wished them joy of the escapee. Mrem subjected to the will of a Liskash noble were never the same again afterwards.

The sound that came out of him next was more sigh than hiss. It was also an invitation for his aide to speak, and Lorssett did: "What do you require, lord?" The lesser Liskash assumed Sassin would require something, and he was right to do so.

"I think it is likely the Mrem will attack us soon—attack us with all their strength." Sassin thought it as likely as the sun's rise tomorrow morning, but he did not say that. It might lead Lorssett to ask embarrassing questions. Sassin did not care to admit to his underling—much less to himself—that his wizardry had gone awry.

As things were, Lorssett let out a small hiss himself: one of admiration for the noble's sagacity. "You will fight them?" he asked.

"I will fight them," Sassin agreed. "Am I a smerp, to run under the bushes when hunters fly overhead?" He hated smerps, partly because he hated everything hairy and partly because they really were pests. They gnawed through wood, they gnawed through bones, and sometimes they even gnawed through solid stone. Whenever they weren't mating, they were eating. They squeezed into cracks you would have thought too narrow to hide even a mite. Their beady black eyes were remarkably ugly. And, while you could eat them, they didn't taste good.

"You are no smerp. You are the lord here. You are the power here. You are the god here," Lorssett declared. Pleasure trickled through Sassin; he couldn't have put that better himself. His aide went on, "When you go to war against the furry beasts, victory is assured."

That also pleased Sassin. But he remembered that victory was assured only after it was won. "We will need to summon all our strength to beat them," he said. "Set that in motion at once. See to it. Use my name in all you do."

"As you say, lord, so shall it be." Lorssett hesitated. "So it shall be from me, I should say. But what if . . . certain others . . . do not care to follow my commands given in your name?"

He was not the only Liskash near-noble through whom Sassin ruled his domain. Very often, it suited Sassin's purposes to leave his subordinates in doubt about which of them held the greatest part of his favor. Very often—but not today.

"Use my name," Sassin repeated. "Tell them that, if they doubt, I will visit them mind to mind. After that, they will doubt no more, but they will not be the happier for it." He would put the fear of their god—of himself—in them.

Lorssett recoiled half a step in fear. "As you say, so shall it be. Our archers, our spearers, our fierce beasts—all shall be in readiness before the accursed Mrem commence to move."

"See that it is," Sassin said. "When those hairy creatures move, they *move*. We cannot act like frogs and turtles and sleep through the cold season at the bottom of a pond. See to it that no one misunderstands or goes slack."

"In your name, lord, all will be done," Lorssett said. It was, once more, the right answer. Which meant... how much? Sassin studied his underling. Did Lorssett dream of snapping with Sassin's teeth one day, despite his sorry lack of sorcery? If he did, he would pay for his presumption.

Again, though, not today. Today, Sassin had to arrange things so the Mrem did the paying.

The wind blew hot and dry out of the south. Rantan Taggah smelled the dust it carried. The transparent third eyelids flicked across his eyes again and again, clearing them of grit.

Get used to it, he told himself. How much dust would there be when the whole Clan of the Claw got moving? Herdbeasts, chariots, wagons, males, females? The folk at the back would be lucky if they could see the folk at the front when the whole long column started west.

And the folk at the front would be lucky if they could see the folk at the back. "Have to keep the rear guard strong," Rantan Taggah muttered. So many things for a talonmaster to think about! The Liskash might try to build a wall so the trekking clan couldn't enter Sassin's lands at all.

They might, yes—but Rantan Taggah didn't think they would. Brothers to serpents as they were, the Scaly Ones were more likely to strike where they reckoned the Mrem weakest, and to hit the column from the flank or from behind. Rantan Taggah did more muttering: "We have to be strong *everywhere*, then." He growled, down deep in his throat. How was he supposed to manage that? Too much space, and not enough males to cover all of it.

A voice from behind him: "What did you say, Rantan Taggah?"

He spun on his toes. "Oh! Enni Chennitats! I didn't hear you come up." Not surprising, that, not when the Mrem were light on their feet—and she especially, being a Dancer. He went on, "I was just trying to figure out everything we'll have to do once we start moving."

"You can't know everything ahead of time," the priestess said.

His mouth twisted wryly. "That's something I already do know. But the Liskash can ruin us—*will* ruin us—if they catch us by surprise. So I have to work out as many ways to keep that from happening as I can."

"We will know—we may know—some of what they do before they try to do it," Enni Chennitats said. "Seeing some way into their sorceries is one of the things the Dance is good for."

"You dragged the truth out of Grumm, sure enough." Admiration filled the talonmaster's voice. *Admiration for the Dance, or for this Dancer here?* Rantan Taggah wondered. Here, at least, he didn't need to wonder long. For both, and especially for the lithe, comely priestess.

When there was time, he ought to do something about that. But there wasn't, not right now, and there wouldn't be for quite a while. The Clan of the Claw bubbled like stew in a clay-daubed basket over a big fire. (The clan females still had a few precious proper pots won in trade with the now-vanished city-states of the Hollow Lands, but only a few. You could be as careful as you pleased, but every now and then a pot *would* break. None of the nomads had the trick to making real pottery—those baskets were as close as they came. If one of the refugees who'd escaped the inrushing New Water knew the art . . . Rantan Taggah found yet another thing he needed to check on.)

How was he supposed to remember pots when he didn't even have the time to think about Enni Chennitats? The clan had carved out this domain south of the Hollow Lands a couple of generations before, grazing their krelprep and other herdbeasts in the flatlands here during the warm season and taking them up into the hills to forage when the weather got cooler and wetter. Now they would have to keep going at all times of the year. The Liskash weren't likely to let them rest and graze their animals as they pleased. Rantan Taggah swore under his breath. What *had* Aedonniss been thinking when he made the Scaly Ones?

Here was a priestess standing beside him. He asked her the question. Gravely, she considered it. "There is no sure answer to that," she said at last. "Dancers have debated it for . . . for as long as there have been Dancers, I suppose. Some say the sky lord put them on earth to give us a proper challenge, and to keep us from fighting amongst ourselves so much. Some say they are not properly part of creation at all, but only Aedonniss' waste, which he forgot to cover as he should have because he'd worked so hard making the things he truly wanted."

Rantan Taggah laughed. "Yes, I've heard that. God-shit!" He laughed again, louder. "I like it."

Enni Chennitats held up a slim hand. She stepped closer to him, which made his heart beat faster. "But there is another possibility. I have never heard that it is forbidden to speak of it with someone who is not a priestess, but I know we hold it close. I will ask you to do the same."

"Of course," Rantan Taggah replied at once, intrigued. "What is it?"

"It could be that the Liskash truly aren't part of Aedonniss' creation," Enni Chennitats said in a low, troubled voice. "It could be that some other god, a dark and wicked god, made them for purposes of his own, purposes that stand against everything the sky god stands for. We do not talk about this much, even among ourselves. It frightens us. It makes us think the world may be a larger, stranger, more dangerous place than we care to imagine. But it seems to explain some things the simpler ideas cannot."

"A dark and wicked god..." Rantan Taggah weighed the notion. After a few heartbeats, he dipped his head to the priestess. "Yes, I can see how that might be so. And he would have made the Scaly Ones in his own fashion, as Aedonniss patterned us, the true people, after himself. That is a very large thought."

"Which is why we hold it close," she told him.

A smerp hopped by. When the breeze shifted and brought it the scent of the two Mrem, it squeaked in fright and dove under a thornbush. Rantan Taggah felt a great tug of memory. When he was a kit, how many smerps had he chased while he was learning to hunt? How many of them had got away under thornbushes or between rocks or down holes in the ground? How proud had he been when he finally caught one? And how horrified had he been a moment later, when it bit his hand, jumped free, and fled?

"Are we even smerps to Aedonniss?" he wondered.

"I doubt it, but he does not hunt us for the sport of it," Enni Chennitats answered, following his chariot of thought perfectly.

That was something. Rantan Taggah wondered if it was enough. The Liskash didn't hunt Mrem for the sport of it, either, but hunt them they did. And when the Liskash did not hunt Mrem, the Mrem hunted them. What else did being blood enemies mean?

Liskash and Mrem even smelled wrong, alien, to each other. Like any kit, Rantan Taggah hadn't hunted only smerps and other mammals. He'd gone after lizards and small snakes, too. (One of the first lessons kits learned—those who lived to learn it, anyway—was how to tell snakes that squeezed from the ones with poison in their fangs.) He remembered how strange their blood and flesh tasted after he made a kill. They were different from him in a way smerps weren't.

He hadn't fully understood the difference then. He did now.

"Someone coming to see you, Talonmaster," Enni Chennitats said quietly.

It was Zhanns Bostofa. Of course it was. Zhanns Bostofa thought himself important enough to see the talonmaster whenever he chose. And he wouldn't be happy with the dispositions Rantan Taggah had made for his herds and wagons. No matter when Rantan Taggah placed them, Zhanns Bostofa wouldn't be happy with it. The talonmaster was morosely certain of that.

And he was right. The heavyset male tore into him as if Zhanns Bostofa led the Clan of the Claw and Rantan Taggah were a lowly herdsmale. Rantan Taggah listened for a little while. Then he said, "That will be enough of that."

Zhanns Bostofa stared at him as if he were a krel-prep that had suddenly opened its mouth to display a daggertooth's fangs. "How dare you speak to me so?" Zhanns Bostofa demanded. With his deep, resonant voice, he might have made a better talonmaster than Rantan Taggah—or at least a more impressive one.

Rantan Taggah was convinced there was a difference between the two. So was the rest of the Clan of the Claw—with the evident exception of Zhanns Bostofa.

"How? Because you're wasting my time, that's how. You should be getting your bundor and hamsticorns ready to move. The clan decided that was the better thing to do after the Dancers showed how Sassin had magicked poor, sorry Grumm into believing the lies the son of a serpent hissed in his ears. If you don't want to come with us, you can stay by yourself—but how long will you last against the Liskash with only the handful of fools who stay with you?" Rantan Taggah enjoyed the rare pleasure of being able to say exactly what he thought.

The snarl of rage on Zhanns Bostofa's face took in both Rantan Taggah and Enni Chennitats. "The way the two of you seem so friendly, I shouldn't wonder if the Dance was faked to get the answer you wanted."

It had never occurred to Rantan Taggah that a Dance *might* be faked. Zhanns Bostofa had taught him something, but not something he'd wanted to learn. He wanted to walk away from the black-and-white male and find someplace quiet where he could try to wash himself clean.

But, shocked as he was, his reaction was as nothing beside that of Enni Chennitats. Her pupils filled her eyes, as they would just before she sprang for a kill. And behind their blackness flamed raw, red rage.

"Fake...a Dance?" she whispered. "Fake the power we have through Assirra and Aedonniss? Come with me, Zhanns Bostofa. Come tell Demm Etter that you think she told a lie about the word the Dance gave us. Come on. I want to watch while you do that. I want to see how much of you is left afterwards." She reached out to grab the male's arm.

He sprang back before she could. He might carry fat around his middle, but he could be nimble when his hide was on the line. And it was. He knew it was. "Here, now! Watch what you're doing!" he said in some alarm. "I didn't say anything about Demm Etter."

"You said the Dance was false," Enni Chennitats answered implacably. "How could it be false unless the senior priestess made it false?"

Zhanns Bostofa made an unhappy noise down deep in his throat. "I might have been hasty," he said at last—more of an apology than Rantan Taggah had ever got from him, or ever expected. But Rantan Taggah was a rival, not a priestess.

And, being a rival, he clawed Zhanns Bostofa while the other male was down: "You might have wanted to piss on things so they'd smell more like you. Next time you need to piss, go find a dry patch of dirt, squat, and cover your piddle with dust the way you're supposed to."

He wondered if that would provoke Zhanns Bostofa to fight. He hoped so. Tearing some strips off Zhanns Bostofa's hide might let him forget the idea of a faked Dance . . . for a little while, anyhow.

Zhanns Bostofa's ears flattened against the top of his head, as if he were ready to brawl. But the plump male turned and stormed away instead. His brushed-out tail showed the fury he was holding in.

Rantan Taggah let out a sigh. "Well," he said, "*that* was fun."

"Wasn't it?" The fur on Enni Chennitats's tail rose up, too. "A faked Dance, a lying Dance . . . I should have torn out his throat for that."

"Yes, you should have," the talonmaster agreed. "When they stood to judge you, I would have sworn he had it coming. By Aedonniss, he did, too."

"Do you know what he makes me wonder?" Enni Chennitats said.

"No." Rantan Taggah wasn't sure he wanted to, either. "But you're going to tell me, aren't you?"

She dipped her head. "Remember how I was talking about how there might be another god besides Aedonniss, a god who's to blame for the Liskash?"

"I'm not likely to forget," Rantan Taggah answered. "What about it?" He didn't see the connection.

Since he didn't, Enni Chennitats made it plain for him: "If that god reached out to touch one of us, what would the Mrem be like afterwards? A lot like Zhanns Bostofa, don't you think?"

Till she first mentioned the idea, Rantan Taggah hadn't dreamt there could be any gods but Aedonniss and his gentle mate. Now, watching Zhanns Bostofa's hunched-over form recede in the distance, the talonmaster found himself a believer—a reluctant believer, perhaps, but a believer all the same.

The driver checked the harness on the two krelprep hitched to the chariot. Only after he was sure all the leather was sound and all the lashings secure did he incline his head to Enni Chennitats. "You can get in, priestess," he said.

"Thank you, Tessell Yatt," she said, and stepped up into the car. The wickerwork of the flooring gave a little under her feet. Everything in the chariot was as light as the Clan of the Claw's finest shapers could make it. The less weight the krelprep had to pull, the faster and the longer they could run.

Tessell Yatt stroked one of the beasts on its muzzle before he came back to join Enni Chennitats in the car. Keeping herd animals . . . That, the Mrem had done for a very long time. The priestess still wondered how her folk had got beasts to draw them and their wagons, though. After all, in a krelprep's nostrils what were the Mrem but predators?

And, perhaps just as much to the point, what were krelprep to the Mrem of ancient days but so much walking meat? Whoever first realized the brown-and-white-patched beasts might be more, might do more, must surely have been a male or female of godlike cleverness.

She looked back over her shoulder. As the trek began, her place was near the front. Behind her, wagon drivers, chariot crews, and warriors on foot snarled at one another. Everyone thought everyone else was getting in his way. Nobody imagined he might be getting in anybody else's way. Mrem weren't always right—Enni Chennitats had no doubts on that score. But, right or not, they were almost always sure.

The driver adjusted the broad shield that would protect them both if—no, more likely when—trouble came. The thick, scaly hide of some mindless hunting

Liskash, cured and boiled in wax, would help ward Mrem against the javelins and arrows the more clever Liskash used.

At the very head of the column rode Rantan Taggah and his driver. He looked quite splendid, his bronze scalemail gleaming red in the morning sun. He pointed to the standard-bearer in the chariot beside his. The standard-bearer raised the pole on which was mounted a hand-long claw cut ages ago from the carcass of a huge, vicious Scaly One. The trumpeter raised his long copper horn to his lips and blew three blasts from it.

"Forward!" Rantan Taggah shouted in a great voice. "Forward, the Clan of the Claw!"

Enni Chennitats's cheer went up to the heavens along with those of the other males and females who could hear the talonmaster. At the back of the column, they would probably be wondering what the fuss was about—if they knew there was any fuss at all.

Rantan Taggah touched his driver on the shoulder. The junior male flicked the reins. He called to his krelprep. They leaned forward and began to walk. Enni Chennitats exclaimed in surprise. Someone had ornamented with gold leaf the four-pronged horns they bore above each eye, so they shone even brighter than Rantan Taggah's polished armor. Now *that* was swank!

Tessell Yatt also flicked the reins. Enni Chennitats took hold of the rail as the chariot started rolling. A warrior accustomed to the battle cars could stand in one of them without needing to hold on no matter how it jounced. She was no warrior, and didn't need to make an impression.

Dust flew up at once. The divided hooves of the krelprep dug into the ground and kicked up the small particles. The rumble of hoofbeats and squeal of ungreased axles all around Enni Chennitats filled her head till her ears didn't know which way to turn.

Something small and frightened dashed away from the chariot in which she rode. A lizard? A smerp? She had no idea. She sensed only the motion down there on the ground, not what had caused it.

Spooked birds flew up from bushes and scattered scrubby trees. Their calls of alarm added to the din. High above them, flying Liskash circled in the sky, riding the columns of warm air that rose from the ground. Enni Chennitats hated being under the leatherwings' cold, too-clever gaze. Some of those creatures had the native wit to spy for Liskash nobles.

She might hate it, but she couldn't do anything about it. The creatures glided high above where spears or even arrows could reach. She'd thought what a marvel it was for the Mrem to have chosen to use other animals as tools. It wasn't a marvel when the Liskash did it—not to her, it wasn't. It was a horror.

She kept looking up every so often. The leatherwings went right on circling overhead. Then, after a while, she saw something she liked even less. One of the flying Liskash stopped circling and sped off toward the southwest, wide wings beating with what seemed to her to be sinister purpose. On and on it flew, its path through the air straight as a spear's.

Tessell Yatt spied it, too. "Cursed thing's heading off to tell Sassin what we're up to," he said.

"I was thinking the same thing," Enni Chennitats answered unhappily. "What can we do about it?"

The driver's tail lashed back and forth. "Not one stinking thing, not that I can see. You're a wise female, though. Have you got any notions along those lines?"

"I don't feel so wise, not watching the leatherwing fly where it will," the priestess said, more unhappily still. "I see the problem, but not how to solve it."

That made Tessell Yatt shrug. "Sounds like a lot of life, doesn't it? Well, sooner or later the Scaly Ones'll try and hit us. Then we'll give 'em what for. Maybe they know where we're at, but that doesn't mean they can do anything about it, right?" He bared his teeth. Whatever lay ahead, he was ready for it—or he thought he was, which amounted to the same thing now.

Sometimes *not* dwelling on what lay ahead was wiser. Sometimes. Enni Chennitats tried to make herself believe this was one of those times. "Right," she said, as firmly as she could.

The axehead perched on the battlement to Sassin's keep. Its kind nested on cliffsides, so the Liskash noble's artificial cliff must have seemed a fine landing place to it.

Sassin held a dead smerp by the tail. He swung the ugly, hairy little body back and forth, back and forth. The axehead swayed with the motion, its enormous eyes avidly following the moving hunk of meat. Sassin might not care for the way smerps tasted. Axeheads weren't so choosy.

Had it been in Sassin to like any other living

things, axeheads would have stood high on the list. They were clever enough to be useful, but not nearly clever enough to be rivals. As far as he was concerned, that made them perfect extensions of his own volition. No, it wasn't liking, but it was as close as he came.

He tossed the smerp into the air. The axehead's long, toothy jaws opened and closed. For a moment, half a digit's worth of bare pink tail dangled after they snapped shut. Then the leather-winged flyer swallowed, and the dangling tail disappeared, too. It cocked its head and eyed him, hoping for more.

Instead, he caught its gaze with his own. The axehead twisted on the battlement, trying to break free of his will, but found itself unable. The foolish Mrem said snakes could mentally master their prey and make it stand still to be devoured. For almost all serpents, they were mistaken. But Sassin had that power—that and more.

He reached inside the axehead's mind. What it had seen was as clear to him as if he'd seen it himself. What it had felt was every bit as clear, but he ignored that. The sensation of flying might have fascinated a hairy Mrem. It left Sassin utterly indifferent. He wanted to know what he wanted to know, and everything else could go hang.

As if from high overhead, he looked down on the outsized smerps—so he thought of them. Oh, Mrem were more clever than smerps, but that only made them more annoying and more dangerous. Sure enough, they were moving west, into his lands. They would pay for that. He would make sure they paid. Yes, indeed!

He studied the formation their leader had chosen. His tongue flicked out, tasting the air as he considered. Reluctantly, he decided that the miserable Mrem had some notion of what he was about. The vermin wouldn't be easy to attack—unless they could be provoked into making a mistake.

And that probably would not prove so very hard. Mrem weren't calculators like Liskash nobles. They acted on impulse, like the animals they basically were. Getting them to move the way he wanted them to move shouldn't be much harder than tricking a hatchling still wet from the juices of its egg.

Somber satisfaction seeped through Sassin. He mentally pulled away from the axehead, leaving it alone again inside its long, narrow skull. It glared at him, as if it could presume to believe he'd had no business violating its privacy so. More often than not, he would have punished it even for such tiny presumption. A god, after all, was not inclined to brook opposition from anyone.

But Sassin found himself in a mood as generous as he was likely to know. So what if the leather-winged flyer resented his mental invasion? It had served him as he needed to be served. That was the only thing that really mattered.

He tossed the axehead another dead smerp. Resentment vanished as it devoured the mammal. As long as he fed it, he could do as he pleased. So it thought afterwards, anyhow. It had had a different view of things while the mental violation was going on. But, again, so what?

The Mrem had a core territory where they and their herds roamed unchallenged. Beyond that, on all sides (save only the north, lost now and forever to the New Water), was a debatable land. They could hold it and use it if they came forth in strength. Then again, so could the Liskash nobles against whose domains theirs abutted. Beyond the debatable lands lay terrain unquestionably belonging to the Scaly Ones. The Mrem had entered those lands only as raiders . . . or as slaves.

Now, proudly, Rantan Taggah led the whole of his folk into the lands Sassin had ruled since he overthrew the Liskash noble whose seat they'd been before. At first glance, Sassin's territory seemed little different from that in which the Clan of the Claw had dwelt since coming up out of the Hollow Lands.

Only at first glance, though. Yes, the grass beginning to yellow under the warm sun was the same here as it had been there. Yes, the same kinds of low, scrubby trees grew in the lowlands and along the banks of the streams cutting across the plain. And yes, the same kinds of birds and leatherwings perched in those trees.

But off in the distance grazed a herd of frillhorns. They were unmistakably Liskash, their bare hides irregularly striped in shades of gold and brown and green. Those stripes broke up their outlines and made them much harder to recognize at any distance than they would have been otherwise.

The wind swung round, bringing their scent to Rantan Taggah. His driver's nose wrinkled. "Faugh!" exclaimed the junior male, whose name was Munkus

Drap. Mrem could eat Liskash flesh if they got hungry enough. They didn't care for it enough to want to herd frillhorns—which was putting it mildly.

Not only that: Liskash herders directed their beasts by mental command. Mrem lacked that power. Maybe a group of Dancers could make a magic that would reach a frillhorn's mind, if it was not too alien for such a reaching. But, once more, to what point?

Something ran toward the advancing Mrem from the direction of the herd: not a frillhorn, even a young one, but something that came on two legs rather than four. For a moment, Rantan Taggah thought the Scaly One watching the frillhorns had gone mad and was attacking the Clan of the Claw all by himself.

But no. As the creature got closer, the talonmaster saw it was only a zargan. The Liskash tamed them and used them to help guide the herds and to fight off predators that might harm their meat animals. Zargan were smaller than thinking Liskash, and ran with their bodies more nearly parallel to the ground than did their masters. A long, stiff tail counterbalanced the weight of head and torso.

This zargan hissed out a challenge as it charged. It threw its mouth open, displaying row on row of sharp teeth. Absently, Rantan Taggah wondered whether the Liskash nobles had bred them for great jaws or they'd had them before being tamed.

The krelprep pulling Rantan Taggah's chariot bugled forth challenges of their own. They would have reared if they weren't harnessed. A Mrem in another car whirled a sling above his head. The stone hissed through the air. It caught the zargan in the side of the head. The beast swayed, then toppled. Creatures of the Liskash kind had uncommonly thick skulls, and often uncommonly small brains inside them. All the same . . . The zargan kicked feebly. Rantan Taggah didn't think it would get up again.

"Well shot!" he called to the slinger.

"I thank you, Talonmaster," the other male answered.

The standard-bearer's chariot passed right next to the zargan. In fact, the krelprep would have trampled it if the driver hadn't steered them to one side. The standard-bearer leaned over the rail and shoved a javelin into the zargan's belly. It went on thrashing even after that; Scaly Ones were notoriously tenacious of life.

"One more beast we won't have to kill later," Munkus Drap remarked.

"True enough, and killing it now cost us nothing," Rantan Taggah said. "That's all to the good. We haven't got the time or the males to go hunting Liskash if they don't hunt us."

"We ought to kill them all," the driver said.

"That would be fine, if only we could. Right now, we can't." Rantan Taggah's head swung toward the right. There was the New Water, holding them away from their own kind. How far west past where they were now did it stretch? Many, many days' travel. The talonmaster was only too sure of that. Many, many days' *unhindered* travel. If they had to stop and fight whenever they entered some new Liskash noble's domain . . .

He almost repented of his choice. Maybe it would

have been better after all to do as Zhanns Bostofa
said, to stay where they were as long as they could.
How long would they take to find the place where
the Hollow Lands ended, where there was a free way
north to others of their own kind? How many of them
would be left when they did?

Any?

But if they stayed on their old grazing grounds,
the Liskash would converge on them from west and
east and south. Even with the survivors who'd come
up out of the flooded lowlands, there weren't enough
Mrem to hold them off. That had seemed obvious to
Rantan Taggah. It still did. What suddenly seemed less
clear, as he set out on this great trek, was whether
there were enough Mrem to complete it.

His hand closed on the hilt of his sword. If you were
going to fail regardless, better to fail doing something,
trying your hardest. Waiting in glum resignation for
death to come to you was more the Liskash way, not
that of his own folk.

And they might win through in spite of everything.

He'd made a face when he caught the frillhorns'
scent. The shifting breeze also took the smells from
the Clan of the Claw to the grazing Liskash. They
cared for the odors of the Mrem no more than he'd
liked theirs. One by one, their heads came up in alarm.
They had big, horny beaks and bony crests edged
with the spikes that gave them their name. One of
the biggest creatures lumbered off toward the south.
The rest ambled after it, showing the Mrem their tails.

That did not necessarily mean fear. A swipe from

a tail like that could knock a male off his feet and leave him broken and bloody on the ground. Even the biggest hunting Liskash—which dwarfed both their own more clever cousins and the Mrem—approached frillhorns with as much respect as their tiny minds would hold.

"Well, if the Scaly Ones didn't already know we were on the move, that herd heading off for no reason would give them the news," Munkus Drap said.

"Don't worry," Rantan Taggah said. "They knew."

As far as Sassin was concerned, all Mrem looked alike. To him, all hairy creatures seemed pretty much the same. They differed mainly in size. In stink, and in nuisance value, they were all variations on a single nasty theme.

His own kind, by contrast, were individuals to him. They varied in size, in pattern, in color, in length of snout and shape of eye, in whether they had a scaly crest over each eye socket, in how tall the crest was if it was there at all, in the shape and thickness of their throat wattles, in . . . in all the details that made them individuals rather than hairy—things.

Here and now, they also varied in weaponry and protection. Some had bows, some javelins, some slings. Their leather shields were mostly small. A few wore caps with the fur still on them. Those Liskash had spirit: if the Mrem caught them, they would die right away—or maybe slowly, if the miserable mammals were sufficiently provoked. Others had helmets and breastplates of leather like that of most fighters' shields. Still others, the captains and commanders, wore bronze in place of leather. Some of the officers decorated their armor with little spikes on helmets and shoulderpieces, so they looked a bit like frillhorns.

Sassin went unarmored. For one thing, he did not intend to get close enough to the front line to expose himself to the slings and arrows of outrageous vermin. For another, he had confidence in the magic that could, and at need would, turn aside the weapons the vermin carried. If you lacked faith in your magic, it was apt to fail you when you needed it most.

Surveying the host before him, he told Lorssett, "You did well in taking my commands to my vassals."

"My thanks, lord." Lorssett was also unarmored, which showed his faith in his master. Putting on heavy bronze would have told the world he did not believe Sassin could keep him safe. It would have told Sassin the same thing—and Lorssett would have been sorry immediately thereafter.

For now, the Liskash noble stepped out in front of the fighters his underlings had gathered. They fell silent; their eyes followed his every move. None of them wanted Sassin's eyes to light on him. The lord's notice was much too likely to mean the lord's displeasure. And the lord's displeasure was bound to mean far worse displeasure for the average fighter.

"Males! Fighters!" Sassin's voice was not especially loud, but neither did it need to be. His followers heard him not only through their earholes but also inside their minds. They couldn't not listen to him, no matter how much they might have wanted to. That gave him a certain advantage over Rantan Taggah, but it was not one he understood.

"Lord Sassin!" the fighters cried. He also heard them with his mind and his earholes. When they shouted his name, he knew how much they feared him. Enough to do anything he commanded. That was as much fear as he required: not always as much as he would have liked, but as much as he had to have.

"The Mrem are coming," he said. "Those stinking, hairy beasts think they can go where they will and do as they please. Are they right? Shall we let them?"

"No, Lord Sassin!" the Liskash answered in what might as well have been a single voice. However much they feared him, they hated the Mrem more. Any Liskash noble could always rely on that.

Sassin knew the upstart mammals loathed his kind every bit as much. He knew, but he didn't care. All you could do with creatures like that was enslave or kill them.

"Will they drive off our herds?" he asked. "Will they trample our egg-laying grounds with their stinking, sweating feet?" Dry-skinned himself, he could imagine little more disgusting than perspiration . . . and his imagination traveled widely in the realm of disgust.

His fellow Liskash felt as he did. "No, Lord Sassin!" they shouted once more. The fighters who carried javelins brandished them. They were ready to war against the Mrem, sure enough. He could see it. He could hear it. He could smell it with his tongue. And he could feel it in his mind.

"Forward!" he told them.

"Forward!" they echoed, brandishing their weapons once more. He basked in their approval, the way an axehead might spread its broad, bare wings and bask in the early-morning sun.

And forward they went. The Liskash had better discipline than the Mrem. With their mental powers, captains and commanders were better equipped to enforce it than the hairy creatures' talonmasters. Logic, then, said the Liskash should usually have got the better of the fighting. So it seemed to Sassin; so, indeed, it seemed to every Liskash noble whose views he knew.

Somehow, logic and the Mrem had but a glancing acquaintance with each other. It wasn't as if the Liskash *couldn't* prevail against the two-legged vermin. They did win their share of victories. But their share always seemed smaller than it should have been, and no noble had ever figured out why.

Lose confidence and you weaken your magic, Sassin reminded himself again. This would be the worst time to do that. He cast his thoughts ahead, toward the enemy. Now they would all be in one place, all bunched together. Now he and his fighters could rid the world—or, at any rate, the world south of the New Water, which was world enough—of them once and for all.

And then there would be peace: peace in which the Liskash nobles could lay and hatch their plots against one another, as they were meant to do.

Sassin could hardly wait.

❖   ❖   ❖

Now that the Clan of the Claw had entered lands the Liskash called their own, Enni Chennitats and her fellow priestesses Danced every morning at sunrise, before the Mrem began to travel. They Danced to thank Aedonniss for bringing the light for yet another day, to thank Assirra for letting mercy come into the world, and, more practically, to spy out traps and dangers that might lie ahead.

It was a tricky business. Just as the Liskash's cheating hides helped conceal them out on the plain, so their cheating hearts often masked their sorcery. Knowing what was nothing and what was a deceptive *nothing* often took both native skill and long practice.

Often, but not always. On the third morning of the Dance, the priestesses had hardly begun to move before they swung in unison toward the southwest. Demm Etter spoke the name they all sensed: "The Scaly Ones!"

"They are on the move," another priestess agreed.

"Straight towards us," yet another said. No one tried to contradict her.

"I had better take the news to Rantan Taggah," Enni Chennitats said.

"Yes, why don't you do that?" Demm Etter sounded— amused? Enni Chennitats thought so. Her ears tingled and twitched. Was it so obvious she liked the talonmaster? To ask the question was the same as to answer it: evidently it was.

Rantan Taggah was talking with Grumm when Enni Chennitats found him. That made sense: the escaped slave was likely to know this territory better than any free Mrem did. But how far could the Clan of the Claw count on what he said he knew? The Dancers couldn't sorcerously test every word that came out of his mouth. If Sassin had set more snares inside him than just the one, he might do a lot of harm.

Without preamble, Enni Chennitats pointed in the direction to which she and the other Dancers had been drawn. "The Liskash are coming. I don't think they're very far away," she said.

When Grumm saw where she was pointing, he shuddered as if in the grip of some strong fever. "Sassin's castle lies over there," he said in his ruined voice.

"Sassin lies whether he's in his castle or outside of it," Rantan Taggah said, and laughed more than the joke deserved. Of their own accord, the claws on his hands came out. A moment later, they slid back into their sheaths once more. He went on, "But if he's coming out, he'll be easier to kill. Easier to get at a turtle after it takes off its shell."

"Turtles don't take them off," Enni Chennitats said.

"Well, if they did," Rantan Taggah said indulgently.

"What are you going to do about it?" Enni Chennitats demanded when he didn't seem inclined to say anything more.

"Fight them—what else?" the talonmaster answered. "They aren't on their way over to play catch-the-string with us. Or if they are, I'll be surprised."

"Are we ready?" Enni Chennitats asked.

"We'd better be. One way or the other, we'll find out pretty soon, won't we?" Rantan Taggah sounded infuriatingly cheerful. Enni Chennitats realized he *wanted* a fight with the Liskash. If anything would get the whole clan behind him, a battle against the ancient enemy ought to do it. After a moment, he added, "Are the priestesses ready to Dance away whatever magic Sassin hurls at us?"

"I hope so." Enni Chennitats spread her hands, palms up. "You never know beforehand. What we can do, we will."

"Well, you'd better go back and do it, then." Rantan Taggah pointed in the same direction. The sky was lighter and brighter than it had been even a little while before. Enni Chennitats could see the smudge of dust low on the horizon there. "You're right—we don't have long to wait."

She dipped her head and hurried away. She hadn't gone far before bugles blared behind her. Warriors yowled and grabbed for their weapons and armor. Not all the krelprep were harnessed to the clan's chariots. Males rushed to tend to that. Females not burdened with kits went off to tend to the herds. It wasn't their proper trade, but they could do it for a little while. The more males they freed for fighting, the better.

"Another battle," Demm Etter said when Enni Chennitats came back to the rest of the priestesses. It wasn't another question.

"Another battle," Enni Chennitats agreed. "The talonmaster wants us to stifle the Liskash sorcery—but you'll already know that."

"I've had news that surprised me less," the senior priestess replied, which left Enni Chennitats nothing to say. Demm Etter gestured to her. "Go on—take your place in the Dance. If you think we face less danger than the males, you're liable to be badly mistaken."

"I serve the clan," Enni Chennitats said. Whatever happened to her would happen to the other priestesses as well. Remembering that made the fight ahead seem a little less lonely. She wondered whether warriors felt the same way. They fought side by side, but one could be horribly maimed while the male next to him stayed safe.

Then Demm Etter raised her hand. They began to Dance, and Enni Chennitats's worries fell away in the task at hand.

"Something tricky," Grumm said. "Sassin will try something tricky. He won't come straight at us. He *can't* come straight at us. It's not in him. He has to twist things, the way a snake has to coil to move."

"Yes, yes." Rantan Taggah heard the escaped slave with only half an ear. He was concentrating on his own dispositions, not Sassin's. He dipped his head, satisfied he had things the way he wanted. Most important, he'd posted Zhanns Bostofa and the plump male's retainers as far out of the way as he could. He didn't want them holding any vital position against the Liskash.

He might have been doing Zhanns Bostofa an injustice. He knew that. But he couldn't get Enni Chennitats's image out of his mind. If there was a dark god, a god responsible for the Liskash, and if that god tried to reach out and get his foul fingers on a Mrem . . . Yes, the result would be much too much like Zhanns Bostofa, wouldn't it?

If Zhanns Bostofa was looking at this same question, wouldn't he think the imaginary dark god's meddling would produce a Mrem too much like Rantan Taggah? The talonmaster bared his fangs. If Zhanns Bostofa thought anything like that, he proved himself no proper Mrem.

Didn't he?

"What is it?" Grumm asked.

Rantan Taggah made his lips come down over his teeth once more. "Nothing," he said, lying without hesitation. He set a hand on Grumm's shoulder. "Aedonniss give you strength, friend. Your hour of revenge is here."

"Revenge." The other male tasted the word. "Well, Talonmaster, it would be better than nothing, but not enough. Nothing is enough. Nothing will give me back my other name."

"I'm sorry," Rantan Taggah said, which was true, and which did neither him nor Grumm the least bit of good. Weighted down with weapons, the scales of his bronze armor clattering on their leather backing, he hurried to his chariot.

His driver bounded with excitement. "We'll kill them all!" Munkus Drap exclaimed. "We'll kill them, and we'll tan their hides, and we'll dig up their eggs and have ourselves the biggest fry the world has ever seen!" Not a whisker's width of doubt clouded his eager mind.

"That would be good," Rantan Taggah said. And so it would, if it happened. But how long had Mrem and Liskash hated one another? Forever, or maybe a couple of days longer. Had either ever managed to destroy the other despite that perfect hatred? Rantan Taggah knew too well what the answer was.

Let me win, Aedonniss. Let me drive them back, he thought. *Let them not hurt my clan too badly. We have far to go, and many more fights to make. We can't be crippled right at the start.... Please.* The sky god might hearken to him. Then again, Aedonniss might not. The god had his own purposes, and put them ahead of his creatures'.

Looking across the arid plain, Rantan Taggah watched the Liskash deploying from marching column to line of battle. The Scaly Ones all looked alike to him. That was almost as alien as their odor. People—people who really were people—had their differences. The only difference he'd ever been able to find among the Liskash was that some of them were stronger than others, and so caused more trouble.

If Sassin was like the other scaly nobles Rantan Taggah had had the displeasure of meeting, there would be no talonmasters' duel, as there might well have been when two bands of Mrem collided. The Liskash were too cowardly to lead from the front.

He knew how the fight would go if it went the way Sassin wanted it. The Liskash would get within missile range and then pelt the Mrem with arrows and javelins and slingstones. Once they'd thrown their foes into disorder, they would swarm forward and dispose of the warriors their darts hadn't disabled.

It could work. Plenty of Mrem forces had gone down to defeat at the Scaly Ones' hands. But Rantan Taggah didn't plan to play the game Sassin's way. He'd told Enni Chennitats the Liskash hadn't come up to play chase-the-string. He aimed to make them play regardless of whether that was what they had in mind.

"Let's go," he told his driver. He waved to the cars behind them. Other leaders would be signaling their groups at the same time. The chariot bounced forward, slowly at first but then faster as the krelprep leaned into their work. Rantan Taggah's body automatically adjusted to every bump and jolt. Was this like travel on the sea? He didn't know. Truth to tell, he didn't really want to find out.

The Liskash went on forming their line. They didn't advance any father, though, not with several squadrons of chariotry bearing down on them. Mrem seized the initiative whether they should have or not. The Liskash were more inclined to yield it and see what happened after that.

They were closer now, much closer. Their archers and slingers went to work to keep the chariots away from their line. They might do a little harm that way, but they wouldn't do much. Rantan Taggah didn't intend to slam into them head-on, anyhow. Just because they made war that way didn't mean he had to.

He tapped Munkus Drap's right shoulder, hard enough for the other male to feel it through his armor. The driver steered the chariot off to the right, around the Scaly Ones' left flank. As often as not, a talonmaster worried only about what was in front of him. What would Sassin do with Mrem chariots rampaging in his rear?

What he would do was make it hard for them to

get there. Not all of his fighters were on the front line. He had a good force of flank guards. A slung stone hissed malevolently past Rantan Taggah's right ear. Another one hit a krelprep pulling a different chariot in the head. The beast crumpled, dead, perhaps, before it hit the ground. The chariot slewed sideways and almost turned turtle.

"Nothing's going to be as easy as we wish it would be, is it?" Munkus Drap asked.

"When is it ever? Wishes are only dreams they don't stand up to the light of day," Rantan Taggah said. He wished Sassin didn't have the makings of a talonmaster who knew what he was doing. He'd known the Liskash noble was a strong sorcerer. But the two didn't always go together. Not always, no, but they did here.

Sometimes Mrem, once they got into a position they fancied, would leap down from their cars and fight the Liskash at close quarters. Sword to sword, claw to claw, fang to fang, Rantan Taggah's folk had the edge on the Scaly Ones. If they could manage that favorable position...

Rantan Taggah wished he hadn't thought of Sassin's wizardry a few moments earlier: one more wish that went a-glimmering. A blast of fear made him shake inside his shirt of bronze and leather. He almost pissed himself on the wickerwork floor, which would have been the ultimate indignity for a fastidious Mrem.

The pair of krelprep pulling his chariot felt it, too. They bugled out their alarm call. The one on the right tried to rear despite its harnessing. "No, curse you, you stupid thing!" Munkus Drap shouted. His voice shook, too. All the same, he kept the presence of mind to crack his whip above the krelprep's back. That, the beast knew, was something to be afraid of in truth. The imaginary panic that filled its mind paled beside the genuine article.

And then, little by little, Rantan Taggah's unreasoning fear also fell away. The first relief came from the Dancers. Sassin's spell might have taken them by surprise, but not for long. The herd animals' response also lent him strength, although more slowly. Krelprep and big-horned bundor and hamsticorns had to be able to fight off magic—so many Liskash hunters, both those with Mremlike wits and those without, used it to stun or terrify their prey.

Beasts that had hair and nursed their young were far less adept at making magic than the Scaly Ones. But they had the power to push it off, to keep their own wits unclouded. In the pushing, they also helped liberate Rantan Taggah and the rest of the Mrem warriors.

"Ha!" the talonmaster shouted. "Is that all the famous Liskash noble can do? If it is, now we make him pay for thinking he's a crocodile when he's nothing but a skittering little lizard." The males in his squadron raised a cheer. By Aedonniss, it was wonderful to have his own spirit back!

He looked back and to his left to see how the other bands of charioteers were doing. He didn't see any of them pounding away from the Liskash. That was the first and most important thing. By the noise and by the dust on the other flank, the Mrem there were already mixing it up with the Scaly Ones.

More dust rose, farther away than he would have expected. Maybe some of the hamsticorns had stampeded in spite of everything the females tending them could do. The big, shaggy beasts had come down from the north with the Mrem. They didn't care for this hot weather, and they really didn't care for the Liskash and their magics. Rantan Taggah couldn't blame them. He was panting and sweating, and just now he too had almost been literally scared out of his mind.

The hamsticorns might want to lumber away. Rantan Taggah wanted to get even. "Let's go get them," he told the driver.

"Right you are," Munkus Drap answered. Rantan Taggah didn't know whether he was right or wrong. He hardly cared. The chariot was thundering toward the Liskash. The krelprep had their heads down. Anyone or anything that stood in the way of a charging krelprep would get eight holes in the front and hoofprints down the back.

Some of the flank guards carried spears. The Liskash *could* fight the way the Mrem did. They preferred not to, but sometimes they had to. If they thought they could hold off a chariot charge, they were out of their minds. Rantan Taggah readied his axe. Whatever the krelprep didn't knock over, he would.

And then a shout echoed in his mind: "Rantan Taggah! It's gone wrong!" It sounded like Enni Chennitats's voice. It *was* her voice. He hadn't known the Dancing could do that, but it was her, all right.

"What's gone wrong?" he demanded, even as he chopped at one of Sassin's scaly followers. Blood sprayed; the Liskash reek filled his nostrils. He chopped again, at another hissing horror. This one ducked away from the blow. One more stroke, and the chariot was through the enemy line. Somewhere up ahead, Sassin would be watching his host come to pieces. Rantan Taggah had never set eyes on his opponent. He had the feeling he would recognize him even so. And he knew he would kill him if he could.

Except Sassin wasn't the only one discovering all his plans falling to pieces around him. "Everything!" Enni Chennitats said urgently. "There were more Liskash—there *are* more Liskash. They must have masked their dust—masked themselves—with strong magic, because we didn't spy it. No one spied it—we were all minding the main swarm. We thought that was everything Sassin had. It seemed like enough."

An arrow darted past Rantan Taggah, so close that the fletching brushed the fur on his arm. He wished it would have pierced him through the heart. Outthought by a Scaly One . . . ! "Tell me the rest of it." His voice was harsh. There would be a rest of it. And it wouldn't be good.

"They hit Zhanns Bostofa's males," Enni Chennitats said. "Right when the burst of fear came, they hit them. And Zhanns Bostofa's warriors . . . They ran away, Rantan Taggah. Everything's going to the demons around here."

He'd known it would be bad, yes. He hadn't dreamt it would be *that* bad. If he and his warriors destroyed

Sassin's army—no, Sassin's *main* army—while the Liskash scattered the females and kits and slaughtered the herdbeasts... Even if he did kill Sassin, the Liskash still won. Plenty of other nobles and uncounted hordes of ordinary Scaly Ones lived south of the New Water. The Clan of the Claw was alone—so alone!—here.

"Pull back," he told Munkus Drap. He shouted to the rest of his squadron: "Pull back, curse it!"

"What? Why?" the driver asked in furious amazement.

The expression the talonmaster used to answer that wasn't even remotely military, which was putting things mildly. Nevertheless, it got the idea across. "They can't do that!" the junior male yowled.

"I didn't think they could, either," Rantan Taggah said bleakly. "Which only goes to show I'm not as smart as I thought I was, eh?" Yes, if everything you were fighting for went to ruin while you were winning your splendid victory, at what price did you buy it? Too high, too high.

A javelin scraped his ear as the driver extricated them from the crush. He wished his bronze helm didn't have holes to let his ears stick out. Better that, Mrem had always judged, than to muffle such an important sense in battle. As the small wound stung and blood ran warm, he wondered how wise his folk were. But then, he had all too many reasons to wonder about the wisdom of his folk right then.

Enni Chennitats had never dreamt of such wild disorder. Mrem and Liskash and herdbeasts ran every which way, all making as much noise as they could. Thanks to the Dancers, she'd got through to Rantan Taggah. She knew that much, anyhow. She would have been happier had she known it would do any good.

Demm Etter handed her a javelin. The shaft was the wrong thickness to feel comfortable in her hand. Demm Etter inclined her head. "Yes, it's a Liskash weapon. Better than no weapon at all." The senior priestess held one of her own.

"What are we going to do? What *can* we do?" Enni Chennitats wailed.

"Kill them. Kill as many of them as we can. Try not to get killed ourselves—the clan needs us." Demm Etter, as usual, was severely practical.

A Liskash wounded a bull hamsticorn with a javelin. The hamsticorn ran toward him, not away. Hamsticorns had no horns. Males rammed heads when they fought in the springtime. Their skulls were thicker than those of any Liskash. *Thump!* The Scaly One went flying. When he hit the ground again—what seemed half a bowshot away—he thrashed like a broken thing that would never be right again. Which, no doubt, he was.

Another Liskash pointed a skinny finger at Enni Chennitats. He seemed astonished when she didn't fall over dead. She felt something in the bottom of her mind, but this Scaly One would never make a noble. And she had magic of her own. Hefting the javelin, she stalked toward the dismayed Scaly One.

He would never make a hero, either. He turned and ran. She flung the javelin at him, but missed. Then she trotted over and picked it up again. She was much too likely to need it again. If she happened to see Zhanns Bostofa, for instance, she would gladly let the air out of his bluster.

"Here they come," Demm Etter said, pointing south.

Sure enough, the Mrem chariotry, or most of it, had shaken free of the enemy and was rolling back toward the rest of the clan. And there was Rantan Taggah, waving frantically as he tried to pull some kind of order out of battlefield madness. Enni Chennitats hadn't tried to touch his mind since her desperate warning; the Dance had fallen into chaos along with everything else. Something inside her unknotted at finding the talonmaster still lived.

Some of the chariots brought warriors up to fight the Liskash who'd hit the column by surprise. Others, Rantan Taggah's squadron among them, stayed behind to keep Sassin's larger force from joining up with the rest. If that happened, everything was ruined.

Then again, everything might well be ruined anyhow.

So much for the gold leaf on the horns of Rantan Taggah's krelprep. It was splashed—splattered—with blood, and parts of it were peeling loose. As swank so often did, it had proved more expensive than it was worth.

Rantan Taggah's spear was gone, too. A Liskash had clutched it as it went into his scaly belly, and his dying grasp pulled it out of the talonmaster's hands as the chariot went past. And he'd broken his axe's handle. He'd shattered a Scaly One's shield with the blow, but he still wished he could have it back. A sword was a weapon you used when you had nothing with a longer reach. Rantan Taggah didn't, not any more. And so—the sword.

He slashed, forehand and backhand, at the Liskash crowding around him. So did the rest of the males in the chariots he'd ordered to stay behind and hold up the swarm of enemies. The Liskash were brave. Though the Mrem had better weapons and better armor for close combat, the Scaly Ones pressed forward as if they didn't care whether they lived or died. For all Rantan Taggah knew, they didn't.

Whether or not they valued their own lives, they wanted the Mrem dead. They slew the krelprep, which were not armored, so their foes couldn't move so fast. That helped them, but perhaps less than they'd hoped. What mattered to Rantan Taggah was keeping the Scaly Ones here from advancing on his vulnerable females and animals. If he had to sell his own life and those of the rest of this rear guard to accomplish that, he would, and he wouldn't count the cost afterwards. That he might not be in any position to count the cost after the fighting ended was something upon which he carefully did not dwell.

After his krelprep went down, he nodded to Munkus Drap. "It won't be pretty from here on out, but it's what we've got to do."

"Oh, yes." The driver sounded ready. Why not? He carried the big shield. Its leather facing was dented from slingstones. Arrows and the broken shafts of javelins pincushioned it. Munkus Drap had broken the javelins off himself—they made the shield too clumsy to handle.

He had a sword, too. He and Rantan Taggah leaped down from the stalled chariot together. A Liskash ran at Rantan Taggah from the left. The foe was on him before he could slash with his sword. He slashed with his free hand instead. Hissing in anguish, the Scaly One reeled away, clutching at his face. A brief yielding softness under Rantan Taggah's talons told him he'd torn out an eye.

"Claws!" he roared. "Claws for the Clan of the Claw!"

The other Mrem raised a cheer. As long as the Liskash couldn't drag them off their feet, their armor and weapons let them take on numbers far greater than their own. Despite courage, the Liskash began to realize they were feeding themselves into a grinder. Their push forward faltered. Even missile attacks flagged. Rantan Taggah wondered why till he realized the Liskash had to be running short of javelins and arrows.

The ferocious warrior called Ramm Passk't leaped on a Scaly One who thought he could fight like a Mrem. The Liskash had a spear, Ramm Passk't only the weapons Aedonniss gave him at birth. That turned out not to matter for long—only until the Scaly One hesitantly thrust the first time. Ramm Passk't knocked the shaft aside and sprang on him. He tore out the Liskash's throat with his fangs, then sprang to his feet with his muzzle all bloody. He roared out something in the Scaly Ones' language.

"What does that mean?" Munkus Drap asked.

Rantan Taggah translated for him: " 'Who's next?' "

Ramm Passk't, gore dripping from his chin, made

a spectacle to give pause to the hardiest of the Scaly Ones. All at once, they stopped coming forward against the Mrem. Standing in their place, Rantan Taggah would have been none too eager himself. Ramm Passk't made the very embodiment of ferocity.

"Let's draw back," Rantan Taggah called to his surviving warriors. "If they come after us, we'll charge them and make them stop. But I think they may let us go."

"Bring them on!" Ramm Passk't shouted. He gave the Liskash his challenge once more. No one stepped out of their line to answer it.

Step by weary, painful step, Rantan Taggah and his comrades fell back. He was amazed how far across the sky the sun had traveled. Hadn't the battle started just a few breaths ago? His exhaustion argued against it. So did the clan's losses. They'd be a long time replacing chariots. Too many warriors they could never replace.

But they were intact, or near enough. They could fight again. They could go on. And maybe they would be able to serve Sassin as he'd served them, only worse.

Sassin was not literally a cold-blooded creature, even if the Mrem sometimes called the Liskash sons of serpents. All the same, he was, and could afford to be, a more cold-blooded talonmaster than any Mrem. His fighters were not friends and comrades; by the nature of things, they were only subjects. And, by the nature of things, expending subjects was easier than sending friends and comrades out to die on your behalf.

All the same, the dunes and drifts of dead and

dying Liskash around the chariots the hairy vermin had abandoned left him dismayed. As he could stop up his earholes and block most sound but not all of it, so his mind could deflect most but not all the agony the wounded projected.

He glanced toward the west. Maybe it was just as well the sun was setting. Were the day longer, the monstrous Mrem might have murdered most of his males. He'd hoped to crush them absolutely, but not everything worked the way you hoped it would. Everyone, even Liskash nobles, got too many unpleasant tastes of that lesson as the years spun by.

Lorssett came up to him. The lesser male would have done better putting on greaves; he had a wounded leg, and clutched a javelin to steady his step. "I did not think you would be rash enough to go where there was fighting," Sassin remarked acidly.

"I did not go to it. It came to me," his aide answered. "I hope this heals. I would not care to limp for the rest of my days."

"I believe you." Sassin could feel his pain, too, however much he wished he couldn't.

Lorssett pointed toward the northeast, away from the sinking sun. "Will you send our fighters after them, to finish them off once and for all while they are weak and off balance?" He swayed in spite of his makeshift staff; he was more than a little off balance himself.

That was certainly how Sassin thought of him at this moment. "If I throw any more fighters at them now, I may have none left by this time tomorrow."

"You will still have some, lord," Lorssett said. "And

the Mrem will be gone—gone! Is that not what you want?"

It was, of course—but, then again, it wasn't. "If I have no fighters, what will ward me and my domain from the rest of the Liskash nobles?" Sassin said. "Not all my enemies are hairy beasts. Some are scaly beasts instead."

"You have the magic to make them keep their distance," Lorssett declared.

"They also have magic—and they would have more fighters than I do," Sassin said. "Far more fighters, in fact. I have done enough here, I tell you." Lorssett only let out a weary, resigned sigh. Angrily, Sassin snapped, "Speak. Come on—out with your worthless thought."

Lorssett did not want to release it, but Sassin's power pulled it from him: "You may know how to win a victory, lord, but, having won it, you do not know what to do with it."

"No? One of the things I can do is make those who doubt me sorry," Sassin replied in a deadly voice. Lorssett's sigh turned to a tormented hiss. Sassin could make pain worse, much worse. And if the Liskash noble felt a little of that himself, he paid the price without complaint.

Night. Defeat. Disappointment. Anger. Anguish. Rantan Taggah had all he could do to make sure the Mrem posted enough sentries out far enough to give some sort of warning if the Scaly Ones tried to attack under cover of darkness.

That wasn't the usual Liskash way. Night was friendlier to the Mrem, whose eyes adjusted to it better. But Rantan Taggah took nothing for granted now, not when Sassin had just beaten him.

He got his wounds salved and bandaged. Nothing seemed bad, or likely to fester. He was luckier than quite a few warriors. All the same, the sting from cuts and ache from bruises left his temper even shorter than it would have been otherwise.

All that meant he went after Zhanns Bostofa as if he were stalking a wild bundor. The only difference was, he would have gone after a wild bundor with more respect than he felt for the plump male. When the talonmaster had trouble finding him, he hoped the Liskash had killed him. That, at least, would have left the other male with some scraps of his honor intact.

But no. There stood Zhanns Bostofa, not far from a fire, with fewer wounds than Rantan Taggah bore himself. The black-and-white male flinched when Rantan Taggah came up to him, but didn't try to flee. He might have understood how hopeless that was. Seeming to shrink in on himself, he said, "Do what you will to me. You would anyhow."

"Why shouldn't I tear your worthless carcass to bloody rags and scatter them around the camp to warn the others?" Rantan Taggah snarled. "You broke. You ran. You came as near as *that*"—he slashed his claws through the air, a whisker's breadth in front of Zhanns Bostofa's nose—"to dooming the whole clan. Was that what you had in mind? Would it have made you happy?"

"No," Zhanns Bostofa said. "I can't stand you—as if that's any secret. But I'm loyal to the clan."

In a way, the talonmaster believed him. A Mrem might betray his clan to another. He would have his reasons for that, whether they smelled good or bad to an outsider. But, in all the tale of years since the beginning, had any Mrem, no matter how wicked, ever chosen the Liskash over his own kind? Rantan Taggah couldn't make himself believe it.

"Are you?" he challenged, furious still. "You pick odd ways to show it."

"Maybe I do." Zhanns Bostofa hung his head. "The fear struck—and I ran. I couldn't help myself. None of us could help ourselves. It was...It was Liskash magic. I see that now. I didn't then. The only thing I could think of then was getting away to somewhere safe as fast as I could."

"What about later?" Rantan Taggah said. "Even the Dancers picked up javelins and threw them at the Scaly Ones. How about you? Were you hiding under the blankets in a wagon?"

"I—I came out," Zhanns Bostofa said. Rantan Taggah's sneer proved even shrewder than he'd guessed. The plump male held out his arm to show off a cut. "I *did* fight. By Aedonnis, I did! That's how I got this."

"A hero," Rantan Taggah gibed. "Why don't you go brag to Ramm Passk't? I'm sure he'd be impressed, too. All he did was slaughter a spear-carrying Scaly One with his teeth and claws."

"Curse it, you posted my followers and me where you did because you didn't think we'd fight so well.

Why are you so surprised when we didn't rip the Liskash to pieces?"

That had enough teeth to bring Rantan Taggah up short for a moment. "If you could fight the way you talk, you would be the greatest talonmaster this clan has ever known," he said wearily. "But you'll fight the next time—see if you don't. I'll put you where I can keep an eye on you. And if the Liskash don't wound you from the front, I'll make sure our warriors finish you from behind."

"I suppose I've earned that," Zhanns Bostofa said. "However you please. I won't let the clan down."

Rantan Taggah had to hope he meant even so much. Sassin had certainly known just where the Clan of the Claw's weak point lay. Yet again, the talonmaster wished Enni Chennitats hadn't made him think about the dark god, the Liskash god, who might or might not exist. That vision was liable to bother him for years. Only too easy to imagine that god reaching a scaly hand out toward the clan . . . and closing it on Zhanns Bostofa.

That thought sparked another. Of their own accord, his claws shot out. Seeing them, Zhanns Bostofa fell back half a step. He had to be wondering whether Rantan Taggah aimed to kill him on the spot, the way the mighty Ramm Passk't had slain the Scaly One.

But Rantan Taggah had forgotten all about him. No, not quite: he was thinking of the plump male in a new and different way. "Maybe," he said, much more to himself than to Zhanns Bostofa, "just maybe, mind you, I deserve to lead the clan in war after all. I can hope so, anyhow."

"What do you mean?" Zhanns Bostofa asked.

And Rantan Taggah told him . . . some of what was in his mind, anyhow.

Enni Chennitats slept hardly at all through a night that seemed a thousand years long. The priestesses were the clan's healers as well as Dancers. None of them got much sleep. Their talents and their knowledge were too much in demand. She cleaned and stitched and bandaged till she started to hate the stink of blood.

The hale males in the clan weren't idle in the darkness, either. They butchered and skinned as many of the herdbeasts the Liskash had killed as they could. They wouldn't be able to smoke or salt or sun-dry all the meat they cut up; some of the hides would go bad before they could be tanned. But the clan was doing what it could to survive and go on. And males and females and kits all stuffed themselves to the bursting point. Somehow, trouble seemed easier to face if you could meet it with a full belly.

Ahead of the sun, the brilliant star called Assirra's Tear climbed into the sky. Sometimes it shone in the morning before sunrise, sometimes in the evening after sunset. It never strayed very far from Aedonniss' sun. Before long, morning twilight turned black to gray in the east.

"Priestesses to the wagons," Demm Etter called in tones that brooked no argument. "We have to rest. The clan will need us again—and all too soon."

How Enni Chennitats wished she could quarrel

with that! But when she opened her mouth to protest, what came out was an enormous yawn. Demm Etter had a way of being right.

Some of the teams drawing the wagons were make-shifts. Everything was going to be makeshift for a while. That was the least of Enni Chennitats's worries. Off to the south, carrion birds and scavenging leath-erwings glided down from the sky to squabble with four-legged prowlers over the feast on the battlefield. The Scaly Ones didn't care what happened to their bodies once they were done with them; they were even less likely to care about Mrem corpses. They held the field, so there would be no proper rites for the dead. *One more thing to grieve over*, Enni Chennitats thought sorrowfully.

Rantan Taggah deployed his remaining chariots to the south of the wagons and herds. He might have been telling Sassin, *Well, if you want to go on with the fight, we're ready for you*. He might have been, but he wasn't. Another battle right then would have torn the Clan of the Claw to pieces.

The only consolation was that Sassin didn't seem ready to start fighting again right away, either. The males who'd got back from the main battle bragged about how many Liskash they'd slain. For once, their brags must have held some truth.

Yawning again, Enni Chennitats climbed into a wagon and curled up into a ball. *What if they need magic? What if they need us to Dance?* she wondered. Sleep smote her before she found an answer.

❖   ❖   ❖

Sassin was coldly furious. By any standards, he'd won a smashing victory over the furry vermin. They should have run back to their old grazing grounds or stayed where they were to try to recover from the thrashing he'd given them. Instead, they headed west, across his lands, as if they'd triumphed in the fighting.

Lorssett had been rude enough to suggest Sassin didn't know what to do with a victory. Sassin hissed softly; he'd given his aide what he deserved for his presumption. But the Mrem, plainly, didn't know what to do after a defeat.

Because they didn't, Sassin would have to beat them all over again. He wondered whether Lorssett had been right even if rude. Doing it when the hairy, yowling pests were all topsy-turvy might have been easier than taking them on now that they'd pulled themselves together.

But, whether Lorssett had been right or not, Sassin knew *he* had been, too: even in triumph, his fighters had taken a fearful drubbing. His magic might have made them advance against the Mrem in spite of that. It might have, yes, but he'd also wearied himself yesterday. He needed time to recover his strength. And he always needed to look at his fellow Liskash nobles. As he'd told Lorssett, if they sensed weakness in him they would be quick to take advantage of it. Mercy was a Mrem notion, and, to a Liskash, an extraordinarily stupid one.

Getting axeheads up into the air to shadow the hairy vermin wasn't easy. Self-centered as any Liskash, the flyers thought only of stuffing themselves with freshly dead meat. They weren't interested in doing Sassin's bidding.

He reached out toward the Mrem with a cautious mental probe. More often than not, that would have been blunted. Mrem didn't have much magic, and needed cumbersome swarms of females to work what they did have, but he wasn't up to using much himself at the moment. Nothing blocked his spying, though. The magic of the hairy pests was in as much disarray as the rest of their establishment after the battle.

Liskash faces were not made to show expressions. Sassin looked the same whether happy or furious. But if he could have smiled, he would have. There was the escaped slave, and there with him the male whose weakness his fighters had exploited. They were in an even more important place now than the one they'd held before.

What was wrong with the Mrem who led that band? Didn't he understand how he'd come to grief yesterday? Did he think it was only happenstance that the Liskash fighters went in where the weak male was in charge? He'd fought the main battle well enough. *More than well enough*, Sassin thought. Had the main battle been the only string in his bow, it would have been a disaster.

Well, what did the Liskash say about the Mrem? That they had no sense of the larger struggle, that they could not see farther than the end of their snouts. Clichés became clichés because they boiled truths down to a handful of words. This one certainly seemed to.

Sassin paused. It seemed to, yes. But what if this

Mrem commander *was* playing a deeper game, trying to lure him into a mistake? That was unlikely, but Sassin supposed it was possible.

He would watch. He would wait. When the time came, he would strike. And, this time, his strike would be altogether deadly. If he sensed trickery, he would change his plans to foil it. But he really didn't think he would need to. These furry nuisances were fierce, yes. They wouldn't have caused the Liskash so much trouble if they weren't. But fierceness and cleverness were far removed from each other. A clever Mrem? The mere idea filled Sassin with cold amusement.

West. Rantan Taggah had known the Clan of the Claw would have a long journey. Till he began it, though, he hadn't truly understood what that meant. How many more battles would they have to fight? Would anything be left of them by the time they got to where they were going?

If he was going to ask such questions, he should have asked them of Demm Etter. If she wasn't the wisest of the Mrem in the Clan of the Claw, he had no idea who was. But the idea never crossed his mind. Instead, he waited for Enni Chennitats to come out of the wagon where she'd rested.

Her fur was rumpled, ungroomed. She yawned enormously, showing off her fangs. Her tongue and the roof of her mouth had dark gray patches on them. Rantan Taggah had never noticed that before. He thought they were charming.

He poured out his troubles to her. When he finished,

she yawned again—not boredom but exhaustion. "We could go back," she said. "We were doing . . . well enough where we were. We could go on . . . for a while."

Her hesitations matched the ones that had made him set the Clan of the Claw in motion. "No," he said. "They'd crush us in the end. It might not happen till after we were dead and gone, but it would happen."

"I think so, too," Enni Chennitats said. "That makes the trek our best chance."

"But it isn't very good, either," Rantan Taggah said mournfully.

"Not very good, but still the best," Enni Chennitats said. Hearing her say the same thing he believed made him feel better. There was no rational reason it should, but it did. She went on, "And if we give Sassin everything he deserves, some of the other Liskash nobles may think three times before they try to block our path. News travels fast among the Scaly Ones. They'll know they can't cross us without paying the price."

"If," the talonmaster echoed. "Everything we're doing now, we're building on a tower of ifs."

"Not everything," Enni Chennitats said. "Sassin *will* hit us again. Chances are, his fighters *will* strike at Zhanns Bostofa again. That's why you've got Grumm traveling with Zhanns Bostofa's warriors for now—just to make it more tempting. And I *can* touch your mind in the Dance. I've already proved that."

"Well, yes." Rantan Taggah remembered the intimacy of that touch, even if it had brought bad news. His blood heated. He willed himself to relax—no time for that now. No time for anything but the fight ahead.

He forced a laugh. "You're right. What else could we need?"

"Luck," Enni Chennitats said seriously. "All the luck we can find, and a little more besides."

"That's what I said," Rantan Taggah replied. "A tower of ifs."

"It sounds better my way," Enni Chennitats told him, and he didn't feel like arguing with her.

Sassin methodically readied his new attack. This one must not fall short. If he'd pressed the last one... That would have been the same as admitting Lorssett was right. No self-respecting god could have done any such thing. Sassin was more than self-respecting: he was self-worshiping. That being so, he didn't worry about what might have gone wrong. He did his best to make sure everything would go right this time.

He made sure his borders were protected, too. The other Liskash nobles wouldn't thank him for delivering them from the trouble these Mrem could cause. As he'd told his steward, they would look at him with grim golden eyes, wondering whether he'd cost himself too dear in the deliverance. And, if they decided he had, they would fall on him and destroy him. Then, no doubt, they would quarrel among themselves over how to divide the spoil.

Yes, I was right all along, Sassin thought: the only conclusion a self-worshiping god could possibly reach.

The weak male and his followers still protected the wagons that housed the hairy females and kits. If the Mrem wanted to hand Sassin the game, he would take it. He made very sure they were not setting a trap. Spying axeheads—he'd got them flying for him again—and his own magic convinced him they weren't.

Lorssett was still limping from his wound. Sassin thought about sorcerously boosting the pain the lesser Liskash felt once more. Not without regret, he decided against it. He needed the things Lorssett could do.

"We are well supplied?" Sassin asked. "Plenty of meat? Plenty of water? We have enough arrows and javelins?"

"Yes, lord," Lorssett said. "All is in readiness, just as you have commanded."

Idly, Sassin flicked a mental probe at his aide. Lorssett was not altogether without magic; he would have been much less useful if he were. But he couldn't hope to shield himself from Sassin's far greater power. And Sassin saw he wasn't lying to please his lord, as aides had been known to do. Things were as ready as anyone could want.

"Come tomorrow, then, we will finish the Mrem," Sassin said. "And, after that, the New Water will wall us off from them for a long time." He wanted to say *forever*, but he didn't. He knew better. Still, the new sea should keep the hairy pests away till after he was dead. That was as close to forever as would make no difference ... not to him, anyhow.

"And we will take all that is theirs." Lorssett understood what victory meant. "And we will have more slaves." With a master set above him, he wanted as many slaves below him as he could get. They reminded him he wasn't so futile a creature as he seemed when viewed from Sassin's perspective. They did, at any rate, when he wasn't face-to-face or mind-to-mind with his overlord.

"Just so. And I will eat their names." Sassin looked forward to that. It was a strange sort of sorcerous pleasure he could not take from his own kind. For whatever reason, Liskash were less intimately connected to their names than were the Mrem. Sassin shrugged. He cared nothing for the whys and wherefores. He only recognized and took advantage of weakness. "When the sun grows hot, when the furry beasts start to *sweat*"—he packed the word with all the loathing it roused in him—"we will put an end to them."

"As you say, lord, so shall it be," Lorssett replied.

"Well, of course," Sassin said complacently.

Mrem in chariots were faster than Liskash afoot. Scouts could keep an eye on Sassin's army and bring word back to the Clan of the Claw with enough time left over for the clan to do something about it. When Enni Chennitats heard shouts of "They're coming!" she knew what she had to do herself.

Had she forgotten, Demm Etter would have set her straight. "Take your places!" the senior priestess called to the Dancers. "All of you, take your places. Hurry, now! No time to waste—and we have to do it right."

Enni Chennitats's place was at the center of one ring of Dancers. She wouldn't be doing much moving herself, not this time. That felt odd: more than a little unnatural. She would serve as the focus of the other Dancers' exertions.

Grumm loped over from Zhanns Bostofa's detachment to stand at the center of another circle, not far from her own. He still had the unhappy, hunched-over stance that had characterized him ever since he made his way back to the Clan of the Claw. Even better than the Dancers, he understood what a desperate gamble they were undertaking. But he *did* stand there, no matter how miserable he seemed. He too was a focus. From him, though, the Dancers in his circle would take. In a way, that seemed dreadfully unfair to Enni Chennitats. Sassin had already robbed him of so much.

They hoped a little more taking would redeem it all. They hoped, yes, but no one could be sure ahead of time. The only way to find out was to try. And so Grumm . . . stood there.

A male—one of the warriors who followed Zhanns Bostofa—came hotfooting it back to the Dancers. "You'd better start, if you're going to do it," he panted. "Looks like all the Scaly Ones in the world coming down on us."

"I thank you, Mm Kafftee," Demm Etter answered calmly. She stood between the two circles. At her gesture, the Dancers surrounding Grumm began to spin sunwise. Those around Enni Chennitats Danced deasil. Demm Etter moved in a rhythm of her own, somehow linking the opposed Dances.

In most Dances, Enni Chennitats would have been so busy concentrating, letting energy flow through her, that she would have paid only scant attention to what was going on around the priestesses. But now she heard the yowls and hisses and crashes and clatters of battle not nearly far enough away. Zhanns Bostofa and his warriors were fighting like males possessed, eager above all else to make up for their earlier failure. The Liskash cared nothing for their eagerness. All the Scaly Ones wanted was to kill.

Enni Chennitats formed Rantan Taggah's image in her mind, as she'd done when the last battle unexpectedly fell to pieces. "Are you there?" she called. "Can you hear me?"

"I hear you, Enni Chennitats." The priestess was assuredly hearing the talonmaster with her mind, not her ears. Even so, it was *his* voice, without the tiniest fragment of doubt. Its very familiarity warmed her. So did his usual directness: "Now—where is the stinking lizard's get?"

"I don't know yet. I haven't heard anything from Grumm." *Heard,* again, wasn't quite the right word, but it was the best one she had. The other circle was trying to get knowledge, direction, out of the escaped slave and give it to her so she could pass it on to Rantan Taggah. Whether they could...

Grumm was what he was—lost and damned, in essence—because Sassin had eaten his surname. But what kept him what he was was the Liskash's possession and retention of that surname. The link between them remained. Up till now, that had worked altogether to Sassin's advantage. Still, a rope was a rope. You could tug on it from either end.

So the Dancers hoped. So they prayed. If Assirra was kind, she would hearken to them. Otherwise, the only Mrem left on this side of the New Water would be a few scattered halfname slaves like Grumm. Better to die cleanly.

Enni Chennitats cocked her ears toward Grumm. That couldn't possibly help, but she did it anyway. She didn't see how it could hurt. Where was Sassin?

Her ears stayed aimed at Grumm, but her body shifted. She hardly realized she was doing it till she finished the move. "*That* way!" she exclaimed, as if Rantan Taggah stood beside her.

"*Which* way?" he asked irritably, because he didn't.

She explained. The mind-to-mind link held more than words alone; she made him feel the direction in which she was facing now. And she could gauge how far away Rantan Taggah was, and also, through Grumm, how far away Sassin was. Little by little, directions and distances converged.

Rantan Taggah and Ramm Passk't stole from one bush, one scrubby tree, to the next. "You'd better know where we're going," Ramm Passk't growled.

"Don't worry about it," Rantan Taggah answered. "If I don't, we'll both end up too dead to care."

"You know how to make a fellow feel better, all right," the other warrior said. Rantan Taggah held up a hand: Enni Chennitats was speaking inside his head, and he had trouble paying attention to her voice and to the one from the outside world—the real world? no, one seemed as real as the other—at the same time.

They'd sneaked around the left wing of the Liskash army. Sassin hadn't set out so many flank guards this time—he realized he'd hurt the Mrem chariotry in the last fight. That a couple of warriors might come on foot? It was such a mad, smerp-brained scheme, it had never occurred to him.

A good thing, too, Rantan Taggah thought. A squadron of archers around the Liskash noble would have pincushioned his comrade and him before they got close enough to do what needed doing. How they would get back again . . . Rantan Taggah would worry about that later, if there was a later in which to worry about it.

"If Zhanns Bostofa doesn't hold them out, I'll do to him what I did to that bad-tasting Scaly One," Ramm Passk't said.

"Someone else will have taken care of it," Rantan Taggah said. "I made sure of that, believe me."

"Too bad," the other warrior said. "I've always wanted his blood on my tongue." His broad shoulders went up and down in a shrug. "Ah, well. It's not like I'm the only one."

"Oh, indeed. Everybody loves Zhanns Bostofa," Rantan Taggah said. Ramm Passk't laughed. The talonmaster couldn't remember the last time he'd said anything so funny.

"Can you see him yet?" Enni Chennitats asked inside his mind. "You aren't more than three or four bowshots away."

Rantan Taggah peered ahead. "There's a little knot of Scaly Ones off in the distance," he reported. Three or four bowshots might not seem like much to the priestess, but at the moment it did to him. "I suppose Sassin is one of them." He almost asked Enni Chennitats to get a picture of what the Liskash noble looked like from Grumm, but he didn't see the point. In any Mrem's eyes, a Scaly One was only a Scaly One.

"Yes. He has to be," Enni Chennitats said. *He'd better be*, was what she had to mean.

"All right. We'll do what we can," the talonmaster said. He pointed at the little group of Liskash. "He's one of them," he told Ramm Passk't.

"Which one?" But Ramm Passk't shrugged again. "It doesn't matter. If we kill them all, he won't get away."

"There you go," Rantan Taggah said. Sometimes Ramm Passk't's ruthlessness could be unnerving even to another warrior.

They sneaked toward the Scaly Ones. Before long, they were down on their bellies. Rantan Taggah tried not to think about all the burrs and fleas and ticks his fur would pick up. He'd groom himself later. If he had to shave himself bare to get rid of everything, he would do that. *Later* hardly seemed real to him, anyhow. He would do his best to save the clan, and after that it would go on without him.

A bare thread of whisper from Ramm Passk't: "Breeze is blowing from them to us. They won't smell us coming. Aedonniss gave us one break."

One of the Liskash stepped out ahead of the rest and pointed north with unmistakable anger—and with an unmistakable sense of command. Sassin had identified himself. Rantan Taggah wanted to thank him. Somehow, he doubted the Liskash noble would appreciate the courtesy.

The talonmaster and Ramm Passk't stalked Sassin like a pair of somo going after a bundor—or maybe even a frillhorn. Somo reminded Mrem uneasily of themselves, though they were easily twice the size of Mrem. They could rise up on their hind legs, but commonly went on all fours. Even the largest Liskash killers thought twice about challenging them.

Closer. Closer still. The rank Liskash scent filled Rantan Taggah's nostrils. It made him want to be stupid, to charge too soon so he could rend and tear and kill. By himself, he might have done just that. So might Ramm Passk't, by himself. Stalking together forced hunt discipline on both of them.

"You're almost there. So close!" Enni Chennitats said. Rantan Taggah froze the beginnings of a start. He was briefly surprised the Liskash couldn't hear her, then remembered he wasn't really hearing her himself.

Sassin was saying something. Rantan Taggah understood only bits and pieces of it: as much of the Scaly Ones' language as any Mrem bothered—or had the stomach—to learn. Something about victory. Something about killing. Something about eating. What else would a Liskash go on about? One of the lesser Liskash turned his head. Rantan Taggah and Ramm Passk't froze. After a few heartbeats that lasted an eternity, the Scaly One looked away.

Rantan Taggah breathed...just barely. One of Ramm Passk't's ears twitched...just barely. The two Mrem glanced towards each other. Ramm Passk't moved first. It was silently understood that Sassin belonged to Rantan Taggah, and keeping the rest of the Liskash from thwarting him was the other warrior's task. Only if something went wrong—as something might very well do—would Ramm Passk't turn his fearsome attention on the chief Liskash noble. When none of Sassin's hangers-on hissed an alarm, Rantan Taggah wormed closer, too.

He didn't know how he decided to stop worming and charge. It seemed more beastlike instinct than reasoned choice. One instant, he was calculating talonmaster; the next, with seemingly no time passing between them, he was raging somo.

One of the lesser Liskash had the presence of mind to throw something at him. He never found out what it was; he only knew it missed. Sassin half-turned toward him. Even across lines of race and hatred, Rantan Taggah read the Liskash noble's horrified astonishment.

The talonmaster felt a tug at his own spirit: magic, hurled his way. But, like the javelin or dagger or whatever it was, the magic missed. Or maybe it hit, but too late. For Rantan Taggah smashed into Sassin, knocked him to the ground, and tore at his belly with hind claws and at his throat with fangs and front talons.

Sassin had claws of his own, and tried to fight back. But one Mrem was commonly worth more than one Liskash in a claw-to-claw fight, and Rantan Taggah was a trained and practiced warrior while Sassin was not. The Liskash noble also tried throwing more magic at his unexpected assailant. Some other Scaly One might possibly have been able to form and hurl a spell in time to keep from getting his throat torn out. Again,

Sassin was not. Rantan Taggah felt the charm try to bite him. Then Sassin lost consciousness and died, and the threat died with him.

Rantan Taggah sprang to his feet, ready to help Ramm Passk't against the Liskash noble's henchmales. But Ramm Passk't needed help from no one. He'd already slaughtered two of them, and the rest were running every which way, as fast as they could go. They might not have been eager to stand and die for Sassin even if he still lived. With him down, all they cared about was getting away.

And, with his will no longer driving them, the ordinary Liskash javelineers and archers and slingers up ahead were suddenly much less eager to mix it up with the Mrem. Clouds of dust hid most of what was going on up there from Rantan Taggah's eyes, but his ears were quick to catch the changed note from the fighting. The talonmaster hadn't been sure that would happen, but he'd hoped.

Ramm Passk't lifted his arm and licked at a bite one of the Liskash had given him. Then he said, "I don't think we ought to stick around here—know what I mean? The Scaly Ones'll be heading back from the fight up there pretty cursed quick, and they won't be glad to see us."

That would do for an understatement till a bigger one—say, one about the size of a frillhorn—came along. "Right," Rantan Taggah said, not about to admit out loud that the formidable warrior could also be dangerous with words.

They trotted away. As they had before, they could

circle around the Liskash army's flank. *Please, Assirra,* Rantan Taggah thought. The prayer couldn't hurt. He'd made this attack not expecting to come back from it. He hadn't resigned himself to death, but he'd come close. Now that he'd succeeded against the odds, all at once he overwhelmingly wanted to go on living.

Enni Chennitats's voice exulting in his mind gave him part of the reason why: "He's dead! He's dead! Grumm felt him die!"

"Now that you mention it, so did I," Rantan Taggah answered. Nobody was going to be dryer than he was, not today.

Enni Chennitats eyed Grumm with a priestess's curiosity. She sometimes thought that wasn't so far removed from the curiosity of a kit poking a bug with a stick to see what it would do. Sometimes nothing happened. Sometimes you learned something interesting. Every once in a while, you picked the wrong bug and got stung—which was interesting, too, but not in a way any kit enjoyed.

She'd thought that, since Sassin held Grumm's surname, it would be released when the Liskash noble perished. That would make Grumm his old self again . . . wouldn't it?

Evidently not. The escaped slave had let out a fierce, triumphant yowl when Sassin died, almost as if he'd killed the Scaly One himself. But then he shrank in on himself again. He wasn't quite so distressed as he had been before, but he wasn't anything like a normal male Mrem, either.

She almost asked him why he wasn't. Unlike a poked bug, he could answer. But, no matter how curious she was, she didn't want to be cruel. She might not worry about a bug's suffering, or a Liskash's, but she did when it came to one of her own kind.

And so, instead, she told Demm Etter what she thought. The senior priestess inclined her head. "The name may not lie under Sassin's tongue any more, but it is not in Grumm's heart, either, where it belongs."

"Where is it? Can we get it back?" Enni Chennitats asked.

"I cannot say," Demm Etter answered. "Now and then, time shows us what we did not know before. It may here. Or"—she lowered her voice so Grumm couldn't hear—"it may not. I think he has gained something by Sassin's death. Now his surname is free to wander, free to find him again if it will, not trapped the way it was before. And I know—I am as certain as I have ever been about anything—how much the Clan of the Claw has gained from Sassin's fall."

"Aedonniss, yes!" Enni Chennitats exclaimed. "Did you see the Liskash run away after he died? What could be finer than that?"

"Their not attacking us to begin with," Demm Etter said, which, once Enni Chennitats thought about it, was plainly true. Sighing, the senior priestess went on, "Too much to hope for, I suppose."

"How many Liskash nobles' lands will we have to pass through before we find our own kind again?" Enni Chennitats asked, disquieted.

"I don't know. I don't believe anyone knows, unless

the Scaly Ones should," Demm Etter said. "I do know this, though: if we win through, *when* we win through, Mremkind will sing our names and our deeds forevermore."

Enni Chennitats wished she hadn't put that *if* in there, even if she'd amended it right away. The consequences of failure . . . Well, were they any worse than the consequences of staying on the old grazing grounds? Rantan Taggah didn't think so, and Enni Chennitats wasn't inclined to doubt the talonmaster. On the contrary.

"Well, well," Demm Etter said quietly. Enni Chennitats followed her gaze. Here came Zhanns Bostofa. He was limping. He had a bandage on his right leg and another on his left arm. But he carried himself with pride of a sort different from his usual arrogance.

He bowed, first to Demm Etter and then to Enni Chennitats. "My males and I, we did what was required of us," he announced, as if he were summarizing a battle for the talonmaster. Rantan Taggah wasn't here, though. The mental link between him and Enni Chennitats had broken when the Dance ended. She hoped he hadn't come to grief after his great triumph.

Demm Etter received the report as gravely as he might have. "You did well," she told Zhanns Bostofa. "You did well—this time—and you were seen to do well. If you and yours had failed, Rantan Taggah's success would mean far less."

Zhanns Bostofa took her qualification with more humility than he was in the habit of showing. "I thank you," he answered. "What is best for the clan is what I want. I have said this again and again."

"So you have," Demm Etter said: acknowledgment rather than agreement, if Enni Chennitats was any judge. The plump male's problem was that his view of what was best for the Clan of the Claw often revolved around what was best for him. This time, those two things truly had matched. Staying alive and keeping a swarm of Liskash from overrunning the wagons was in Zhanns Bostofa's best interest as well as the clan's. Too bad only a desperate emergency created the match.

"And now we can go on," Zhanns Bostofa said grandly. "Since that is the talonmaster's decision, I will not stand in the way."

Until the next time you do, Enni Chennitats thought. The black-and-white male would soon forget his humility. He would go back to being himself. And he could no more help acting obstreperous than hamsticorns could help shedding their long pelts in the springtime.

One of these days, he would go too far. Or he might actually turn out to be right, in which case it would be hard to keep him from becoming the clan's new talonmaster. And what would become of the Mrem then? Enni Chennitats didn't want to think about that.

And she didn't have to, because a sentry shouted that he saw Rantan Taggah and Ramm Passk't coming back from the south. All the Mrem started yowling joyously at the top of their lungs. Enni Chennitats didn't hold back. Killing a Liskash noble and getting away with it was worth celebrating any day of the month.

❖   ❖   ❖

Rantan Taggah had never dreamt he might get tired of males making much of him. He'd really never dreamt he might get tired of females making much of him. Ramm Passk't hadn't got tired, except perhaps in the most literal and happy way. Rantan Taggah wouldn't have been surprised if half of next year's kits had sandy fur and uncommonly broad shoulders.

After Sassin's death, the Liskash in what had been his domain stayed away from the Clan of the Claw. Maybe the unexpected triumph of the Mrem intimidated them, at least for the time being. Maybe they realized the clan would soon be gone, and then they wouldn't have to worry about their hated enemies for a long time. And maybe they were so busy plotting among themselves about what would become of Sassin's lands that a detail like the Mrem hardly seemed important. Chances were every one of those things held some truth.

Which held the most, Rantan Taggah neither knew nor cared. He rode at the head of the Clan of the Claw, in a chariot Zhanns Bostofa gave him to replace the one he'd lost in battle. He felt uneasy accepting the other male's gift, which was putting it mildly, but saw no graceful way to refuse. Zhanns Bostofa tried to give him a team of krelprep, too. Those he did decline. He used krelprep from his own herds, and would train them up to the standard of the pair that had died on the battlefield.

He checked the territory ahead with the same care he would have used to check under flat rocks for scorpions and centipedes before laying his blanket on the ground. The Scaly Ones had a sting worse than any from some crawling thing with too many legs.

The clan was nearing what Rantan Taggah thought to be the western edge of what had been Sassin's land when Enni Chennitats walked up to him as the Mrem were setting up camp for the night. "Will all the other Liskash nobles fight us the way Sassin did?" she asked.

"By Aedonniss, I hope not!" Rantan Taggah burst out. "I hope they'll leave us alone. If I'm by myself, without a bow or a sling, I'll leave a somo alone unless it decides not to leave me alone. I hope the way we served Sassin will make the rest of the Scaly Ones think three times."

"What if it doesn't?" Enni Chennitats persisted.

"Then we keep fighting them and keep beating them till they get the idea," the talonmaster said. "Or they beat us. In that case, you can stand beside Zhanns Bostofa and say, 'I told you so.'"

"I don't want to stand beside him. Just being near him makes my fur want to twitch," Enni Chennitats said. She set a hand on his arm. "I'd rather stand beside you."

Far and away the biggest reason Rantan Taggah hadn't cut a swath like Ramm Passk't's through the clan's females was that he'd hoped to hear something like that from her—or to work up the nerve to say something like that to her. He hadn't. Sometimes— often—it was easier to risk his life than rejection from someone he cared about.

"Well," he said, and then "Well" again. He tried

once more: "Where do we go from here?" That was better, but not, he feared, very much.

"West, of course," Enni Chennitats answered, which startled a laugh out of him. It wasn't that she was wrong—she was right. "But wherever we go from now on, we go together."

"Yes," Rantan Taggah said, and he'd never felt so clever in all his life.

A Little Power

S.M. STIRLING

And so Rantan Taggah spoke and the way was open. But he walked in blood and wept. "Why," he demanded, "have you abandoned us in this forsaken land?" But there was no answer and the call to arms came again. There was no rest for three days and three nights.

Then when the demons had been cast asunder, the Dancer Enni Chennitats told Rantan Taggah to sleep and he did. In his dream Assirra appeared. She stood tall with golden fur and eyes that glowed with the green of Spring. Around her the earth sang and stirred, bringing forth an unending vista of great fields of grass and grain in which countless herds grazed.

"Lead our people home," She commanded. "Go West and take them to the promised lands. Lead them and they will be free."

And Rantan Taggah knew that there was not greater need than to be free. So he sharpened his claws and regained his faith. On the next day he told the clan of his vision and Enni Chennitats Danced it until all understood and agreed.

And so the people began to be free.

—*The Book of Mrem*, verse forty-two

PROLOGUE

THE PLAINS BAKED UNDER THE SUN, AND THE long yellow grass hissed like the ghosts of angry warriors as the herds grazed under watchful eyes or paused beneath gnarled, thorny trees. The hills stood blue with forest in the distance, and tendrils of their green followed the watercourses; in season the wings of the birds filled the sky. From time-weathered citadels of stone the magician lords of the Liskash folk waged their wars with swords and spells and poison and knives in the dark, rising and falling in a cycle that changed little but the names.

So it was; so it had always been.

But the wild Mrem were coming, and nothing would be the same. Nothing, ever again.

The great hall of the goddess Ashala had walls of sandstone colored like pale gold, with specks of mica that glittered in the hot sunlight of these lands; it rose to the height of three tall Liskash standing on one another's shoulders. The timbers that bore the roof were of a hard dark wood that had been hauled laboriously from the far mountains and each one was richly carved in images that told of her power and the legends of her ancestors. The air smelled of fear and ancient death.

The wall behind the throne was stuccoed and inlaid with colored tiles in a design of the rayed sun in splendor, Ashala's personal symbol. Before the tall-backed throne of wrought night-black wood and beaten gold the stones of the floor had been blackened by fire.

That was where the goddess staged her executions. She could burn anything to ash with her mind and frequently did so, especially those who had displeased her. Sometimes it was a limb or an eye, sometimes the whole of them, depending on the depth of her displeasure.

The hall was high but narrow, and nobles crowded back to make an aisle for Hisshah, the daughter of the goddess.

Hisshah stood, nervously waiting for her name to be called, controlling the impulse to flick her tongue over her fangs and thin narrow lips. The dry, musky scent of the packed nobles made her heart beat faster, but her face was calm. She did not think the ultimate punishment would be hers today. She was, after all, her mother's only heir.

"Let Hisshah approach the Divinity!"

She walked carefully towards the throne, keeping her stride slow and long and the sway of her head and tail regular. All of the high Liskash of the court were gathered and she would not show weakness before them. Hard enough to do as she was shorn of all the jewels that marked her rank, save those embedded in the scales of her forehead in a sigil that marked her as her mother's.

She'd been proud of the mark at five summers; now at twenty it infuriated her to be *claimed*, like a piss-pot or a rug.

Her mother wore no jewelry at all; instead her whole body glittered with tiny embedded gems, one to a scale, a privilege she reserved for herself alone. Ashala sat on her carved throne of ebony and gold still as a statue, her yellow eyes cold and the pupils narrowed to an S-slit.

At her mother's orders it had been two weeks since Hisshah had fed or, more importantly, drunk. Only a people as strong as the Liskash could endure such deprivation. Now she was to be humiliated as the final, and to her, the worst, phase of her punishment. But she would not stumble, she would not weave drunkenly down the aisle; though her head was swimming. She would show herself to be a proper heir to the throne. Knowing that one day she would be sitting there meting out rewards . . . and punishments . . . made it possible to endure this.

Ashala watched her daughter's slow but steady advance and grudgingly respected her for it.

The weakest and last of my clutch and very disappointing since the moment she broke the shell, which she barely managed to do without dying of exhaustion. Still, mine, *which is to judge by high standards.*

Hisshah could move small objects with her mind and perform some basic magic, but her powers were trifling and no training had been able to discover much more. The one thing she could do well was ward her mind. She'd gotten that from her father.

The impossibility of reading his mind was what had made Ashala kill him in the end. There was just no telling what he might be plotting. And unlike his last daughter his powers had been formidable.

It's time I had another clutch, she thought. *Try again for something better while time enough remains for the hatchlings to reach maturity while I can guard them.*

But she dreaded the negotiations, as well as the proximity of a powerful male and his entourage.

The last one's minions had spied on everything and then they'd all refused to leave.

No wonder I killed him, Ashala thought with satisfaction.

It had been cleverly done, too, if she did say so herself. They suspected, naturally, but they couldn't prove anything, which meant less chance of a feud. Of course, those suspicions might make it difficult to find a new mate. But not impossible. Her domain was rich and she had much to offer in the way of favors. It was always a balance, of course; you wanted a strong heredity for your offspring, but not strong enough to make it likely they'd succeed in killing you, and not from a mate so strong that he'd succeed in doing so himself.

If anything her disappointing remaining offspring might be the sticking point. How her children had all managed to kill themselves or each other, except for

Hisshah, was a source of amazement. Perhaps she'd erred on the side of recklessness when selecting the sire. Certainly *she* had always showed an adequate degree of patience.

Yes, she would set things in motion. It was her duty, and duty was not to be shirked.

At last Hisshah was crouched before her in the posture of submission. *It wouldn't have taken any longer if she'd crawled*, Ashala thought in contempt.

She waited until she sensed the court getting restless. Her people were still by nature, but their eyes had begun to move, and nictitating membranes to flicker.

"Why, Daughter, do you make me punish you?" Ashala asked.

Hisshah went from crouching to completely prone, plastered to the floor from snout-tip to tail-tip in one long exclamation point of submission.

"I beg your forgiveness, great goddess, it was never my intention to insult you."

"And yet, you did. By suggesting that I might bring food and drink to you and your cohorts as though I were a mere slave."

"It was only meant to be a small joke, great one." Hisshah writhed in humiliation. "No one could ever take such a thing seriously."

"My dignity," Ashala snapped, "and your loyalty should never be the subject of jokes! I am tempted to have you flogged for your insolent tongue!"

There were a few shocked, involuntary hisses at that. She would not, of course. Hisshah was, at the moment, her only heir. And there were some things that underlings did not forget; too much disgrace would make it impossible for the heir to reign securely. Again she waited, until the moment was almost too stretched.

"Tomorrow you may drink. The day after you may have food," she said at last.

"The goddess is gracious," Hisshah said to the floor.

"Rise up!" Ashala snapped. She'd thought of a way to punish her daughter and perhaps help to thwart the danger that marched towards them.

When Hissah was on her knees once more she continued, "Perhaps you have time for jokes because you haven't enough to do. I have decided that some of the Mrem require training as soldiers. I shall give that task to you."

"Thank you, great one," Hisshah said, her voice clear and firm.

Inside Hisshah's third stomach had clenched. Make the Mrem slaves into soldiers... Clearly impossible!

If it were possible it would also be dangerous. What is my mother thinking?

She knew of nothing that could prompt such a mad idea. Her mother had soldiers enough to make any ambitious neighbor wary, and as much territory as could be dominated from a single holding. It must be a scheme to further humiliate her with an inevitable failure.

"You may return to your chamber," her mother said. "My steward will attend you to answer any questions you may have concerning the Mrem and whatever weapons are available to arm them." She waved her hand in dismissal.

Hisshah rose and bowed, then backed away for ten steps until she could turn and leave the hall. When she was gone it would be prepared for feasting as hers was the last business of the day.

Tomorrow I will drink. And the next day I will eat and I will eat well, Hisshah promised herself.

A pleasant thought occurred to her. If she was to make Mrem into soldiers, she would have to discipline and punish them. Perhaps she could eat a few.

I always was partial to mammals, she thought.

Two days later, Ranowr squatted in a circle of friends and fellow slaves, together in the dust outside the low opening of the barracks entrance. There was a sort of familial resemblance amongst most of them. Their short, downy fur was grey with darker grey stripes and most had white bellies and hands. Two were yellow with darker stripes and one was a solid grey.

There was nothing unusual in the circle; they often sat together so, gathered in front of the dormitory where the adult males slept. But tonight they waited for Tral to bring them word that old Sesh was gone, devoting the hours of sunset and night to him, as the heat faded out of the stone walls of the compound and the colored band of stars stretched itself across heaven. This time of the cycle was more natural to Mrem in any case.

The Liskash had decreed that he was too old, sick and feeble to be worth feeding and so should be allowed to starve. There wasn't enough food to share with him, so Tral, their healer, had given him a sleeping draught from which he would not wake. The circle would mourn him, remember his life and honor his passing.

And so, they sat silently waiting.

That was where Hisshah and her small group of guards found them. The arrival of the Liskash made all of the Mrem crouch, eyes down and hands flat on the ground.

Hisshah, known as the lesser goddess to the Liskash and the young goddess to the Mrem, looked them over.

At least they're reasonably well disciplined, she thought. *But how can I turn creatures so cowed and worthless into soldiers? Mrem haul weights and scrub and carry.*

"Which of you speaks for all?" she asked.

"I do, young goddess," Ranowr said.

"Come here and kneel before me," she commanded.

When he was before her she studied him. He was taller than most Liskash, and broad and sturdy like all of his kind. He looked healthy and strong, and probably wasn't really tubby; that was the disgusting fuzz. The steward saw to the health of the slaves. And while it was true that a weak slave was a worthless slave, you didn't want them too frisky.

Still, if they're to be soldiers perhaps I should increase their rations, she mused. *If anything goes wrong, I can tell my mother than it is all her fault.*

That thought made her hiss slightly with laughter; blame flowed downward, gain upward; so the world was. She would ask the steward; he was the expert on Mrem. But for tonight, the first night she would be eating after her long fast, she had other plans.

"Which of your fellows can you spare?" she said, with a hiss of command.

She watched Ranowr carefully for any sign he might make, but he remained motionless. Some of the others were less controlled. One toward the back, with nicks in his ears and a grizzled face, looked sharply at Ranowr. It didn't take a deep knowledge of Mrem to know that he was older than the others.

She pounced.

"That one!"

The guards moved forward and took him by the arms. Hisshah and her party began to move away.

"He's a good worker," Ranowr said, still kneeling, his eyes carefully down. "Skilled in the care of bundor and hamsticorns."

Hisshah paused and turned to look at him in disbelief. "Are you asking me to show...what is it you call it...mercy?"

The word had a rather odd contour, as if it weren't really suited to the Liskash throat.

"Please, young goddess," Ranowr said, lowering his whole body.

"I didn't think it possible, but you have amused me," she said. "I am pleased. I shall send you some meat later." Then she turned and continued on her way.

The Mrem captive gave his companions a long last look before the guards hustled him off.

Ranowr and the others, stunned, returned to their circle.

"Fesa was a good Mrem," Ranowr said grimly.

It was the ritual phrase that opened the mourning circle. He glanced at the departing group of Liskash with Fesa in their midst.

If the gods created us, why do they treat us so cruelly? Why do they hate us so?

Because they did. They must. Yet it made no sense to create something and then to hate it.

And we hate them.

Just being near them made his skin crawl and pelt bristle and tail stiffen and bottle out, his ears flatten themselves as if for battle. But that could be because they had so much power.

"Fesa was a good worker," said another, bringing Ranowr's thoughts back to the mourning circle.

"He was good with the kits," added Krar.

Truth be told they were all good to the kits. Where any one of them might be your own, treating them all well just made sense. Still some were better at it than others and Fesa had been one of those.

"They'll be missing him," Ranowr agreed.

Tral entered the circle.

"Sesh will not wake," he announced. Looking around he asked, "Where's Fesa, he should be here, he was Sesh's oldest friend."

"Fesa is no more," Ranowr said. "The young goddess took him away."

The words were bitter on his tongue. Fesa would die a hard death tonight. And the meat Hisshah would send, if she sent it, would be from his corpse. A calculated insult. But they would burn it to ashes and scatter them in the wind. The only freedom any Mrem could hope for.

Stunned, Tral took his place in the circle.

"Sesh was a good Mrem," Ranowr intoned.

They spent the best part of the night remembering both of them.

The practice field was hot and silent; the guards on the outer walls moved to look occasionally, and there were bleatings and hootings from the stock pens, and a little twitch of wind flicking sand into eyes.

"Watch carefully," Hisshah said, feeling loose and confident in the familiar exercise and the welcome heat. "Overhand down-cut, angled right to left."

She tapped the mock sword on one part of the practice post, then mimed a downward slice that would have struck the neck of an opponent. The sound was muffled, for the training weapon was wrapped in tightly woven grass rope to lessen the jar to the wrists.

"Backhand cut, angled up, right to left."

She hit the post on the other side, where the gap between the hip-bone and the lowest rib would be—a clear target into the meat, with organs and big veins beneath. Even if it didn't penetrate, a powerful strike there might rupture something essential; certainly it would knock the wind out of your enemy, leaving them open for a killing blow.

"Then you tie them together with their mirror-image."

She struck, down, up, down and up, into the space where the angle of the neck would be, letting the blade's weight carry it down past the target to loop back and up and down at a slant again, like an X.

A muffled *clack* as padded wooden sword struck the hard pell, then *clack* and *clank* again.

She did it again and again, faster and faster until the mock sword seemed to blur and her body as well, weight shifting from one taloned foot to another. When she was finished with her demonstration she tossed it to Ranowr.

"Now you try."

Ranowr took the practice sword and carefully assumed the stance that Hisshah had taken. Then he swung the sword. He tried going faster and faster as she had until he struck the post square on and knocked the practice sword out of his hand, unconsciously flexing his wrist against the sting. The curved length went end-over-end into the watching group of his fellow Mrem. They dodged aside, and then one caught it and brought it.

"Pick it up," Hisshah said. "Do it again. Control the location of the strike. You should be able to put it between one scale and the next, as hard and as fast as you can strike. Precision first, then speed, then force. Look into your enemy's eyes, not at where your sword will strike. See that with your hands."

The Mrem actually wasn't bad. She'd done that much sooner during her first try at the post. But then she'd been much younger.

They were working on the small practice field between the outer and inner walls. It held two rows of ten practice posts in a field of clean raked sand and was longer than it was wide; spear and arrow-targets stood at each end. The whole was fenced with rails and it was within smell of the stables.

Hisshah walked back and forth as she watched her first student. She hated being this close to them. Their smell made her sick; a heavy, meaty scent that was suffocating. And the sight of their furred skin was loathsome unless you were hungry. Her mother couldn't have found a more subtle punishment if she'd tried for seven rainy seasons and a day.

Still, they were strong and supple and reasonably quick, it was just possible that they might be trainable as soldiers. That is if you were looking for troops that were utterly expendable. They'd never have any finesse, being mere brutes, but they might have some utility.

I hope we won't regret this, she thought. *We might regret it more if they do learn than if they don't.*

Weapons in the hands of slaves struck her as risky at best. Even if your own soldiers were infinitely better than the Mrem would ever be.

Speaking of which, there was Captain Thress leaning against the fence observing their progress, dangling his helmet by the strap in one claw and enjoying the hard dry heat. His other hand rested on the stone pommel of his war-sword, and his long narrow head moved slightly as he followed the action.

"All right," Hisshah snapped, "all of you pick up a sword and begin. If you drop the sword, pick it up and keep going. Watch this one."

As the Mrem hurried to follow her instructions she walked over to the captain.

"They're not as bad as I expected," he observed. "For absolute beginners."

Which is exactly what I thought, she noted with some pride.

"What are you doing here, Captain?"

"I came to see Mrem learn to fight," he said. "Thought I might learn something."

"Mrem know how to fight," Hisshah said. "Not all of their scars come from whippings."

He made a wry gesture with his mouth, showing a line of conical fangs.

"True," he agreed. "Truth is, it is always a . . . interesting to see what you are up to, lesser goddess."

She stared at him. He had been going to say amusing, she knew it. One day he would regret his insistence on emphasizing her lacks every chance he got.

"Have you no duties, Captain?"

He slowly blinked, letting the lids sweep in from either side in an insolent gesture.

"I would have come in curiosity at some point. The great goddess's notion is so unique."

He glanced at the Mrem. "I think one of them grows weary of your exercise."

Hisshah's head whipped around on her long flexible neck. One of the slaves was pausing between strokes. She started towards him, picking up a practice sword from the pile. Maybe she should demonstrate the strokes on a Mrem.

Ranowr sat in his place before the dormitory barracks, feeling aches in muscles he hadn't known he had. The young goddess had instructed them for hours, demanding more and more speed. He thought they'd done well for their first day.

And Mrem are as fast as they, or are so after the first few strokes. Faster if the weather is not hot, though we do not remind them of that. Most of us are larger and stronger, too.

But if he felt this bad now he dreaded the morning.

The young goddess was training ten of them, including Krai, who was something of a rival. Hisshah had told them that they would be responsible for training other Mrem to fight with sword and spear. He wondered if they'd learn to use the bow.

Or will they keep that weapon for themselves?

That wouldn't surprise him. What surprised him was that the Liskash were training them at all. It was a mystery like much of what they did and said; as if they walked on the ceiling rather than the floor, or walked backwards.

He suddenly smiled to himself. While the males ate their dinner he'd seen the beautiful Prenna in the distance. The only pure white-pelt Mrem amongst them all, with pink kittenish skin around her eyes and lips and a warm sweet scent. She'd seen him as well, and in the way she'd stood had told him that she was pregnant with his kit.

Ranowr grinned with his whiskers forward, feeling a warmth within at the thought. He would know which kit was his, especially if it was as white as its mother. He sighed in happiness. He'd never heard of anyone knowing their own kit. But he and Prenna, in their brief moments in the mating shed had formed a forbidden bond.

They'd been chosen at random to mate, the way the Mrem always were when the Liskash decided they'd need more slaves in the future. When he'd been thrust into the shed he'd been struck by her beauty. White fur, slanted green eyes and a delicacy of form that surely even the oblivious Liskash must appreciate. When he had gently embraced her, he whispered his name in her ear. She'd met his eyes and answered softly:

"I am Prenna."

"No talking!" the Liskash guard had snarled.

"He hurt me," Prenna had gasped.

"You animals are disgusting," the guard had said. "Don't hurt her," he added to Ranowr. "I hate this duty."

Then he'd turned his back and Ranowr and Prenna had made love.

That's what it was, Ranowr thought. *Making love. Not rutting like beasts.*

He did love her and now she was bearing his kit. He wanted to tell someone, but who could he trust? Any such relationship was strictly forbidden.

So it will be our secret, he thought, wondering if they'd ever be together again.

A bitter thought, that someone else might lie with her when the Liskash again decided she should breed. It was like a hot coal in his heart. But there was nothing that could be done about it. He sighed, lonely for her and sad at both their fates.

For a moment he imagined them running away together, living in freedom, just them and their kits.

He shook his head ruefully. It could never be; the Liskash owned the whole world. If they escaped the goddess Ashala they'd be swept up by some other Liskash god or goddess, one who very possibly would be even more cruel.

We'd probably be killed outright.

The way the Liskash seemed to hate Mrem made it almost a certainty; they killed even when it wasn't in their interest. Here at least they got enough to eat. Not as much as they wanted, but enough. In any case, he'd never put Prenna in such danger.

In his youth two slaves had broken the rule and been found out. The female became pregnant and was tortured until she gave up her lover's name. They were bound together and the young Mrem were made to bury them alive. He'd never forget their struggles as they tried to keep their heads above the dirt; the terror in their eyes.

Afterwards all the females from the oldest to the youngest were whipped to remind them that their bodies belonged to the Liskash. Now you never saw a female alone. Ranowr sighed and rubbed a sore muscle. He heard a sniffling and looked over at a group of kits. One had his arm around the shoulders of another who shuddered with sobs. He rose and went to them, kneeling on one knee before them.

"Are you hurt?" he asked.

The one who had been weeping wiped his eyes and straightened up with a sniff.

"No, sir," he said in a surprisingly steady voice.

Ranowr smiled. "Good. I thought something must be wrong." He waited a moment. "Is something wrong?"

The little face crumpled at the sound of a sympathetic voice. "I miss my mother," he choked out.

"Of course you do," Ranowr said laying his hand on the kit's head. "We all do. All I can tell you is that it gets easier with time."

The kit rubbed his eyes, he must be seven summers old; that was when the Liskash separated the male kits from their mothers.

"Why can't we all stay together?" the kit asked.

"What's your name?" Ranowr asked.

"Fesa."

A cold chill touched the back of the leader's neck at the name. He thought again of Fesa being led away to his death and took a deep breath.

"Well, Fesa, you're well grown now and have to learn how to be an adult. Since you're a male you must learn that from males. The Liskash have decided that males and females should live separately. And so we do. If you ask me why that is, all I can tell you is that is the way things are."

"But why?" the youngster whined.

"Because that is the way the Liskash want things to be. They are as gods to us Mrem and so we must do as they say or they will destroy us and we will not live at all."

He stroked Fesa's head. "Better to be sad and sore than dead, don't you agree?"

Fesa and the other kits nodded, their eyes big.

"It is something we all must learn," Ranowr said patiently. "Just as we all must lose our mothers and sisters. You must be strong and learn to find friendships with these your agemates. Do you understand?"

They nodded again, obviously dissatisfied, but knowing they weren't going to get a better answer.

Ranowr smiled and nodded to them, moving back to his place among the older Mrem.

Such is the path to adulthood, he thought. *Full of half explained realities, revealed one layer at a time.*

Four weeks later Hisshah snapped:

"Like this!"

She drew the battle sword at her side; it moved like a living thing compared to the clumsy padded practice weapons, glittering as if scaled. Then she demonstrated the complicated move she was trying to teach the idiot Mrem. Its tongue dangled out, and it dripped.

They were so disgustingly *damp*.

"The spearhead is coming at you. There is *force* behind it, enough to split your breastbone. But that means the attacker is committed to the line of his attack. His weight is moving forward and he cannot alter that quickly. *Strike* so and it will go over your shoulder, and the force will carry him forward so that he cannot withdraw the point and strike again at once. Then turn your wrists and body and cut down the shaft at the hands. *So* and *so*. Two movements like one. Do it right this time or I'll flog the skin off you!"

The Mrem slowly imitated the move and got it right.

"If you took that long to do it to the enemy you'd be dead!" Hisshah shouted. "Unless he stops to laugh and hisses the tongue out of his jaws! Do it faster, you fool!"

The Mrem tried and failed. Before he was halfway through the maneuver Hisshah kicked, her taloned foot thudding in the Mrem's leather-clad middle. The cheap armor took most of the impact, but he wavered breathless, then fell to the ground as she sheathed her sword and reached for the whip slung at her belt.

"Young goddess," Ranowr said, greatly daring, "I do not think we can do it the way a Liskash could. We are made differently. Our arms and shoulders do not bend in the same ways."

Hisshah halted with her whip raised and stared at him. Instantly she saw that he was right. They did move differently. Instead of the short, sharp, efficient motions of her people, the Mrem seemed to...to *ooze* from place to place. They had speed, but it was of a different quality.

We are wind. They are water, she thought with satisfaction. *Perhaps I am concentrating too much on form, and not enough simply on what works. Still, I can't afford to lose face.*

She gave the unfortunate Mrem before her one hard stroke with the lash.

"Interesting," she said smoothly, coiling her whip.

She poked her victim with the whip handle. "Go and practice that maneuver."

Then she gestured Ranowr over to her. "What is your name again?"

"Ranowr, young goddess."

He kept his eyes carefully down, but his heart thundered. Who knew what she might do to him for his boldness?

Hisshah stared at him. "Ah, yes," she said at last. "You are making a habit of asking me for mercy." She sniggered. "If you are trying to teach it to me you're wasting your time. I will not learn it, I do not wish to learn it. Look at me."

Cautiously he raised his eyes and stared into her golden ones. She did not blink, but he did, twice before she spoke again, with the disconcerting up-and-down motion of the eyelids that made the Mrem gaze so alien.

"But it is possible that you may have something to teach," she said at last. "You are the best of your fellows at following my instructions. Even so, I've noticed that you do not imitate me perfectly. Perhaps you are right, perhaps your kind cannot faithfully follow our movements. But I think you can be taught to fight. I shall concentrate on training you. And you and I will amend any moves that you feel are too... sophisticated for your rough form. Then it shall be your task to train your fellows."

She nodded. This could work. "Now," she stepped back, "show me how you would perform the move I've been trying to teach."

They worked together for the rest of the afternoon, while the other Mrem practiced their maneuvers unwatched. But Ranowr could feel his people watching him and the young goddess. There would be questions asked this night.

He still found it hard to be around her, but he

also felt they were making progress; finding ways to wield the practice sword that matched his limbs and allowed him to gain the speed she wanted.

Hisshah was pleased. Finally they were getting somewhere. And dealing with just one of the creatures was at least a little easier. This one, it seemed, had a brain that he could comprehend.

Ranowr, using the altered overhand cut on the practice post, struck it so hard that the sword broke. He held the hilt awkwardly and glanced at Hisshah in apology.

She stood stiffly, but only said, "Get another."

Inside she was horrified. The sheer strength of the creature! She'd never seen anyone break a practice sword like that and for a moment she felt cold with fear.

It is good that a slave is strong when you want him to break rocks or haul timbers or lift water, she thought. *If the slave can hit you, that is another matter.*

If this hairy crew decided to, they could tear her to pieces before anyone could react. She only had two guards with her. Tomorrow she'd bring more.

No one said a word to Ranowr during dinner, at all. He could sense them looking at him, even though he kept his eyes on his food and he wondered when they would have it out.

He was not surprised when it was Krar who spoke first.

"I thought you would get a beating for breaking that sword, Ranowr. The young goddess seems to like you though."

The others murmured agreement, sounding amused, rather than angry.

"I think what she liked was that we were getting some results," Ranowr said calmly. "If it keeps her from beating us to death for failing to do what she wants I'm prepared to work closely with her."

He snorted. "Not that I have a choice."

The others chuckled at that. But Krar pressed on.

"It's unnatural, a Mrem working one to one with a Liskash," he said.

"Well, Krar, if you don't like it then you can always refuse to cooperate. I'm sure the young goddess will understand and applaud your delicate sense of propriety. You will be groomed by her own paws and given succulent fish to eat from a golden bowl."

There was outright screeching laughter at that and Krar settled into silence, glaring at Ranowr.

Are you jealous of me? Ranowr wondered. *I'd let you have my place beside her if I could. Aren't you old enough to know that a Mrem has no say in what happens to him?*

He finished his food and took the bowl to be washed. Then went in and lay on his pallet, curling up with a paw over his nose. He was in no mood to socialize tonight. He was just drifting off to sleep when Tral came in and touched his shoulder.

"I would speak with you," he said formally.

Ranowr rose with a grunt and followed the older Mrem out.

Tral led him away from the circle and the dormitories until they stood in an empty space between outbuildings.

Ranowr glanced around. They wouldn't be overheard here if they were careful. He looked at Tral expectantly.

"I have seen something amazing," the older Mrem said, his voice trembling. "If I hadn't seen it with my own eyes I wouldn't have believed it."

"Just tell me, Tral. I'm all ears."

His stood erect to show the truth of his interest, and his whiskers bristled forward intently.

"I was speaking to the steward about some of the kits having bird pox and needing to be isolated lest they all get it. When I was walking back I saw some guards leading a Mrem bound with chains towards the prison."

"A Mrem in chains is something we've all seen before, Tral. What's so amazing about that?" Ranowr asked impatiently.

"It was a stranger," the healer said. "And he was wearing a warrior's harness like the soldiers wear, only made for a Mrem. He struggled and they were finding it hard to hold him. He clawed one of them badly and almost broke free. Finally Captain Thress clubbed him on the head and the soldiers dragged him away."

Ranowr opened his mouth to speak, then closed it and licked his nose instead, taking in a sharp breath of amazement. He felt as though he'd been knocked upside his own head by an overseer's club. What Tral was telling him was impossible. They'd always been told that they were the only Mrem in the world and that the great goddess's many times great grandfather had created them to work for their Liskash masters.

Certainly they'd never seen any Mrem but those who lived and worked in Ashala's territory. No Mrem was a stranger. They at least knew each other's faces.

And for a Mrem to harm a Liskash and not be instantly killed for it was unheard of. And...

"In a war harness, you said?" Ranowr asked.

"Yes, like, but unlike the Liskash gear. Made for a Mrem, no doubt of it and richly made at that. It looked as good as the one Captain Thress had on."

Ranowr's legs felt weak and he went to a crouch in the dirt. His whole world was shaken. That there might be other Mrem somewhere had never occurred to him. He'd always believed that the slaves of the Liskash strongholds were the only Mrem in existence.

He stood. "I must speak with him," he said. "They took him to the prison?"

"The place of pain," Tral agreed.

Frowning, Ranowr stood in thought. "I will find a way." He looked Tral in the eye. "Tell no one of this. Swear it," he demanded.

"I so swear," Tral agreed.

"Good. You took me aside to talk of the bird sickness among the kits. In fact you should tell me of your meeting with the steward and what he said. It sounds like we'll be without the kits' labor for a few days."

"At least ten days," Tral said and told him everything.

It was almost a comfort. The other thing... it was too *big*. When he thought of it, his mind felt like it was reaching for something just out of sight. *Meanings* kept tumbling in on him.

❖   ❖   ❖

Hisshah sat at the council table idly staring at the triangular designs of blue and green inlaid in colored stones on the white walls, focusing on the shifting play of light through the narrow windows and ignoring the other eight councilors. They were all were waiting for Ashala and the captain to arrive; the most active thing in the room was a thin blue trail of bitter incense-smoke in a little silver censor.

Thress and Ashala were often together and not for the first time Hisshah wondered if he was her mother's lover.

Ashala entered the chamber briskly and the council all rose to their feet and bent their necks, as if for a bite. Thress followed on her heels and hastened to his place. The great goddess sat and with a gesture commanded them to be seated also.

"For some time now," Ashala began, "we have been facing a crisis involving wild Mrem."

The councilors stared at her for a moment, then cast surreptitious glances at one another. All except Captain Thress, Hisshah noted.

"I had hoped that our neighbors would handle the situation before it reached us, solving the problem and weakening themselves . . . which would solve other problems," her mother continued. "But they have failed to do so. It seems several thousand Mrem and their animals are aiming to cross our land in an attempt to join their fellows beyond the new sea. So far, despite the odds against them, they have succeeded."

She leaned back in her thronelike chair and folded

her hands beneath her chin, curving her neck in a meditative S-shape.

"I am of two minds about whether to stop them altogether or to harry them across our domain as fast as they can move. But I'm inclined to the latter. If it were easy or free of cost to wipe them out, someone would have done it by now. Let them go—and become someone else's concern."

She glared at everyone at the table, then sat forward, placing her hands before her on the table.

"However, we have a more immediate problem."

Here she glanced contemptuously at the captain. "We have captured one of their scouts. Which would have been a good thing if the captain hadn't allowed him to escape in the main courtyard in front of everyone."

"Is there any way to keep this from our Mrem?" Hisshah asked.

"Do you ever even try not to be stupid?" Ashala snapped. "Of course, *our* Mrem know about it. I did say this happened in the main courtyard. That matters less than what we make them think it *means*. If you control meaning, mere facts become irrelevant."

She leaned back again, raising her hands. "At least I think I did say it happened there in the courtyard."

"Of course, great goddess," Hisshah muttered.

Hatred for her mother burned cold in her breast. If she'd had her mother's power the older female would have been ashes long since.

"The question is how to contain it. I have decided, if it becomes necessary, to tell our slaves that demons have taken the form of Mrem in order to confuse them and must be killed."

She gestured, three fingers and grasping digit.

"That is why we've been training Mrem soldiers. The wild Mrem may be reluctant to kill their own kind and while they're engaged with the slaves we will flank them and kill as many as we can. Our aim will be to get them running. That should minimize any damage they can do to our herds, buildings, waterworks and such."

"Great goddess, we should annihilate them!" Thress said, slashing his claws down the table.

"Oh, be quiet," Ashala hissed, her voice heavy with disgust. "And stop marking the furniture! Our neighbors did not send one word about this invasion. Doubtless they hope we will do exactly what you want, thus weakening ourselves and making it easy for them to strike."

She glared at her daughter. "Tell me that the slaves have become minimally competent by this time."

"Some have, great goddess," Hisshah said. "But not all by any means. It has been only a month. I was not told that I had so little time."

"A point," her mother admitted. "You will increase the pace of their training. Our scouts report that we have less than twenty days before we are invaded. I'd rather not lose all our slaves; but if we achieve our main goal it won't matter. After all," she said with a smile, "if we made them too competent they'd be too dangerous to have around in any case."

Glancing at Thress, she continued. "Captain, in

light of your idiotic failure this day, I find that you need some oversight."

She turned to her daughter. "In addition to your training duties I would have you take on that oversight. You will approve the captain's orders for the day. And he will seek your permission if there is a need to change them or if he needs to request anything. You may issue orders to the guards if you see a need."

The captain sat up straighter, moving slowly, his face carefully blank.

"Yes, great goddess," he and Hisshah said in unison.

Hisshah felt pleasure like a long cool drink after a day spent curled on a hot stone. Seeing someone else humiliated, especially one she so despised, made a nice change. She would have to see how she could make this even more unpleasant for him.

"And you may select a score for your personal guard," the elder goddess added.

Saksh, the head of Hisshah's personal guard, pulled his thin hard lips back from his teeth in disgust.

"What I hate most about Mrem is their smell," he said. "Like herd beasts, but ranker."

"Except they talk," Hisshah pointed out.

He clicked his tongue. "That's so wrong!"

She laughed; he had a point. Maybe she was growing used to them, the smell didn't bother her as much now. Though they smelled riper than ever as they struggled to teach their fellows what they'd barely learned themselves.

The idea of thousands of them coming to fight made her blood run thin and fast. The sight of their straining bodies instinctively made her want to strike them down.

They're too strong, she thought. *And who knows if they can be controlled by telling them the females and kits will pay if they don't fight?*

That had been her suggestion.

It probably wouldn't be a factor to a similar number of Liskash, but they're odd that way.

There was no indication from their behavior today that they knew about the Mrem prisoner. They seemed wholly focused on learning to fight. But they were slaves, good at dissembling. Lies were a slave's weapons, after all.

Except that we are giving them spears, shields and spears and *their skill with lies. And they are Mrem, stronger than we give them credit for.*

One of Thress's guardsmen came trotting up to her. He crouched and offered her a wax message board.

She read: *I await your approval of my orders.*

Below, those orders were listed. Fury filled her, flashing like lightning through her veins. How dare he prod her!

With every appearance of calm, she said to the guard, "Tell the captain I shall send a messenger in a short while. As soon as I have a chance to review his orders. Perhaps next time he could arrange to send them earlier in the day."

She smiled as an idea came to her. "Tell him that." She gestured as regally as her mother. "You may go."

"Ranowr," she called as soon as the guard was out of earshot, "come here."

"The young goddess says that your orders are approved, but that you should substitute Ssen for Thash at the main gate. Also that you are to get your orders to her the night before or early in the morning."

Kneeling, his hands on the ground before him, his eyes respectfully down, Ranowr waited for the inevitable blow. Thress was known for his temper and his punishments even of other Liskash. To Mrem the captain was still more vicious. He waited, braced, his heart thudding rapidly.

Thress looked down on the Mrem slave, his blood tight in his veins, until he felt as if his scales would stand on end and vibrate. He took a deep breath, and his rigid tail seemed to quiver with it.

"How dare you speak to me so?" Thress finally asked in a calm, steady voice. "I am superior to you in all ways, you filth!"

He raised the short, thick whip that was the mark of his rank and began to strike Ranowr until the skin broke. Thress continued the beating, his breath whistling through his teeth, spittle flying. Liskash from the guard gathered round and watched silently, while Ranowr covered his head and face with his arms as best he could.

"Captain Thress," a cold voice called. And called again before it was heard. Hisshah stepped between the guards, her hands on her hips. "How dare you beat my messenger?"

"He was overbold in his delivery of your message, Hisshah." The captain wiped spit from his chin. "I felt discipline was in order."

"And I feel that you have overstepped yourself, Thress."

She deliberately drew his name out in a hiss, equally deliberately choosing to omit his title.

Glancing at the bruised and bloody Ranowr, she tsked.

"You will be useless today. Go and find some light duty. But be on the practice field tomorrow morning."

She waved a hand in dismissal. Ranowr struggled to his feet, bowed his head and staggered off.

"Now, Thress," Hisshah said turning back to him. "Let me instruct you in how you will treat my messengers in future."

She drew a small, sharp knife and carefully put a point on one of her claws until the tip was nearly invisible, holding it up and turning her head this way and that to examine it.

Ranowr went to get a drink and to wash his face, splashing the stale warm liquid out of the stone trough and then rubbing at the fur with his wrists. Then he found Tral.

"The skin is broken," the healer said after examining him. "But not too deeply." He gently applied an ointment. "You'll be stiff for some time, and will have to watch how you move or the wounds will open again."

Ranowr snorted; how he moved was not his choice. "Who's doing latrine duty at the prison today?" he asked.

It was a chore for which they all drew the short straw at some time. Lately he'd been exempted because of his training. It was time he took on the unpleasantness. Light duty, the young goddess had said.

"Sigowr is to empty the piss pots today," Tral said. "He's chopping wood right now by the smithy." He gave Ranowr a searching look. "Are you going to try to talk to the prisoner?" he whispered.

"Why else would I volunteer?" Ranowr asked with a pained grin.

"It is forbidden."

"Everything is forbidden that is not an order. I will talk with him. It's lucky the Liskash are so fastidious about waste and so are giving me the opportunity."

That was true; it was an oddity of the Liskash. Leaving the waste buckets to overflow would be yet another indignity they could visit on their prisoners, but even the torturers wouldn't stand for it.

He slapped Tral on the shoulder and went to find Sigowr to tell him of his reprieve.

I hope they're not busy torturing their prisoner, he thought.

There weren't many prisoners locked up at this time and Ranowr quickly found the one he wanted by the smell of his bucket. He walked slowly through the cool dimness of the half-underground prison, beneath the arched stone ceiling that made this like a tunnel. Iron grills showed to either side.

"You there! You're a Mrem?" he asked softly, turning his face away to keep an eye in either direction and letting the wooden buckets in his hand clatter a little to cover the words.

"I am," came a tired voice; the words were oddly accented, but easily understandable.

"Who are you? How did you come here?"

"My name is Canar Trowr, I am a scout. Your soldiers captured me. That's all I'll tell you."

"My soldiers?" Ranowr said with a laugh. "Do you think I'm a Liskash? Do I sound like a Liskash? Do I *smell* like a Liskash?"

"You sound funny," Canar Trowr answered. "But any Mrem who works willingly for the Liskash is an enemy and I would kill you as soon as I'd kill them. Traitor," he added.

"Willingly! None of us work willingly for the Liskash. We work so they won't kill us or starve us or burn us with their minds or eat our kits. I was born here, all of us were and we were told that we were created by the Liskash and only tolerated because we work. If we don't work, if we try to fight we are killed.

"But where are you from?" Ranowr demanded eagerly. "How did wild Mrem come to be? Did you escape from the great goddess's domain?"

The prisoner laughed outright, not a sound often heard here.

"Your great goddess lied," he said flatly. "Hard to believe of the noble Liskash, but they lied. They're not gods. They never created us. There are thousands of free Mrem and I am one of them."

Ranowr thought for a moment, stunned. *Not gods, the Liskash are not gods.*

He forced the thought away and bent his mind to more practical matters.

"I don't know how many thousands would be. I know hundreds, how many hundreds is that?"

"Ten hundreds is a thousand," the prisoner said. "And we are more than ten times that many. We journey toward a land of Mrem hundreds of thousands strong."

Ranowr caught his breath. So many, unimaginably many. He heard the prisoner shift his weight and chains clinked.

"Can you get me out of here? I will lead you to them. You could come with us."

"Get that dung cart moving!" a guard shouted.

Ranowr hastily emptied the bucket and shoved it back through the hole.

"I'll try," he whispered and moved on.

Through his shock and the whirling awe of a world huger than he could have imagined, resolve hardened in him. He would free the prisoner, and Canar Trowr would lead all of them to freedom. Now that they had a place to go.

"Today when you deliver my message you are to stand straight and look Captain Thress in the eye," Hisshah commanded.

She was smiling, quite happy at the thought of Thress's reaction to such boldness. She'd have to be hard on Ranowr's heels to make certain the captain didn't kill him, because she intended the slave to be her messenger every day.

Her message was much the same as the previous one, his orders were approved with minor changes. But, oh! how he would burn.

The damn smerp means to kill me, Ranowr thought bitterly.

He blinked. This was the first time, even in his thoughts, that he'd been so disrespectful. But he felt justified. Thress would undoubtedly beat him again.

"Yes, young goddess," he said aloud. He took the wax tablet from her and trotted off.

This time Thress went at him with claws and teeth. Ranowr dodged and backed, covering his face with his arms and letting a swipe knock him down; then the kicks started, the killing claws poised.

It was *almost* worth it to hear the frustrated rage in Thress's hisses, the rage that could not be assuaged. Would still scorch like lava even if Ranowr died.

Once again, more quickly this time, Hisshah intervened; Ranowr coughed cautiously, felt no broken ribs grating, and stood blinking in the bright dry sunlight. As they returned to the practice field Ranowr could tell that she was elated by the captain's humiliation.

"Tonight you will deliver a message to the gate guards, I'm changing the password. You will do this every night."

"He will kill me, young goddess," Ranowr said.

"No, he won't," she said blithely, with a lithe flex of tail and neck. "He wouldn't dare. If he were to displease me so much the great goddess would punish him. He is being disciplined and he knows it. He would be very unwise to resist his punishment. Don't worry, I won't let him go too far. It is my plan that he should come to recognize you and dread your coming. That should please you, Ranowr. That a Liskash will dread your coming."

She laughed gaily. Ranowr throttled a snarl with a massive effort of will that left his male ruff bristling; thankfully a Liskash wouldn't know what that meant. The hideous thing was that it *was* almost worth it to think of the guard captain trembling in fear at the sight of a Mrem face.

Nevertheless, Thress will kill me.

Necessarily, slaves were better at reading their masters than the reverse, and Thress was on the verge of madness. Ranowr would have to find a way out soon. First he must find a way to kill the great goddess. She had the power to burn out their eyes if they were anywhere near her. If she didn't just set them all alight. He glanced at Hisshah. She was so full of hate, perhaps she hated her mother, too?

"Perhaps the great goddess would not want him too humiliated," he ventured.

Hisshah pressed her lips together. "He will not show weakness by complaining," she said, with notably false confidence, and added:

"Be silent now."

And she hastened her pace. Ranowr's heart smiled within him. She didn't trust her mother. And that probably meant she hated her.

Though she probably feared her, too. How could you not fear the great power of fire born from the mind? In a way, it was a pity that the younger Liskash had only the small power of—

Ranowr blinked. A thought scurried, like a little seed-eating beast in dry grass. His mind stalked, ready to pounce.

That night Ranowr cornered Tral away from the others.

"You can talk to the females' healer," he said. "I need to know how many females and kits there are. Also I need to know what supplies they have charge of, where such are located and how much they have. I will find out how many of us there are."

"Are you trying to take over the steward's job?" Tral asked, puzzled.

"No, I am preparing us to leave. I will free the prisoner and he will lead us to thousands of free Mrem. He doesn't know that yet, but if we come with our own supplies I don't think he can complain."

Tral was aghast. "Free?" he said and went silent. "What are thousands?" he asked at last. "Are they soldiers?"

"Thousands is a number. But I think they all are soldiers; if they were not, would not the Liskash have killed them or made them slaves?"

Agreement dawned in the healer's eyes, and his astonishment-slack face firmed.

"We just have to find them and we'll be too many for the Liskash to attack."

Shaking his head the healer warned, "It could never work, Ranowr. The Liskash are armed and they are more than we are. We can't just all decide to go, it's impossible. Think of what the great goddess will do! Think of the kits!"

"I am," Ranowr said grimly. "I'm thinking of them growing up thinking the Liskash are gods and therefore impossible to fight. I am thinking of something we've never known, Tral. Freedom! We can do it, I know we can. If I can work it right they'll be too busy to worry about us. But first I need to know how many wagons we have, how many krelprep, how much food we can carry. Where are the bundor and hamsticorn herds and how many of them can we take with us. And we need to know all of this soon."

"What makes you say that?" Tral was clearly frightened.

Perhaps by the size of the idea, perhaps thinking his friend had gone mad.

"They've sent out a scout, the one the Liskash have captured. The Liskash have moved our training forward. Why else have these things happened if not because the free Mrem are close and coming closer every day."

Ranowr clawed the air before his own face and lashed his tail. "We must act!" He put a hand on Tral's shoulder. "Are you with me?"

The healer took a deep breath and held it, then nodded.

"Maybe freedom is worth dying for," he muttered. He looked up at Ranowr. "Can I tell the female healer why we're doing this? She'll want to know; she's not stupid."

Ranowr thought about it; it was a danger, but Tral was right. He was going to have to trust people if this was going to happen. Hard to do; the Liskash had raised them all to watch one another and to report any strange behavior. But for this to work it couldn't just be him and the healer.

"Yes," he said. "And she should tell those she trusts." He smiled. "Be convincing, my friend, be very convincing."

When they got back to the circle before the dormitory Ranowr began to question Retys, who supplied the herders. Asking him what exactly he did and how many he served.

"There are eighteen herders for the hamsticorns, we have less of those, only about three hundred or so. Twenty-three take care of the bundor, four hundred of them at least and they're more frisky. I just bring them supplies and take their count of the herds for the steward's records. What I mostly do is stare at the back end of my krelprep as I go from one herd to another."

"What's it like to drive a krelprep?" Ranowr asked. "Are they difficult to manage?"

"Why do you ask? Are you angling for my job, Ranowr? Being the young goddess's favorite too hard on you?"

They all laughed, for by now the others were listening.

"No," Ranowr said casually. "I was just curious. Sesh once said to me that knowledge is never wasted."

He shrugged. "And I've always had an interest in krelprep. Did you ever ride one?"

Retys burst out laughing. "Me? Do you think the Liskash would let a slave mount their precious riding beasts? They'd whip me for thinking of it, and you too, so you'd better watch out."

Ranowr decided to take that advice and watch out. Tomorrow he'd ask someone else something just as casually. The need to hurry was on him. Who knew what shape the Mrem prisoner was in by now or would be in a few days?

And the great crowd of free Mrem were on the move; he couldn't risk his people being left behind.

Thress had taken to carrying a club for the sole purpose of using it on Ranowr. He could always get in at least a few solid hits before Hisshah stopped him.

"Why do you persist in annoying me?" Hisshah asked the captain after once again catching him at beating her messenger. "You know I'm the great goddess's only heir. One day I will sit on her throne and your life will be in my hands."

"In your hands?" Thress sneered. "What would you do to me? Pout me to death? You will never sit on her throne, never! She could still have a clutch. And then you would have a whole new set of young rivals to worry about."

He stopped short as though shocked at his own temerity. But he didn't back down. Hisshah felt as though she'd been doused in icy water. She glared at him.

"One day," she said softly, "you will regret those words."

Then she turned on her heel and walked away, Ranowr following.

"Young goddess," he asked, "why do they think you have no powers?"

"Because it's true," she snapped. "I can move small objects with my mind and that's it."

"Could you tie a knot inside a bottle?" he asked.

She hissed a scornful laugh. "Yes, easily. And what good would that do me?"

"If I could do such a thing," Ranowr said fervently, "I wouldn't have an enemy left alive."

Hisshah missed a step and then continued on her way.

"You have enemies?" she asked casually.

"Not many, but I do have them. Thress for one."

She spun and slapped his face. "You grow over-bold," she snarled. "Do not think because you can use a practice sword that you are more than a slave. You will be silent now."

They walked on in silence, but Ranowr was pleased. He knew he'd planted the idea he wanted in her mind.

Hisshah's mind churned. Thress would never have suggested the great goddess having another clutch if he hadn't heard her mother mention such a thing. This was bad. Her whole life hinged on being the goddess's sole heir. Without that prospect she'd be nothing.

And what did the slave mean about tying a knot inside a bottle? Did he mean what she thought; that you could tie a knot inside someone's head and kill them that way?

She liked the idea. No one had ever thought of it before. It was . . . it was *deliciously* sneaky. It meant you didn't need to be strong enough to destroy in bulk, from the outside, battering at someone.

It hinted that the Mrem were even more vicious than her people, which was unnerving. She listened to the slave's footsteps behind her. She should practice . . .

No, this one is too useful. I don't think Thress would be as insulted if I sent a new Mrem messenger. I'll start on small animals. There are always smerp in the barns.

Satisfied she walked on, busily thinking up tonight's new password.

Then she hissed laughter. She would make the password *Mighty is Thress.*

Because if you pronounced that with the soft, wet, mushy accent a Mrem's mouth-parts gave to the words, it meant something a little different, or could be mistaken for such. If you had been driven mad by frustration anyway.

Tickle me, Thress.

Her hissing grew as loud as water flicked on a heated bronze griddle.

In the short time he'd had Ranowr had collected just about all the information he needed. People were growing curious about his newfound thirst for knowledge, but so far no one seemed to find it too strange. The kind of strange they'd report to an overseer.

But now he needed to bring in more people. Today he would start with the hardest to convince. Krar.

He did not like Krar, who was a rival and a close one at that. Ranowr was speaker solely because he was marginally more popular. There was no room in their relationship for being friends. But he respected the other Mrem. Krar was smart and capable when he wasn't letting jealousy get in his way and would be a valuable ally.

Tral had volunteered to come along to back up what Ranowr had to say.

They found the other Mrem mending a fence in an empty practice field.

"Krar, I would speak with you," Ranowr said.

"You can speak with me during supper," Krar growled. "I don't intend to court a beating by chatting with you when I should be working."

Ranowr picked up one of the fence rails and held it in place. "Now I'm helping you. So you shouldn't suffer any ill."

"What about Tral?" Krar asked indicating the healer with his hammer. "What's his excuse for being here?"

"I need to confer with the speaker about something. Don't worry, they won't ask what." Tral glanced around, then continued, "Though there's no one to ask."

Krar gave an impatient hiss and began hammering in a peg. "What do you want?"

"I want to be free and to free all of our people," Ranowr answered.

Krar snapped back as though Ranowr had burst into fire, his eyes wide with disbelief.

"Are you *mad*?"

"No. And there is a real chance for us."

Ranowr told him about the strange Mrem and what his arrival portended. Then he explained most of his plan, holding back only the parts he himself was uncertain of. When he was finished he studied his rival, waiting for his response. If it was the wrong one he was prepared to kill him. But he hoped that Krar would see things his way.

"I can't believe this," Krar said, shaking his head.

"It's true," Tral said. "I've seen the prisoner myself."

"But so much relies on chance," Krar insisted. "Does everyone know what you're planning?"

"Just us," Ranowr told him. "But we'll have to tell everyone soon. If we wait too long they'll kill the prisoner, or the free Mrem will be past the great goddess's territory."

He waited, watching his rival think. After a long pause he asked, "Are you with us?"

Krar took a deep breath. "I don't know," he said slowly. "It's so much to think about."

Ranowr shook his head. "I can't give you time to think about it," he said. "We need to know now if you're with us."

He leaned close, holding the other Mrem's gaze with his own, letting him scent his determination.

"Think quickly, but carefully."

"Think what this could mean for all of us," Tral said passionately. "To do what we wish, when we wish, to own our own bodies, to know our kits. To be free!"

"It's madness," Krar said.

"Madness to stay when we could go," Ranowr told him. "This is our one chance. If we don't take it then we deserve to be slaves."

Krar nodded slowly, his eyes on a distant thought. Then he met Ranowr's eyes.

"You know I hate you."

"You don't hate me," Ranowr said with a laugh. "You just want me not to exist."

"You can say that because you've never had to live in your shadow." He licked his lips. "What do you want me to do?"

"Back us up when we talk to the others. Help me convince them in spite of their fear. And help me make any possible traitors more afraid of us than of the Liskash."

Ranowr held out his hand.

Krar looked at it, then up at his rival.

"You don't want much, do you?"

"I want to be free. I want *you* to be free. Then if you wish, we will take spears or swords or knives and you can see about making the world one where you don't have to think about me."

A smoky light came into Krar's amber eyes.

"Take his hand," Tral said impatiently. "You know it's the right thing to do."

With another deep breath Krar shook his head, but grasped Ranowr's hand.

"I know I'm going to regret this," he muttered.

"Maybe we all will," Ranowr said. "But it's still the right thing to do."

❖   ❖   ❖

Hisshah approached her mother's riding krelprep cautiously; it was an unpredictable beast that liked to kick and bite. It pulled its muzzle out of the feeding trough and looked at her across the polished saccar-wood railing, its skin gleaming with health and careful grooming.

It had bitten her, almost trampling and killing her twice while her mother looked on, waiting to see if her daughter could control it. The animal was a beauty though, strong and sinuous with fancy yellow-and-green markings. She hated it. She stood looking at it for a few moments, then she struck.

First a push at the nervecord within the spine, which caused the beast to bellow in confusion as its legs collapsed. That was delightful, but painfully loud, and Mrem slaves would come running to see what the trouble was—they would pay for any injury to the prized beast. So she cut off its air, just a little *pinch* within the windpipe. She watched it thrash helplessly, its golden eyes rolling in panic. Then she ended it, grasping at the delicate tissues of its brain, like dragging mental claws through jelly.

It collapsed, kicked, voided and died in less time than it took to think the words, so much dead meat, its colors dimming already and its tongue lying out across its teeth.

Hisshah smiled. Her mother would be displeased; she'd been proud of her mastery of this willful beast. But Hisshah was thrilled. This had been the first large creature she'd tried out her new power on. And it had gone exactly as she'd expected. Her whole being was alight with joy. She had a great power. As great as her mother's if less spectacular.

I feel ... I feel so happy. *Happy as I have not been since I was a little hatchling.*

She looked around; no one had heard the commotion, it seemed. With a soft laugh she turned and walked from the stable. Her mother would be so annoyed.

The guard struck Ranowr with a couple of light blows, almost for form's sake. Then he said wearily:

"What's the password for the day?"

"*Mighty is Thress,* master," Ranowr said cautiously.

Three of the closest Liskash warriors hissed uncontrolably. One of them clapped both hands to his snout, covering his nostrils in horrified surprise. Another's spear clattered on the stones, its steel head clanging with a discordant ring that died into the sudden stillness of the morning. A third was backing away, his lips and nose squeezed tight, his whole head jerking with the need to hiss laughter.

"*What was that?*"

"Master! I said *Mighty is Thress!*"

This time he *did* say it, working to keep his tone hard-edged and crisp like one of the rulers. He was almost as horrified as the guards at the—unintentional—slip. For a moment he thought Thress would die then; veins were visible under the fine scales beneath his throat, and his pupils opened until they were ovals that were almost round.

It was exactly the sort of petty but cunning spite the young goddess would come up with.

"Go," Thress said, his hands trembling; his voice was beyond rage, almost pleading. "Go, go."

The Liskash was turning to his subordinates even as the Mrem backed away. Hissing and snapping-stone shrieks rose as he walked away.

Soon, Ranowr thought as he walked away rubbing his arm.

He had everything in readiness; the wagons and tack were arranged for a swift departure under the guise of a new efficiency. Stores of food and blankets and tents were ready to hand, allegedly in the event of a neighbor attacking. So far they'd gotten away with everything and the steward was pleased that they were working so diligently.

It's easy to work hard when it's for your own benefit, Ranowr thought grimly. *We'd never have shown them how hard we can work, otherwise.*

"You were seen leaving the stable," Ashala screamed, her voice echoing through the hall. She pounded her fist on the arm of her throne. "Tell me what you did to my krelprep!"

"What makes you think I did anything to it?" Hisshah asked her mother boldly.

Ashala paused. This was most unlike her daughter, who, though on her knees where she belonged, was otherwise upright, instead of her usual cowering posture and was meeting her eyes. She leaned back in her throne. If there was one thing she'd learned in her years as ruler of this domain it was that such a change of attitude could be dangerous.

"What were you doing in the stables?" she asked.

"I merely visited my own krelprep to see how it fared."

"You never visit your beast," Ashala reminded her. "You hate krelprep."

"I'm not fond of them, it's true. But we're about to go to war and I don't intend to walk."

Hisshah paused. "What happened to your krelprep?"

Ashala glared at her. "As if you don't know," she growled.

The younger female returned the glare with a look of innocence.

"You know I would never go anywhere near your krelprep. It's tried to kill me twice. What could I possibly have done to it without getting in reach of its teeth?"

"It's dead," Ashala said through clenched teeth.

"What happened to it?" Hisshah asked.

Hiding her glee was as hard as anything she had ever done. Boldness seemed to be working. At the start of this conversation she'd thought she'd be receiving a whipping by now. Possibly that she'd be a bubbling grease-stain on the stones.

"We don't know. There isn't a mark on it," the great goddess said.

"There's been some sickness in the barn, the hostlers have been complaining of dead smerp and worrying that whatever killed them will spread to the krelprep. Perhaps that's what happened to yours."

Indeed I know for a fact that's what happened to yours, Hisshah thought. "Perhaps we should clear that barn and burn it down."

Ashala was still visibly angry, but also thoughtful. What her daughter had said was not unreasonable.

Thress leaned over and whispered in her ear.

"You could have poisoned my beast," the great goddess said.

Hisshah gave an exaggerated sigh. "If I tried to give food to your krelprep it would have taken off my hand. And if I bribed a stabler to give it food he would report it to you instantly."

She raised her hands. "Has anyone made such a report?"

It was beginning to feel like she was going to get away with this.

Once again Ashala looked thoughtful, once again Thress whispered.

"Did you kill my krelprep?" she demanded.

Hisshah stared at her for a long moment.

Why not now? she asked herself. Now is as good a time as any.

"Yes," she admitted. "I couldn't help myself."

Her mother's eyes flared and she knew herself in danger. She still thought she was safe from burning, but she could see that her mother was thinking about it. She readied herself to strike.

"That thing hated me," Hisshah said. "It wanted to kill me, but I didn't want to die. It was me or the krelprep, Mother. Which would you rather have alive?"

Ashala actually blinked in surprise to hear her daughter call her *mother* in open court. She looked out at the assembled courtiers and then frowned at her heir. If Hisshah was clever enough to be able to kill a beast so much stronger and more vicious than she was then perhaps she was too dangerous to have around. She prepared to strike her.

"You can be replaced," she said at last.

"No, I can't," Hisshah said.

The great goddess stiffened and her eyes rolled back in her head, foam formed at the corners of her mouth and her body bucked three times. Then she slid bonelessly from her throne to lie on the burned spot where so many others had died.

Hisshah licked her lips and brought her breathing back under control. She'd felt a wave of heat just as she struck and knew she'd survived only by dint of the unexpectedness of her attack.

She mounted the dais and sat on her mother's throne.

She smiled at the stunned courtiers.

"Remove that," she said to the guards, gesturing at her mother's body. "But save the gems, I'll be wanting those." The guards looked from her to Thress and she felt a flash of anger.

"It is by no means settled that you should take the great goddess's place," the captain said. "I demand that you rise from her throne!"

He grabbed her arm and yanked. Hisshah made his legs fail him and he almost dragged her from the throne as he fell. She put her foot on his chest and kicked him over backward. He drew a dagger as he fell and would have thrown it but she struck again, leaving him paralyzed from the shoulders down.

"Stop her!" he shouted. "Strike her down; she can't get all of us."

"Oh, yes I can," Hisshah assured them, though she wasn't sure herself. "I'm keeping the captain alive because I have a score to settle with him. But any of you who wish to die on his behalf I'm willing to oblige."

She met the eyes of those she thought might rebel and saw them acknowledge the truth of what she was saying. She looked at the captain's second.

"What is your name?" she asked, though she knew. She knew everyone in the compound.

"Sheth...great goddess."

Hisshah smiled at him. "You are now captain of my guard. Have Thress taken to the prison."

Once again she indicated her mother's body. "Have that removed."

"Can't you see what she's doing?" Thress screamed. "She's a murderer, she must be stopped!"

Well, so was my mother, Hisshah thought. *Many times over. She killed my father and countless others, often for nothing more than her own amusement. Where was your outrage then, my little captive captain?* She considered taking his voice, but no, she wanted him to have a voice. Soon she would hear him in full cry.

"Captain Sheth?" she prompted.

The new-made captain gestured to the guards and they began hauling the two bodies away.

"You will regret this!" Thress warned them. "She'll kill you all!"

Once the still shouting former captain was gone Hisshah turned to her court.

"I am prepared to accept your oaths of fealty now," she said kindly.

The scent of fear was dense and sharp, and her nostrils flared. This wasn't as spectacular as burning, but in its way . . .

Better, she thought, and smiled.

One of the nobles stumbled as he came forward to grovel and swear.

Much, much better.

Tral hurried up to Ranowr where he was practicing strokes with Krar.

"I just saw them drag the body of the great goddess from the hall," he gasped. "It was really her, the body was glittering with jewels and the guards were dragging it by the feet and they were dragging Captain Thress out, too."

Ranowr stared at him, his breath frozen. This was it. This was what they'd been waiting for.

"Set everyone to gathering the food and the wagons," he said to Krar.

To Tral he said: "Inform the females and then meet me at the prison with two Mrem and a handcart. Bring your medical kit."

Then he headed for the guards.

"The young goddess needs you in the great hall," he told them. "Something terrible has happened. I think Captain Thress has struck down the great goddess."

Saksh, the head of Hisshah's guard stared at him for a moment, then slapped him.

"How dare you say such a thing?" He pulled out his whip. "I'll have your back in shreds for that!"

Just then a guard came running up to them.

"The great goddess is dead!" he gasped. "Captain Thress is fallen!"

Saksh stared at him, then at Ranowr. "You and your fellows go back to your dormitory and stay there!" he ordered and ran off with the other guards trailing him.

Ranowr then nodded at Krar who began rallying the other Mrem and then headed for the prison at a run.

"The young goddess has commanded all the guards to report to the great hall," he told the guard at the prison gate.

The guard looked uncertain, but he'd been given orders by this Mrem before. He immediately turned the problem over to his superior.

"We've just been given charge of Captain Thress," that one said. "Why would she order us to abandon him?"

"Because he's safely locked up and she needs your support?" Ranowr suggested.

The guard weighed that in his mind and decided that it made sense; everyone knew rewards and punishments flew full and wild during a change of power. He blew a whistle and the other guards came running.

"Fall in," he ordered and they marched off.

Ranowr watched them go in disbelief. *This is going almost too well,* he thought and headed into the prison. As he rushed down the corridor he heard Thress's voice from behind a door. Pausing to glance through the grill he saw the captain lying motionless on the dirt floor.

Seeing him, Thress narrowed his eyes. "You! Her pet! Come to gloat, have you?"

"No, Captain," Ranowr said. "I have neither the time nor the interest." And he was gone.

He removed the bar from the door of the Mrem's cell and entered. Canar Trowr lay panting on dirty straw, no longer chained. Chains were no longer needed. His feet were a bloody mess as were his hands. As was most of him. Ranowr's heart went cold. If they were too late it was all for nothing. Tentatively he reached out and touched him.

Instantly the prisoner sprang alert, only to sink back again.

"Who are you?" he asked in a voice that grated.

"Ranowr. I've come to get you out."

Canar Trowr laughed weakly. "Surely you could have waited a bit longer?"

"Not if we want to get out of here. Can you walk at all?"

"No. But I will anyway. Help me up."

He did so. There wasn't a place he could touch that wasn't wounded, but aside from a few groans the prisoner kept his pain to himself. Then, when he was upright and leaning heavily on Ranowr they stumbled awkwardly from the cell.

Once outside Tral and the others were there to meet them with a handcart. They stared at the prisoner; the two helpers in amazement to see a stranger Mrem, Tral in horror at his wounds.

"Take him," Ranowr said, "hide him. As soon as you're ready head for the gates. That's where I'm going now."

"That is what the new great goddess has commanded," Ranowr said for the third time.

"But it makes no sense!" the guard said.

"Still, those were her orders. Perhaps it's a loyalty test," Ranowr suggested, hoping that would move the stubborn fool.

The guard looked over the Mrem's shoulder and blinked. Ranowr followed his gaze. The first wagons were coming in sight and the gate remained closed. He'd been telling the guard that the Mrem were all to gather at the great bundor herd until Hisshah called them back, but the guard persisted in resisting.

Ranowr turned back to him, his face and manner calm. Everything about him proclaiming, "I am following orders. What about you?"

At the wagons' inexorable approach the guard's resistance crumbled and he shouted to his fellows to open the gates.

Watching them go through Ranowr saw Prenna sitting in one of the wagons. She met his eyes and raised a hand shyly. He smiled and gave the barest nod and ruffle of whiskers, then she was gone.

Now his people were on their way, he had one last thing to do. Towards the end of the slow-moving column he found Tral.

"The sleeping draught that kills," he said, "does it work on Liskash?"

"Even better than it does on us," Tral said. "They're so much smaller."

"Give me what you have," Ranowr said. "And give my love to Prenna for me."

Tral handed over the flask. "What are you saying?" he asked.

"It may be some time before I catch up. Don't wait for me," Ranowr told him. Then he turned and trotted away.

Hisshah was glowing with pleasure. She had accepted the oaths of all of her mother's court, her court now, and had just finished deciding a case that her mother had been neglecting in favor of the plaintiff she hated least.

Suddenly Ranowr was there, offering her a goblet of wine.

"You must be thirsty, great goddess," he said, smiling.

She was parched, but also suspicious. How had he gotten into the great hall? And whence this good will?

But then . . . he has been very useful. Dangerous, but useful. A cunning Mrem could be even more useful in the future. I must sleep. If I make him hated enough, he will help guard me . . . perhaps a Mrem guard? I need never fear their trying to overthrow me . . .

"It is the custom here," she said, "for the one who offers wine to taste it first."

He took a sip, then offered the goblet again.

"You might as well drink it all," she told him. "I won't drink from the same cup as an animal."

Still, part of her was gratified to think that even the Mrem were pleased to have her as the new great goddess.

Ranowr hesitated. "It is so fine," he said. "Never meant for the likes of me."

"Drink it," she insisted, watching him closely.

He did, gulping it down in four swallows. "It's good!" he said. "Thank you, great goddess."

She laughed and reached out a hand for another goblet. He took another from the tray and filled it for her. Then she also gulped the fine wine down, gaily smashing the cup to the floor where it shattered, the dregs splattering a few unlucky courtiers. She laughed at that.

"Wine for everyone!" she said. "I would have us drink a toast to my new reign."

As the servants began to circulate, she gestured to Ranowr for another cup and he quickly filled one for her.

When everyone had been served she raised the goblet she'd been sipping from and exclaimed, "To a new day!"

And the cup slipped from nerveless fingers to shatter on the ground.

She was suddenly ice cold and her heart was laboring, darkness was narrowing her vision. Hisshah drew a deep breath and tried to rise only to find it impossible.

No! she thought. *Not now! Not when I've won!* She turned her eyes to Ranowr. *It was him. He'd killed her!*

She tried to speak, tried to curse him, tried to kill him. Nothing worked. Her breath was coming hard now and the dark was closing in.

Ranowr suddenly dropped to his knees, dying himself from the poison he'd put in the wine.

"You . . . die . . . too," she manged to hiss.

"I . . . die . . . free . . . and for . . . my people," he said, laboring. "You . . . just . . . die."

Her eyes closed. There was one last whispered sound: "Prenna . . . our kit."

Then nothing.

Battle's Tide

MICHAEL Z. WILLIAMSON

And on the thirtieth day there rose before the clan a great mass of demons. And Rau wondered at their number. The Claws gathered and they too saw it was too many, but Aedonniss entered Hress Rscil and spoke to them, saying go this way and that and to strike as I instruct so that my own legions can join in the battle.

So those in the claws took heart and fought with courage. But this was still not enough, for the most evil Sassin was powerful and his minions countless. Warriors fell and there was no one to fill the ranks.

Then the Dancers came forth and stood with the warriors and everyone wondered. So the claws once more took heart and both fought on even as many more fell.

Seven days and seven nights they fought, warrior and Dancer side by side, carving their way through a numberless horde. And finally when those who remained were exhausted and unable to even raise their weapons Aedonniss caused the sea to come forth.

The waters rose and with them came a roar of vengeance. In the foam could be seen the face of every Dancer who had fallen and rising above the water on a silver chariot rode great Cmeo Mrist, priestess and lover. And the demon's minions were torn asunder by the waves. But the warriors of the clan were touched by not a single drop.

And so the way was once again open.

—*The Book of Nrao*, verses eighty-four to eighty-six

NRAO AVELDT LIKED HIS WAGONS AND HIS SPIES. In the colder lands to the north he had been an upstart. But here the Clan of Three Fangs was powerful enough to have even torn land from the Liskash. Times had been hard, still were, but the clan leader did not regret his decision to take his people south. At least he hadn't until a few weeks ago, when the waters came.

He sat under the broad shade of his residence in a wicker chair, enjoying a drink of grer, fermented arosh milk. It refreshed the body and let his mind think clearly. He had much to think about. So did his advisors, seated in a ring with him on carved wooden chairs. His son Nef Esnrao benched quietly attentive off to the side, learning actual rulership along with the parchment lessons he took. The boy looked distracted, his long tail twitching impatiently from side to side, but Nrao understood that was partly an exploitation of his age. He was wiser than many suspected. He was tawny and handsome, certainly his mother's son as well as his. Nrao's warm, golden coat was striped with black on cheeks, wrists, tail and ankles. Distinctive markings, the seer Ingo said, for a male of distinction.

Nrao Aveldt's neighboring Mrem sometimes mocked his taste in politics. They preferred decorated Dancers and large warriors. His corral of wagons, the extended wall and defense works around it, the shapers who maintained all, and the monies spent on distant rumors amused them.

He had Dancers and warriors, too. His warriors knew several fighting styles and tactics. His Dancers studied a variety of dances and incantations. When a fight came, the wagons moved his warriors rapidly, and he could place them in superior position to the enemy.

That was why his steading was larger than any within knowledge, and why he was amused at the mirth sent his way. Hidebound traditionalists would fall by the wayside. His clan was one of the first to take southern land from the Liskash. The ancient enemies were still licking their wounds. This meant he had some of the best water and grazing. They held a large if dusty savanna with three large rivers and numerous wells and oases. Clan herds beyond count browsed the tall grass. So it had been for over five years, an ideal home for a growing clan, but now...

When the sea broke through to the Hot Depths, he'd dispatched scouts, diplomats and spies to draw maps and tell him all they saw. They were here now, to counsel him on all they knew.

Nrao Aveldt began, "I would like updates on each aspect. Talonmaster Hress Rscil?"

It would be hard to miss Hress Rscil, the talonmaster, with his oiled fur looking darker than its natural tan tones, worn and abraded harness he seemed never to remove, and flat but heavy muscles. Next to him were spear, javelin, battle claws and knife, neatly leaning against the bench. He had come directly from fighting practice.

Hress Rscil spoke in his deep, confident voice. "The refugees continue to gather and approach. One large band has gathered the remnants of several clans. Few are a threat directly, but all need food and water. I still suggest guiding them west and then north to the cool streams and woods. It is not long before we will have to do the same. Isolated there is no question that eventually we will fall. We must also keep the way open until then for others who are farther in. Their strength will be needed." One ear twitched as he finished.

Nrao Aveldt said, "While I bear them no ill will, sending them ahead provides useful information, and has some effect on the cursed Liskash."

"Yes, Clan Leader." The talonmaster was practical, of course.

"Seer Ingo?"

His elder philosopher, aged but spry, his fur tufted and ticked in white, leaned against one arm of his bench and said, "Land itself, the Hot Depths, was taken from the earth. It was not prime land for anyone with fur, but all of its dwellers must find a new place to live. The weather is still changing, and more than we expected. The sun will draw much rain from this large new sea, and drop it to the west. This will improve growth, but will also cause new rivers and erosion."

Nrao Aveldt nodded acknowledgment. "Will that cool things enough to hinder those annoying Liskash?"

"I don't know yet." Seer Ingo did not lower his ears in shame. It was safe to be unsure around Nrao Aveldt. He knew not all answers were cast in bronze. "It may enable or hinder them."

"Can we use that land?"

"We can. It could prove rich eventually, but it would take development of grass, then scrub, and repeated burnings to make a rich soil. We'd need to transport earth borers, naked tails and goats to provide dung and dig it in with claw and hoof. Also, the Liskash will object."

Nrao Aveldt smiled and said, "They'll object, but it might not be an issue, if the climate is not to their favor. Watcher Tckins Mestri?"

His head spy leaned forward slightly. The Mrem was slim and very average looking. His dull gray coat was healthy but ordinary. He wore harness of a trader, the pouches stuffed with items and valuables. It was a suitable disguise for his comings and goings.

"Nrao Aveldt, there is much going on between the Liskash and other Mrem. People fled the flooding in all directions, some to be captured by Liskash, others crowded and displaced. They caravan and fight, as the talonmaster has said, to seek homes farther north, and west around the New Sea. Liskash fight with them, and each other. I can't speak to the long term of the region, but movement west is our only option. East is desert and sea, south is Liskash, north is the New Sea."

The clan leader said, "That is certainly an issue. Do you believe it's worth it to move now, though?" Tckins Mestri trembled slightly at the question.

"I believe we can find a good position early, run wagons to small strongholds to keep them supplied, and build a solid steading. The Liskash are fighting amongst themselves. We might find a defensible position north of the hills, without needing to fight our own kind."

"That would be good, but is not the only consideration. We must have enough people to occupy and hold the land against violent Liskash and displaced Mrem. Priestess Cmeo Mrist?"

The only female present, the priestess had the circling symbol of the Sky Lord around her neck. The bronze of the medallion stood out against her glossy black fur. She stretched out a hand. The very grace of it attracted the attention of all the males, but it was what she said that mattered. Her round, gold eyes were sincere with concern.

She spoke, "Aedonniss does not speak directly. We must infer. If this is to be a new, rich land with a broad sea to fish in, and has caused much distress for the Liskash, it is clear he is offering us an opportunity. He does not guarantee it will be easy, or successful, but I feel he wants us to try. Challenge is what makes Mrem great, over those indolent, lazy Liskash."

Nrao Aveldt saw it, too. There was risk, though

it was manageable with preparation and forethought. There was also the chance of great expansion. Rich territory, plentiful food, and perhaps a secure border against the scaly Liskash.

"Then first, I will have the wagons checked, and meat dried."

Oglut was excited and nervous, though he'd never let the underlings know that. His fathers had built this palace of carved marble and scented wood through the power of their minds to control others. His limits had always been those who could also force others to their will. Now some of those who had lived in the lowlands were gone, or had lost their slaves. He sat on his throne and thought.

There seemed no end to the water. Where there had been rich holdings now there would be nothing. His own lands had been considered too high and cool. But now his holdings were intact and the riches he had coveted lost. Where he had once ruled at the edge of the lowlands, now he would control the far side of a new ocean. At least if it stopped rising before the whole world was flooded.

There was potential for great expansion, with Sassin and Ashala dead and their holds in tatters. Then, those accursed Mrem who had challenged them in the warm jungles were also fleeing ahead of the New Sea. Most went north to the cold lands they had been spawned in. The few heading directly west would be easy to incorporate as they reached the range of his mind. It was a silly game they played, but what could one expect of semi-sentient mammals with no mindpower? They weren't good for much, but could serve as a buffer against other attacks, rather than waste more valuable lives.

The New Sea would also bring rain and growth. More food meant more slaves, and a finer godhold. He needed to move quickly, to secure it before someone from far south did so, or it got overrun by those accursed hairy Mrem from the north.

He pondered it all while sitting on his favorite throne, comfortably fanned by slaves, caressing the new female he had recently acquired, and occasionally sipping from a golden goblet of wine. He enjoyed his godhood. He put that aside and chose action. Yes, it was time the boys grew up.

Oglut wished for his servants to appear, and shortly they did.

"I am moving to secure the empty godholds of Sassin and Ashala, to claim the slaves and resources that they abandoned. I need my chariots and guard ready. My sons will lead the campaigns."

Then he called his sons.

Mutal arrived, young and eager with trappings worthy of himself. He had had his scales gilded and painted in handsome colors to resemble a mosaic. His garments had been woven of the finest cocoon strands and dyed regal purple. Behind him, dull-eyed Mrem servants carried his gilded weapons and armor on plush pillows. Buloth didn't appear at once. He was big enough now to be a slight challenge. That was another issue for Oglut to address.

He waited for Buloth, who arrived with hints of incense and sage smoke. His costly blue and yellow raiment was askew. Had the boy been breathing dimweed again?

Oglut spoke to him first.

"I have decided to annex the lands left vacant by our departed neighbors, all the way to the coast of the New Sea. Once this is done, there will be a large godhold for you, so you need not wait for my demise."

"Thank you, Father." The boy, now grown, didn't seem appreciative, but smug.

Oglut frowned. Perhaps Buloth did not understand the gift he was being offered. "Rather than you fight me for control, you can have a new holding, and larger than this one. Mutal," he said, shifting his gaze and his power to the younger male, "you will have my holding, or a large part of it, what you can control, when I am too old to rule. If we expand further, it may be larger as well."

"Thank you, Father. It is a great offer, but I wish you long life." The younger one, at least, was sincere.

Oglut dismissed the comment with a wave. "Of course I will live long, but I am older than you. We will plan now to secure our new lands. I will have Buloth ready at the east with an army, to expand as far as possible along the new coast against the furry pests as the weather warms. Mutal, you will go south. Success awaits us. All we need to do is be ready for it."

His sons smiled in approval, as did he. No back-stabbing or mind-forced retirement as a helpless elder needed. They could have three large holdings now, and his sons would expand after he died. If one of them died in the process, it would just mean more for the other, and for himself.

Oglut was pleased. Some of his hatchlings would die. Those who survived would have lands of their own that would take them many seasons to secure. They would have no time to turn on him and try to claim their inheritance early. And by the time they were strong, he would be much stronger.

"By the end of this season you will all be lords of your own lands," the Liskash finished.

No need to offer them his already stable holding. He hadn't lived this long through trust. They could create their own. Their triumphs would reinforce his own borders and set them up as shields for his realm.

If the Mrem and their beasts showed up after things were secure, they'd just make useful slaves.

The massive hide tent that served as both the residence and command center for the clan was nearly full. None could twitch their tail without hitting another. There was a strong scent off the moist fur of the nervous Mrem as those Nrao Aveldt had summoned stood and sat inside, sheltered from a light rain. The two dozen Mrem waiting were of every size, color, and type. They seemed to have nothing in common; none carried himself like a warrior. But then that was the idea. Most appeared to wear the tools of merchants or tinkers. In reality they were the eyes and ears of the clan.

All were strangers to each other. Nrao Aveldt had never before called in so many of his scouts and spies at one time. Ears and tails twitched as the normally solitary and cautious Mrem watched each other with calculating eyes. None were armed, but all labored to keep their claws sheathed.

The clan's spies usually sent messages in code, or brought reports back after a tour of merchanting or as envoy. Rarely did they report in person and always in private. Just being known to the other put them at risk. Nrao Aveldt had ordered them all in quickly when the full extent of the water's rise became apparent, sending replacements with the call. Those Mrem were not as experienced as the existing spies, but this was how they learned. Those who survived. Nrao Aveldt and the clan needed every fact now, but still had to keep up their guard, even at a cost.

Also, Hress Rscil's scouts were on a steady rotation, to map the New Sea and watch for migrations. Nothing but Liskash had lived in the very bottom of the Hot Depths, but the river courses were lush and fertile, to the point where they evaporated. With the flood, a few tribes had moved north, more south, an unknown number west, where they would be massively outnumbered by the Liskash.

Every eightday, he met with Hress Rscil and the incoming scouts personally, and received updates from his advisors. He would not move until he knew conditions were right, but then he'd strike like lightning to exploit the opportunity.

Today, he had both a spy from Afis's domain to the west, north of the Liskash, and the scouts from the coast. He waited on Seer Ingo, while Nef sprawled on his bench and stropped his claws. Annoyed, Nrao reached out one of his own claws and dug it into the post between the boy's. Nef flared his ears back, nodded and sat up.

"That is better," Nrao Aveldt said. "Now, pour wine for the guests."

"Yes, Father," Nef Esnrao said. He might be young, but the trappings of courtesy came easily to him. He should make a good leader one day.

Refreshments and a casual atmosphere, Nrao Aveldt found, made information more forthcoming. Some rulers demanded strict formality and adherence to rank. He was first among them, and deserving of respect, without the need to be ego-fluffed. When all were served, he sat among them, his pupils spread wide to show friendliness and interest.

Sicht, the spy, wore well-made harness, as befitted his position as one of the trade ministers to Afis's holding. He was comfortable enough with Mrem of status, and politely took a drink and a sweetened meat chew, pounded with honey and dried frusk. They were unhealthy, but delicious.

The two scouts were politely subordinate, but their smell and the proud set of their ears said they knew they were trusted to report honestly. Hril Aris and Flirsh Arst brought out their notes, and stood to consult with Seer Ingo. The old male unrolled his larger map, cut from the whole hide of a draft-bred arosh stretched out, and the three gathered to mark it. Nrao sat back enough to let them work, while watching.

Shortly, Ingo glanced up at him. "The flooding of

the warm lands is causing more rains, and dampening the hills. They are green with growth. It has drowned many Liskash and those Mrem who were passing through."

No Mrem chose to stay in what had been stale and hot lowlands. But through that desert had been the shortest route to the rich, open lands in the south. Nrao's father had led the clan through, though not without losses to the heat-loving Liskash that thrived there.

The scout's tail flipped with concern, flapping against two startled spies behind him. He seemed to not notice. "The water has come quickly enough that the great lords there are broken, but thousands of Liskash fled ahead of it. They can only reinforce those who were already trying to destroy us."

Nrao Aveldt let the tip of his tail lash as well. "Obviously we must stop that before it commences."

Hril, as senior scout, said, "The rise is measured in handspans a day, but it has spread over a huge area, and periodically inundates a depression with great force. Everywhere as it rises and the rains come the land is thick with muck because nothing has time to grow where once there was desert. The water slows, but still claims more land every day. Some days the waters are calm, then it suddenly rises quickly and pushes deeper inland, only to pull away again. But each time it remains over more land."

The scout's concern was obvious as he finished. "We searched every direction and route. Deep water blocks every path back to the lands of our ancestors. It would have taken days to run at the narrowest point. But there is no crossing the swirling sea that covers those routes now. To sleep near the water's edge is dangerous. One scout who ventured too far out into what we thought were shallows was pulled away by powerful, hidden currents. No more clans will come to reinforce us: no one can cross. Those of us south of this new sea are alone."

Nrao Aveldt had never seen a sea. He would have to correct that. He did understand there were plants that grew submerged, vicious reptiles in the depths, and even primitive animal-like things, fast but edible, near the shore. That was something else to explore. If they lived long enough to explore anything, the clan leader reminded himself, stroking a whisker.

Hress Rscil traced roads and paths on the broad parchment with the tip of a claw. Two disappeared into the new coastline. Three others were very close. All those routes north were broken. That particular bay would have a lot of shore traffic, if they could secure the area. If there were some way to cross it on water . . . but it was far too broad and stormy.

"Seer Ingo, what about crossing the water at some later time? Can boats be made larger?"

The sage tilted his head in assent. "With heavier timber, yes. We have none now. That might come from the hills as thicker forests grow."

"I am not worried about it now, but after this campaign, I think it a worthy pursuit for our artificers to ponder."

"Noted."

Nef Esnrao, leaning over their shoulders, suddenly pricked up his ears eagerly.

"Father, what of caravans? Should we have more warriors along that route, against conflicts or bandits?"

Nrao was proud of that. "A good question, Nef Esnrao. Most insightful for your age. Hress Rscil?"

The talonmaster nodded and raised his ears. "The caravans can support each other in proximity, and I don't foresee them fighting, although water could be an issue. But it's not a bad idea to reinforce the garrison on Steep Slope. They can conduct escorts and patrols. Outpost Master Shlom is one I well trust."

"Please. I will arrange supplies for you."

Hress Rscil said, "But this is all temporary. All of us must move, and I concur on doing so soon. The later we wait, the more desperate we will be." His ears showed his agitation.

"Soon, Hress Rscil. We must be prepared."

By midday, Nrao Aveldt had updated his strategy and plans with the new information. He offered all parties a lunch of fresh roasted mottlecoat liver with salt and ground sharproot, and gave orders for following spy missions.

It was time to discuss stopping the Liskash mind threat.

The clan leader wondered how the Dancer could look graceful even just sitting. Cmeo Mrist was beautiful and moved with a deadly grace that entranced all males. Nrao Aveldt also reminded himself she was also the second most powerful Mrem in his lands.

He wondered what she saw sitting there with even her slitted eyes still as she waited for him to speak.

"Cmeo Mrist, the spies bring me disturbing news. Oglut is the name of the Liskash godling in the east. From reports, he is powerful in his mind magic. He bound even Mrem warriors in the fight."

She stared at him, subtle changes in posture and a twist of her tail showing she was attentive and clearly listening. He realized Dancers rarely engaged in the skirmishes that his warriors had faced as they moved south.

"Once a warrior is actively fighting with an opponent, he should be intent on the task and not susceptible to distraction. So it has been for generations. Oglut overcame that. My scouts saw him enter a battle against those fleeing the waters and bind the warriors to his mind. The Liskash then turned them against their own clan brothers."

"I see."

"That means we must bind them back. Priestess, what can we do?"

Cmeo Mrist sat back and stared at the panel behind him, her black pupils spread so wide they swallowed up the golden irises. He let her do so, realizing the meditation for what it was. He often stared while thinking himself. Hers, though, was much more intense, even to watch. She fingered the symbol around her neck and her eyes slackened, then focused sharply on nothing.

Nrao Aveldt sat still also, not wishing to disturb her. These things worked in their own time.

She blinked and said, "We must strengthen the Dance."

"Very well. How so?"

"If we have more Dancers, and closer to the warriors, they can exert more power. Distance is very important. The power weakens quickly."

"Closer, you say. That's awkward, in a battle formation." The clan leader twitched his ears.

She said, "Ideally we would need to be in the formation."

That was a striking and uncomfortable suggestion. It made his fur bristle, and he wanted to forbid it at once.

However, he had to consider it fairly.

Mixed with warriors. It hadn't been done. That could mean there was a good reason not to, or that it hadn't been thought of.

He took a sip of his drink and said, "I will summon the talonmaster. Return in an eighthday."

"Yes, Nrao Aveldt." She bowed respectfully and left.

A messenger ran for the talonmaster, but it took time for him to clear the field and arrive. Nrao Aveldt used that time to consider. A central clearing in the formation for them? Several smaller ones?

Talonmaster Hress Rscil arrived shortly, his fur puffing in sections as the muscles underneath twitched. His face remained calm, but his body betrayed his tension.

"Welcome, Talonmaster," Nrao Aveldt greeted him. "I want to explore the idea of putting the Dancers into the warrior formation."

Hress Rscil fluffed and said, "Clan Leader Nrao Aveldt, have I given you cause to doubt my abilities?"

Nrao Aveldt hastened to reassure him. "Not in the

slightest, Hress Rscil. I could find no finer warrior.
This undertaking of mine seeks to provide you, and
the greatest warriors of Mrem, with stronger shields
against the Liskash. Do you have doubt in *my* abilities?" He asked it without rancor, but it was a test.
Not of Hress Rscil's loyalty, but of his willingness to
argue against Nrao Aveldt.

"None. My concern is that battle is traditionally a
male pursuit due to strength. Females fight well, but
are better in defense. Also, Dancers will not be fighting. They will be Dancing. If we lose large numbers
of Dancers—females—the entire steading suffers."

Nrao Aveldt dipped his head in assent. "I agree with
that assessment and its logic. However, by combining
your strength with their resistance, and with a goodly
support of wagon drivers, we can take and hold a
deep piercement into Liskash territory. Desperate
times may be ahead. Any tactic we can add that will
forward our aim is worth exploring."

"Then I propose we test it as we go, and use known,
working tactics if it proves unsuccessful."

Nrao Aveldt had that exact thought, but decided
it made a good bargaining point.

"A sound idea. We will discuss this, Cmeo Mrist
and you and I and others, in a few days. For now, I
wish for both groups to become more familiar."

Hress Rscil's ears perked out and he twisted his
mouth. "I will try. It's an untested concept, and requires
adjustment to our formations."

"We will discuss it now, then," Nrao Aveldt decided.
"Hress Rscil, I offer you some grer."

"Thank you, Nrao Aveldt. I accept."

Nrao Aveldt sat patiently. Hress Rscil calmed down as he first gulped, then sipped the cool, tangy fermentation. A scribe stood back, waiting for attention, and the clan leader gestured for him to approach. The Mrem did so, and hesitantly proffered a bark tablet of provision accountings for the pending expedition. It was more than Nrao Aveldt had planned, but a reasonable amount. He marked it, and dipped a claw in ink to make it official, then handed it back.

Shortly, Cmeo Mrist returned.

"Greetings, Nrao Aveldt and Talonmaster Hress Rscil."

"Priestess," Hress Rscil said.

Nrao Aveldt nodded. "Welcome, Cmeo Mrist. Hress Rscil has urgent matters to discuss on our plan, so I moved the meeting. I hope this is workable."

"I will make it so," she said. She curled into the bench opposite him and drew her feet up onto the seat. Her tail wrapped up around them.

"Good. This is a private meeting," he said, and looked over at the recording scribe, who nodded, stood and left the hall. He looked at his son, who stood poised as if to depart, but he looked as though he would like to stay. "Yes, Nef Esnrao, you may remain. Remember this is a most secret meeting, not for discussion even with Ingo or your other teachers."

Nef was so solemn and earnest that Nrao almost smiled.

"I understand. It is a matter of the steading."

"It is." He turned back to Cmeo Mrist and Hress

Rscil. "I wish you both to be free to raise objections and offer input. My concern is that the plan work, not that my ego be assuaged."

His advantage, of course, was that he meant it. He was hard to sway from a course, but did accept reason, and appreciated argument even if it distressed him.

There was silence for a moment, then Hress Rscil said, "Clan Leader, Priestess, with respect, this is what I find: My warriors are unused to the presence of females. This causes them to either loiter as near as possible to the females, hoping to attract their attention, or to cavort and exhibit, for the same. I fear that in battle they will uncontrollably lash out to prove their heroism, or gather around the females to protect them. This means they will not be fighting the enemy in a coordinated fashion. They'll fight more like scaly Liskash, not like Mrem."

His ruff was raised in agitation.

Calmly, Nrao Aveldt said, "I understand the problem and believe it. We must find a way around it. Cmeo Mrist, please explain your plan."

Cmeo Mrist said, "I will assume we can resolve this problem." She looked irritated, too, however, grasping her tail to stop it from twitching. "As I explained to you, by having the Dancers closer to the warriors, I believe we can provide a stronger protection against spells. This means we need some warriors to protect the unarmed Dancers. I thought it easiest for both to put the Dancers in the middle, surrounded by warriors."

Hress Rscil said, "The logic is sound, but you are not a warrior, nor are you used to dealing with warriors, and the special mindset they need. It is one of brotherhood, not of a male for his family, or a potential family."

Nrao Aveldt intended to ask, but Cmeo Mrist beat him.

"Then what do you recommend as a solution?"

Hress Rscil's ears popped, but he calmed down and replied, "How close must you be? Would behind a rank of wagons be close enough?"

"It might," she replied. "But my thought was to be close enough for the warriors to hear and be inspired by the chant. There's more power in it. It's hard for me to explain, but during practice, I can feel the power of it, and the closer, the stronger, and being part of it is of course so much more."

Hress Rscil said, "It's logical. There's also the logic that warriors don't do well that close to females."

Cmeo Mrist cocked her head and her pupils narrowed. "Yet the Dancers don't have this problem. Are you suggesting your warriors lack this discipline?"

Hress Rscil's fur brushed up all over and his claws twitched.

Nrao Aveldt said, "Careful! This is a conference, not a challenge." He eyed them both. Aside, he saw Nef wide-eyed in worry at the clash of wills. The boy was still for once.

Cmeo Mrist's pupils spread out to normal. She said, "While I meant that to be provocative, the question remains. Are not the warriors disciplined enough to keep their positions?"

"What?" the talonmaster snarled.

Hress Rscil needed a moment to calm down, and Nrao Aveldt allowed it. He sipped his drink and waited, without indication of unease. It occurred to him that his own ability to choke down his instincts might be a large part of what made him so effective. He never rose to a challenge unless it suited his purposes, and ignored jabs and pokes that others dueled over. His neighbors slapped at him hoping for a reaction, but also afraid they might get one, and so kept their distance.

Hress Rscil drank his grer and shook his head. "It is not so simple as it sounds, Priestess. Yes, my warriors will take my orders, well and willingly. What I am describing is their nature to protect females, and to seek mates. This will cause them to shuffle in close to keep the females from harm, and to be aggressive, within the limits of their orders, but not at the ideal level, to show their bravery. Females encourage what is best in the male, but an army is not about one warrior, it is about the whole."

"Fair enough," she said. She turned a hand over, the picture of feminine grace. The clan leader understood well what the talonmaster's concerns were. "Then the question remains, what can we do to make it work better?"

"I don't know," he said, with a toss of his ears. "Any concentration of females is going to cause this, I fear. This is why they are used in the defense, while the males campaign in the offense."

Cmeo Mrist offered, "What about several concentrations, then? It's not ideal for our trancing, but it might be done."

Hress Rscil pondered, as did Nrao Aveldt. He didn't understand the workings of magic, the Dancers, and trance. As a former talonmaster, he understood how to place warriors. This would be complicated. The idea was a sound one, but was implementation possible?

Hress Rscil finally spoke. "It is possible. I advise against it, because it means manipulating each element by itself, or requiring the warriors to manage greater details, and fallback plans if one should take more casualties than another."

Nrao Aveldt said, for Cmeo Mrist's benefit, "Yes, it is best they have only their fist of fellows to move and be concerned with."

Cmeo Mrist drooped her ears and slumped. "That is all I can offer. We will do our best wherever you will have us, but closer is stronger."

The talonmaster seemed genuinely unhappy to have won the debate. Nrao Aveldt appreciated that. So when the idea hit him, he felt sorry for what it would do to the poor Mrem's mind.

"What then," he said, "if we evenly disperse the Dancers?"

Both stared at him. Hress Rscil's tail twitched. Cmeo Mrist arched her mouth and flexed her ears. They were both too surprised to respond.

He continued. "The original idea didn't go far enough. Everything Talonmaster Hress Rscil says is true. But, if we mix the Dancers throughout, there's no clustering, and the warriors can show their best mettle without pressing the formation."

Hress Rscil said, "It might be the whole formation

will surge forward. It also means the females will be exposed to attack, especially by thrown weapons. There will also be arguing for position."

"Not from my Dancers," Cmeo Mrist said tightly. "In this context, you must think not of females, but of Dancers. They are as necessary to the fight as warriors, and not all females, nor even more than a few, can serve thusly."

"Necessary, but not necessarily on the battlefield!" Hress Rscil roared.

Nrao Aveldt held up his hands for calm and said, "No plan is without flaw. Can this be done? Does it solve more problems than it creates?"

Hress Rscil growled a sigh, and untensed his ears.

"It means a great deal of work, and drill, and instruction for the warriors."

Nrao regarded him sincerely. "I can think of no one more capable, and worthy of the songs afterward, than you, Hress Rscil. Call your drillmasters. Cmeo Mrist, prepare the Dancers."

"I shall, Nrao Aveldt." Cmeo Mrist faced Hress Rscil fully and said, "It appears we will be working together." She extended one claw.

Hress Rscil smiled, propped his ears up, and hooked her claw with his own.

"Thus are legends created," he said.

Oglut supervised his sons' preparations in the fenced field outside the keep. They had a tendency to loiter before acting. That was so animal. It was best to keep them a bit hungry, and a bit aggressive.

He set Buloth's forces against Mutal's in a war game. The young males set up their battle lines for Oglut's approval. Buloth needed to be ready first. His target was farther away, so Oglut concentrated upon his preparations.

"You place the Mrem at the rear," he called, seated on a comfortable bed on the back of a trunklegs, a behemoth mammal with leathery gray skin and a prehensile snout. "So they can eat anything that dies on the way, either by falling out, or native life stirred up by your passage. Remember they must eat meat, unlike our more advanced digestion. If a creature is lamed, kill it and give it to them. It motivates the others, and also keeps them aware of the vileness of these hairy beasts."

Buloth said, "Yes, Father. Also, I will put the mammal herd beasts in front, where they can eat grass before it is trodden. They make good emergency food."

Oglut nodded. "They do. Not the tastiest, but adequate nourishment for slaves."

Buloth's gray tongue darted across his lips. "I have decided I will kill and roast a Mrem before any battle. The smell will motivate them to my desires."

That was very amusing. Oglut chortled and flicked his tongue. A whiff of breeze brought him the smell of a cook fire at that moment. No Mrem, but something savory. Yes, that was a fine suggestion.

"Very good," he said.

Buloth said, "I have enough food for me and my assistants. The rest will scavenge as we go." He sounded most eager.

"They are well fed to start. They will have good endurance and be pliable."

"Thank you, Father."

"Are you ready to take control of them now?"

"Yes, Father! I am ready and privileged."

Oglut felt his son probing, enveloping. Buloth was strong enough, but not confident. That would come. He also had mixed feelings to find his son was not as powerful as he. Less of a threat, yes, but also somewhat inferior in mind. He might improve with practice, though.

In a few moments, Buloth had taken command of a two-thousand-creature army, plus a few personal retainers and some stupid beasts who only needed a vague prodding to haul carts. All their wills were bent to his. It was not as complete a command as Oglut would have had, but it would do.

It was time.

He thought rather than said, *Go, Son, and teach the furry little turds a lesson. You may start on your holding now.*

His son's mindvoice came back clearly. *I hear you, Father, and am grateful. They will be brought into the whole.*

He turned to Mutal. "See what your brother has accomplished, and learn."

"I will, Father," Mutal said, earnestly. In his mind, Oglut picked up a well-developed sibling rivalry and ambition of his own.

Success was within their grasp. He had bred well.

❖   ❖   ❖

The warriors were of two minds. Either the females were a too-welcome distraction, or they were a hindrance. Talonmaster Hress Rscil felt as if he could pluck out every hair on his body in frustration. His tail was constantly moving as he watched his subordinates mediate arguments and order the warriors back into line.

He found himself in daily conference with Cmeo Mrist, starting the first day. They used his chariot, with an erected sun shade, as a platform for observation of the drill field.

"This is not going well."

"It will. It is a new thing, and will take getting used to." Cmeo Mrist sounded confident. Her eyes were bright and calm, and her expression serene.

"Indeed," he said, wiping sweat from his eyelids. "How are the Dancers?"

"I don't know entirely. I see one substantial problem, though, that must be resolved."

"Yes?"

She fluffed slightly, and her ears flattened. That was surprising. The Dancer had very good control of her elegant body, usually. It must be significant.

"Several of the warriors have been most condescending to the Dancers. It is not only rude, it will undermine their confidence, and their empathy."

"Yes, that must be addressed," the talonmaster agreed at once. Indeed. That would not build a cohesive force, and as she noted, could undermine what they had. "What is the nature of these comments?"

"Several to the effect that females are not suited

to battle, only to defending the house. Others that they can't possibly manage to keep up with such powerful warriors."

Hress Rscil couldn't help but grin.

"That first would be from the older ones, the second from younger ones."

Cmeo Mrist couldn't suppress a smile in return. "It was."

"It will be hard to break." He sighed. "I have some ideas, but you must support me."

"Of course," she said with a cordial lay of her ears.

"I'll start on that in the morning." He could start now, but he wanted time to think, and it was a hot day, dusty and gusty and more suited for a nap. He'd have to call a break shortly.

Cmeo Mrist said, "Well, I must thank you for your understanding."

Talonmaster Hress Rscil regarded her evenly. "You are welcome, Priestess, but I must be honest."

"Yes?"

"I share some of that sentiment myself. However, my clan leader has given me orders, and I will comply as best I can. I expect as much from those I command."

She almost sighed, and her ears drooped slightly. "I understand. I also will do the best I can. Of course, I'm not happy with such . . . instinctive behavior." He knew she'd wanted to say *undisciplined*, though she did not. "I will trust you to address it."

"Thank you," he said. Fair enough, and he'd continue to give her the benefit of the doubt.

He wasn't sure she'd feel the same way tomorrow.

Barely after dawn, the training resumed. Hress Rscil watched from atop his chariot as the drillmasters motivated the warriors in the cool air and dew-damp earth.

"Crawl! On your bellies. There are leatherwings overhead, and hurled spears and rocks. If a filthy Liskash sees you, you'll drool and do his bidding. Now up and run! Run like the filthy Liskash wants you carnally. Down! And crawl!" The nearest leader clapped his hands together to make his warriors move faster.

Rscil had talked to his drillmasters, and by "talked," he'd told them bluntly what behavior was acceptable to him, and thence to Nrao Aveldt. A general lesson and motivation now would be followed by individual attention to any comments, and further group activity would continue until the problem was resolved. As an additional incentive, he'd spread the snide word that any warrior who didn't feel capable of marching with females had his leave to return to the herds. That resulted in hundreds of flattened ears, but no desertions.

They might hate him, but they would obey.

Cmeo Mrist looked rather nonplussed at the warriors crawling through sand and brambles, jumping, charging, diving. It was painful and exhausting, and mildly degrading. Still, it would enforce the rules.

They drilled all day, and there was clear resentment, but better response. One side benefit, Hress Rscil thought, was that no warrior would quit if the females didn't first. Nor was anyone foolish enough to challenge the clan leader, the talonmaster, or even a drillmaster on the matter. He was satisfied.

Two days later Cmeo Mrist reported, "The comments have stopped. Muttering, however, continues. The Dancers are dealing with it, including joking about it. With respect, a warrior of great ability need not boast. His skill is apparent. The boasting only serves to point his insecurity. Especially with Dancers, who can sometimes read feelings."

"I will relay that," Hress Rscil agreed. "Some of the warriors will feel put upon, that they have been felt in such a manner." It struck the talonmaster that he had watched the graceful Dancers, and their movements had inspired the occasional less than chaste thought. Had Cmeo Mrist or the others sensed this? He dismissed the concern and plunged ahead,

"I have a suggestion, a delicate one, if I may," he said. His proposal was a bold one, and could have repercussions if not taken well.

She raised her brow hairs and said, "It's necessary that we agree that we are not enemies, and can share sensitive things."

He hoped the Dancer was referring to what he was about to propose.

"One matter, which I feel is legitimate, is that this will be a long march with stiff battles."

"Go on."

"The warriors fear the Dancers are graceful but not strong, and I use that term in the physical sense, and will not be always able to keep up with the claws."

"I see," she said. "Yes, I understand the context. And what do you propose?"

"I would like to conduct training routes as well

as drill. A few hundredlengths at first, building to greater distances."

"That makes sense," she agreed. "To make it interesting, I propose three thousandlengths to start."

Talonmaster Rscil took a moment to eat that. While not a great distance, it was a healthy route for warriors, and a fair approach to battle. Eventually, he'd like twice eight or more thousandlengths. Cmeo proposed starting at more than an eighth of that at the start. Of course he appreciated the offer. It would speed training, and make a better showing for them. Could they do it, however?

"Are you confident of that?" he asked.

She sniffed. "Warrior, what do you think females in camp or town do? They butcher meat, haul wood, walk herds, fight predators. It has been years since we fought to defend the town, but you've heard and seen herding station battles. Besides, I will guarantee none will drop out. If they fall, it will be from exertion, and demonstrate they have the courage to give all. Surely that will serve some measure?"

Rscil admired her assessment of the situation and appreciated the cooperation. "Either will serve great measure. I admit to knowing little apart from war, and I value your advice," he said.

Cmeo Mrist chuckled and rumbled in her throat. Her eyes twinkled.

"This information is a lack of your warriors, and ironic being as we know so much of our neighbors and enemies."

"It is," he agreed. "Does any male ever understand a female? Or the reverse?"

"I understand you better than you think, Hress Rscil." Her eyes bore a flash as she raised a gourd for a lap of water.

Her glint made him most delighted and uncomfortable at the same time.

To cover his confusion, he said, "I will see to the plans for these routes."

As he left, he heard her growl a much louder chuckle.

Before dawn the next day, Hress Rscil looked over the warriors at morning gathering. Some were stolid, relaxed, attentive. Some were eager and itchy to start. A few looked disdainfully at, or away from, the Dancers who were clustered together at one side of the field. Everyone's tail twitched with impatience.

Cmeo Mrist stood nearby, a bundle next to her. It was smaller but similar to his, with water gourds and dried meat for meals. She had a dagger and short javelin, to his full panoply.

"Today we march," he shouted, and the drillmasters echoed him. "Follow me!"

He turned and picked up his bundle, then started at a brisk but steady pace toward one of the well-worn paths of the settlement. Cmeo Mrist matched him and fell alongside, with Senior Drillmaster Gree on the other side. The old, scarred clan drillmaster was just called Gree. No one knew his full name or even if Gree was his taken or given name. Rscil himself was unable to recall and anyone of lesser status knew better than to ask. Gree had counting beads, and a very reliable pace. He also had a very craggy face with claw scars and torn ears. He'd fought in many border raids. Cmeo Mrist looked like an unearthly being in comparison, glossy black, trim, dainty and graceful.

It was early and dark, cool and misty, but would be warm soon enough, from exercise and the sun. His chosen route was south, between several copses that led to the Great Desert, many days' walk south. There had been forest here, until Mrem had harvested it for building, and to clear grazing land.

Nothing was said for a time. Gree kept count, shifting beads on the string. They were drilled copperstone, the rich blue that became ore when heated. Rscil shifted his pack slightly, to relieve pressure on his back. Cmeo Mrist kept pace well enough. She took more steps with shorter legs, but seemed unbothered by the exertion.

Behind, the lines of warriors and Dancers stepped off, with drums beating a time. The rearmost ranks had to wait in order to move. There were noises of shuffling and shifting, occasional curses from the drillmasters, but shortly, it evened out and they were all en route.

Gree counted aloud as he reached the first mark. "Seventy-six, seventy-seven, one hundred..." Then he resumed a barely audible mutter under his breath.

Hress Rscil said, "Gree can be trusted with all information. So, Cmeo Mrist, did you advise the Dancers on our plans?"

"Only as you did the warriors. A route march, with water."

His ear twitched acknowledgement. "Very well. I hope it turns out as it should. Though I do wish Mrem had the endurance of arosh. Even a few thousandlengths is barely a morning's work for them. It would last us all day."

She said, "In exchange Aedonniss has given us our brains, and not as slaves to Liskash, but as individuals."

"Indeed. Our tools are our strength." He gestured slightly with the javelin he carried over his shoulder. It was cast and hammered, ground to a fine, gleaming edge, decorated with etchings and chiselings of praise to the sky god. He observed that hers was as well made, though it had not seen service.

It was a hot day, and dusty, with little wind. Despite that, Hress Rscil could smell the army. The whole didn't smell too fatigued yet, and he could tell the females by their different scent. They managed. Behind, the arosh hauled light carts for any injured. Inevitably, someone would step in a rut, take sick from the sun, or otherwise need to be carried. The Liskash usually left casualties to crawl or die. Mrem made sure to recover them, both for practicality and in compassion.

Gree counted, "...seventy-six, seventy-seven, four hundred..." The tempo was perfect.

A while later, a thought struck Hress Rscil. He turned to his companion. "Cmeo Mrist, it seems to me that a good route march is a bit like a Dance. Ideally, every warrior should have the same stride, the same speed, and move in an even line."

"A bit," she said. She sounded a little breathy, but still fit. "This is another benefit of mixing the Dancers.

We can help keep the time, with our drummers." She signaled behind her to the female drummers at the head of the file of Dancers. They stopped playing their complicated rhythm of worship and changed to a rapid double-beat that matched the pace the marchers were keeping.

Hress Rscil found it lightened his step. "The drums are enticing. Once they are steady, I look forward to them and walk with them."

"That is part of the magic," she said. "The Dance, the drums, the chants, all reach the brain, and keep it focused and free from distractions and mind magic."

She sounded somewhat winded now, as Gree reached a thousand paces. Hress Rscil used that as an opportunity to say, "We are two-thirds to our turnaround today. Yes, I will arrange for the drummers. Let us be quiet a time. I wish to listen to the army and hear for trouble." Quiet would also save breath.

They strode on, Cmeo Mrist occasionally quickening to catch up. She didn't fall behind, but she did have to work at it. Rscil made a point not to slow his pace. His warriors knew how he moved, and this was to prove a point.

When Gree counted one thousand five hundred lengths, Hress Rscil stopped and raised his arm. He turned, shouted, "Circle and rest!"

It was obvious the Dancers hadn't seen this maneuver before. Some warriors broke out of ranks, formed eight points with spears jabbed into the ground, and the rest swarmed through brush and behind rocks looking for threats. In beats only, the area was secure, with watchpoints on a few rises to supplement the defensive positions, and a clutch of small lizards, rodents and eggs piled next to a fire lay and ready for Hress Rscil's orders.

"In rotation, eat and rest!" he shouted.

One of the drillmasters struck a fire plunger, coaxed out the tinder, and blew it under the lay. The fire caught, and there was a frenzy of skinning, skewering and placing of meat for a quick roast. Someone placed a pot to boil leaves, and the groomer-surgeons dropped tools into another pot to boil clean. There were some blisters and small lacerations to attend to, male and female both.

Across the warm, hummocky field, that scene repeated with other groups, each of eight fists. The Dancers watched with growing admiration. Rscil was pleased.

Satisfied, he sat himself, on his pack. Gree was already comfortably squatting, and Cmeo Mrist cautiously stretched out on a blanket. She stretched the pads of her feet to ease them.

"They will take turns on watch and eating, then?" she said.

"Yes, with a few mouthfuls of fresh meat to improve this harness leather," he said, holding up a flat, translucent piece of dried mottlecoat meat.

She tightened her face and flattened her ears. "Are some of them eating...those?" The plants the warriors were chewing on looked like weeds, unappetizing weeds at that. The brown seed packets looked very different from the rich crops Mrem raised in more peaceful times.

"Emergency training. Some seed pods contain enough substance to keep one alive a few days. The spies and scouts practice that in case they have to escape without supplies."

"I see. It just seems so unappetizing."

"It is, and causes digestive trouble without practice. They eat a mouthful now and then for preparation."

The females had grouped themselves apart from the males, which he approved of. There was some mingling, but it seemed courteous and appropriate. Two latrine pits were dug, one east and one west, to allow some modesty. Those would be filled as they left.

He allowed an eighthday for food and rest, with light naps in the sun. It was arid and clear in their part of the world, but not too warm. To the north, though, he could see clouds above the New Sea. The sun drew water that would fall to the west. With Gree on guard nearby, he allowed himself to take a short sleep. Cmeo Mrist had already curled up on her blanket to nap.

On his order, the warriors rose, drew in the circle and formed into ranks. The Dancers shuffled among them, and did so fairly quickly. They were learning.

He felt a little stiff himself, being no longer a youth. Still, this was something he could manage, and he led off with a shout.

The day would be pleasant at rest. It was hot for striding, and they all panted and sweated much of the way back, but almost all made it without issue. Before supper time, they were within the low stone walls of the city.

At the warrior compound, fresh towels aplenty waited with clear water for wiping fur and cooling down. Gree immediately acquired a large bundle from the caretakers, and brought them over. He handed a large one each to Cmeo Mrist and Rscil.

"It went well, I think," Cmeo Mrist said, neatly cleaning dust from her coat. She was most careful to wipe around her eyes and in her ears. "Only three Dancers fell out, and all are older. So did two warriors, both saying they were injured."

"Yes, some Dancers are older than any of the warriors. An old warrior becomes a smith or farmer. That is something I had not considered." He scrubbed his face and drew his whiskers through the soft cloth.

"Acceptable?" she asked.

"It is," the talonleader assured her. "Have the comments lessened?"

She smiled. "From what I've heard, they lessened throughout the march. It was my Dancers who had comments. They found the exercise boring."

"We must do this, as boring as it may be, regularly before we begin the long walk to the war. Though Nrao Aveldt tells me it won't be many days. He awaits more information."

"So I was told also," she agreed. "Do you prefer more practice?"

"I always prefer more time to drill," he said. "However, there's a point where it's more important to get on with the task, rather than boring and tiring the warriors."

"I understand."

Once clean, they both walked up the cobbled road to Nrao Aveldt's broad house. Hress Rscil pondered that he typically ate with the warriors except when the clan leader summoned him. As a warrior himself, he was not mated, and never bothered with a servant. His own house, made to be easily broken down and carried in a wagon, was small, with a sleeping bench, sitting bench and a hearth. Someday, perhaps, he might settle down with a mate and need a larger dwelling. He glanced speculatively at Cmeo Mrist. What would such a one be like as a mate?

Nrao Aveldt greeted them, and he nodded in courtesy, ears out.

Hress Rscil offered, "Our training goes well. A little more is desirable, but we stand ready to leave on your word."

"Excellent, Talonmaster. And you, Priestess?"

Cmeo Mrist said, "The Dancers are fitting in better, I think, and there is less unrest with their presence. I will defer to the talonmaster's advice, but I believe they are ready."

"I concur," Hress Rscil agreed.

"I am glad to hear it," Nrao Aveldt said. "I have word from one of our observers. There are Mrem held captive by the scaly worm's accursed mind magic. He saw them without harness. They differed in height and face, as well, so two clans. Oglut binds them to his bidding and forces them to the basest of chores."

Hress Rscil said, "I think Aedonniss speaks to us. Territory, improved land, two Liskash tribes eliminated and the third made easy. Succoring our fellow Mrem from such desolation is the pointing star. How are the preparations?"

Nrao Aveldt said, "Eight eights of wagons threefold, each with five eightyweights of meat, darts and tools."

The talonmaster did some mental calculation. "It will be enough. If you wish, let us plan to move an eightday hence."

"I do wish. Aedonniss guide you, Talonmaster and Priestess." He looked wistfully around at the dusky horizon, dark to the east and mottled pink in the west, his tail flat against his body.

"It will be a challenge to leave our home for new lands."

Hril Aris checked the time. The moon was full and almost full high. It took some study, as it didn't rise as high here toward the north. It should lower again to the far south, if the philosophers were right. They claimed the world was a ball 29,000 thousandlengths across. A huge distance. More than three times that around.

All he knew was that they'd wagoned, walked and now slunk and crawled 650 thousandlengths. They had spears, slings and large packs of dried meat, and would have to return unseen. They would be heroes; no scouts had traveled this far and fast. Spies took their time and sent missives of gathered stories. Scouts watched directly. It was thrilling to be so far, well within Liskash territory, but unseen. Their splotched coats of brown and tan were supplemented with crushed ochre and bark, so they blended with the ground. More importantly, though, were their abilities in stealth.

The river below flowed into the New Sea, helping

fill it, ripple by ripple, as the massive waves tumbled in from the far east. Oh, to see that. Reportedly, it was a waterfall two hundredlengths high, four thousandlengths across, acting like a hose for a waterwheel, blasting across the former Hot Depths, flooding villages and driving herds before it.

But the river was their current task. It would have to be crossed on the way north, and they needed an easy ford. The hills were a poor choice, for the thin air, steep slopes and rocky terrain, not to mention being much closer to several Liskash strongholds. Lower here was less predictable, constantly shrinking, but probably the only practical choice.

"River" was charitable. It probably was one farther down, where it was inundated by the New Sea, now only a few thousandlengths away in a pointed bay. Here though, it was a broad stream over rocky shallows, filled with cobbles and pebbles and a few larger rocks from uphill. It would be easy to ford across. He had to decide if they should do so, and explore further, or just record this location and report back.

The rocks were a bit odd, and looked tumbled and displaced. He'd have to consider what had caused that. Large beasts pushing? An army? Earthquake? Recent heavy flooding? Perhaps that. The banks were scoured. The rocks seemed not to match, though.

It was a cool evening, slightly damp, and quite pleasant on the whole. His fur was slowly soaking up dew from the air, but it wasn't so cold as to be a problem. The wind brought wet, pungent smells from the east.

His musing was interrupted when his fellow scout, Flirsh Arst, whispered, "Do you hear something?"

Hril Aris flared his ears and listened. There was something.

"Thunder?" he muttered back, but it went on and stayed steady, but got closer.

"Earthquake?" Except there was no shaking.

Then there was a little tremor. Only a little, faint and again, oddly even.

"Downstream," Hril Aris said. He couldn't believe what he thought he saw.

"It is the sign of Aedonniss," Flirsh Arst hissed reverently.

The river was flowing backward, in a solid wall of water. It was the new sea pushing up to claim more land.

Hril Aris stared, still outside but shaking within, as a wave six Mrem high rushed below in an almost sheer wall, the air seeming to hold it straight. He saw rocks tumble before it, weeds and branches thrash.

Then he understood, for once he had seen the Great Sea.

The moon called the sea to her, causing it to rise on the beaches. The sea broke in waves, twice a day, retreating in between. But beyond this the new sea filling was still sloshing like a wine cup set too hard upon a table. When both forces joined, the water ate more land.

Here, though, the New Sea narrowed in a long indentation caused by the river's former valley. It was quite deep further along, and looked like a water funnel. When water was poured into a funnel...

The moon poured all the water of the sea into that small funnel twice a day. It rushed higher and deeper up the long valley, tumbling rocks, disturbing growth, ripping mud from the ground. Nor would it move in waves; there was nowhere for it to go with the weight of a sea behind it. It would stay here, retreating slowly over a quarter day, gradually releasing back into that long bay. The reeds and grass would look scoured by flood, but the rocks would remain upstream and tumbled, in odd contrast.

He realized that as the sea continued to rise, this whole plain to the mountains could flood. It would become impassable, and make a great strategic barrier against attack.

It was even possible some of these foothills would become islands.

"Let us go," Hril Aris said with a faint smile. "We have seen what we need."

If they could move the clan across it soon, they would have a sea to protect their rear.

It certainly was lush, Buloth thought. The rains greened things up tremendously. They also cooled it down somewhat. Hopefully, that would change once the New Sea was full. For now, he kept a wrap over his shoulders, and ate nuts for the fat. Tonight he'd have another warm fire and tasty meat. He had to eat almost as much as a mammal did in this climate.

The soarers said there were Mrem to the east, and moving west. That was serious. It was his territory, not even mapped yet, and the vermin were moving in. He praised the flying beasts, bid them wait their time, and find out more. There were also Mrem in the south, trying to move into this territory.

Buloth enjoyed the campaign. He could feel his mindpower increasing with practice, and he was grateful to his father for this opportunity. As they advanced, he drew in more animals, a few stray workbeasts, and even the population of a small village by a stream, all to add to his army. At times, he could even feel insects and snakes drawing to him. He rewarded his fighters by causing many rodents and digging lizards to stand up and wait to be harvested. He'd learned that well-fed slaves were happy slaves. He attributed his gains in power in part to that. His father was frugal to the point of stinginess, and kept them hungry. Distractions like hunger, though, weakened the grip on their mind. There was a positive side of that as well, though. He had no desire to be mind-linked to a slave upon its death.

Later that day he did feel the ugly touch of Mrem to the east, scrabbling through the hills. They were refugees from the river valley into the Bottomlands, distressed, tired, sore and hungry. That would make them hard to manage. However . . .

Yes, they'd eat well on the rats he'd just suggested present themselves. That would settle them down in a camp for a time. He determined where to the east they were, and maneuvered the army that direction. Their camp would make a convenient place for his army to rest, after he incorporated them.

The trunklegs turned in that direction, and he

decided to take a nap in the swaying carriage, atop the fluffy mammal-hide mattress he'd brought.

Nrao Aveldt received the scouts in his home, and made sure they were offered good refreshments, of grer brew, honeyed mottlecoat livers, and less rich, overbearing fare, like the delicate graygull stewed in arosh marrow and water.

They sat at his bidding, drank copious amounts of brew in guzzle rather than lap, followed by even more herbed drink. He didn't mind. They needed water and energy and salts. Formal manners were for formal occasions. This was about information. He let them make a start on replenishing their withered hides while he called for Ingo and Tckins.

The scouts were eager to report, but did so between mouthfuls of soup and meat.

Hril Aris pointed at the spot on the map with his spoon and said, "The water rises, slower, but steadily. It occurs to me that as the ground flattens and widens, the rise will be slower, but it doesn't mean the far flooding is less."

As he limped in the door, Ingo said, "That is correct. I am awaiting an architect with measuring sticks to return from the coast near the Great Flood. That will tell us more."

The other scout, Flirsh Arst, added, "All is chaos. The sea also comes and goes." He indicated the movement with his hands.

Ingo said, "That is the tide. As the moon circles overhead, it draws water up toward it. It should be a footlength or so different, but that can matter in the marshes. Perhaps being a new sea the tides are stronger?"

Tckins Mestri said, "It is more than that in the narrow valley here," he pointed at the map. "This used to be Cracked Mountain Pass. Now it is a stream, as Hril Aris has said, and water beats against the rise twice a day."

Ingo said, "Yes, with nowhere to go to spread out, the water must splash high, much like in a bathing tub."

Tckins Mestri agreed, "Any advance will have to work around it, higher up the mountains or around, or time the approach carefully. It's like a flash flood in the desert hollows, twice each day."

Nrao Aveldt tapped his chin with a claw. "This interests me greatly. It's a predictable barricade we can hide behind and sally from, that can't be removed. It's intermittent, but impenetrable during that time." *And more than that,* he thought.

"We will find more," Hril Aris said eagerly. He and Flirsh Arst were justifiably proud of the information that they had brought home. Nrao Aveldt nodded.

"Please. An accurate schedule is most desirable," Nrao Aveldt added.

"At once," the Mrem scouts agreed.

They drew on the map and told of their observations, then Nrao Aveldt gave them leave to go rest.

"You serve well," he said, placing a hand on the shoulders of each of them. "We will all be grateful to you."

Once the scouts departed, the clan leader grinned to himself, and scratched his ear in thought. He sent a

messenger for Talonmaster Rscil. It was time. Aedonniss had given them the tools they needed.

He turned to his son, Nef, watching from his
favorite bench.

"Do you see what I do, young one?"

Nef was maturing quickly. He'd sat still for most
of the council.

"Father, the water has power. If it moves rocks,
can be harnessed to move rocks for us, or to cut
more ground."

Leader of the Three Fangs Clan Nrao Aveldt was
proud of his son's insight. "Yes, cutting ground is what
I have in mind for now, and moving rocks later."

Then, with no one around for the moment, he
grabbed the boy in a tussle. They laughed and snarled
and sweated until the day's scribe rumbled a reminder.
They sat back and recovered their breathing.

"Scribe, you may take a break for an eighth. I
thank you."

"Thank you, Clan Leader. I will return." The Mrem
bowed slightly and walked out.

Hress Rscil arrived, dusty from training. Yet another
reason less formality was good. There was no delay
while his talonmaster cleaned and put on a polished
harness. He took Rscil and led him to a bench in the
corner of the enclosure.

"Hress Rscil, this is in private, because I have a
most exciting strategy in mind . . ."

Talonmaster Hress Rscil was pleased with how the
long march was going, given that they were leaving

the Veldt forever. He was not a sentimental Mrem, but he had felt a pang turning his back on their home for the last time. From that moment forward, they would be strangers anywhere they went.

They were far north and west, well into the foothills. Drizzling rain and cool temperatures prevailed, which wasn't particularly comfortable, but was much better than dust and heat.

The first three days involved a lot of wagons interspersed with walking, and some minor coordination problems with replacement wagons. The station masters simply hadn't believed the numbers involved and had assumed error. Rscil's presence had been all the motivation they needed to sort it out quickly. They furnished what they could, and soberly accepted the orders that they'd move out with Nrao Aveldt's large caravan.

They'd passed through the territory of Rantan Taggah and Jask the Long, who were gone leaving ghostly camps and empty keeps. The spies reported their progress as somewhat successful, but desperate and harried. The Three Fangs clan would not be so scattered. Rscil's warriors would be followed by Nrao Aveldt's, also heavily supplied and prepared for a long journey. They gathered and hunted to improve their rations, not simply to survive.

Their people numbered fifteen thousand and more, a staggering count. Two thousand of the clan's best fighters and Dancers were with Rscil, entrusted to break trail for the families, young and elderly. It was good, he thought, that warriors weren't permitted to mate until older. It was one less distraction. Of course, that was the reason they found the Dancers interesting, even out of season.

Once past the road shift caused by the bight in the New Sea, they'd turned north, dismounted and walked. Days passed eating dried meat and berries, a little honey, supplemented with stew of wild game and chopped tubers. It was nutritious enough, though not satisfying.

The Dancers managed well enough. The warriors bore it stoically. The drovers and others in support made no protest. Each day's march, though, was a struggle, with some shorter than others to allow recuperation.

Water was the main thing. When it rained, all the wagons opened to let cones gather it into barrels. They filled at every stream and pond. It rained on the third night while they bivouacked, and broad leather sheets became catchments for every container possible. The water would hold.

Which only left how they'd work and fight.

While it was easier to hide in low areas, dispersed, a good high ground was stronger and more defensible. This land was rolling and hummocky, but there were a few viable positions.

Talonmaster Rscil considered the location of his battle stronghold carefully. His force was limited and casualties had to be minimized. That was necessary for Nrao Aveldt's wishes, and his own survival. He would not waste his Mrem.

He chose a broad hill, not very high, but with steeper sides. It would be hard to approach, hard to attack, except by the accursed leatherwings. Spears would do for those. To counter ground troops, they would construct a fortress, but one with many surprises for the enemy.

Under his direction, the warriors, drivers, haulers and the stronger females went to work. The drillmasters snarled in friendly fashion, indicating placement. Everyone dug, making a low rampart around the hill, surrounded by a now much steeper approach. There were two entrance ramps, one facing the territory ahead, one back toward their holding.

The younger warriors used the large bronze tube hammer to set their stakes into the rampart, and the fist leaders followed along, each with their rope and thong, lashing them into a solid defense. The wagons, their wheels blocked, made a defensive inner circle. A large, frontal assault might still overwhelm the post, especially if the attacker was willing to trample his own warriors, but it would give enough time to mount and depart, or at least flee on foot. The wagons were left packed, and items only withdrawn as they became essential.

It was tough, panting work, and might have to be done several times, but it would leave them with a trail of defensible positions. All Nrao Aveldt's group would have to do to augment it was drive their own stakes in the existing rampart.

That done, watches were set, well-hidden firepits dug for food, and latrines cut to drain downslope, rendering those areas even less approachable. If there was time, more earthworks and stakes might go in. It was not nearly as good as a stone castle, but stronger than the natural terrain.

Once done with that, they rested a day. Progress would be slow. Clan Leader Nrao Aveldt's neighbors would laugh at this, as they had at many of his practices in the past. They'd prefer to rush headlong. Nrao and Rscil preferred to minimize risks. Those left in camp would be charged with reinforcing it daily until no longer needed, starting with more earth, then adding any rocks or timbers they found.

Buloth took great delight in the acquisition, or near-acquisition, of more slaves for his army. He was somewhat nervous, and fought not to let it show in front of his senior servants. Ahead were the Mrem escaping from the Hollow Lands, numbering some two hundred. He cautioned his lead slaves to restrain themselves, and they simply trudged over the landscape, like the mindless beasts all non-Liskash were. He prodded his drivers and beasts to move ahead, to give him range. He sat back in his padded seat aboard the trunklegs and patted his hands together in gleeful anticipation.

One hundred and ninety was his improved estimate. A little closer.

It was exciting. He could feel their minds, feel them becoming distinct entities, and knew they were unaware of him. They were beyond that next ridge. Some suggested they were on watch, but they were not atop it yet. He knew of them, they not of him. He grinned.

Suddenly it clarified in his mind, like melted sandglass. One hundred and eighty-eight exactly. Three of them approached the crest of the ridge. He continued to approach but focused on them. They were near the peak, he could feel their unease and then...he had them. He felt for the symbols, but could make nothing of their harsh, unorganized language. He pushed what he needed, though, and one of them turned and signaled below. Then they began back down.

A little while later, he felt the minds of the others in his circle. He stretched out, felt a mass shriek of panic and fear, then a huge swell as their minds fell under his. It was almost sexual, the warm flood of power and anguish, and then they were his. They could not withstand him. They must see their new master!

His beasts topped the ridge, he looked down on his new vassals. The dull eyes of the Mrem refugees stared up at him. It was not the welcome he would have liked, but he loved the sensation that all the creatures he could see belonged to him. With a casual hand, he suggested his army build its camp for the night around his new charges.

To drive home the point, he set the filthy furbags to work digging cesspits.

Buloth could feel his power growing day by day. It was a combination of practice and distance from his father. That made sense and also proved the need to set his own godhold a safe remove from Oglut's domain. They could be allies. They could not be cohabitants. The weaker Liskash didn't matter; he could control them if he wished, or ignore them to their peace. Only a few were worthy of godhood, though, and while they must mate to keep the lines pure, otherwise, distance was needed.

He'd been directed northerly, and there were allegedly Mrem that way. He wasn't keen on north. North was cold, and hard on people. However, it was now a lot more moderate, and humid, than the previous time he'd been here with his father. It seemed to be true the weather was changing with the New Sea. He'd have to make sure to see it, after he secured a godhold. He'd have to go to it to assuage his curiosity, he thought wryly. Creatures would take his orders. The sea would not.

A few more gis of distance should be enough for now. That would put him beyond the Low Mountains, and create an easy border at a safe distance. He could always relocate his capital at a later date. The labor was free, after all.

He pondered the power his mind gave him, to take peripheral information from entire gis away, if one of his slaves saw something, and then to integrate it into his plans. The future belonged to Liskash.

It was at that moment that he saw a flash of Mrem wagons, well within the borders of his godhold. Buloth growled and grew tense, and sought the source of the vision. There. That one, and through it he saw the filthy creatures had even constructed a crude fortification, of sticks and mud. Somewhat like ants they were, but far too clever for stupid beasts.

He flicked a finger in their direction. That excrescence would have to be dealt with at once.

He directed the slaves to abandon their digging and walk. If he was satisfied with their progress, they could eat tonight.

❖   ❖   ❖

In a crack in a grassy hillside littered with fractured rocks, Hril Aris felt the vile punch of Buloth's mind. He focused on the grass in front of him, absorbing its smell, its color, its springy coils, fighting to be one with the grass, not that mind. It worked. He wasn't enslaved.

To his surprise he realized he had gained information from that brief but intrusive touch. He knew that mind was sending a large army toward them, based on something seen by a creature in thrall to it. That spy had to be one of the browsing pebbleskins they'd passed earlier, or even one of the leatherwings drifting overhead in lazy circles, may Aedonniss curse them. Given all that, it would be best to wait for dark for him and Flirsh Arst to move. The reptiles were not only slow and cold, they couldn't see in darkness, either.

He gestured to Flirsh, and they both crawled deeper into the crevice to await the night.

It took all their training not to panic. Their fur fluffed in fear as well as for warmth, and they huddled like kits. Hril listened and felt the thud of footsteps. He lost count of the number of reptilians who came past, from little scavengers to herd beasts to adult, armed Liskash in singles and small groups. Even a trio of bedraggled, half-starved Mrem caught in the spell wandered not far enough away for comfort. He and Flirsh didn't speak, but he knew they were both terrified of winding up just so—brainless, pitiable slaves of a scaled monster. He wasn't sure if it would be better to rescue those Mrem or kill them in mercy. All he and Flirsh had were knives and hand axes, though, for food and shelter.

Eventually, dusk gave way to darkness. They eased themselves out of the crack in the rock, and he led the way, fur stiff and heart thrumming, in a low, silent slink between rocks and tufts, toward the distant fortification, which didn't feel as safe now.

After a few hundredlengths of aching muscles and grueling fear, he deemed it safe to rise and walk erect. When he was sure there were no other creatures about, they ran.

Hress Rscil received two panting, dirty scouts, and served them bowls of water and a plate of soft meats at once. They guzzled and lapped the water, and smacked down the meat between comments.

Hril Aris said, "The Liskash approach, or at least their slaves. Too many reptiles to count. A trio of starven Mrem. Eights of small beasts, with that look of mindless focus."

"How far away are they?"

While Hril Aris drank some more, Flirsh Arst said, "Over the next hills. They will arrive within two days, if they continue this way."

"You didn't feel the spell?"

Hril nodded. "We felt it. We avoided it by thinking like plants. It felt angry, focused. I believe he knows we are here. He intends conquest."

Rscil flattened his ears.

"That was inevitable, but perhaps it's a little early. Still, the world is what Aedonniss decrees. We will get to try our new tactics soon, it seems."

It was then that a distant shout was relayed by a closer watch. "Liskash are sighted on the hill!"

The scouts rose, but Hress Rscil gestured for them to stay. "Drink, eat, sit a few breaths. Your bravery is needed again, but I would have you in best health."

He turned and stepped out of the tent to give orders.

When Hress Rscil shouted "Form up!" Cmeo Mrist shivered in thrill and fear. This was it. They were going to test her belief that Aedonniss' dance and chant would protect them from reptile mind magic. If she was wrong, they would all be filthy slaves of a filthy lizard. If she was correct, they only had to fight for their lives against them. She gathered her females together, waking a few from sleep.

Many of the Dancers were agitated, and their smell, fur and ears reflected that. A few even lashed their tails in fear.

"Hurry now!" she cajoled, urging them toward the sound of the talonmaster's voice. "The warriors need us in place." She didn't say "Depending on us." That seemed too heavy for the moment.

Warriors sprinted past her, with shields, javelins and swords, some with daggers and pouches, a handful with stiff leather visors against sun or stones. They fell into line surely, and with a few shuffles were in perfect formation. Despite eightdays of practice, the Dancers didn't look nearly as neat or skilled. It was nerves. That, and perhaps Hress Rscil was right about the different ways males and females fought.

They looked it, too, with their fur and ears like that. A few warriors betrayed eagerness, or trembliness. The Dancers, though, were nervous or afraid. Cmeo Mrist had to stop that.

She waited for the initial orders from the drillmasters to echo down, then called out herself.

"Dancers, now is the time to be put your trust in Aedonniss and Assirra and the Dance. We are here to fight as warriors, to make the males even more powerful and sure. We act as their shield against the filthy mindrape of reptiles. Stand fast and ready."

It wasn't a bad speech, though not entirely what she'd wanted to say. Rscil had coached her carefully in how to phrase it so the warriors wouldn't be offended. It increasingly was obvious to her that the warriors were rather sensitive Mrem, and needed constant reassurance. Still, they were expected to wade into battle and perhaps die. She would hold her tongue and phrase it to honor them, if it helped.

It did seem to work. The eldest and youngest Dancers steadied a bit, and that spread throughout the troupe. The eldest of them had some experience with violence, but the youngest had no grasp of it. In between were the many with enough knowledge to know fear, without the practice to handle it. Together, though, they had their years of training, and the eight-days of practice they had with the warriors. It might not be enough, but it would have to do. Cmeo Mrist nodded to Hress Rscil. They were ready.

He nodded back.

❖ ❖ ❖

Buloth sat at the peak of the hill and looked below. He had an excellent vantage point of the entire valley. The terrain here was drier and coarser than farther south, due largely to this being out of the old cloud line before the New Sea. His godhold would end not far from here. Still, these filthy furred things were in his territory, and would never go away of their own accord. They were intruding now, from the desolate wastelands they spawned in.

He sat under the awning of a comfortable tent, with a bed stuffed with fluffpods and dressed in trunkleg hide, tanned to supple softness. He had a fine clusterberry wine, delicious shoots and tubers, and a delicate stew of some fast running bird his domestics had brought for him. Nothing could be finer, if he could only eliminate the rotten mammals.

It was amusing to see this stronghold of theirs, all mud and sticks and rocks. No carving, no hewn stone, no buttresses. They showed the sophistication of savages generations past, as he'd seen on a hill near his father's capital, that had been a Liskash holding lost in the dawn of time. That was all this kind could aspire to.

Still, they might eventually learn to build, and that would be problematic. The time to eliminate a pest was when it was first found. That meant now.

He could see them frantically running around, and forming neat little squares. They really were like birds or insects in their simplicity, unable to work independently and lacking the mind to control others. He smiled faintly and pushed his army forward.

✧   ✧   ✧

Upon boarding his chariot, Talonmaster Rscil first made sure his warriors were arrayed as they should be, then that the Dancers looked right, with Cmeo Mrist nodding approval from the ground. After that, he checked that those defending the followers on the redoubt were on the ramparts with arrows, stones and javelins, and the gates ready for instant blocking. Only then did he turn his gaze to acknowledge the enemy. It was a thought out policy, and it was also a visible display of his respect for his own and contempt for the scaly ones. He checked his own weapons by touch. He had a fistful of javelins, a heavier stabbing spear, and the bronze gripclaws he'd use up close, if any lizard survived to reach the chariot. It wasn't wise to wish for that, but he'd enjoy it if it happened. In front of Gree was a box of heavy, weighted darts.

Up the hillside were creatures. He couldn't tell precisely what type since they wore enveloping leather armor and helmets with spikes or crests, and clouds of dust surrounded them, but their arrangement made it clear they were organized, and therefore hostile. They were either Liskash or controlled by them.

He knew he had the best scouts because he was not surprised, knew the approximate terrain, and already had his warriors ranking up. Against that was foreign terrain with a much easier supply line for the enemy, but he'd maximized his chances.

Hress Rscil watched his warriors stand unmoving in formation, and the Dancers hold their now familiar places among them. The terrain was clear, but uneven, with rills, dunes and rises, occasional patches of scrub and a bare fistful of trees. As battlefields went, it was excellent. However, it would take maneuvering, and besides the usual unblooded warriors, there were the Dancers. He was concerned, but they could not be his first priority.

The talonmaster watched the attackers' movements to determine their strategy. Quick was good. Planned was better. They were a loose formation, but steady at the low end of a charge as they advanced down the hill. Probably, they were at a brisk walk, and their weight and the slope pulled them forward. Loose, though, and not a proper square of ranks.

"At the pace, advance!" he ordered. Gree heard him, and tapped the chariot's fast-running arogar into a trot. They were valuable beasts, and could speed him anywhere. These two were well-blooded and as experienced as any old soldiers.

Hress Rscil decided they might as well take the fight to the enemy. There was no advantage to waiting further, and he hoped to disrupt the obviously less well organized Liskash formation, if it could be called that. The enemy came forward in clumps and groups, but not in lines. He had to resist the urge to underestimate them, rabble but with twice the warriors he commanded. And if their lord was on the battlefield, all would be of one mind.

The talonmaster was concerned that some of the force he faced might be Mrem. There appeared to be some familiar shapes. They had fought a few of their own kind before. The enslaved Mrem all had shared the same expression of pain and horror. Most had also fought to the death. In a perfect world, Aedonniss would let those be captured alive in this battle. But to do that the clan would have to hold the field against a determined, often suicidal foe and have the time to subdue those Mrem controlled by the Liskash lord. Rscil sighed and flicked a claw. In this world, they would likely have to be killed. There would likely be no choice. His best and most veteran were in front, and some mixed among the rest. He trusted them to do what was necessary.

Still, it would not do to underestimate that force. More dust rose as they advanced, and they were on higher ground for now, coming down from the mountains. They would be motivated by whichever Liskash styled himself their "god."

The Claw drillmasters kept up a steady, encouraging shout as they advanced, until Cmeo Mrist started her chant. In moments, the other Dancers voiced with her, and the thump of the claw's drums soon matched those of the Dancers' footbeats.

It was an inspiring sound. It looked...odd. Even after long practice, to see the Dancers twisting forward between paired ranks of warriors was disconcerting, and felt slightly wrong, and even unmasculine. Better than being enslaved in mid spear thrust, Rscil reminded himself. If it worked...

There were some slight ripples in the ranks as the enemy became visible. Liskash in plenty, some mounted on several eights of beasts, behind a charging wall of literal meat—herdbeasts including mottlecoats, pests, scavengers and some lupins, anything the ruling

Liskash could stir up and control enough to drive forward. Yes, there were Mrem approaching too, with their body language and fur showing extreme distress. Poor creatures.

Behind them was a mass, not really a formation, of scaled Liskash. Most were spear armed. Many held round shields made of some sort of plant. The fighters stood a bit taller than the Mrem, with thick legs ending in splayed toes. Their scales were mottled, tending toward shades of gray, green, and tan. The Liskash warriors' reptilian heads were long and ended in a long toothy mouth that on most sagged slightly open. Yellow and white teeth, sharp and longer than a claw, were visible even in the distance. Few of the Liskash wore any armor and fewer held swords. Those who rode were better equipped, carrying long lances with bronze points, backed up by two long, curved knives in leather belts.

Then the smell of the enemy mass hit him. The reeks of fear, anger, despair, anguish and the stench of unwashed bodies from enslaved Mrem and uncared-for animals all rushed up his nose. He winced, sneezed, and shook his head. The Liskash didn't care about their slaves so their slaves did not care for themselves.

"Forward!" the talonmaster shouted.

The horde came on fast, and there were more ripples, and he realized one significant problem. The chanting of the Dancers drowned out the encouragement and orders from the drillmasters. The formation was more ragged than he liked.

He pointed, and Gree cropped the arogar into

motion. Together they hurried down to the front line
of warriors.

The talonmaster shouted as he went, matching the
first drillmaster he passed. *"Keep your spacing! Keep
your spacing!"* He hoped to turn that into a chant
itself. Gree repeated the command. A couple of others caught on, and it spread.

It worked. Fist leaders within the ranks echoed it,
and order improved. Rscil neared the front and hefted
his bundle of javelins, then checked the bronze claws at
his side. He would be in the battle directly. The front
two ranks tossed their first volley of bronze darts. They
whistled as they flew and landed among the animals and
slaves with deadly effect. The talonmaster knew, though,
that their darts and javelins would have more effect
against a cohesive force of thinking beings than they
were having on the disorganized gaggle of dull-witted
slaves being driven into the clan ahead of the Liskash.

Then the oncoming wall of enemy smashed into
them, and a fistful of leatherwings dropped from the
sky to clap their wings low over the first group of
Dancers still chanting behind the front line of warriors.

Instinctively those Dancers hissed, snarled and lost
their Dance. A couple of the front Dancers froze; the
rest nearby fluffed and arched and poked at things
running between their feet and flapping overhead,
dancing around in disgust or surprise. One stretched
her claws and ripped a tear into a low-flying leatherwing. Two others tore at a small snarling beast that
had been driven through the warriors, until it came
apart in gobbets of flesh and bone.

That was manageable, but the Dancers' aggression caused a complete break of the two ranks of warriors behind them. They hesitated, unsure if they should shove their way past or wait. Several tried to rush in front to form a block around the Dancers, leaving a gaping hole in that line behind the unarmored females. Some warriors from farther behind broke ranks and ran to defend the Dancers, exactly as Hress Rscil had feared. They exposed more of the Dancers who were behind them and those too stopped chanting. The sensation of calm that the drums and chanting had instilled was fading.

The slaves and wild beasts were dead or fled. The smell of blood and fear was tangible. Drillmasters shouted, their strident orders almost lost in the din as the first rank now thrust and stabbed the leaping Liskash. They left the spears impaled in scaled muscles and drew swords and bronze claws, as the second rank poked their points between the fist warriors in support.

Well enough, Talonmaster Rscil thought, for a battle. He had withdrawn to a slight hill where he could overlook the field after the first surge had been broken. Despite the chaos among the Dancers behind them the clan was holding its ground. It was apparent the Liskash fighters were less skilled, but there was a great many more of them than the clan had warriors. Already he could see masses of Liskash beginning to flow around the edges of the clan.

"Fifth and Sixth Claw, split and wing! Either Flank!" he ordered, and nothing happened. The chanting was distracting at this point, and didn't seem to accomplish anything. He heard his order relayed, and long moments later, those units ran to take positions angled back and on both forward flanks.

This wasn't something they'd practiced enough with the Dancers. Upon seeing those warriors battle run, rather than jog into position, those females with the Seventh Claw reacted in fear, drawing up, fluffing up fur and claws for a fight, and disrupting the last two ranks, which he needed for support. For a moment the talonmaster felt despair, knowing that all was lost. But as he looked about it was clear that nothing had been decided. It took him a moment to realize the despair was not his, but a weapon of the Liskash. A few of the warriors near Rscil looked to him, ears low and teeth barred.

Cmeo Mrist and some others shouted and gestured at the laggard Dancers, pushing the last few into position and leading them in the Dance. Their chanting rose once more, and the talonmaster felt the Dancers' spell in his mind. It returned with a feeling of exasperation and motherliness, or perhaps big sisterliness. It helped, and he saw the warriors gingerly form back toward some semblance of order. Swiftly, the peace in his mind was restored. With a near obscene hiss the formerly wavering warriors of the Clan of the Three Fangs tore into the Liskash.

Then the talonmaster had more to worry about, as he was in front right of the formation, with Liskash, stomp lizards and a pawful of ragged, sickly-looking Mrem charging at him. Gree was ready as soon as Rscil slapped his shoulder, drew up fast, and grabbed his own weapons. They each tossed four darts in quick succession, and one from the Liskash flew close between them from somewhere, its fletchstring brushing his whiskers and making his fur puff even more.

The flankers fanned around him and chopped their way forward, which was good, as the arogar were crippled and dying in whinnies, riddled with spears and cut by blades. For now, though, it was a platform from which to direct the fray.

They had a good front, and could manage an envelopment, but it was thin, only the two ranks. The Third and Fourth Claws had recovered, and he pointed and shouted for them to be general reinforcements to replace casualties.

The Dancers had pulled back, or rather, Cmeo Mrist had pulled them back. They were a few lengths away, but seemed comfortable enough there, and their chant was in full, deep resonance, an angry snarl of defiance. The drums were abandoned, and it was clear that Cmeo Mrist and three of her senior Dancers were holding the rest together.

The clan's drillmasters at either end, realizing communication was impossible and seeing opportunity, began enveloping, their claws going from folded back to arcing around. That slowly put more blades against fewer Liskash, and the Mrem clambered over the bleeding green and tan enemy bodies. That also disrupted the lines, but that was for a positive reason.

Suddenly the talonmaster saw more coming. A lot more. On the crest of a hill ten long javelin throws away, another thick rank of spear-armed Liskash waved and shouted in their guttural, hissing equivalent of speech. With every clan warrior already engaged, there was nothing left to stop these new enemies from sweeping behind and trapping the entire clan. Or worse yet, slaughtering those of the clan who were too weak to fight and were waiting in the distant wagons.

"By the flanks *arch back and fall back!*" Rscil shouted. "*Arch back and fall back!* First Claw slow backstep!" The talonmaster took a deep breath. This was going to be difficult. "First Claw slow backstep. Everyone hold the line!" Others picked up the shout, and with dignified poise, the claws on both ends of the clan drew back, never turning away from the new force of Liskash. This formed a deep V as the center retreated faster than the flanks.

Whoever was commanding the Liskash must have realized what the formation was doing. As they reached the clan position, parts of the new Liskash force tried to get behind the V, but that meant running at an angle through the rush of their own fighters. That helped to disrupt the entire mass of charging Liskash. As they were hit by darts and confused, it became apparent that the Liskash warriors were simply not skilled enough to complete the maneuver. Nearly all turned to fight along the insides of the V.

The clan continued to draw back. The Dancers formed into two clumps, one each side of the point of the V, and moved smoothly back, a good distance behind the warriors.

At least the retreating claws had left a good crop of bodies for the scaly beasts and their lord to consider.

By the time the enemy reinforcements reached the place where the battle had been, the retreat was four hundredlengths back and still moving, still leaving a lot more dead lizards than Mrem, and stable in movement. The second force of Liskash attacked. It halted before even reaching the battlefield. Those who had been attacking the claws hesitated and desultorily retreated, just turning and bumbling off. A few darts and javelins took a few more in the back, until the drillmasters ordered a halt to it.

"Hold javelins!" The First Claw's drillmaster shouted. The cry was immediately taken up by the others.

"Why?" a warrior yelled back. "There's more of these overgrown pests to kill!"

"We'll need them for another battle, lad!" the drillmaster bellowed.

The warriors shrugged. One of them stooped to the dusty ground and came up with a fist-sized rock. He heaved that at the retreating Liskash. A lizard caught it in the back of the head and sprawled face first on the ground. The Mrem's fellows cheered and felt for more stones.

While not as effective as edged weapons, the rocks did cause a certain amount of damage. Several casualties were inflicted before the staggering Liskash were out of range. And, the barrage of stones made the warriors, many wounded and all reeking of Liskash blood, feel better.

It was a grueling march back to the wagons and fort, but the claws were left in peace, for the moment.

❖   ❖   ❖

Buloth was delighted, lounging on his comfortable bed in the fading light. He'd lost slaves, yes, but he'd beaten back this force of individuals. Most amusing that they thought lining up in rows would match the power of his mind. It organized them, but they gave up some of their vaunted independence. More than his own slaves gave up; all he cared was that they attacked the enemy. How they chose to do so was their problem. These creatures, though, had voluntarily crippled themselves, and relied on shouted voice orders.

It might take several battles, but the outcome was inevitable. The stronger mind—his—would win and acquire more slaves.

Thinking of that, he tried to tally old slaves, new slaves, and any casualties. He could feel the latter whimpering and hurting, but lacked the strength to twist them into death. They'd just have to suffer, so he shut them from his mind. Surviving slaves were down a bit. That was annoying. Buloth wondered if it were possible to count casualties in the even lines of the mammals. He'd remember that for next time.

Meanwhile, he should regroup his force, feed them enough to carry on, and then advance on the furry beasts again.

This whole venture of developing his own godhold was quite exciting, and very informative. He shivered in anticipation that once done with his he might even be on terms with his father.

Mutal wouldn't matter, nor even hinder, if Buloth managed to absorb his father's holding. When the old Liskash died or was frail, his slaves were Buloth's for the taking. Then a simple advisory to his younger brother that he was assuming the minds should do it. There wouldn't even be a need for fighting. Yes, that was a good plan.

With that settled, it was time to quickly crush these encroaching creatures and secure as much space and as many minds as possible, both for the prestige, and for the practice.

But first, dinner. He'd vowed to roast a Mrem. Now would be the time. He called his cook.

Hress Rscil's tent was imposing in presence, even being no larger than the others. Perhaps it was the finer weave of the russet-colored fabric, or the small but comfortable and beautifully carved benches. Perhaps it was the guests, or just the presentation, but those within felt a sense of awe.

They had much to discuss. They were alive, with some casualties and low morale. That was first. Cmeo Mrist, Rscil and Scout Hril were all dusty and worn, but alert and waiting.

"I will start with my assessment," Rscil said, not ungently. "It was bad, but to be fair, not terrible. The Dancers panicked when battle joined, recovered somewhat and stayed out of the way. Obviously, we could not practice real combat beforehand. Cmeo Mrist?"

The priestess looked somewhat embarrassed. Her whiskers slicked back and her ears lay against her skull. The tip of her tail twitched back and forth.

"Yes, they were scared and are. I saw the warriors

stuck behind them, but couldn't move fast enough to help clear the way. It did not go as we had hoped."

"What do you suggest?"

"More practice is needed," she said without hesitation.

He was impressed. She asked no respite, but was eager to press on. Was it safe to do so, though?

He said, "I don't dismiss the idea, but I insist on proven tactics for future battles. Let the Dancers be close to the rear—they proved comfortable in that position—and let my warriors have their cohesive mass."

Cmeo Mrist said, "Hress Rscil, I understand your caution, but we are less effective further away. We must make this work." She gripped her tail to avoid fidgeting, and her ears betrayed agitation. She felt that strongly about it.

"With respect, I saw no effect to speak of. Morale was higher than normal, but much of that was taken away in the confusion. Then a number of warriors rushed to worry about the females instead of the fight, exactly as I warned." He finished and braced for the return.

Cmeo Mrist was remarkably calm in response.

"Hress Rscil, how many did we lose to the thought stealing of the Liskash?"

"Why, none, that I'm aware of."

"Very well, it has worked that much," Cmeo Mrist concluded.

Rscil said, "That was with Dancers in the rear, as I propose."

"I prefer that they stay with the warriors. We will train them not to hamper the battle."

"We will see," Rscil said.

Hril said, "I have a little favorable news to add."

"Yes, Hril Aris?" the talonmaster asked, his ears betraying his curiosity.

The scout stood and paced, tail twitching. "Talonmaster, Priestess. First, let me offer that this godling of theirs appears inexperienced. He let his warriors loose enough to retreat, with no thought for gleaning or the wounded. I have other scouts and a few teamsters recovering javelins, swords, harness, and there are some wounded we can treat. We have mercied several, and there will be more. When convenient, we also mercied the Liskash wounded, regardless of their condition. I feel pity for them as slaves, but have no desire to friend such creatures. Their javelins, also, are being taken to the bronzewrights to be straightened and sharpened. We will use them. Some arosh and arogar have been butchered. I included yours, Talonmaster. With no disrespect to fine animals, but they are meat." He bowed slightly.

Hress Rscil said, "Of course. I would expect no less." A fine scout, and a potential Master of some kind. Hril Aris's pupils swelled with the compliment.

"Thank you. Also, just before this council, we sighted eight and four Mrem who were held by the Liskash. They fled west and slightly north, back toward the New Sea."

"They broke the mindbinding?"

"Yes, apparently when our retreat started."

Cmeo Mrist said, "When our voice was surest. As I predicted."

Hril twitched as Rscil leaped to his feet, but it was not a threat.

Instead, the talonmaster said, "Cmeo Mrist, we will drill our warriors and our Dancers so that we do better next time."

Rscil knew it would not be quite so easy, but he would take the risk. He, all of them, would be remembered for generations once this was done. He only hoped it wasn't as spectacularly brave failures.

Cmeo Mrist raised herself tall and said, "Talonmaster, as if things are not complex enough, it seems the Dancers can fight if they must, without weakening their voice, as long as they are in the formation."

"Yes, we have agreed," he said. What was she leading to?

She seemed a bit hesitant as she said, "How many javelins have we recovered from the Liskash?"

That was a striking notion.

"I see we must drill the Dancers as well."

The warriors were not entirely happy with the decision to continue with the Dancers. They let it be known. Drillmasters reported hearing angry comments from their fists of warriors, and voiced their own complaints.

On the one fist, Hress Rscil understood both their need to release anger after the battle, and their frustration at a formation broken, with fellows left dead. Some two eights had been succored and would probably live, though many would never be fit to fight. Eight other eights and three had either died, or needed mercy. There would be other battles, and they were only two thousand and a few.

On the other, it must be driven to the haft that they were bound together.

Hress Rscil called the claws to order. "If you are unhappy, you may walk back to our steading in defeat. The warriors will remain for our glory. We'll wait to begin practice until those who wish to leave have gone."

The complaints quieted to mutters, and there was much shuffling, some bristling, and flattened ears. None wished to abandon the others, nor bear the shame attached. It was also clear there was no retreat, except as a whole. Individuals wouldn't manage the trip, except a few hardy scouts, all of whom stood with Hress Rscil. They could form parties, but what if they were attacked, to then die unknown in shame and ignominy? And if this campaign were successful, what chances would they have of mates and land?

He and Cmeo Mrist watched from his chariot, led by two precious replacement arogar. The practice, no doubt spurred by the threat of disgrace, was much more vigorous, and the Dancers moved with urgency.

A drillmaster shouted, "Step aside!" and the Dancers gathered in pairs, leaving gaps for supporting warriors to use. It was also hoped this would be their default movement if agitated, with enough practice.

Gree took over, ordering, "Advance!" and the supports flowed through the Dancers, who resumed their normal spacing.

"Retreat!" "Flank right!" "Flank left!" "Envelope!"

Rscil watched with satisfaction tempered by caution. They knew the moves, and with better relay through the fist leaders, the orders propagated across the field in heartbeats. It was going much better since they understood the faults of the first attempt.

Cmeo Mrist said, "I am more confident, now that they've seen battle."

"Only a little," he said. "I wonder what will happen the first time one dies."

The Dancer hesitated. Her lovely eyes turned sad. "I don't know."

"Pardon me if I seem brusque. There's some increase in resentment, given that the Dancers were in some part a hindrance, while suffering no harm. Even the benefit of spells is hard for a warrior to grasp and see."

"I understand," she replied. "How did the retreat go? It seemed to me to be orderly."

"Surprisingly so. The Dancers moved well enough, and the warriors were busy focusing on line and fighting."

"I felt the Liskash was happy with it. We retreated from him. It built his ego."

He felt rage fill him as it had not at the end of the battle. "Is this something you see as a positive?" he snapped. "Because I don't feel the benefit."

Cmeo Mrist laid a long, very soft paw on his arm. "Please bear with me for a moment, Hress Rscil. I need information."

"Go on," he prompted, corralling his temper.

"How did our casualties do in retreat?"

"If I understand your question, we gave a lot more

than we took, but there was very little succor for those we had to leave."

"Would a further advance have meant more?"

"For us? Yes. For the enemy? It's hard to say. Cursed Liskash don't retreat as they should, and killing them seems to only lead to more of them."

"What if we planned to retreat?"

He flared his nose, ears and eyes at that, then considered the question as a matter of strategy.

"I think I see," he said. "We face off, take a smash, fight an orderly retreat killing as many as we can. We stay cohesive, and the scaly godling believes he is doing well."

Cmeo Mrist's eyes danced eagerly. "Could we repeat it?"

Rscil considered. "Possibly. If we could fake an actual panic..."

"How often must we do it, or can we do it, to even the odds?"

It shook him from his pondering. He took a breath of the rich, fresh air and remembered the story he had heard.

"Oh, that. That's not the goal. The goal is to get near the godling and kill him, which destroys the entire army's will to fight. Our task is to protect the clan as they move along the shore. We will all meet up in good time."

"Does that mean a concerted thrust?"

He tensed and felt his fur fluff. "There is a specific plan for that, but it is not for sharing. I require that you not try to read it from me." He bristled his whiskers and hoped she'd comply. Now was not the time for any such intimacy.

"I understand your caution. Of course I would do no such thing." Rscil chided himself for not trusting her. She was diplomatic, and honest, and a fine companion.

He said, "So let us continue to improve the legend."

Upon next daybreak, the warriors were in much better spirits, and slivers of sweetened dried fat for breakfast boosted their morale. They'd worked hard in attack formation, and been praised.

That changed when drill started. The first few practice retreats were accepted and went well. Obviously, it was important to be able to disengage.

However, with each iteration, the fidgeting and fluffing of fur increased.

Between the fourth and fifth, one of the drillmasters, Chach, approached the chariot, sought assent, then came close.

"Talonmaster, with respect, when will we return to practicing attack? The warriors feel they are being punished."

He shook his head firmly. "No punishment, Chach. We will practice attack shortly. The Dancers need more drill than the warriors to ensure things work. At least one retreat is likely, and significantly important if we are to save our fellows. Attack will follow. We need an orderly retreat, and we can fight as we do so."

"Mrem warriors are not much for retreating, Talonmaster."

Hress Rscil acknowledged his warrior's brave soul. "We do when we must, and we do so well. In this case, think of it as a planned strategy to bring us more lizardlings to kill. We will kill as we advance, and again as we retreat."

The Mrem grinned, and reached to flick his whiskers. "That I like. I don't like, and can tell you the warriors don't, having to leave wounded fellows behind."

Rscil nodded. "It is a terrible burden. However, we lost fewer in retreat than in advance, and less than in a prolonged clash. Remember, our enemy is the godling. His slaves are nothing without him, and merely obstacles."

"It's a hard idea, Talonmaster, but a bold one, in its twisted, backwards way."

"You may spread the word that I am confident in our ability to attack, but want to make our retreats equally painful to the scaly pests, who are twisted and backward themselves."

"Thank you, Talonmaster. I shall." He nodded in respect and strode away.

Rscil kept the exasperation from his ears. He didn't care for it either, but it had to be done. As they moved north, they'd certainly be attacked from behind.

The warriors were most disgruntled at the idea, even in acceptance. Rscil, with plain harness, loitered upwind of a fist campfire that night. An honest appraisal of one's support was necessary.

Someone grumbled, "I don't care if it does inflict casualties. Retreating is just unMremly. Do we retreat the whole way north, guiding them with us, leaving our fellows in a trail for the rest to follow?"

Another replied, "We'll advance as well. We just

have to draw the damned things out. Remember they have no endurance."

"They have numbers. We should be striking through their mass like a spear, to destroy this godling."

"Well, Talonmaster, why don't you tell us how it's done?"

"Hish," the second Mrem said dismissively. "I don't need to be a talonmaster to know that hurting enslaved lizard things won't win this. Poor, disgusting bastards. Lesser animals and not even the dignity of being themselves."

Yet a third offered, "Well, honestly, I don't like it much either. It'll be a sad day if our proud claim is that we retreat better than anyone. But if we win that way, I suppose eventually that will be the respected thing to do. At least when fighting Liskash."

An older, raspier voice said, "It's like that always. My mentors lamented the loss of individual bravery into this cohesion, but we beat everyone with it. Theirs lamented the longer-ranged javelins as cowardly, and detested slings. Styles change and advance."

"But do you like it, Frowl?"

"No, I don't. But while I'm fist leader, we'll do as the drills and the talonmaster say, and do it well. Forget that we're retreating. Just plan on being the smoothest, neatest, proudest fist, with the highest pile of lizard bodies."

"Urrr, I guess a pile of dead lizards rather proves the point."

Rscil smiled. A snarling warrior was a happy warrior, and would do as he was ordered. As the old timer

had said, this wouldn't be possible with the styles of
Nrao Aveldt's grandfather.

At two other fires in other areas, the grumbling was
the same. The warriors didn't like it, but they'd do it.

As he returned to his tent for another late night
council, there was a hissed alert from a sentry.

In moments, warriors rose, clutched whichever
weapons were closest, and dropped low to spring
lightly on all fours. They moved quietly, more so than
untrained people in daylight. Seasoned warriors, good
warriors. Rscil was proud of them.

In moments several impromptu fists formed up.
The warriors might not be of the same fist, but they
would make it work. Some moved to the edge of the
embankment. Others prepared to defend the gate.

At the same time, a drillmaster took several other
fists to the far side, and as other warriors were apprised,
they filled in around the perimeter. A noise could be
nothing, or a threat, or a feint.

A warrior awatch on the rampart gave signals. Past
each side of the guard post a fist flowed through tunnels made for the purpose, and sought to envelope
the gate.

Rscil watched the signs while seeking a spear himself. One of the warriors recognized him, stiffened
silently, and offered his spear while drawing his claws.
Rscil took the spear, twitched eyes and ears at him,
and turned back.

Several warriors were atop the traps, prepared to
block the zigzag entrance with tumbled rocks.

Rscil was talonmaster, but the sentry on the rampart

was the Mrem in charge. It would be foolish to step into the middle. He watched and waited for a signal. A secret part of him hoped for a small scuffle in which he could be only a warrior. He missed that part of his life.

Then the sentry raised his hand for a hold, while gesturing with his javelin for a foray. The two fists in the tunnels scurried from sight. Beats later, they returned through the gateway, leading and surrounding eight and three prisoners.

They were Mrem. Scrawny, scraggly, unkempt, but Mrem, carrying Liskash-style spears and very crude rawhide harness. They stared around in nervousness and fear, tinged with a scent of despair and shame.

One of them acted as spokesman for the rest.

"We tank you of our rescue. I be Trec."

The fist leader asked, "You were held by the Liskash?"

Trec nodded nervously. "Liskash, yes. Held in bond and contempt."

"How did you escape?"

He opened his hands and gestured at the others. "At battle ending mind helding break. I gather we and walk, intent normal."

"Are there others?"

"Might so. I hope."

The fist leader said, "I must take this to Hress Rscil."

"Hress Rscil will come to you," the talonmaster said, coming into the open. "I am still a warrior, after all."

The fist leader—Ghedri, if Hress Rscil remembered correctly, nodded in respect and stepped slightly aside. He addressed the newcomer.

"Trec, I am Hress Rscil. We move to conquer the Liskash, and occupy this territory."

Trec looked wistful and sad.

"If we can only live to see that."

Rscil knew what he was asking, and it fitted his needs to have insider information.

"You might. Will you serve under me, as we smash them?"

Trec looked him up and down. "How addressed you, leader?"

"I am titled Talonmaster."

Trec extended his hands, palm down toward Hress Rscil.

"Hress Rscil, I accept as Talonmaster mine."

The others held hands forward in agreement.

"I welcome you," Hress Rscil said. "Mrem, see that they are fed lightly but often, clean water, help them bathe, and find them rest. We will march again tomorrow."

He turned and walked back to his quarters.

On the whole, it had been a good day.

Buloth threw a copper pitcher at one of his senior attendants. The Liskash picked it up without a word and took it away with him. The young noble wasn't happy at losing slaves. The stress of battle had to have done it; he was not as strong as his father yet. That was a good lesson for him. Not just the mind magic, but the ability to retain it in harsh conditions. That would come with practice. Today, he meant to get practice. His gold flecked eyes narrowed with determination. Those retreating Mrem would not find him so easy this time.

He wanted to pretend he wasn't concerned about the escaped Mrem. He didn't need to pretend. No one here was aware of it, nor concerned. He enjoyed this lone power. How would he manage that with mates and children? That would be something to think on later.

For now, he didn't have to worry about the nasty creatures, and he found his mind focused sharper when it only had reptile brains to manipulate. They were cleaner, more advanced, less chaotic. He could control them better, and it felt as if he had more. That might be something to examine, too. If he could select the best, most tractable slaves, he could do more with them. The rest would have to be used for more menial tasks until they broke properly to his control, or be used where they could die heroic deaths for his greatness. Yes, he liked that notion.

There was much to explore here. First, though, he would flank and crush those nasty little vermin.

He selected a wine for his victory, and had his handserver put it aside.

He also decided Mrem did not taste good. No amount of seasoning made that gamy meat palatable.

Hress Rscil had doubts about his strategy. His warriors didn't like retreating. He had new, untested weaklings, to be honest about it. He had most of the clan's Dancers and warriors and their lives or independence to lose. There was no par, no gracious drawing of lines. Either he crushed the helpless slaves of this Buloth, and that creature himself, or he and all his people became mindless shit-handlers for the thing.

Still, it had worked once by accident. Hopefully it would work again by design.

The warriors were drawn up, with the eight and three new recruits mixed among them, and the Dancers. The warriors looked more concerned about the newcomers than they did about the Dancers. Rscil found that a relief.

This time Cmeo Mrist rode with him, with a spear to defend herself in need, and a loudcone like his own for directing her Dancers. All knew it would be a retreat. None yet knew the whole story on why.

It started as before, with a steady march toward the encroaching force that swarmed down the hill at a run.

This time, though, the clash did not cause the Dancers to snarl and panic. Many flinched or fluffed in aggression, but all kept their positions. The line held, and worked, and hordes of enslaved fighters fell squirming in reptilian death. It took so long for them to die. Eights of beats they'd thrash and twitch, long after their blood and their life had left them. Did they have no afterdeath to retreat to? Was that what kept them tied to the dead flesh? Was the mind magic grip that powerful?

He was almost distracted by those thoughts, but a javelin whipped past again, the bronze scarred from edge to edge combat, and bright as it missed his eye. He swore, and Gree galloped them closer to the line as a taunt to the enemy and a salute to his own. He would be closest during this retreat. Cmeo Mrist chittered slightly from nerves, but gripped the bound edge of the chariot and stayed still.

Then his divided attention returned to realize another mass of Liskash was spreading to flank them. Advance, retreat made no difference. There were thousands of them. Possibly an eight of thousands.

He raised his cone and shouted, "Drillmasters, divide the claws at the middle and retreat in two elements! Divide at the middle and retreat in two elements!"

The talonmaster burned and cringed inside. This was a complicated maneuver they'd never trained for, but it might give them enough frontage to save themselves. This was not to be a winning battle. He must just hope that the clan survived this one.

It worked to start with. Claws Five and Six, and Seven and Eight spread out to match the flanking forces. Three and Four split in two and clustered behind the lead ranks. The Dancers stepped aside, and then formed two shallow arcs that deepened into broad Vs. Once again, the slaughter started, a short backstep leaving clumps of twitching bodies for the attackers to maneuver around. That broke their advance and slowed them, and the Mrem butchered them as they came.

It worked so well that there was an even chance to advance, slightly. Hress Rscil flared his ears. *That* was useful. Perhaps that could be developed. Instead of a flat front, a dagged one.

Several Dancers broke from the mass and dragged wounded warriors to the rear, where a wagon waited to haul them far back. Some of them might survive, with herbs and washing and fire.

Then the retreat started in earnest, and it didn't look as if the warriors were faking fear. They were massively outnumbered, but laying about with claw and shield at any limb offered. Not many Liskash died, but eights of eights were crippled or maimed and would never fight again. He watched a leatherwing beat down, attempting to disrupt the movement with its wingtips. One warrior slashed off a tip with a keen spear, and a Dancer hurled her javelin just right, into its breast. It screeched, beat away just far enough to collapse into the Liskash lines.

Cmeo Mrist hopped down from the chariot and ran toward the formation, leaving him to wonder what had taken her. She didn't act bespelled, and she ran toward the battle, so he waited to see what happened.

He shouted for more reinforcements on the right flank, which was taking the brunt of the assault directly in front of him. The fighting had pushed close to where Rscil stood. He and Gree hurled their barbed darts into the encroaching mass in rapid succession, scoring an eight of wounds each.

The retreat suddenly erupted, with those cursed refugees turning to strike defending Mrem marching beside them. Hress Rscil snarled. Once a slave, always a slave. His warriors responded instantly to the attack. The refugees were no match for warriors on guard against them. He watched one smashed in the head from behind, another stabbed, others beaten and driven to the ground. The damage was done, though. Brave warriors had been outflanked and died, and the formation damaged. Some claws fought with but a single line of Mrem now. Too many of his warriors' snarls had turned to pain and fear instead of anger and challenge.

The Liskash were winning, and looked ready this time to press the attack all the way back to the fort. He sensed this was their end, and determined only that they'd all die before being turned into plants waving in something's mind breeze.

"Shallow the Vs and retreat!" he shouted. That would expose a wider, thinner front, but there was no choice. They couldn't make it narrower. The nasty Buloth had seen their maneuver and planned to defeat it. He was not so stupid as he seemed before.

"Reinforce the Vs in twos!"

They would also leave many brave warriors wounded or dead on the field. Those who survived would be enslaved. That was too much to think about.

At that moment he felt Cmeo Mrist's presence.

Courage, warrior, it said, and he felt it directed at him. The snarling song, the waving javelins, the shifting dance, gave him a calm measure of strength.

He heard her again, giving orders through their minds. Yet it was not unpleasant.

Dancers, heed the Dance, heed me, and advance.

Then something amazing happened.

The clan's retreat continued, with bloody precision. The Liskash charged into their formation, were slashed, stabbed and tossed into small heaps that became obstacles. Occasionally, a Mrem fell, sometimes in death, but more often from a crippling but treatable wound. The scouts had recovered some of these fallen last battle, but many had been lost. But then the talonmaster worried it was beginning to look like they were all lost.

Hress Rscil stared in bemusement and spine-fluffing appreciation as the reserve line of Dancers chanted and danced right through a portion of one claw's defensive rank, which drew aside briefly in surprise, then locked behind them. Two warriors made to follow, remembered their orders, and stayed.

But for whatever reason, the magic worked. The Liskash didn't notice the Dancers walking right through their mass. They even seemed to step aside for them. The Dance wove taillike through them, twisting past wounded Mrem who were offered two shoulders each. The chant continued, while their Dance disrupted a little, but seemed to hold.

They worked their way across the Vs, then the Liskash parted to let them back at the Mrem line. Two warriors stepped aside for them, and they twirled right back through with the wounded in arms, right past his chariot. Eights of warriors had been saved. Cmeo Mrist, her fur stained by the blood of a Mrem she had assisted, flared her nose and spread her ears as she passed.

There was one tragedy, made worse for its uniqueness, as they finished. The spell weakened as they reentered, and some hulking, green-skinned thing noticed them, enough to jam a blade into the spine of the last, and youngest Dancer. She convulsed and died with a shriek.

Then the Liskash weakened again, and drew back. This time it was orderly. They fought their way out of reach, fell back in groups, hurled rocks and javelins, taunted the Mrem, then ran.

"Let them go!" Hress Rscil ordered.

He decided not to discipline a few eights of warriors who hurled javelins into the retreating masses. A dead Liskash was a dead Liskash.

Hress Rscil shuddered in relief that the battle was won. The line had been so thin, so frail. Any rush from the Liskash would have smashed through and destroyed them all. The godling seemed to know only the crudest of tactics. Advance, envelope, reinforce. He lacked any skill in maneuver or strike. It proved they weren't particularly bright, just possessed of an evil grasp.

However, it would be foolish to assume another wouldn't be better. This one might have been a child or a fool. The next might not be.

The message dispatched to Nrao Aveldt with his swiftest runners advised of their situation, tactics, supply level and location. The plan to swing around the hills was not sustainable. Instead, they'd have to move north fast, and try for the river valley the scouts found. They'd have to cross between surges of sea, and hope not to be pinned by it if they were attacked. It was like a gate that opened twice a day, and moved along the fence a bit more each day.

With luck, the messengers would intercept the

resupply wagons and have them divert. Even with gleaning, javelins had been lost or broken. Wrighting took charcoal and fine clay. They could hammer damaged ones straight, and treat them in the fire, but there were limits to repair.

With all that done he had to address the aftermath of the battle. The warriors fed and drank, as did the Dancers. He heard the discordant snarls of Cmeo Mrist and her senior Dancers performing rites over their youngest dead, and two others. He gave them credit, though: they'd fought well and bravely when death came to their ranks.

Rewards and accolades would come after one uncomfortable matter. Punishment. Outside, the drillmasters, several fist leaders and a fistful of Dancers awaited as witnesses and advisors for him. He stepped out of his tent into the improvised parade field, where Trec and four surviving refugees waited. Refugees? Escaped slaves? Inadvertent traitors? What status should he give them?

For now he settled on name.

"Trec, you and your Mrem betrayed my warriors in the midst of battle. I will hear your argument."

Trec staggered and shook his head. "Oh, my Talonmaster!" he shouted, and fell to his knees. "Buloth's power did us caught, into mind squirming beneath and within. I stabbing one of your warriors ere I knew, then to strain against, tried." He held forward his left leg, lacerated by his own javelin edge. "Resisted, but not enough. Shamed I survive, that your warriors beat me down alive, not dead."

He turned to address Trec's appointed commander. "Fist Leader Chard."

"Yes, Talonmaster." Chard was stiff-faced, dirty and twitching in the after tension of battle.

"Tell me of Trec's fight."

Chard twitched his whiskers as he took a breath, and said, "He fought weakly due to his health, but with eagerness. I know of three wounds he inflicted on Liskash, and perhaps a death. Then he turned on Cysh, and was beaten down with hafts and fists."

"Fist Leaders, is this true of the other four?"

Nods and ears of assent said that was so. Fist Leader Braghi said, "This one, Cir, killed three and wounded two. We saw him turn and stopped him before he did more than inflict a scratch." He held up his forearm. The bandage indicated it was somewhat more than a scratch.

Hress Rscil wanted to be diplomatic, and to encourage others to defect, mostly for the information they'd bring. A few more spears, wielded by half-starved, untrained drifters, whose minds were bent to a lizard, were not of much military consequence. He couldn't have them near him, though.

"Trec, Cir, Gar, Hach, Leesh, stand and hear my ruling."

The remaining four of them stepped, or rather, limped forward, and stood proudly. They were scared but determined, and would die like Mrem for their shame.

Hress Rscil said, "Your mind was not your own, and you fought to maintain it. I hold no charge against you. I will move you into the van, however, for your courage. At worst, you may earn an honorable death. At best, perhaps you will turn back to yourselves, and put this false godling beneath you. Until then, you will be guarded by others, with respect and in support."

Trec spoke for them all. "We will honor in live or die, and thankee for mercy and wisdom."

He nodded, flared his ears, and said, "Priestess Cmeo Mrist, is there anything that can be done to strengthen their minds?"

She spread her ears and said, "Perhaps. I will work with them."

"Now I will publicly praise you and your Dancers for saving two eights and seven wounded warriors with your Dance through the battle."

There was a snarling cheer.

She bowed with a smile, erect tail tip twitching. "Thank you, Talonmaster. It was a proud privilege for us."

He went on to praise eight and six warriors who'd shown remarkable courage when reduced to a single rank without nearby flankers, fighting with the inspiration of Aedonniss and holding the line. Two had done so when Trec's Mrem had attacked their fellows. He discreetly referred to "wounded in battle," not "stabbed in the back."

"That is all for now. I respect you all for your fight and magic, and you, our drivers and handlers for your tireless work. I must coordinate our withdrawal from this fort, though all things willing, we will return and garrison it, build it and declare it a town before long. All be sure you are prepared to move tonight."

Cmeo Mrist caught up with him as he entered his tent.

"Talonmaster Hress Rscil, if I may ask, what did you see of the spell this time?"

With only a little reluctance, he said, "The chant and dance broke the spell. It does work." He waved to the other bench.

"Yes," she said as she sat.

"I noted that Trec and his cohorts were furthest from you, and ceased hostility as your Dance left the formation, surrounding them on all sides."

"It does work," she echoed him.

"You have no more Dancers to add, and we may face larger armies. How will you manage?"

"Stronger spells and louder songs," Cmeo Mrist said. "Think of it as complement to your warrior shouts."

"I see," he said. He had an idea. "Would more music help?" Cmeo Mrist's eyes widened with curiosity.

"It might. There are spells that incorporate layers of voice harmony, of horn."

"We have used baghorns in battle. They are great for signaling."

She brushed her whiskers and smiled. "I remember those from the route here. Why aren't they used in battle? You could choose tunes for messages."

That was a startling idea. Music was more about feel than thought, but of course Dancers felt things differently.

He clamped down on his interest in this shapely,

brilliant female, and said, "I will add that to the long list of things to study, after we have won this war."

"Thank you, Talonmaster," she said, with a warm lilt that had to be purposeful, and meant to tease him. "Then can you arrange a meeting with your horners? I'm sure we can develop something."

"I will do so. We will win in our next engagement, I am sure."

"As am I, needing only my faith of spirit. And in you."

She stood and pulled the curtain as she headed for her own tent.

Buloth shivered in elation, riding his bulky steed at the rear of his army. There they were, the hairy mammals, in their crude, dusty, smelly little hilltop camp, and here he was, with a thousand warriors a bare gis away, approaching in foggy darkness step by measured step, each creature in a slow, methodical advance. If he'd got the trick right, they felt pain for making noise, and nothing for proper advance. With practice, he might offer them pleasure, as disgusting a concept as that was, but it would improve motivation with simpler minds. That wasn't a subject he intended to discuss with Father. He'd save it in case of need.

They approached closer and closer, and he heard scrabbles and voices and movement. He couldn't read the Mrem, though. There were a few, but not enough. Those cursed priestesses of theirs. They interfered with his mindspells. He'd not only kill them. He'd humiliate them first, in the most carnal ways possible, with the filthiest beasts.

Then the mental fog cleared and he realized he'd been cheated. There were fewer than fifteen Mrem in the camp. He silently and angrily ordered the charge, and flogged his trunklegs into speed. He would be first, and take vengeance personally.

He dismounted and ordered two large stilts to carry him up the slippery slope. Twenty warriors flanked him against attack, and they burst in bounding turns through the back and forth of the gateway.

Rocks crashed and smashed into his guard; he tumbled and rolled to the slippery, sharp ground as the stilts were crippled, and found himself and six guards facing the Mrem. He reached out to grab their minds.

Nothing happened.

They were drunk. Something fermented, something smoked and something eaten. They were wailing, insane, mindless hairy beasts, armed with rocks and javelins and frothing at the mouth as they slashed and beat at his guard.

In moments they were all dead, though one moaned and twitched. Perhaps not dead, but what did it matter? It would be soon enough. Let it enjoy its pain for daring to attack a Liskash god.

Buloth staggered around, realized he'd been hit stingingly in the leg, and recovered his composure, outraged at the events. Then he saw the bandages on the dead Mrem.

These were all wounded, left behind drunk and drugged to fight him, with no purpose other than to kill a few Liskash before they succumbed to their injuries. They lacked even the grace to die with dignity.

But the rest were gone. He could chase them through the dark, but he suddenly realized he was afraid. He was in a furious panic and knew it. Those fuzzy beasts were better than they should be. How could they do this? They were stupid, barely intelligent, with no mindpower. They couldn't know what he planned, yet were ready for him. They'd retreated and slaughtered his slaves on the way. The second day, he'd spread for envelopment with a massively larger force, and they'd split to match it, then retreated again, and destroyed more. Now they retreated entirely, and with little loss.

The slaves lost in the first bout had come back to him in the second, then he'd lost them again. Were they so mind-damaged? Had he done that? Too much hold, too little? Part of this was Father's fault for not giving him more instruction. The servants taught him literacy. They could not teach mindholding. Father's fear had caused him to fail.

The toll in slaves and beasts was terrible. Nor had he acquired replacements. It felt as if he'd lost numbers in the last day. How? Why was his mindpower slipping?

The numbers were so bad he'd even made an attempt at having the wounded bandaged and carried, in hopes they'd heal. Limping slaves might not look the best, but at least they could stop javelins for the others. That he was reduced to this shamed him to a yellow tinge, even without other gods to see him.

His only recourse at this point was to retreat home and beg for reinforcements, and ask for advice on his failure.

He might not be ready to be a god yet. It hurt his ego, but he was a realist, as Liskash were.

He let the servants strike the pavilion and the banners, douse the fire and pack the wagons. He would ride home proudly but without fanfare, and ask Father to help him fix it.

Buloth reported in his best manner. Father sat on his carved and padded throne, listening in annoyance.

"Father, as I noted, I enslaved a hundred and eighty-eight Mrem, and pushed two strong attacks—"

"And botched them disgracefully," his father said vocally.

Buloth swallowed. That was not a good sign.

"I tried my best, but I need more counsel," he said, diplomatically, and willed himself to present that way in mind.

Father snorted and took a swallow of wine. "More counsel? You need more intelligence. Unbound animals outfought you."

"They did not bind. I tried surely. The ones I had bound also broke." He kept it as factual as possible, but he was afraid it sounded insufficient.

Clearly your mind is not strong enough, came the reply.

It is, he said. *I felt them, counted them, even turned some traitors back once amongst the enemy. There was interference. Their priestesses . . .*

Priestesses? his father roared. *Animals don't have religion. They have superstition at best.*

As you wish, but that is how they presented.

Buloth knew it was fruitless. Father would not believe until he felt himself, which hopefully wouldn't happen, as it would mean Mrem here, in the stronghold. But Father was not finished.

You have wasted my slaves, shamed me in front of the world, and made it necessary that I now do your job myself. Your younger brother will take my place. He has proven worthy.

Buloth had earned his father's scorn. *I abase myself, Father.*

You'll do more than that.

He felt a warm little trickle, then a crushing weight.

Buloth gasped and spasmed, fell to the ground and described a running circle with his feet as his own hindmind crushed his heart.

The last thing he heard was his father's voice.

"Even a son has a price in slaves."

Hress Rscil felt vindicated. He'd pushed hard for them to move north and east, then east along the side of the hills. Ahead, the setting sun reflected off the New Sea and turned the water crimson. That was all anyone talked of, once it came into view. It also kept them moving, too excited to want breaks. He insisted, though. Rest was necessary for good health. They might be in unending battle soon enough.

They camped on a hummock, with a hasty berm reinforced with stakes they'd hewn en route. Those had taken the last four days to gather, with the scrubby trees hereabouts. Hunting parties brought in some game to stretch their salted and dried rations. There were even some tubers that worked adequately in stew, if there was enough frusk and other fruit to cover it.

They could smell the New Sea, and hear faint rushes of water. At first it was disturbing, but quickly it became familiar and relaxing. The smell was of muck and rich earth, and some musty mold. This would be productive land.

The next morning they were afoot, moving quickly and eagerly to this New Sea, larger than any lake. At midday they reached it. Even seasoned veterans halted in wonder at the sight. Hress Rscil was as awed as the others.

Gree said, trying not to sound too eager, "Talon-master, I propose we allow a rest and play time."

Rscil grinned at him. "I agree. In shifts of three, an eighthday each." Not that he didn't think it was a fun idea himself, but he recognized it would be a distraction until they all got it out of their systems.

Then they'd move north, and try this most bold of tactics, based only on information from scouts. This was a new way of war, and he wondered how it would be fought generations hence.

Cmeo Mrist was very beautiful, erupting wet and slick from the water, her glossy black fur clinging to her form. He looked away to avoid being distracted. Perhaps after this campaign he could consider a mate, but could any female compare with one as brave and intelligent as she?

The water was turbid and lukewarm, like runoff from a camp station for watering beasts, not at all refreshing. Bits of plant floated in it, and bubbles of deep decay rose occasionally. It was shallow, except where it dropped off suddenly, this being a plain at the edge of the hills, with the former Hot Depths east and below. It took only a short time for the polish to wear off for Rscil.

He formed them back up, and had the scouts and watchers move out to clear the way. They still had a long way to go on this new route, and at least one legendary battle.

There was surprisingly little grumbling, and the break seemed to have refreshed the Mrem, as well as inspired them, with this mucky, bitter water that lapped at the land. In short order, they were moving north. He studied the narrow but obvious tidal flat. How did one decide where the land ended and sea began? Especially with the sea changing?

Rscil walked, though he could ride. Occasionally he'd mount chariot and patrol around the army, to offer encouragement. Then he'd dismount to walk again. It saved the beasts, and let every Mrem know he walked with them, not above them.

It was good that he did so. It helped keep the pace even. Stragglers would be at risk, though he did urge them to greater speed.

"Dancer, I saw you fight. This is but a walk. You are well up to it!" "Wright, you hammer bronze all day. Move that strength to your legs." "Warrior, you don't want to be late for the glory."

They were in good spirits, just fatigued. A long march could do that. He kept up the encouragement and had Gree at the van slow their pace slightly. Faster was preferred, but arriving all together and fresh to fight was more pressing.

Before night, a message came from ahead. A watcher sprinted back through the lines of wagons, slowed for the approach, and came alongside Rscil.

"Talonmaster," he said, "we have sign. Drag and trail of an army, and fresh filth marks of Liskash scouts."

"Thank you, Arschi. I will note both and send all the scouts out."

Indeed he would. This was almost the end.

Oglut was very, very annoyed. Mutal had been unable to secure the south against the remains of Ashala's godholding. Several offspring warred for position, leaving the entire area a shambles of discord and starvation. It would take time to resolve, and would have to be rebuilt from the bottom. However, Mutal had marshaled his creatures and brought them back largely alive. His report indicated that much fighting went on between the new aspirants and the stray Mrem. That was something that should be left for now. They could kill each other until Oglut was ready to move on them.

It had not been a great campaign, but it hadn't been the disaster that Buloth's was. There were now reports from his distant eyes of two Mrem mobs near the New Sea, south of the hills and moving north. This was after the ridiculous behavior of moving west. The new environment was prime for reptiles, not the steaming, stinking furries. If he didn't know better, it seemed as if they'd meant to conquer his territory, and now were fleeing north. There were tens of thousands of them.

If Buloth had done his job, at least one of those packs would be slaves, scattered savages or slaughtered now. Instead, there were two, and he'd have to deal with them personally. One son was a former incompetent and now corpse, the other competent but untrained.

What annoyed Oglut most was it was his own fault they lacked in such skills. Still, there'd been no way to trust them with that power until there was expansion room. Between the cool continent to the north swarming with mammalian vermin, and the two strong, warring factions to the south, there'd been nowhere to go. Now there was, but it was a mess.

He called for his beasts and handlers, and pushed the army and loose auxiliaries into movement. This would be an excessive slaughter.

Hress Rscil pushed the army on into the night. They grumbled and snarled under their breaths, but he could tell they were at least as excited about meeting with Nrao Aveldt's force. That would make them stronger.

The original plan was for Hress Rscil to drive around the hills, north of Oglut's city, drawing that army along. He'd have the advantage of speed and a good map they couldn't know he had, and that would free Nrao Aveldt's force, with the civilians, to move north unmolested. With river, sea and hills, they'd have all the terrain advantages.

Now, they had to guard Nrao Aveldt's rear, and challenge the approaching Liskash. He hoped it would work. It had to. They still had terrain, and from scout reports, the Liskash were heading to meet them.

It was profound how this sea had changed the world. The filling of a ditch, albeit a large one, was destroying entire kingdoms not anywhere near the Hot Depths.

Shouts from ahead roused him from his musing. They'd run into the tail of Nrao's army. Warriors sent up cheers and yelled greetings to their mates. Drillmasters had to shout them back into order, but they had smiles on their faces as well.

It took most of an eighthnight to actually find the clan leader. There were that many warriors, and Dancers, and wrights and drovers. Add in the dark and few lamps, and it was a chore. Eventually, though, he heard Nrao Aveldt's gravelly voice nearby.

He called, "Clan Leader, I greet you."

The golden-coated male turned suddenly, and a smile spread across his face.

"Talonmaster! Well done!"

Hress Rscil bowed his head as the failures of the last several eightdays rushed into his mind. "Not so well. We are forced to an alternate plan."

Nrao Aveldt put a hand on his shoulder. "Still within our plans. I have your reports, but would share grer and hear first hand."

"Certainly."

It felt good to sit on a bench in Nrao Aveldt's tented wagon. It was big enough for four to talk or one to sleep. The grer drove the damp and chill from Rscil with its fermented warmth. Nrao Aveldt waited patiently until he was ready to speak.

Comfortable, and with big slabs of fruit-laden dried fat at hand, Hress Rscil told his tale. Their body heat warmed the small tent, though the humidity clung to their fur.

Nrao Aveldt sipped his own drink. He was polite and attentive, and seemed eager for the upcoming fight. When Rscil finished his story, he spoke.

"I am pleased by this. You have found a tactic that will work well in this position, even better than we planned. The Dancers have proven their worth. We can beat the lizards' mind magic and their army. I am sympathetic to the former slaves, but I agree they should be offered the chance to die bravely, or win through. It is the only way for them to be free."

"Thank you," Rscil replied.

"It is only days until this comes through." Nrao Aveldt warned.

"Then a new home?" Hress Rscil hardly dared consider it, it was so far out of his plans. Nrao Aveldt understood. He smiled.

"Yes, then a new home, but I will need you behind until we are out of danger. Then you will build a fortress. Do you still prefer Outpost Master Shlom?"

"I do. He commands well without supervision, and I will leave seasoned drillmasters with him." Hress Rscil assured Nrao Aveldt.

The clan leader's throat hummed with approval. "Excellent. Our welcome in the north will be better if we leave a strong position here, I believe. Then let us rest and prepare for the fight."

Nrao Aveldt stretched, shifted and curled again on his bench. He tilted his cup and drank thoughtfully.

"You do realize, Hress Rscil, that we could have left in small caravans and likely been unseen, most of us, spreading out across the north. We would sacrifice our steading, perhaps half the clan, and our past, but our bloodlines would continue. My son suggested it, in fact."

Hress Rscil was uncomfortable with the idea.

"A bloodline is more than just blood," he said.

"Yes, that is why it is only a desperate last plan. We must remain a people." Nrao Aveldt emphasized his words by slapping the wood. He raised the crockery bottle for a refill as shouts came from outside. He placed it on the table and scooped up a javelin. Rscil followed suit, and both were outside in moments, with Nrao Aveldt's guards and servants falling in around them.

There was a Liskash present, but only one, looking somewhat bruised and worse for wear. Two scouts held him by his scaly arms. He was greenish yellow, and well concealed in darkness.

Nrao Aveldt spoke at once to his talonmaster. "Do you have anyone who speaks their oily tongue?"

Rscil said drily, "I rather hoped one of your spies did."

"They are busy elsewhere," Nrao Aveldt said, without elaborating.

Rscil thought. "Then no, but wait." Possibly . . . He turned to a scout. "Send for Trec, among my camp."

Nrao Aveldt said, "Ah, one of the escapees you spoke of. Good."

The Liskash didn't fight, and his expression was creepily blank. No ears, no smile, little way to tell what they thought, if they thought. Though at least some of them built castles. He did seem to twitch whenever the grips on him were lightened, pondering escape.

"Hold him well," Rscil said.

The warriors nodded and all but sat on the cold-skinned thing. He struggled a few beats, then seemed to accept his position.

Trec arrived in short order. Despite the long route and field rations, he looked fitter and fuller than he had when he'd dragged his worn self into their camp. That said much.

"Greetings, Trec. Are you skilled in the tongue of these creatures?"

"Talonmaster, and you are the lord?" he asked, turning that toward Nrao Aveldt.

"I am. I greet you, Trec. I will meet with you later."

"Understood, lord," he nodded and turned back. "Talonmaster, no one I known speaks language this. Do not the commoners project thoughts. They only hear, and not much."

"That is unfortunate. I am reluctant to kill him in case he is expected. He may also prove useful to send a message back, as well, if we knew what to say."

Trec said, "I can translate you thought hearably, I think."

Clan Leader Nrao Aveldt didn't want to think overly on that. The poor Mrem had had those disgusting creatures in his mind. That by itself helped color his response.

"Tell him this: 'Go tell the slimy lizard we await him.'" He gestured, and the guards hauled the lizard upright.

Trec strained, gripping his head and shivering until he drooled. He sank slowly to his knees. Suddenly, though, the Liskash stiffened and recoiled, whipping around and reacting in horror, even while on the ground.

Trec stood and said, "I did my best."

"For us?" It was harsh, but a valid question.

Trec nodded and took it like a Mrem. "I did, Talonmaster. My mind is breakable to rulers of they, but not here, and not of things like that." He pointed at the now panicky Liskash.

The sentries looked to Talonmaster Rscil for assent and, receiving it, prodded the creature with the butt of a javelin. The Liskash trotted unsurely away, before increasing to a run into the damp, foggy darkness.

Rscil smiled and said, "Aedonniss and Assirra willing, we shall meet this Oglut in a day or so. For the first and last time."

Nrao Aveldt said, "I hope that optimism is well-placed, Talonmaster."

"It is. You will be impressed."

The clan leader observed, "It's near dawn. We may as well awake and on with it now."

Rscil was exhausted, but concurred. The sooner

they arrived on their chosen terrain, the sooner they'd be ready for battle.

The next day, they reached a wide, shallow river in a loamy plain, and Hril Aris assured them it was the one he and Flirsh Arst had observed. It flowed steadily over the rocks, and they certainly did look disturbed. They were wet, as the tide retreated.

"On this side we have a wall to stand against," he said. "Across, we have a barrier against attack."

Hress Rscil nodded. Though it was more than that.

"For half a day at a time, yes. It is as you describe." Timing was critical, though. "We will bivouac here," the talonmaster ordered. "I want stakes and pits."

Then they'd await this creature who styled himself a god. In this terrain, they had a steep hill to east and lapping water to the west. With a river as a third side, they'd pin him down regardless of his meaningless slaves, and eliminate him.

Oglut was in his tent at a meal when his servants brought a messenger to him. The creature was worn, abraded and weak. He also seemed reluctant to speak.

"Out with it. I am in a hurry," he said. The roasted trot bird was most tasty. He belched up its essence and inhaled it.

The Liskash trembled. "Great Oglut, the message is unpleasant."

Tell me.

"The message was . . . speak to slimy reptile of our presence and impatience."

Oglut grew cold. His entire body grew still from

that comment. It had been a very long time since anyone had spoken to him thus.

The messenger cringed and huddled, awaiting a terrible backlash. Oglut stared down at him.

"I will not kill you," he said. "That is the message. If the furry filth wish to meet me, they shall." He ripped the location from the scout's mind, enjoying his flail and gasp as his mind was violated. "I must go to the New Sea anyway. I will do so to drive their broken bodies into it."

To his servants he said, "They are at the steep mountain creek, above what used to be the cataract. We go there now. Toss scraps to the slaves and get my carriage."

He looked down at the nervous, hesitant creature before him.

"Stand. Get ready to march with me."

One didn't kill messengers. One could, however, move them to the front.

"They come!" was the call.

Talonmaster Rscil woke to it. He'd had a couple of eighths of rest at least. It would have to do. It was morning, but he'd been up most of the night, conducting his own reconnaissance, placing stakes to mark key points, and examining approaches.

"Form up!" he shouted as he sprang from his cot. He heard Nrao Aveldt shouting, and Cmeo Mrist, Gree, several other drillmasters calling out their orders in response.

Once out in the sun, he checked its position. If the

chart the scouts had was correct, it was a full eighth and a quarter until the river filled. Behind them was a wide, muddy flat, strewn with rocks, deadwood and debris, with a shallow river splashing leg-deep down the middle. It was poor protection, though harder for the enemy to cross while under defensive fire. If the Liskash came down from the heights, though . . .

The scout Ingo's report had detailed times based on the position of the moon, and a prediction of eventual depth. This narrow beach would soon be a shelf under the sea, probably within a month. The hardscrabble cliffs above and west would be the shore then.

The warriors were well-blooded, and all his Dancers too. Nrao Aveldt's claws were somewhat less so, as they'd marched straight here. Between them, though, it should be fine, he told himself. They were side by side, filling the beach from cliff to water, as the drillmasters had been instructed. The line between them was apparent to him, but probably not to a reptile. It was a weak spot. One of several.

Several fists of scouts scurried up the cliff, to hold high ground against a flank. Nor had a force come around the mountains. South was the distant, dusty mass of a Liskash army, led by some godling or other, hopefully Oglut himself.

Whoever it was approached slowly. Rscil realized they might be standing a long time. Given that, he ordered, "Rest in place!" and indicated to the nearest drillmasters to give Mrem turns to relieve themselves, drink water, grab a chunk of meat, even if they weren't hungry.

It was almost a stately advance, of a formal meeting. Except neither the Mrem nor Liskash cared about dignity or formalities with each other, only about killing the other as a threat.

Dust in the distance informed him that the enemy was close. Here they came, in the advance, moving to a faster walk. They were perhaps five hundredlengths from the south bank.

"Watch for leatherwings and attacks from the cliffs!" Rscil ordered.

It was none too soon. There were leatherwings all over. High above, the scouts shot arrows and slung stones at them, but the enraged beasts stooped and dove at them. That kept many away from the army on the ground, however the flocks seemed endless.

Several soared down the cliff and over his formation, only to be slashed by warriors and Dancers. They quickly gave up and retreated, cackling and cawing in pain. The warriors on the cliff kept up a barrage to speed them. Sending a prayer to their bravery, he turned back to the approaching Liskash.

"Steady!" the talonmaster commanded loudly, trying to sound assured, as a stampede of wild animals bore down on them, ahead of the approaching Liskash army. It was large, mostly lizard and all ugly, until the lead beasts piled into the narrow angled trenches they'd cut across the ground. Shrieking and stumbling, they piled up in a wreck of bodies and dust, flinging grass and debris. It was an abattoir of legendary scale, with the smallest animals racing through to be speared, the half-sized game lamed and injured in the pits, to be smashed under the hooves and claws of the tumbling, trumpeting wall of large meat.

If they survived this battle, the Mrem would all eat very well indeed.

Oglut seethed. These too-clever furballs did seek to challenge him. He gurgled gleefully as a soarer flung one of them from the rocks to dash to its death below. He sent them to gang up on the cliff-scaling creatures one at a time, if that's what it took.

But ahead, madness. The stampeding animals were to smash this neat little box, crush the stinking beasts under claw and foot, and leave only scattered, panicked individuals for his army to finish off.

Some had made it through near the water. There, the Mrem slashed and fought, their proud formation broken into groups who could only prod at trunklegs with their bronze spears. Oglut had his mind and the trunklegs' weight.

Farther inland, though, where those pits were, was a shambles of broken, screaming things. If he could kill them with thought he would, not from mercy, but to shut their wails. They were beyond distracting, they were painful.

However, the mammals numbered a few thousand, and he had tens of thousands. They cared for their lives; his slaves did not. All that was necessary was to advance past the blockade of dying meat, then charge. If they could be stuffed into the river, they could be drowned.

The beasts were actually in advance. He laughed to himself.

He would not fall for the tricks his worthless son fell for. For one thing, they couldn't get past the crippled stampede or their own traps.

He gave his orders slowly and carefully.

Talonmaster Hress Rscil, now aboard a wagon, which was sturdier if slower than a chariot, studied and planned while the advancing army wove cautiously between and over dying, kicking beasts. That said all that was needed about this godling. Death and pain of others were tools for him, with no compassion at all.

But Aedonniss and Assirra had brought them here at this time. They guided their Mrem.

He raised his loudcone and shouted to Nrao Aveldt. "Now, as we agreed!" Then he raised it to his drill-masters. "Slow retreat!"

This wasn't a fighting retreat. This was a maneuver for position. They maintained line and spacing, though it was awkward while stepping backward on rough ground.

It was unnerving to see thousands of Liskash moving cautiously, slowly, across the beaten ground, under the mesmerizing spell of their master. However, that made it clear it was Oglut they faced, not some lesser lord.

Next to him, Cmeo Mrist raised her cone and said simply, "Dancers, now!"

Their wailing, resonant song rose instantly to full volume, with a tight chatter of drums that resolved into a strong beat. The borrowed baghorners sounded off, punctuating and reinforcing the song.

❖   ❖   ❖

Oglut gritted his teeth. First the shrieks of the beasts, now the wauling song of those cursed Mrem. Was it their death song? He hoped so. Even here, it hurt his mind, made concentration difficult. It must be horrible up close. A quick check into the mind of a forward warrior indicated it was so. Ugh.

His army made it through the obstacles, and had only a quarter gis to go to reach them. Soon enough he'd hear them make other noises, ones no more pleasant, but much more enjoyable for him.

Now the fuzzy things changed direction and advanced again. Whatever they were doing, it wasn't going to help them. With these gone at last, he'd solidify to the north and send Mutal south. It might be time to sire a new brood for the future.

He took a gulp of a good wine for fortification, rose up on his carriage's dais, and ordered a charge. He'd follow right behind them to enjoy the view.

Talonmaster Hress Rscil had told Clan Leader Nrao Aveldt he would be surprised. Indeed he was.

The band advanced with precision, for these were not slaves. Each one was a willing, trained Mrem, their minds and actions linked in a joining that could only be called magic.

The Mrem kept the pace and the beat, in a steady, mesmerizing thump of left feet. The warriors advanced in identical, perfect pace, their rows as straight as an engineer's string. In and among them, the Dancers moved in their own special way, arms punching and flailing at the air in unison, the motions rippling in waves from van to rear. Their unified chant inspired even at this distance. Under it all, the drone of the baghorns buzzed like angry bees, simultaneously adding to the power whilst distracting from anything else.

Those head tosses looked flamboyant and artistic, but meant each Dancer stared down the length of her row every two steps, and did not look long enough at the advancing Liskash to be distracted. For the warriors, the gyrating Dancers were visible peripherally, and gave them reference points for their own lines. It didn't hurt that they were lithe females, either.

Ahead, the mass of Oglut's army advanced. They came now in a solid but uncoordinated group, with a little forward swelling in the middle, a dip of less brave or driven to the sides, and a slight swelling at the flanks by those Liskash who almost hesitated. The narrowness of the new beach throttled them into a tighter bunch. They moved well, not hindering each other, and with some shuffling, the braver moved to the front.

The main concern was some flanking maneuver on the high ground to the east. Nrao Aveldt squinted up that way, his pupils narrowing to slits. The slingers, archers and javeliners had been tolled heavily by the leatherwings. He hoped enough remained, though the ground up there seemed inhospitable to most, strewn in boulders and clumps of stalky grass. A few stray beasts and a fistful of Liskash scrambled up, to be shot down. It was the far side of the battlefield, but not far enough.

A good battle was won before it was engaged, by

having all avenues accounted for, and good position and movement. This was a good position. The fanning Liskash slipped down the bank and piled up again, sorting themselves out, but wet, muck-sheened and visibly frustrated.

There was always that fear, though, that it wasn't enough. It only took a wobble in the front to create a gap that became a hole. How would this formation fare? Rscil reported very favorably, but Nrao Aveldt hadn't seen it in person. Trust fought with insecurity. He gripped his own chariot rim. Oh, to be in the fight. But now as clan leader, he must defer to others. He led them all, not just the warriors. He had the sea flank, Rscil the hill flank. He'd rather they were reversed. The gooey ground underneath hindered the chariot. It might be best to dismount. With a nod to his drover he did so.

It worked well, so far. The warriors in the first two ranks seemed calm, collected, and held the best spacing he'd ever seen. They strode and strode. Diagonally behind them, the Dancers waved those short spears overhead and side to side, keeping a perfect line. Their motion was almost mind magic itself. It drew one in, commanded one to watch. There was good and bad in that, as the enemy approached rapidly, already across the river's shallows and climbing the bank.

Then it was on.

A wave of leathery reptiles charged forward, swelled out against the Mrem, broke and tumbled and fell. In beautiful, glittering, musical balance, the warriors struck the incoming bodies and tossed them aside to the females. The Dancers' spears twisted, flashed and resumed their shaking flutters. The scaled beasts thrashed and twitched, their bodies reluctant to release souls already dead.

Forward momentum stopped, each rank pulling up and trying to maintain spacing from the one in front. The ranks stacked up, but kept even for the most part.

With only minor ripples, the Mrem came to a stop and kept a solid, impenetrable front of shields and spears. The oncoming enemy could only advance and try to overwhelm them frontally, past broken bodies and across a pot-holed savanna.

The tactic worked. The reptiles and a handful of sad Mrem under godling control advanced again, as the cajoling demands in their minds fought with their fear. They were many, and directed, but not inspired. They arrived in a ringing clash, and fell in clattering heaps. The Mrem were many, and were inspired and each an eager, thoughtful self building a greater whole. No single death could stop them; were Nrao Aveldt or Hress Rscil to die, the battle would continue. As some few warriors and Dancers fell, others stepped forward. The formation was built of courage, discipline and art.

And magic. Oglut put forth his will. Nrao Aveldt could feel it, a mighty darkness clutching at his mind, his spirit. He shuddered himself, this far away, and watched in fear as a ripple swept through the combined band.

But that was all. A ripple, then nothing. The overwhelming force of a lizard who styled himself a god was no match for the proud minds of cooperating Mrem. His grasp for control evaporated. Then it slipped from those he already held. His entire army could be seen to hesitate, shiver, stop for a moment, then collapse on itself. Some few pressed half-livered attacks. Others cowered down where they stood, trembling in abandonment and fear. Most retreated from a walk to a panicked sprint, ebbing back in a softer, weaker wave than the attack.

The Mrem advanced slightly, but only slightly, holding the perfect dance, the perfect advance and moving forward in step on step across the plain. Hress Rscil shouted, as did the drillmasters. The energy, the power, the motion and sound of the Dance let the bristling spears add to the magic, and nothing Oglut had mattered.

It was time, though. To the west, the lapping waves built, and the gravelly loam between it and the Liskash narrowed quickly.

"Retreat," Nrao Aveldt ordered the nearest drillmaster, and his flank began to withdraw. Others caught it, and the order flowed forward and through the mass. Hress Rscil nodded and shouted it. The other drillmasters echoed it, and the formation marched through itself, with the lead warriors now holding the face of the V.

It was a struggle to keep aligned as they backed across the river silt. Nrao Aveldt had never been so proud in his life.

Oglut felt a surge and a shift. That was odd. His power felt suddenly much greater. He seized it and pushed his will, urging all his slaves into the attack.

He was sure he'd acquired a number of Nrao Aveldt's warriors, who would sow chaos in that very pretty formation, and bring it to a boiling incoherence the rest could overswarm. His warriors and beasts hesitated, regrouped and charged.

It hit him too late what he'd felt. It was not the sudden gain of the attacking Mrem. It was the recovery of some of his slaves, who had actually broken from his mind. He cursed, and flogged them mentally, demanding they charge or face even greater agony. They slowed, but continued.

That was fine, even for the mindweak, because the Mrem were in retreat. They were pulling back across the river now, and lacked the heart and spleen to face his mind and his warriors. He would press now, then pursue. The muck and water would slow them. Their care for their skins would be their end.

Talonmaster Hress Rscil felt strangely calm, despite hot sun, sticky mud and the sun beating down on him. Then he sloshed into the river and felt chill. He sought gaps between pebbles with his feet. A fall now would be disastrous.

Even though their plan called for abandoning the carts and chariots, temporarily, his guts flopped as they did so. The drovers and javelin throwers dismounted and ran, to fall into the ranks where they could. Many did not make it to that relative safety.

Ahead, hundreds of soulless eyes stared at him from Oglut's mind-ravished slaves. They took little care as they slid down the gullied bank, from tangled grass to sodden mud, then onto loose rocks. They crashed through the growth and over downed limbs, to splash into the water.

It was up to his waist now, and he looked around to monitor progress. It went well enough, but the lines grew ragged as bodies fought the current. The water was cool, though, and cleaned his fur. That probably wasn't fair exchange for hindered movement. He was in a deeper, slower pool at the bottom of some cascades hissing above him. Others were ankle-deep in rocky, tickling shallows. Some were in rapids between the two.

The other problem became apparent. He cared about holding formation. The cursed Liskash didn't. They high-stepped and waded and dove into the current, eager to reach the Mrem because the monster in their brains told them to. They threw themselves against javelins, to die and drag those into the water in their bodies.

"Darts!" the talonmaster shouted, and a flurry of bronze-tipped and weighted points arced from the front rank.

The water ran red downstream of him.

Then he was knocked under and felt a spear point tear past him, slicing his arm. Some of the Liskash had made it obliquely up the hill and across the rocks above. Rscil felt three or more, and he struck out with his spear, while clutching at his waist for his battle claws. Another jab missed, but he was still under and being held. His arm burned and his lungs started to.

The spear was jammed in the riverbed, so he could only use it for support, as cold water shoved at his nostrils and throat, sloshed in his ears and pulled at him. He got a fist in his battle claws, though, and raised them with a grin that he restrained just in time to avoid choking.

With a firm thrust and shove, he accomplished two things. He pushed his head above water, and he sliced the guts of his rightmost antagonist into tatters that leaked and bled in a boiling surge of color.

The talonmaster swung his battle claws gleefully around and watched for just a moment as a Liskash's expressionless face shredded like a wind-ripped tent. The thing convulsed and thrashed and at last made a squealing sound as its feet kicked and it fell away. That freed Rscil's spear, but he left it in the chest of the third, that clutched at it and drooled blood as Rscil swam downstream, spitting gory water.

Quickly, Rscil assessed. There were other melees in progress, as Oglut's slaves tried to overwhelm them by sheer numbers. The live Liskash used the twitching dead as stepping stones, and seemed determined to catch every Mrem point they could.

It would work, Rscil realized. They'd run out soon enough, and then, regardless of claws and teeth, they'd be buried under revolting lizard flesh. He watched one catapult itself over its predecessors, clear a gap in the First where no one had any longarms left, to land amid the Dancers, who snarled and howled and ripped it apart with javelins and claws.

Three beats later the Dancers were back in formation, panting and glazed red, but singing and waving.

But a glance back showed that Claws Eight and Seven were scrambling up the north bank, reaching down to help the Dancers ahead of them. There were holes in the front, where the bravest had died, but Aedonniss—and especially Assirra—willing, the rest would get up that bank, and have high ground from which to stab the disgusting lizards.

We'll be heading north soon enough, he told himself.

Then the talonmaster ordered, "Quick now, and even! Thrust and block! and thrust and block! and step! and thrust! and step! and thrust!" His arm hurt, but he ignored the pain. Almost everyone near him showed small wounds.

At least the nearest heard him over the din of dying Liskash, and swung their points in unison. It worked, creating a wall of bodies again that hindered the advance until the water dislodged some into the shifting ripples.

Then they were all on the silt and debris of the north bank. Sharp gravel had never felt so wonderful. The talonmaster pulled at the nearest warrior and Dancer, shouting, "Keep position! And keep dancing!"

He could hear left feet stomping as the retreating claw took back its position. Those farther back passed forward their spears, keeping their javelins for themselves.

Rscil hadn't heard that roar before, but he knew what it meant.

"*Retreat at the double!*" he shouted. "*Retreat at the double!*"

He heard someone echo it before the sound was lost.

If they could only get up that slippery bank...

❖   ❖   ❖

Oglut saw victory. A sheer wave of dispensable slaves, petty criminals and mindweak inferiors hurled themselves against the lead Mrem. They might hide it from his sons, but he saw that the front rank had all the stoutest and best. Beyond that were lesser-built males and even females. Crack that façade and the rest would flee.

They were moving faster, already, eager to retreat from him. They slipped and clambered backward up the bank, using their spears for support and traction. He had them, and now for the kill, and once he tasted their anguish, he would draw them into his fold and make them his. They would entertain him, clean the herd beasts, scrub latrines, all the lowest tasks.

He urged his trunklegs on, drawing his high-wheeled chariot, bedecked in its glittering silver and bluestone, in a bumpy ride down the bank and across the mud. It wasn't dignified, but none would notice. With enough speed, the animals managed not to mire, though they did struggle. His wheels sank, but dragged and rolled, and then he was in the river, up high, looking down on the puny victims. A wounded one waved an arm before him, and he steered to crush it under the left wheel, feeling a rise and crunch as he ran over its ribs.

It was then another distraction on the left caught his attention. He glanced over, and froze in wonder. Was it magic? Some trick of a storm? But the sky was clear and blue, and a rushing wall of water roared toward him, brown with dirt and spitting froth and weeds.

Was their damnable god real?

The far flank disappeared under it, others turned to

run even before he gave the order, and a handful of Mrem scrambled farther up the bank, as one slipped and submerged. He had no time to balance that small frisson with the searing hatred and disgust welling up inside. The water was easily twice his height as it rose over the chariot, tumbling him with it and bruising him with heavy river cobbles that smashed and burned. He sealed his nostrils and grasped for support, but the chariot was atop him, the trunklegs thrashing upside down and tangled as they drowned, and he knew he was to follow in moments. He recalled he'd wanted to see the New Sea. It had even come to him.

He pressed forth his will for his surviving slaves to fight in reckless, unending abandon, but knew it was pointless. Stupid creatures. Many had run from the far dry bank right into the path of this flood.

He felt them crying, panicking, dying, and a swell of elation from the cursed mammals, then the odd burning of water inside him.

After that, there was only the sighing of the waves.

Cata

**JODY LYNN NYE
& JOHN RINGO**

They Danced and the minions of evil perished. But the minions were many and they were too few. Finally the Dancer stood assailed in her body and mind.

"Guide my claws," Cassa Fisook prayed.

And Assirra heard her and entered her. And so filled with the power of Assirra, Cassa Danced as never before, with such grace and purpose that no demon could stand before her. And thus to her the goddess had given to the dancer an awful gift and Cassa began to worship Asirra with the Dance of Death.

—*The Book of Bau*, verse ninety-seven

Catas are stories of beauty and pain.
—Ancient Mrem saying

SHERRIL RANGAWO TIPTOED SOFTLY INTO THE pavilion under cover of the music, careful not to disturb the Dancers' ritual. As counselor to Their most august Sinuousnesses, he had the privilege to view but not interrupt. He wished they had been resting; how satisfying it would have been to be able to make a grand entrance and fall at their feet exhausted! He had thought about it all the way back from Ckotliss, the stronghold of Tae Shanissi. The very relief he felt at being alive at all, let alone in one piece made him want admiration and sympathy. He promised himself now to be stoic and modest, all the more to make those waiting admire him more. Since he wore no weapons, he made no sound as he slid into a fold of the heavy hide tent. His charcoal-gray fur allowed him to blend with the shadows to await the end of the ritual. The chamber, the center of the Lailah clan's mobile city since they had left their flooded valley many leagues to the east, was formed of rectangular tents open to a central square that let in the sky. Under the hot sun of noon, the Dancers danced. He breathed the sharp, leather-scented air, and watched.

The slender, black-furred females wove a hypnotic pattern, sliding in and out among one another, as if they were attempting to weave a complicated knot out of pure energy. He could feel it, though he was far more sensitive to nuance than sensation. Sherril marveled at the ancient story unfolding before him. No matter how many times he had seen the Tale of Creation, it never palled. That young Dancer at the back, though—she needed more work on her portrayal of the Burgeoning Garden. Too clumsy. He would not dare say he could do it better himself, but he wagered his attempt would show more grace than hers. The rest, though, exhibited litheness and power that made him lust after all of them. The beat of the white skin drum, the wild fluting of the twin-pipes, and the pinging of the lyre only made his blood pump harder.

The priestesses leaped over and rolled beneath one another, drawing power in three dimensions. They wore bracelets and anklets of jeweled silver or gold, as well as charms around their tails and in between their toes. The metal glittered in the sun. Their fur seemed to glitter, too, dusted as it was with powder crushed from precious stones. Sherril smelled the fragrance of their fur warmed by their efforts and the heat of the day. A senior Dancer, Cleotra Mreem, caught a glimpse of him out of the corner of a brilliant grass-green eye. She did not waver for a moment, but shot a meaningful look to Cassa Fisook, the head priestess. Cassa Fisook looked toward Sherril. The dance changed, slowing down. The hot energy began to melt away. Cassa Fisook whirled and leaped as lightly as a leaf until she was in the heart of the circle. Her Dancers came to a halt, facing her. Their voices sounded low in their throats, a gentle burr. She made gathering gestures with her arms, collecting the last of the power. Her long hands tucked it into a ball that she offered to the sky.

The chief of the Dancers bore a few gray hairs around her chin and nose, but was otherwise the upright, slim female who had protected, and mothered, the Lailah tribe of the Clan of the Claw for over thirty years. Her training and condition were so thorough that she was not even breathing fast. Sherril was exhausted from having run all the way from the center of the city.

Her chief servant Petru Keoh oiled into view. The huge, nearly all-black male was adorned even more ornately than his mistress. His many bracelets clashed together on his heavily-furred arms and legs, and he had dusted himself copiously with golden glitter. Sherril hated to admit it, but he envied Petru Keoh his thick ruff that made the ladies swoon with pleasure, not that the big gelding ever noticed. He brushed Cassa Fisook's fur smooth and sprinkled her with fresh sparkles, blue and green this time. Tiny, jeweled glints twinkled from the sable depths of her coat. He moved to adorn the rest of the Dancers, more sparingly, with the exception of that imperious senior female, whom he decorated copiously with precious red glitter. Petru Keoh was not above playing favorites, Sherril thought with a snort.

"I see you have returned," Cassa Fisook said. "Alive and well?"

Anyone with less self-possession than Sherril Rangawo would have lowered his head at the reproof. The ritual had been performed to protect him and his escort on their journey. Dancing magic took a great deal of effort and energy. Not to have revealed himself immediately was an error. The priestesses could have stopped much earlier, but then he would not have seen them dance. To Sherril, it was worth the possible tussle on the ground with the Dancers or their bodyguards. He strutted forward.

"I am here," he acknowledged. "My mission is accomplished, and I have brought us all back without hurt or loss."

"What news, then?" a deeper voice inquired.

Anyone with less self-possession than Sherril Rangawo would have jumped through the open roof. The Dancers parted. He saw Bau Dibsea lounging on a pile of cushions at the edge of the Dancing ground. The talonmaster glared at him. It was one thing to preen before the females. It was quite another to show off before a well-tried warrior with many kills to his name and a reputation for nipping holes in the ears of obnoxious subordinates. Inwardly, Sherril Rangawo cowered, but he covered his discomfiture as well as he could. He bowed.

"Leader, I bring news."

"I assumed as much. Let us hear it."

Dancer Cassa Fisook settled on her purple-dyed cushion beside Bau Dibsea. Sherril knew Bau was being honored to witness the Dance because of what might come later, but Sherril Rangawo knew differently. He was pleased to have information that the talonmaster did not. Cassa Fisook gestured to him.

"Sherril Rangawo, come forward and tell us what we must know."

Sherril gestured at his person, flicking a morsel of dust from his breast.

"Your Sinuousness, forgive the state of my fur. I haven't had time to wash since I returned."

"No matter," the Dancer said. "It is more important that we hear what you have to say."

Cassa Fisook twitched a finger, and Petru stepped forward. The valet held a painted wooden tray on which balanced a beaten-silver pitcher and a silver cup. Not the first-quality cup, as should have befitted Sherril Rangawo's station. He let out a hiss under his breath as Petru poured out wine for him. Petru retorted with an almost inaudible snort. He knew that Sherril could say nothing. He was going to get away with his insult. *One day*, Sherril Rangawo vowed, he would make the valet pay. But the Dancer swiveled her ears toward him. Sherril offered a drop to the God, Aedonniss, and his gentle bride, Assirra, then drank deeply. If he had been alone he would have drained the cup in a gulp. Sherril Rangawo didn't realize how dry his tongue was.

"What says the lizard?" Bau Dibsea demanded.

Sherril looked longingly at the cushions, but Bau

Dibsea did not invite him to sit down. Cassa Fisook was kinder. She waved to Petru, who arranged a seat just under the lip of the tent where the heat would beat down on Sherril's back but his face and toes would be cold. *That's two,* he thought. But he curled up on the down-stuffed pouch and tucked his feet beneath him.

"Greetings to you, Dancer Cassa Fisook, and Talon-master Bau Dibsea, from Tae Shanissi, lord and self-proclaimed deity of the sovereign city-state of Ckotliss, master of ten thousand and a domain of great span and fertility."

"Gack!" Bau Dibsea spat. "Even their names are sickening to say."

"Did he hear you out?" Cassa Fisook asked, ignoring the male's interruption.

"All my words and movements were heard, lady," Sherril said. He sipped more wine to wet his tongue. The heady fragrance helped dispel the foul dust of the road and the cloying smell of the Liskash city. "He and his lords listened to me in the great hall of that stone keep that we observed from the ridge. He gave me sweet water to drink and flat cakes of some foul grain or bean that I ate only out of courtesy. I explained exactly as I was instructed to that we are peaceful travelers in Lord Tae's land. The mountains and the sea preclude our passing to either side of this valley, so we must go through. That we want to do as swiftly as possible. I also requested to trade for supplies to see us on our way."

"And . . . ?" Bau Dibsea asked, impatiently.

Sherril hated to be rushed. The Liskash were more appreciative of his full explanations and the spooling out of the Lailah's journey from their homeland. He wrinkled his nose slightly, sweeping his whiskers back.

"He is agreed, Talonmaster."

Bau sprang to his feet. "Excellent! Then we will break camp at once. Will he provide us with guides or maps?"

Sherril patted the air with his palms. "Not so swiftly, my leader. There is a price."

"A price?" piped up Ysella Ehe, the young Dancer who had stumbled. "What price? They enslave our kind. I hear they even *eat* them."

"Ysella!" exclaimed Cleotra, the Dancer with lush, sleek fur dusted with red. "It is not your time to speak." But it was not a formal council, and the young one had asked a question the rest of them wanted answered.

"We are not to their taste, except as slaves," Cassa Fisook said. "But it is true, Lord Tae might demand such a price."

"In truth, I saw many Mrem in the city," Sherril admitted. The sight of scrawny, ill-kempt Mrem yoked to a wagon as if they were beasts of burden or carrying heavy loads behind their Liskash masters was a deep insult. Their faces wore despair that he could not and did not want to imagine. The Mrem in the noble household looked as miserable, though not as ill-fed or groomed.

"None of us will submit," Ysella insisted.

Cassa Fisook gave her a look of kindly patience.

"No gift is ever really free, my daughter. There is always a price, even if that is simple gratitude. What do they want?"

"It is not as onerous as slavery, Your Sinuousness," Sherril said. "Lord Tae said that he is a student of our race. He wishes to know more about us. He admitted that once a Mrem's mind is in his thrall it ceases to think as one of us. Lord Tae said he was perhaps too quick to subsume something interesting. He would know more of our culture and customs."

The Dancers murmured among themselves.

"So he can conquer ones like us more easily?" Bau growled. "Knowledge is power!"

"How does he want to learn about us?" Cassa Fisook asked.

Sherril opened a hand. "Before we pass through his land, Lord Tae proposes to have representatives of our tribe visit him in his citadel. They will be welcomed as guests, free to come and go as they please—with certain restrictions, naturally. He would hear our songs and poetry, see our art, and learn the history of our people. He specifically said he wished to meet the Dancers."

"To deprive us of their magic," Bau said at once. "Once in, the visitors are certain to become prisoners. I am wary of his intentions. My warriors will feel the same."

"It is quite understandable that he wants to know us," Cassa Fisook said, blinking her wise green eyes. "It is also undeniable that it might be a trap."

"Whoever goes in will have no assurance of getting

out," Sherril said. He felt his own sacrifice was going
unnoticed. After all he had been through! "As I had."

Bau snorted. His golden eyes gleamed. "We are
well aware that you have just gone into the serpent's
mouth and emerged unscathed," he said. "You want
gratitude; you have it. Well done. Now, we must plan
to achieve the same with a greater number."

Cassa Fisook saw the disappointed expression on
Sherril's face and regarded him with sympathy.

"Your deed will not be forgotten, my friend. It
shall be added to the annals of our tribe. Rest now."

Sherril feigned a convincing collapse into exhaustion
though he held up a hand to protest. "That won't be
necessary, Your Sinuousness. I am prepared to lead
our visitors back to Lord Tae's stronghold, immediately
if necessary."

Bau was fooled neither by the sudden show of
weakness nor Sherril's self-sacrificing offer.

"The elders and warriors need to hear slimy Lord
Tae's proposal," Bau said. He flicked a hand toward
a white-and-black mottled servant. "Go tell them to
gather in the hollow up on the ridge. I will address
them there. We will decide which of us will go into
the trap." The servant bounded away, running.

"I will give them a full report, of course," Sherril said, complacently. "They will want to know how
many doors lie where, how high the walls are and
how many guards stand upon them."

Bau had to hand it to the old scamp. He would
gladly have done without him—would rather have done
without him—but he realized now that he could not.

For the same reason that they had sent Sherril there as their emissary, he would be of great use on the return journey. Sherril had well-developed survival instincts. He seemed to sleep with one eye open, and no one had yet caught him off guard for any of the beatings that he had earned and undoubtedly deserved. Sherril was capable of preceding you through a doorway but ending up behind you as if he had the dinos' own evil magic. His powers of observation were legendary throughout the camp as he had been in their own land, many leagues behind them to the east. If he had been able to wield a spear or hold up that bulk of his longer than three breaths in a fight, he could easily have maneuvered himself into the position of talonmaster. But no one would ever trust him. Bau knew better than that. But he always managed to find himself a vantage point. He *was* a Mrem. Better to give him his chance than to have him working against the group because he was thwarted.

"Very well, then. Come and make your case."

The high hollow amid the thin-branched trees made a natural amphitheater. The remaining warriors, only three hundred sixty in number, settled themselves on the cool earth. With a hiss and a meaningful look, Cleotra made the younger females settle down and stop whispering. Only twenty-three Dancers and apprentices, out of fifty that had lived in the old land before the floods came, had made it this far. She fervently hoped they would lose no more. Her friend and fellow Dancer Nolda Ilu lay in a cool spot on the

grass, attended to by a couple of the apprentices. She
was due to kitten any day. Her last pregnancy, even
in the safety of their old home, had almost finished
her. Cleotra feared that having to give birth on the
road would be too much for her. The baby in her
belly kicked once in a while, showing the outline of
a tiny foot, as if impatient to be free. Cleotra begged
the tiny one to wait, at least until they knew they had
safe passage through Ckotliss.

Many of the females of the clan were near to their
time. By all rights they should be making up nests for
themselves in a comfortable corner of their homes,
laying in special treats and nourishing foods to see
them through their confinements. Mrem females liked
to give birth in private. The custom, admittedly, was
a throwback to their uncivilized days, when males
hoping to force females back into estrus would kill
kittens who did not bear their scent, but Cleotra simply
didn't care for an audience when she was on her side,
straining to produce her baby. No one would dare to
watch her in that undignified time! She cherished her
son and daughter, but was glad that no siblings for
them were in the offing.

Everyone had had to fight their natural urges to
beget more young, at least until they were safely on
their way to rejoin the clan on the north side of the
new water. It wasn't easy when so many of the males
were attractive and virile, and the tantalizing spice of
spring was in the air. It would be the most natural
thing in the world to choose this year's mate from
among the ebony-coated warriors and tear the night

apart with longing cries and wails of satisfaction. Look at that foolish child, Ysella, making eyes at the lieutenant of the guard. She had not even had her first estrus yet! Luckily, Scaro Ullenh's gaze was wandering among the mature Dancers, as if he had a hope of mating with one of them! It wasn't for want of trying; that was sure. There wasn't a female of bearing age he had not propositioned, many times, over the course of the last months, including herself. Handsome he was, to be certain, with a deep chest, a narrow waist, and strong, springy thighs, but what an ego!

Nature was against them. Cleotra believed—she must believe—that Aedonniss had not turned his face away from his children.

On one side of the ridge lay the verdant valley ruled over by the odious Liskash. On the other was the desert through which the Mrem had lately come. Personally, she liked the heat, though it was making her luxurious fur come out in handfuls. She refused to think the shedding was the result of a lack of decent food. Rations had become distressingly thin. They usually were at this time of year, just before the first planting of spring, but she and her fellow Dancers had sworn to make do on what scanty supplies were left, along with the results of hunting. The local wildlife, mostly lizards and other mindless Liskash-kin, fled on their approach. Cleotra was sick of chameleon stew, fried iguana and roasted flitter—when the hunters were lucky enough to get sufficient food for all the tribe.

She missed meat, red meat. Once when she woke from a dream of eating a thick, juicy haunch of venison, she almost cried. When she got over the disappointment, common sense had returned. Oh, she could have pulled rank and demanded a piece from a herd beast that died on the road. Those carcasses were a rare treat, and there were plenty who needed it more than she did. What easily-digested and most nutritious food they had must be saved for the very young, the sick, the elderly, and the warriors. None of the herd beasts could be spared. They were being used to haul wagons at the moment, but they would form the kernel of new herds when they reached the safe haven where the rest of the Clan awaited them. Out in the desert, there were few palatable sources of meat, almost all Liskash-kin. The sea, which had flanked them on their right all the way from their drowned home, was too perilous for all but line fishing, an unreliable and slow process. The rest of the Mrem could, and did make do on what was left, dried meats, pulses, insect-ridden grains and the disgusting small prey they could snare or shellfish they could dig out of the sand. Sometimes Cleotra hated being so responsible.

She could almost have borne a further trek through the desert better than what lay before them. From the hollow on the ridge she could not only see the valley of the Liskash, but she could smell it. The black earth, fresh and smelling of rain, had been freshly turned for planting, and lay in neat squares awaiting seed. The sour-sweet odor of composted manure did not sicken her, except possibly to make her homesick. Her mother's household should have been planting now. All those farmers, swept out to sea! She lifted her hands to the sky and swayed them in a pattern of prayer to Assirra. *May their souls be at rest.* For a while when the Lailah had started traveling to the west, Cleotra had felt their presence, but only as far as the borders of their land. The dead had stayed behind. Cleotra missed the comforting sensation. In its place, she felt the imposition of the Liskash's magic. And the stench.

Who would have thought that magic had an odor and a sound of its own? Since childhood, when she had joined the corps of Dancers, the magic of the Mrem's prayers had been a part of her life, her coming and going, her lying down and rising up, the food she ate, the air she breathed and the people she loved. Though she had Danced many a ritual for protection from them, she hadn't had to interact with Liskash nobles, until one month into their journey the Lailah had to fight against one who had suddenly noticed that the tribe was cut off from its kin and vulnerable for the first time. He had tried to take over their minds. Only Cassa's swift realization that something was wrong had saved them. She had whipped the Dancers out of bed and made them dance for their lives. Their talonmaster at the time, Mowar Echirr, had driven back the Liskash's forces. Cleotra had never forgotten the unbelievable smell of decay that had permeated the camp, and the off-tone of everyone's voices, birdsong and frogsong. When the Liskash noble fell, everything returned to normal.

She was aware of it now. Lord Tae felt at them with his mind. He was powerful and dangerous. How she hated being at his mercy!

So did her kin. They muttered and yowled among

themselves, speculating as to the news. Bau strode into
their midst, attracting more gossip. He had buckled on
his war harness and donned his bronze clawed gaunt-
lets. The bronze gorget that protected his throat was
buried deep in his black and white fur ruff. Instead of
the flint-toothed spear he might carry into battle, he
held the staff of leadership, a wrist-thick pole carved
down its length as a braid. The teeth of enemies stud-
ded the turns and folds of wood. From the top dangled
strands of hide on which were strung faceted crystals
that twinkled and danced. It was used by the designated
speaker of the moment because no Mrem could keep
his or her eyes off the swaying strings.

Bau snarled and bashed the staff on the ground.
Gradually, everyone turned to look and fell silent. Bau
fixed his lamplike golden eyes on each of them in turn.
When they met Cleotra's, she shivered. He spoke.

"We are now entrusted by Rantan Taggah to open
the way for the rest of the Mrem and find a path to
safety. We are now the tip of the talon for the Clan of
the Claw. Two weeks ago, we passed what has survived
of brother Rau's Three Fangs. They were supposed to
lead next, but you saw in what poor condition they
were after their battles.

"The Clan and our herds are hungry and tired.
It is up to us to find a way west. We have found it,
we hope, but as our scouts report, there's a hopeless
bottleneck. A fortress greater then any we have seen
before. Greater than that of the Liskash Rau defeated.
The alternative is not an attractive one, and a sand
desert in which many would die."

Some of the gathered Mrem stirred nervously. The hot sands were a friend to the Liskash and doubly dangerous. The leader raised his voice to regain their full attention.

"Where once we were just a small clan concerned for ourselves, now us, Rau, and all who must join together are of the Claw." Bau paused and held up one hand claws extended. "Now our talons must be swift and deadly."

He paused, letting his words have effect. Then, in a more even tone, continued.

"You are aware that four days ago, we sent Sherril Rangawo to negotiate safe passage for us through the lands down there." He gestured down the slope toward the wide valley, then turned to point at Sherril, who preened at the attention. "But there he sits! You can see that he has returned safely. The Lord Tae Shanissi has agreed that we can proceed unmolested…" Bau's voice was drowned out by a chorus of pleased yowls. "Bury it, you fools! You know it isn't that simple! This is still a Liskash we're dealing with. Nothing is straight-forward. The weakling dinos always have a reason. They always want an advantage. This is it: in exchange for allowing the tribe to pass through the land, he demands a *cultural exchange*."

"They can't understand culture," Drillmaster Scaro Ullenh said, with a scornful flip of his tail.

Bau nodded agreement. "Not ours; not yet. That is what he claims he wants. We are interesting to him." He held up a hand to forestall the outbursts. "No, I don't really believe him. I think it is just a means of gaining power over Mrem, though I do not yet know how he plans to achieve that. We will not know until it's all over and we've shaken the dust of his realm off our feet. But we can't stay here on the edge of his lands forever. There are too few of us to fight, though we'd take many times our number to Aedonniss with us. To go back and choose another route would cost us months more of travel. I do not lie to you; we have little food left for us or our beasts. We need to trade or buy, and no one else is near enough to sell us grain. We lose Mrem and herds on the road every month we must travel. Those who go to perform for Lord Tae will likely save many lives. I do not pretend that those who go will come back, alive or unaltered. The Liskash magic has robbed many Mrem of their names, minds and freedom. We could lose all those who go into the citadel. Therefore I ask for volunteers."

Nearly all the warriors leaped to their feet, yowling their willingness. Bau couldn't help but feel pleased. They knew it was suicide, but that never stopped a true Mrem. He had to weed out the foolhardy, the inexperienced, those who were too young or too old, and especially those who did not rise until they saw their fellows spring up.

"I would die for the sake of the clan!" declared one warrior, shaking a fist above his head.

You're not going, Bau thought to himself.

Then one he knew and trusted heaved himself to his feet, a stocky, grizzled male with scars on his arms and chest. Emoro Awr led a squad of picked warriors. Every one of them feared his wrath, yet strove for his approval. He prided himself on bringing all those under his command back, alive or dead. Bau nodded. Here was the first of a strong band.

"Emoro, will you lead a force to accompany our people into the city?" he asked.

"To Aedonniss' gate, if need be," Emoro said. "And back again."

He wasn't bragging, only stating what he believed to be true. Bau was pleased. He crossed to Emoro and put the staff into his hand. The strands of crystals danced and twinkled. All the Mrem's eyes followed.

"Choose your fighters."

Emoro looked around. It was a tribute to the old male that no one looked away, or sat down, to avoid being chosen. In fact, most of the young ones seemed eager. Bau watched with interest as Emoro made his decisions. He forewent most of his usual band, tapping instead fighters who were more than cadets but had seen only a few battles.

Bau frowned. "Will you choose none of your own warriors, brother?"

Emoro flicked his tail. "I don't want to leave the clan with inadequate defenses."

"You won't," Bau said, slightly amused. "We'll make do."

"All right, then." Emoro pointed to Scaro, who had been one of the first to rise. "You'll be my lieutenant, Drillmaster Ullenh."

Scaro threw his chest out. "Of course, my Clawmaster! I am proud to serve."

Emoro returned the staff to Bau, who immediately passed it to Cassa Fisook.

"The choice of a Dancer must fall to you."

The elder female sighed. Her bright green eyes looked sad. "I would go myself. There is much more I would teach my students before I am confident that knowledge is safely stowed in their memories, but I am growing old. There may come a time when infirmity might cause me to hold you back. Better I give myself to this task. If I were not to come back, others could carry on. When the Clan of the Claw is reunited, that lore that I had not passed on to my Dancers can be restored to our collective memory."

"There is another way," Bau reminded her. In his heart he feared the loss of any of the priestesses. They protected the clan in ways that he and his warriors could not, and they were the guardians of their history and customs. Nearly three-quarters of the fighters could fall before it would mean the same as being deprived of one of the remaining Dancers. "We can go far to the south and skirt Tae's land. It will add greatly to the length of our journey, though."

"All the more reason for me to undertake it," Cassa said. "Petru, you will come with me, won't you?"

The valet cast himself upon the ground on his back before her, throwing up a cloud of scented glitter. "Anywhere and anywhen, my mistress."

"No," Cleotra said, alarmed. She rose. "I will go, Cassa Fisook. You can spare me. You have others who know as much as I."

She said it, though she didn't really mean her humble words. Cassa smiled at her kindly.

"No, my dear. I cannot 'spare' you, but I will be

grateful if you will make this journey. You will be better than I."

"Never that, Cassa!"

"Don't underestimate yourself, my dear. I expect you to succeed me one day." She turned to the talon-master. "Bau, this is our Dancer."

The talonmaster bowed deeply to Cleotra Mreem, flicking his tail in wide arcs. "Your Sinuousness."

She accepted his obeisance.

"The rest of us will work for your safety while you are in enemy ground," Cassa Fisook said. "But you should not go by yourself. You, too, should take," she smiled, "a lieutenant."

"Me!" Ysella Ehe sprang up at the military term. She glanced at Scaro and ducked her head immediately. The warriors all chuckled except Scaro. If her unrequited passion had gone unnoticed before, it was not now. He looked perturbed and slightly horrified.

Cleotra moaned to herself. That girl would be nothing but trouble, mooning after the randy warrior in the midst of danger.

"No, child," she said. "Stay with the others. It will be safer."

"I am not scared of lizards," Ysella said scornfully. Why did no one take her seriously?

"And what is the source of your courage?" Bau asked, gently. He had a daughter her age.

"The Dancers can stand against all," Ysella insisted. "When we Dance, the power of Aedonniss flows through us."

"I think not," Cleotra said. "Remain here, my dear.

You are the next generation. Give yourself time to grow up."

"Cleotra Mreem!" The girl's golden eyes widened with dismay.

"Take her," Cassa said, unexpectedly. "You may need her energy."

Cleotra frowned. To concentrate upon their rituals, she needed to focus. If she was worried about one wayward youth, that distraction could break the vital link between her and the others. Ysella picked up on her concern.

"I will serve you," Ysella promised. "I will be the best apprentice you could have. I will be obedient. No one will work harder than I."

Cleotra did not want to, but she relented. "All right. I will hold you to your word."

"I won't fail you!"

"Mistress, I must go, too," Petru said, rubbing his cheek against Cassa's ankle.

"You, my friend?" Cassa asked, looking down on him fondly. Petru blinked at her.

"Of course. Who will care for the lady Cleotra and Ysella in that barbaric city? Who will see that their coats are brushed smooth and that every bracelet is polished to the sun's own gleam? Who will see that they have food that is fit to eat? Aedonniss alone knows what filth they consume behind those walls!"

Sherril perked up. A valet in his train? He had felt like such a supplicant in Lord Tae's court before, with all those lizards running to and fro to serve the noble's every whim. To show that he was a Mrem of substance, worthy of having a servant of his own, would elevate his status. Besides, should they survive to return, there would surely be an opportunity to take a measure of revenge upon the obnoxious creature.

"I would be grateful if you would allow him to accompany me, Your Sinuousness," Sherril said.

"Granted, then," Cassa said. "Prepare, then. We will Dance you a farewell."

Even Sherril could feel the power rush through him as they left the encampment early the next morning. The Dancers surrounded them, throwing their arms toward them as if casting garlands around their necks, then bowed, arched and twirled again and again. The twenty picked Mrem warriors marching in two files on either side of him looked proud and a little sheepish. They were prepared to die for the clan if they must. Sherril, for his part, had no such intention. If he could impress that skinny, furless creature in the citadel with their magic and wisdom, he would be a hero.

Emoro Awr, with Scaro at his side and Bau hanging over them like a stormcloud, had debriefed him thoroughly as to the architecture and garrisoning of the citadel. He had been made to describe every doorway and window he had seen, the thickness of the walls and the height of every ceiling. How many Liskash were there in the courtyard, and how many within the keep itself? How many captive Mrem? When did the sentries pass? What form of locks on the doors? How many wells and fountains? Had he spotted dungeons or cells of any kind? What about armories?

Sherril was proud that he had forgotten none of these details. Plus, he had offered information for which they had not asked. Lord Tae had a practice of overruling his captains on a whim. All of his people were afraid of him; Sherril could tell by their posture and the way each measured its words when it spoke to him. He had two tasters to sample his food. He kept pets. Six small flying lizards fluttered around his throne, eating tidbits and leaving messes on every surface. They bit visitors, soldiers, servants and whoever else was unlucky enough to get close to their sharp little beaks. Emoro and Scaro exchanged glances. If they needed a distraction, Lord Tae's flutteries might prove useful.

"And their food didn't kill you," Emoro noted. "Good. Better to find out on you rather than someone who's really valuable, like a Dancer."

Sherril took that in the spirit that he hoped it was intended, for the greater good of the clan. The playful glint in Scaro's eye left him uncertain.

He felt like an old hand, leading the others down the sloping track with the rising sun at their backs and morning dew clinging to their leg fur. Some of the scouts who had actually discovered the scarcely used road accompanied them part of the way, then turned back as the party reached the well-traveled, packed-gravel road that led to the city.

They were not traveling lightly. Four young bullocks whose loss the tribe could not really afford hauled two-wheeled carts behind them laden with bags and bundles. Sherril deplored the quantity of luggage, but he had been overruled at every protest. Weaponry and armor for the warriors, that he approved and understood. Anything that the Dancers required for their comfort and the performance of their art, he neither caviled nor begrudged. Food, wine and clean water, naturally, in case nothing came their way along the road. Gifts for the Lord Tae, to show their appreciation for his forbearance. But two carts brimmed with parcels containing the personal belongings of that cursed valet, Petru! It was an outrage. Pots of scent, boxes of glitter, bags and bags of jewelry and other adornments, none of which was necessary to their journey. Grooming tools the likes of which he had never seen, as well as many other things he had glimpsed but did not recognize. Sherril had complained of the additional responsibility of looking after the possessions of a mere servant. The Dancers championed the big nuisance, of course, but to his surprise, so did Emoro. Sherril was surprised. He never thought of a soldier like Emoro even noticing an ephemeral like Petru. Sherril took the information in to muse upon later. He had learned a lot since they had left their homeland, and had been able to use much of it to his benefit from time to time.

Numerous carts with big, heavy, flat wooden wheels creaked along, drawn by thin-pelted cattle or huge lizards with round feet like tree trunks. The drivers, lower-caste Liskash, small of stature, eyed the warriors suspiciously. Sherril scorned them. Liskash were physical cowards. They were even less inclined to physical interaction than he was. They covered their hairless skins in woven cloth that had been dyed in terrible colors and worn in combinations that hurt him to look at. He hated to give Petru any credit, but his garments and adornments pleased the eye at least.

The Mrem felt uneasy in the midst of so many of the enemy. Sherril believed in the power of the gods. Aedonniss and Assirra would help them withstand an attack. Though these merchants all had guards walking with them and a few carried vicious little green-skinned lizards on their carts to prevent pilferers, they were more interested in making it to Ckotliss's marketplace by the start of business rather than tangling with a party of heavily armed Mrem surrounding a stunning, proud, lithe, black-furred Dancer jingling with bracelets and anklets on her dainty limbs. The child, Ysella, trotted along behind, looking like an afterthought.

The smell overpowered Sherril's delicate nose. He had had the forethought to bring with him a cloth soaked in crushed lily petals. He raised it to his face to mask the odor of the Liskash, their beasts and the endless piles of dung that the creatures deposited.

As Sherril thought it, a green-and-blue-skinned beast over five Mrem-lengths long with baskets of nuts draped across its spiny back lifted its heavy, conical tail and let a heap drop directly in front of them. The Mrem had to hop to avoid stepping in the steaming mass. The drover, sitting on a saddle just at the base of the huge creature's neck, opened its flat mouth and emitted a staccato hiss. Other Liskash nearby joined in the merriment.

"I'm not sure, but that strikes me as a deliberate

insult," Scaro said, wrapping his long fingers around the shaft of his spear. The merchant stuck his ugly chinless face in the air. Scaro growled under his breath and sidled forward. Sherril put a hand in the center of the guard's chest.

"The difference in our species means that what strikes one of us as funny will be lost to the other," he said in a low voice, keeping a wary eye on the Liskash merchant. "That which is cruel or kind is open to a certain amount of interpretation. But, yes, that was an insult, and no, it would be a very bad idea to respond."

"He should know better than to interfere with us," Scaro growled.

"I don't take threats from slaves!" the Liskash hissed.

"Who are you calling slaves?" Scaro demanded.

The Liskash looked superior. "Those mangy bags of fur who don't know their place."

"My place is at your throat, tearing it out of your body!"

"Scaro!" Emoro snarled. The lieutenant stood for a moment, staring at the Liskash. "Did you get your pads dirty?"

"No, sir!"

"Do you care if you get your pads dirty?"

"Well . . . no, sir!"

"Then let the lizards have their joke! We'll laugh all the more heartily when we reach the other side of the cursed water. Do you hear me?"

"Yes, sir," Scaro said. He resumed his place in the file.

"Aedonniss bless me, but if a little dung offends you, then you'd better never eat meat again! Everything poops, boy. Even those ugly warts sitting up there." Emoro gestured at the merchant, who was very pointedly not listening. "Picture that one squatting, if you want, with those ugly purple trousers down around his ankles trying to grunt out his last meal. Don't look too dignified, does he?"

The males in the ranks chuckled. The merchant's neck inflated as if he were a frog. The Mrem broke into open howls of amusement. He turned, his big round eyes bulging out of his ugly flat skull. He clenched his fist. The laughter died away. Sherril Rangawo felt something evil begin to stir around them. A noxious odor flavored the air, clawing at his throat and the inside of his nose. The miserable Liskash was putting a curse on them!

"It would go ill," he said, aloud, to no one in particular, "if we reached Lord Tae and had to tell him that his invited guests were treated badly by one of his own subjects."

At the mention of the noble's name, the rider's neck pouch deflated. The Liskash turned and hunched over the neck of his mount.

Sherril spat out the terrible taste in his mouth. All of the Mrem rolled their tongues to rid themselves of it. The Dancers in particular seemed most troubled by the sensation. Ysella gasped and extended her tongue as if trying to spit it out. Petru rushed forward to cluck solicitously over Cleotra and Ysella. He hurried back and stopped one of the bearers to rummage among the bundles in his cart. Petru drew from it a stoppered bottle and a bronze goblet chased with a pattern of flying birds. He poured liquor into the goblet and offered it to Cleotra. She took a sip, then nodded. Ysella took her draught and made a face, but got it down.

"Make sure all are treated equally," Cleotra instructed him. Petru bowed. He brought the goblet to Emoro, then Scaro, then each of the males. Sherril waited impatiently for his turn.

At last the big servant undulated up to his side. Sherril pretended not to notice the delay. Petru offered the cup. Only a few drops remained in the bottom.

"I will need more than that to restore me," he said.

The words reached the ears of the Dancer a few paces behind him.

"Give him what he needs, Petru," Cleotra said.

Petru shot a reproachful look at her, though it was tinged with deep adoration. "Lady, I am. He recovered better than most on his own!"

Cleotra widened her eyes. Petru grudgingly tipped a tiny measure of potion into the goblet. Sherril drained it. The strong liquor raced through his veins like hot lightning. The smell of the lizards lessened immediately. He stood up straighter.

"Thank you," he said, handing the goblet back to Petru. Even better than dealing with the effects of the malicious magic, he had made the valet do something he did not want to. Perhaps he could leverage it into further service. "Now, my fur has become slightly disarranged. If you would brush me, it would settle my nerves. And," he added with a daring glance, "I would like some of the sparkling powder sprinkled over my shoulders. Perhaps the blue?"

"Now, let's just address one misconception before we go one step farther," Petru said, putting his big hands on his hips. "I am not *your* valet. I do not serve you. I serve the Dancer Cleotra. If I have any time left over from my care of her, that time belongs to this young one, Ysella. They are the most important people in this caravan. I will see to their well-being, their meals, and *their* grooming. You are the leader. Lead. I will not interfere with that."

The warriors behind him laughed.

Sherril was disappointed, but he waved a hand diffidently, as if it did not matter at all what the valet did or what the warriors thought. "Very well. Back to your place. We must turn at this next crossroads."

He knew that Petru glared, but he pointedly did not look back. Too much terrain lay ahead of them, and too many dangers, not so easily dealt with by veiled threats and herbal remedies.

"How ugly!" Cleotra said, staring up at the edifice at the heart of the city. After an entire day's walk they came to stone-and-mortar walls the thickness of two Mrem-lengths. Upon those walls were carved lines in the language of the Liskash. She puzzled out the inscription, and discovered that it was a warning. Anyone passing inside the walls of Ckotliss was considered to have taken an oath of loyalty to Lord Tae Shanissi. Woe betide those who broke that oath: they would be punished with lashings and spikes. The rest of the carving went on to detail in what way those spikes would be administered. Cleotra shuddered. To either side had been carved likenesses of a noble, with huge crystals set in the eyes. Cleotra found their stony stare unnerving, and was glad when they went through the gate and could no longer see it.

She followed the escort under gates perforated with secret peepholes and arrow slits, and into a courtyard large enough to encompass three or four good-sized Mrem farms. Before they had emerged into the sunlight, they were surrounded by Liskash warriors who leveled pole arms at them and disarmed her escort. Once all spears, bows and knives had been confiscated, they steered the Mrem toward the center of the citadel.

Inside the confines lay dozens or hundreds of smaller buildings, it was difficult to say, since the whole place fluttered with small tents, lean-tos and laundry on lines. Bundor, hamsticorns, krelprep, and many other animals ran wild within the space, looked after by dead-eyed Mrem or Liskash children with little care for their charges. She had always felt an antipathy toward Liskash but fought against it. A Dancer must embrace life, whatever form it took. There was simply something about them that made the hair down her spine stand up in a fighting ridge.

The curtain walls were meant to protect Liskash and their goods and cattle in case of attack. Few of those coming and going that evening lived there. The exodus as they entered was heavy, many thousands of dinos finishing their day's toil and going home. Lord Tae and his household enjoyed relative isolation in the keep.

Within the walls, the feeling of being imposed upon was stronger than ever. The sensation had built ever since they left the mountainside, until it impinged upon her mind like a headache. She took comfort in the rhythm of the Dance beating in her soul. It meant she was not separated from the other Dancers. They were with her now, as always. The Dance was a protection for which she was grateful. The sun had baked them on their journey, but the air was damp as if the valley was full of water, and now that the sun was setting she felt chilled. While it was a relief not to feel dried to leather, the sensation of being cold and damp added to their perception of vulnerability.

The squared, pyramidal center block loomed over her almost ten Mrem-heights. The walls had been built of stone and covered with painted plaster. The covering must have peeled away often in the humidity. Liskash on ladders with buckets slathered a new coat over the exposed blocks. Cleotra spotted several different levels colored many different shades of ochre. The lip of the tower itself gleamed in the setting sun as if made of gold. Polished metal would make it difficult to hook a grapple or claws to pull oneself up. It could be done, though. In her childhood, she had made much more difficult ascents, she thought mischievously.

One would think that since it was the most prominent building for a hundred leagues that there might be some attempt to make it beautiful. If it had been an animal, Cleotra would have said it was molting because of some parasite.

Flanking it were two smaller, similar towers made of wood, neither close enough to the main tower to leap to it. Lord Tae or his ancestors took no chances of ambush. They were also ugly, their purple-gray timbers clashing horribly with their taller member. If pressed for a compliment, she would have to say that the three towers were nicer looking than any of the clothes of Ckotliss's inhabitants.

Petru echoed her very thought.

"Surely it would be better to go naked than to wear *that* tunic and *those* trousers," he said, as a Liskash strutted by, resplendent in a turquoise-dyed tunic that went well with neither his nether garment nor his pale blue skin. Cleotra smiled to herself. She adored Petru, and he was devoted to her. They understood one another. One day he would be her personal valet.

Large, muscular Liskash warriors in plate-sewn hide armor and heavy helmets patrolled the walls. They vanished into square towers in which she could see archers crouching. Flying lizards swooped in and out of the guardhouses, no doubt carrying messages and intelligence for the garrison. With such powerful magic at his command, whom did Lord Tae fear?

Surely not them. The Lailah was such a small tribe. They had come to supplicate him. She did not like the thought of begging a dino for their lives, but her pride must bow down and serve the needs of the clan. Ysella's ridge was up, too. She felt the overwhelming power of the noble. She hissed to herself, and her eyes flashed at the Liskash escorting them. They did not seem very impressed by her or by Cleotra.

Good, the Dancer thought. *They see us as harmless. All the better.*

"We are here as peaceful envoys," Sherril kept reassuring the Liskash captain. The spears and bowmen made the Mrem nervous. "The warriors are an escort of honor for our Dancers. The Dancer Cleotra must be protected and kept from outside interference, you understand. And of course, I am a person of great importance among the Mrem. I would not come unaccompanied. I did not before, if you recall. The weapons are only to keep us safe from brigands and thieves on the road, not to attack our host or his loyal servants. You are loyal to Lord Tae, are you not?"

This last question made the bright blue spots on the captain's cheeks pale to gray.

"You dare to question me?" he hissed.

That put the proof to what Sherril had maintained, that Lord Tae ruled by fear. Cleotra dreaded meeting him.

The minister put an innocent hand to his chest. "You must not think that he has sent me out among you as a *spy*," he said. "I am but a humble visitor from a distant land. My question is an innocent one."

Innocent or not, it set the rest of the lizards on edge. Sherril strutted ahead of them, even outside the ring of bronze-tipped weapons that ought to have contained him. Cleotra wanted to laugh out loud. She was almost sorry she had not had Petru adorn him when he had asked. Perhaps she would grant him that favor later. His daring was as great a protection as the Dancer's rituals or Emoro's warriors.

The guards marched them around to the west side of the great keep. At the wooden tower, they came to a halt. A ladder made of sticks tied together with ill-cured hide thongs rested against the wall.

"Go on, then," the captain said. "Up and over."

Cleotra looked up. Three Mrem-heights above her was the first occupied level. To either side of the ladder were doorways set into the wall. Many lengths to the left along a very narrow walkway, nearly at the corner of the building, was another ladder leading to the second stage. Above that, at the center of the wall, a third ladder led to the roof, where two Liskash guards with ruddy-colored skin peered down at them.

"Which of these quarters is ours?" she inquired.

"Inside," the captain said. His pikemen braced their weapons as if the question was a threat. "Go."

Emoro barked out orders. Two of his warriors took their place to steady the ladder. He swarmed up it like a kitten a sixth of his age. Six males followed him. They spread out to await the Dancers' ascent.

"Come up, Your Sinuousness," he said, extending a hand.

Cleotra ascended to the stage and waited for Ysella to join her. The child was wide-eyed with nerves. She took the girl's hand and squeezed it. Ysella gave her a nervous glance. She was doing well. Cleotra was relieved that the girl was holding up.

"Aedonniss will protect us," she said.

Sherril made as if to climb up, but Petru shoved past him. He put one foot on the bottom rung and shot a smug look at him.

Cleotra shook her head. Their feud bid fair to put them all in danger. She was going to have to speak sternly to Petru, although little good seldom came from interfering with the valet. He was like a boulder rolling down a hill. He tended to crush anyone in his way, though usually for the sake of someone else, such as Cassa.

Sherril, his ruff fluffed out with annoyance, joined them. All but five of the remaining warriors and Scaro came up.

"Well, go on!" the Liskash captain ordered.

"My men and I stay here," Scaro said, in a tone that brooked no disagreement. "My clawmaster's orders. I guard the entrance to their quarters. This is where they are domiciled while they are guests of Lord Tae; this is where we wait until they come out again."

The dino grunted. He was not smart enough to puzzle this out himself. He did seem to know that Mrem were faster and more nimble than his kind, so there would be injuries even if he summoned help to make all the pesty visitors stay in one place.

"Lord Tae did say that we could come and go as we pleased," Sherril called down to the captain. The Liskash frowned, drawing his low brow even lower toward his muzzle.

"Very well," he said. "I will see what is my lord's will. Go on. Up and over."

People lived within the walls of this pylon, Cleotra

observed. Through an open door she spotted a female in an ugly orange shift tending an egg lying on a bed of straw. The top stage, though, was no more than a walkway half a Mrem-length in width. The Lailah tiptoed along it. The captain directed them to the other end of the wall to a ladder. Cleotra looked down.

Below them were two more stages with doors in the wall, but at the bottom was an open courtyard with a fountain where more guards waited.

"A fine trap," Emoro growled, echoing her very thought. "Kick away the ladders and we'd be fish in a tidal pool, ready to be scooped up."

Cleotra closed her eyes. She reached inside herself and felt for the strand of warmth that tied her to the other Dancers. They were there, comforting their distant sister. She sensed Cassa's warm wisdom, the love of her fellow priestesses, and a more remote touch that she had always associated with Assirra. Cleotra sent a quick prayer to the goddess to plead with her husband to protect them, and felt a surge of energy in return.

"We are not alone," she reassured Emoro. "Aedonniss is strong with us."

"The gods be blessed," the grizzled clawmaster said. "But we may need earthly strength to supplement His gifts."

They climbed down to the ground level. Night had fallen by then. Torches lit the square with feeble, twisting spires of yellow light. Cleotra was hungry and footsore. The sound of the water tinkling in the fountain made her want to go and dunk her head.

She longed to wash the dust off her face and out of her ears, but that would not be dignified. Instead, she played with the leaves and ropes of vines hanging from enormous metal openwork baskets on poles around the fountain. The desert through which they had been trudging for weeks had no such lush greenery. The scent soothed and pleased her.

The captain conferred with a small, skinny male in a long checked tunic and rope sandals. The male counted them.

"There were twenty-six," he said, his throat pouch swelling impatiently. "Where are the other five?"

"Outside," the captain said. "They are standing guard."

"I have nothing in my instructions regarding that," the functionary said. His black eyes were no more expressive than pieces of slate, but his voice sounded as fussy as any court official she had ever met. "They are all supposed to be here."

"*You* go tell them to come inside," the captain said flatly.

The steward shrugged. Impatiently, he waved a hand, directing the Mrem toward the most remote corner of the courtyard.

He pointed at a trio of dark, low doorways, then gestured at Cleotra, Petru and some of the guards.

"The first third of you, in that chamber. The next third, and the next third. Go on!"

Cleotra peered into the first room. It reeked of something dead and plenty decaying. One narrow rope bed stood in the corner of the unlit stone chamber. The press where she kept her dancing veils was larger.

The bedding, if she would dignify it by default, had black and gray streaks on it, she dared not guess from what. Debris, including piles of dried leaves that had drifted or were kicked inside from the plants hanging over the fountain, filled the floor. Furiously, she turned to the official.

"I will not sleep in that rathole. And I do not sleep in a bunkhouse. I will have my own chamber. Now!"

"This is where you are assigned!"

"Nonsense!" Petru bustled up to the steward. He was half again as tall and twice as broad as the skinny Liskash. "We need eight rooms, not three. We will have the entire row."

"Those are occupied!" the steward said, though he looked frightened.

"Unoccupy them! We are guests. Unless you would like our soldiers to empty them for you?"

"I do not listen to slaves!"

Petru poked the steward in the chest with a sharp, blue-enameled claw.

"We-are-not-slaves."

The steward looked to the guard captain for help. The captain stood back, his arms crossed, his face impassive. He was not going to participate in any functions that were not in his orders. With an aggrieved sniff, the steward began to knock on doors. Self-important-looking Liskash peered out. He murmured to them in an apologetic tone. The Liskash glanced at the Mrem in terror or annoyance and slammed the doors. Cleotra was mortified at the thought that she might have to occupy a chamber with common soldiers, but her worries were soon assuaged. The doors opened again, one after another, and the Liskash within bustled out, their possessions clutched in their arms.

As soon as the rooms were clear, Petru took charge, setting aside the least objectionable chamber for the Dancers, one for Sherril, one for Emoro, four for the guards, and the last for himself. Cleotra sniffed the air. The chambers reeked of mildew and dead rodents, possibly the remains of the previous occupants' lunch. It would have to be cleaned before she set foot in it, but it might do. She had not slept under a solid roof for some time.

"The Lord Tae will send for you when he wishes to see you," the functionary said, peering down its long, skinny nose at them. "Be quick when he calls, or you will suffer the god's wrath."

"We do not wish to cause trouble," Petru assured him.

The steward blinked his black eyes at them. "You already have, but Lord Tae will deal with that."

Cleotra steeled herself. She would undoubtedly have to dance for her life. To do that, she needed rest, but there were some lines she absolutely would not cross. She turned to Petru. "I will not sleep in there, not like it is."

"I will see to it, Your Sinuousness," he reassured her. "Stay here by the fountain." He stroked her shoulder and stalked over to the nearest claw of warriors.

"We are at a disadvantage here," Emoro told Sherril. "I don't have enough warriors to patrol all four walls. We are trapped in this place. Liskash could swarm over those walls and we'd be easy targets. I would feel we could control the situation better in a low building, say an inn?"

Sherril gave him a peevish glance. "We are being honored with rooms near the main keep itself," he said. "I had to stay near the main gate when I was here last. Lord Tae is showing us favor. We need his approval. It is better to do what he wants."

"What if what he wants is to see how quickly we can die?" Emoro asked.

"You are not the diplomat here," Sherril said, his neck ridge rising along with his temper. "You are the escort only. Be silent except where you have advice to offer."

Emoro's eyes glinted. "This is my task," he said. "Bau sent me to make certain that we would be safe. This is not safe."

"It will have to be for now!" Sherril said. He loomed down at the shorter clawmaster. "Make it work!"

Cleotra sprang up and bore down on both males, letting her voice rise to a war-cry.

"No more arguing! Unless you both want me to treat you like the kits you sound like!"

She got up and stalked around the fountain, letting the vines conceal her. She did not want to see her traveling companions for a time, even though she could still hear them.

"At least the priestess didn't kick your backside, the way she did on the road," Emoro observed.

"I didn't start it this time," Sherril said. "Stick to your tasks, and I will stick to mine."

Petulant children.

Ysella trembled in a corner as Petru bullied the Mrem warriors into cleaning the foul chamber with broom and shovel. It wasn't just the stink, but there was something pressing against her mind from the inside. She fought against it, as Cassa and Cleotra had taught her, but it was difficult. She was sensitive to emotion, as all Dancers were, a prime reason that she had been accepted as an apprentice. It made her more receptive to the rhythm of the gods, but it was not that easy to live with.

When she was nervous, as she was now, she comforted herself by singing the lullaby sound her grandmother made when she was a small kit. It was a cross between a chirp and a trill. If only Scaro had come in with them! He was a male to be reckoned with. None of those horrible Liskash could withstand his might. She daydreamed about falling into his strong arms and being carried away to a romantic bower where they would declare their everlasting love for one another. She knew it was a silly fantasy, since she was a Dancer and he was only a soldier, but perhaps she could find a way to overlook her superior rank. He would be such a splendid mate! The rolling muscles of his back, the way he waved his tail, the spring of his long feet all melted her into a puddle whenever she saw him.

The elders ignored her as they held a conference outside by the fountain. She could hear them and see them well enough.

"What do you think, lady?" Clawmaster Emoro asked, properly yielding authority to Cleotra.

"Lord Tae seeks to control us in here," the Dancer said. "The force of his mind is oppressive. You can smell him."

"I am sure he can hear anything we say," Sherril said. "And much of what we think, though I feel more protected than I did on my first visit. It must be your presence, Dancer," he added, as Cleotra glared at him.

"Do you feel our ritual left you unguarded?" she asked, her green eyes narrowing to slits.

"Oh, my lady, no!" Sherril exclaimed. "It is only the proximity to the Liskash lord that gives him the strength to probe us as he does. If we were here too long, and without your ties to Aedonniss, our minds would fall quickly under his influence." He pricked his ears toward the walkways, where Mrem slaves climbed down the ladders with baskets tied to their backs. Any harness or jewelry that those poor creatures had owned in better days had been taken from them, along with identity, history, even independent thought.

The inference was not lost upon Ysella. If the New Sea had not drowned their homeland, she might never have had to face the horrors of the lizard-kin. Her granddam lived far to the north of her settlement. It used to be all they needed to do to visit the old one's steading was to travel through the hot, broad valley as the sun crossed overhead twice from right to left. Now, it would take months, if not years, to rejoin her. She was sure that her granddam lived. A faint connection still existed between them. Oh, but Granddam was so far away!

Ysella yearned for her days as a kit, when she could

climb into the old one's warm embrace and be nestled close. Her own parents had died in some accident—no one had ever really told her the tale. Her brothers had gone to the warriors' camp soon afterward, and she had been apprenticed to the hall of the Dancers.

Now all those buildings were gone in the flooding. The elders had all said the sea could not rise higher than the mountains at the west end of the great valley. They talked about the safe crossing they could make there. Behind them, various tribes of the clan had scorned them for retreating so soon. Ysella burned with shame. She chirruped to herself. The warriors looked down kindly upon her, especially one young recruit with a mask and chest of banded bronze fur. In an all black coat, those markings would be considered flaws, but to Ysella they looked like sunlight, a welcome sight in that dark place.

"May I help you, Dancer?" he asked, holding out a long, slender hand to her.

Shyly, she put her fingers into his, and was surprised by his strength as he hauled her upright with a quick jerk. She hastily smoothed her fur and straightened her necklaces. She closed her hand on the amulet of Aedonniss and Assirra that she had been given to celebrate making her first Dance as an apprentice and felt a warmth from it that was not from her own body heat.

"Thank you," she said. He gawked at her, as what warrior might not? Dancers had an innate grace. She recalled Cassa Fisook's stern lessons that it should be reflected in their manners as well. "What is your name, warrior?"

"Gilas Aulor. I know your brothers, Your Sinuousness. They said you were very beautiful." His eyes shone. They were the same bronze as his breast-fur. "It is true."

"Thank..." Ysella began shyly.

"Presumptuous kit, get on with your tasks!"

They jumped apart. Scaro stood there, his tail lashing from side to side. Ysella looked up in pleased surprise. The lieutenant must be jealous of the young male! She gazed up at him, her pupils spreading. Scaro moved to one side and took her arm, pulling her out of the way. Ysella preened, enjoying the feeling of his strong muscles and sinews under his fur. Oh, he did care for her! He just could not say it because of the differences between their ranks. She wondered if that day came when, long after Cleotra had taken Cassa's place as senior priestess, she, Ysella, ascended to that position, she would be able to act upon the feelings that she knew she and Scaro shared for one another. But she couldn't wait that long. He was here now, and so was she.

She ran a claw tip along Scaro's muscular arm. The fur rippled under her touch. She shivered with excitement and peered up at him out of the corner of one green eye. He didn't look down. Ysella realized that they were not alone. Scaro must not want to reveal his feelings before an underling.

Gilas finished sweeping and left the room. Behind him, a female Mrem shuffled in, fresh bedding in her arms. She kept her eyes low.

"Hello, lovely lady," Scaro purred. He let go of

Ysella's arm and moved into the path of the newcomer. "And what is your name?"

She looked up at him with terror in her eyes. Scaro moved closer and took the sheets and featherbeds out of her arms. He tipped her chin up with one finger, the claw carefully retracted.

"No need to fear me. I'm friendly. I could be your new best friend. Where do you live?"

Her jaw opened, but no sound came from her mouth.

"Silence is good, too," Scaro said, wrapping her in a solicitous arm. "Perhaps you would just like to show me?"

She shook her head, wide-eyed. Scaro pressed further.

"Maybe you don't live alone. That's fine. I don't mind having more than one of you at the same time. I think you will find that I am equal to all things. Shall we go?"

Before Ysella could translate this baffling interchange, a hand smacked Scaro in the ear. His eyes went wide and he whirled, claws out in a defensive stance.

"I thought I'd find you up to your tricks!" Emoro said, the corners of his mouth upturned. Scaro let go of the serving Mrem and saluted his senior officer.

"Sir!"

"I suppose there's a reason beyond wanting to seduce the locals that you came within instead of remaining on your post?" Emoro asked.

"Oh, he wasn't..." Ysella hastened to assure him. "He was just trying to make friends with her! She is very shy. She doesn't talk."

Emoro frowned, his heavy brows making his eyes into yellow slits. "Scaro, it ill befits a warrior to have children make excuses for him."

"I didn't ask her to!" Scaro protested. The serving Mrem slipped out of his grasp and rushed out of the room, her eyes fixed on the floor. Ysella drew herself up at the insult.

"Clawmaster, I am not a child," she said. "I am a Dancer. Please treat me with the respect of my rank. I would give my life for the Clan of the Claw as readily as you."

"Of course, dear little one, of course," Emoro said, in a soothing voice. "We all hope it won't come to that. Well, Scaro? What is it?"

The officer looked a little sulky. "A messenger came from Lord Tae. He wishes us to visit him this evening. He wants to learn something new today, he said. The rest of my warriors protect the way in to this building. I have come to escort you out."

"Right, then," Emoro said. "Good thing you didn't shout it from the roof like you do your other business." He grinned and nudged Scaro with his fist. Scaro grinned back. "No time for that until we get home again, do you understand me?"

Scaro's eyes narrowed mischievously.

"Clawmaster, there's *always* time. It doesn't take that long." He and Emoro shared a juicy laugh.

Ysella looked from one to the other in bemusement. They couldn't mean sex as such a casual encounter, could they? She had always thought every coupling was supposed to be meaningful! That meant that he was

trying to . . . that servant girl . . . he *wouldn't*, not when
he was just starting to understand his feelings for her!

Ysella started to chirp to herself. Emoro took her
by the hand.

"Come on, girl, I mean, Priestess. We have to get
moving. Don't want to leave Lord Tae wondering."
Emoro led her out into the courtyard.

Gilas hurried behind them, his broom in hand, and
saluted. "May I escort the priestess to the court, sir?"

"Yes, good idea," the clawmaster said absently.
"Look after her."

Gilas beamed shyly at Ysella. She flattened her ears
in displeasure. A recruit. A green, untested warrior to
be *her* champion? Not likely. She opened her mouth
to protest to Emoro, but he turned away from them
and bowed to Cleotra. She received him regally. Ysella
wished she had her composure.

"Priestess, my officer has just informed me that
Lord Tae wants his visitors tonight."

"What?" Cleotra snapped, her tail swishing. "We
have had no time to rest or eat!"

Emoro looked apologetic. "We're at his pleasure,
lady." He handed her a packet of field rations from
his own kit. "Eat this. It will do for the meantime."

Cleotra looked at it in disdain. "I am sick of pieces
of leather and sticks of wood. And Lord Tae will have
to wait until morning."

"We must go, Your Sinuousness." Sherril stood up
and smoothed his fur into place. "This is an opportunity to make a good impression. If we are willing
to do his bidding in small things, he will take it into

account. A small sample of your talents, or the poetry of our people, of which I have memorized the many sagas, will whet his appetite for more."

"I do not jump when I am bid to jump!"

Ysella glided over and knelt at Cleotra's side. "He will worship you, Cleotra. He will. He won't even notice the rest of us, he will be so entranced with you."

Sherril huffed into his whiskers. Ysella regarded him meekly. He was a very important Mrem. She had probably offended him. She looked to see whether Cleotra was inclined to punish her.

The senior Dancer seemed much more inclined to take out her temper on Emoro. Her tail lashed impatiently, and in spite of the dimness of the court-yard, her pupils had contracted to slits. She bared her claws and slashed the air impatiently. Ysella winced. Cleotra whirled.

"Petru! Fetch my green veils and bronze anklets. Bring the sistrum and the dombek."

"Yes, Priestess," Petru said soothingly, from very close by. He appeared at her side, a huge black shadow, his fur dark and fluffy as though he had risen from a restful sleep. Painted hide bags and cases hung from straps over his massive shoulders. "All is prepared already. All you need to do is concentrate upon your art, lady. May I adorn your fur before you go? A little brushing, perhaps, to make you feel fresher?"

Ysella could feel tension fading from all of them as Petru fussed over the senior Dancer. The horn-backed brushes in his hands whisked down Cleotra's body, fluffing the sleek black fur up one way, then smoothing it down the other. Fur would have flown in every direction if Ysella had groomed herself like that, but not a single hair seemed to float in the dank air. All of it was caught in the bristles. With a lick of his forefinger pad, Petru slicked back her whiskers, untangling a few until her face was a mask of perfection. From a pouch Petru took a pot of glamour dust and sprinkled it on her fur. This one was gold, meant to impress. It picked up yellow lights in Cleotra's eyes. Ysella craned her neck hopefully toward him, hoping that he would brush her a little as well.

Cleotra noticed the state of her fur first. "And the child, Petru," she said. "I don't want to be disgraced by her."

"You won't, Priestess!" Ysella exclaimed. But she was happy to be taken in hand by the valet. She luxuriated in the sensation as the brushes danced over her body, from nose-tip to tail-tip. She stretched under Petru's ministrations, feeling the weariness depart from her. Cleotra favored her with a superior smile.

"If only you were that graceful in Dance, Ysella," she said. "And Sherril, please, Petru."

The valet paused for a moment to flick a pinch of blue dust over Ysella's coat. It was the first time she had been allowed glitter. She preened happily, enjoying the pinpoints of light. Petru, with a look of impatience, scrubbed down the advisor with less tenderness than he had used on the Dancers, and sprinkled a bare fingerful of silver dust on his dark gray coat.

"You look so handsome, Sherril," Ysella said admiringly.

Petru let out a small hacking noise. Cleotra ignored it and clambered gracefully up the ladder. Ysella followed her, going over in her mind all the movements of the Dance. They kept her from thinking too deeply about the Liskash awaiting them.

There's nothing to fear, a thought slipped into her mind. *Trust the noble Lord Tae. He has given you safety here. Calm. Let yourself be at peace.*

It was good advice. Ysella gave in to the soothing thought, and mounted the first rung.

She had said she was willing to give her life for the clan; she just hoped she wouldn't really have to do it.

Emoro took point beside the dino guide, a low-browed, heavyset creature almost his own height with slate blue skin and a flat mandible. He didn't need to look back to know the rest of his warriors spread out in formation. He was too old a hand not to know that the peril from the Liskash came from the minds of the nobles, not from their snail's-pace battle tactics. Two skinny, red-scaled lizards held guttering torches aloft.

"Let's go," the guide urged them. His beady black eyes wore no expression. Emoro gave him a blank look in return.

"Are we ready?" he asked the lady Cleotra, as Petru fussed over her. A small portion of her leg fur had become disarranged as they had come over the pylon's confining wall. The valet hastened to smooth it out. Emoro watched his sure strokes with admiration and impatience.

"Not yet." Petru straightened up and surveyed

Emoro with a measuring eye. "You can't go like that, Clawmaster. You'll be a disgrace." He moved in on him and began to brush his short, grizzled coat.

"No...!" Emoro roared.

"Yes," Petru said, meaningfully. Emoro submitted, but with a snarl on his face and lowered ears to show that he disapproved. He wished Petru wouldn't make a spectacle of him like that in public, but if he ordered him back into line, he'd pay for it later, in private. That payment was often delightful, though. He hoped all those days weren't behind them. Scaro let out a hiss of scornful merriment. Emoro growled low at him.

"You wait your turn, Lieutenant," he said. "We all have to look pretty for court."

"Never!" Scaro said, his eyes twinkling. "I'd rather be rough and ready, Clawmaster."

Petru snorted. "Ill-kempt is not a fashion statement."

Emoro said nothing. Scaro and Petru didn't make a secret of their disdain for one another. It had come to blows once in a while.

Petru didn't make too much of a show of his ministrations, nor did he reach for the sparkling dust with which he loved to adorn himself. Emoro thanked Aedonniss for small mercies, and nodded to the dino to lead the way. The torchbearers moved out ahead.

"Make way!" they cried in hollow, piping voices. Lizards couldn't possibly have any balls, not with kitten cries like that.

Lanterns or stinking, guttering torches hung on every corner and at the doorway to every domicile, however humble. The Liskash couldn't see in the dark like Mrem, so if they wished to go abroad at night they had to herald the way with artificial lights. Emoro did his best to avoid looking directly at any of them, lest the miniature suns blind him to movement in the shadow.

He spotted plenty of that. The sorry-assed Mrem of this town—curse every dino back to the egg!—came and went about their tasks, all of them round-shouldered and droop-tailed. Not one of them looked as if it had had a decent meal in months. It would be his pleasure to take their host by his scrawny neck and wring the life out of him for the humiliation of his fellow Mrem. He was grateful for the protection of the Dancers. He'd faced Liskash without Dances performed behind his force. When a noble was nearby, he felt a strong urge to drop his weapons and surrender. Common sense had taken point, though, and he killed the enemy with all the more ferocity thereafter. He kept the image of the last Liskash he had speared in the forefront of his mind, to refer to in case he forgot how dangerous and treacherous the scaly worms were.

The closer they got to the keep, the more he could feel an oppressive sensation around his head. Lord Tae was trying to influence his mind. He ground his sharp molars together.

None shall pass! he thought. He hoped the others could withstand it. Cleotra must have felt it, for she began to chant quietly to herself. After a startled squeak that told Emoro the girl had to be nudged for inattention, Ysella joined in.

"Aedonniss, how this place smells!" growled Neer, one of his seasoned warriors, two steps back and two to the left of him. "Reminds me of that hole in the wall up near the south border we cleaned out, Clawmaster, remember . . . ?" His voice died away. That border was gone, along with all the towns to the north of it. No doubt the Liskash had lost plenty of their kind when the water began to flood the Hot Lands, but Emoro didn't care about that. Everyone he knew was missing friends or relatives who had been caught by surprise.

"Aedonniss decided He needed another body of water close to us, Neer," Emoro said stoically. "We don't question the gods. We just take orders. Right?"

"Right, sir," Neer said thoughtfully.

The warriors felt naked without their arms. At that moment, Emoro was certain his best war-claws were mounted on the wall of the gatehouse-keeper's hovel. He understood how little choice they had in approaching this lizard-lord as supplicants. His warriors could defend such a small group with no trouble. They were well-schooled in hand-to-hand fighting. Aedonniss grant they wouldn't have to use any in the next few days. All he had to do was get a fat counselor and a couple of spoiled Dancers back and forth to their camp. That was all. Hah! All!

With all the fanfare, their small procession gathered quite a crowd of onlookers in the short walk between the walls of the lower tower and the main keep. This building, unlike the two smaller ones flanking it, was surrounded by guards. Emoro studied their placements. Not bad, but too much space between sentries in the dark. On the other hand, an enemy would have to fly—and get past the leatherwings circling overhead—to pose much threat to Lord Tae, and this was the cork in the bottleneck blocking the Mrem from passing safely to the west. They were only the first of the tribes that would come this way. Others were no more than weeks behind them. This mission must succeed, so Emoro could not indulge his deep-seated wish.

As the smaller keeps were built, so was the larger one. There was no gate. At a ladder, carved and pegged from an exotic wood and polished smooth with wax, the Liskash urged them forward with spears lowered. Emoro counted guards on duty, how far away they were, and how well armed. He might need this knowledge later; he might not.

He sent Scaro up the ladder first with four warriors. They swarmed up and stood waiting on the first stage. Scaro sent him a hand-signal to say that the walkway was wider than on the smaller building. He nodded.

"Up you go, Priestess," he said, holding out a hand to Cleotra. She scorned him, like the fancy bitch she was, and clambered up without help. Petru passed within a hair's-breadth of him, grinning under his whiskers. He put his hand into Emoro's and stepped up onto the rung after his mistress.

Emoro brought up the rear of the party, behind the last warrior. It was a long way up to the smooth metal lip hammered onto the stone around the top, and a long way down. He took a good look at the courtyard before he made the descent.

The building was deceptive in its size. From the outside, it looked much smaller than it was within. The pylon-walls contained a courtyard that could hold a thousand people. The black and white checked floors were made of fitted and polished squares of stone that felt pleasantly cool under the foot, but were no doubt slippery as river eels when wet. The evening dew was falling. Emoro watched his steps cautiously so as not to slide.

"This is horrible," Petru said, just audible to his fellow Mrem. "I think, yes, that I may be sick. Could this have been worse designed?"

Emoro had to concur. The colors of the Lord Tae's home clashed on the eyeballs, even by torchlight. Against the walls, which were painted, as far as Emoro could tell, in bright blues and greens from copper minerals, hung vast tapestries of red, orange, purple and brown. They had orange-and-purple checked borders that matched cushions on the couches that had been arranged before these hideous works of art, if a blind Mrem was led up to feel them and told that's what they were, obviously so people could study them at their leisure. Emoro would rather have gone on maneuvers over shards of volcanic glass with a double-weight backpack.

Two lines of heavyset guards in metal-studded leather armor stood in the very center of the courtyard. Emoro did a quick count and got four eights in each. Three officers commanded each line. They wore bronze plates sewn to their leather tunics and had crested helmets with low snout-pieces. The chief commander, discernable because he had a white Mrem tail depending from his helmet, curse him to the depths of the sea, marched out before the Mrem got within ten paces of the line and shouted.

"Halt there!" he ordered.

Sherril undulated out of the group, elbowing Emoro aside. He made an elaborate obeisance. "Greetings, Commander. We are to meet with the Lord Tae."

The commander pointed a leather-gloved finger at a pair of doors with a pointed arch behind him.

"There is where you will have your audience. Stay back behind our lines and do not attempt to cross them. Anyone to approach the throne too closely will die! This is the order of His Godliness, Lord Tae Shanissi. State your names."

Sherril bowed low. "Then we heed the order. We are the representatives of the Mrem of the Lailah tribe. I was here only four days ago. I am Sherril Rangawo. I present the Dancer Cleotra Mreem and her apprentice Ysella Ehe." That self-aggrandizing heap of fur was going to ignore them! Emoro growled low in his throat. Sherril glanced over his shoulder with a haughty sneer, but he turned back to Tae. "And the senior warriors who have escorted us to your presence, Clawmaster Emoro Awr and Drillmaster Scaro Ullenh."

Petru cleared his throat meaningfully, but Sherril did not speak again. Emoro stifled a grin.

"Welcome to you, and welcome back, Sherril and your companions."

A reedy voice echoed forth. Emoro blinked. Through the wide doorway he saw a thin, very short Liskash with pale blue skin the color of a winter sky seated on a stone chair on a platform eight feet or more above the floor. His black eyes bulged in his narrow face. His skull was rounded except for a narrow ridge of scales that ran from just above his eyes over and down the back of his head to his collar. His raiment was bright orange with narrow black lines. Bronze ornaments jingled on his sleeves, and tall, vividly colored feathers stuck up around the collar like a picket fence. Statues of the Liskash lord in various outfits and painted garishly to match stood on plinths all around the room. The costume he wore that night was depicted on the third figure to the right of the doorway. Lord Tae could behold his own image whenever he chose.

"I shall be ill," Petru said, feelingly.

"That is hideous," Scaro said, in a rare moment of concord with the valet.

Sherril bowed again. "Greetings, Lord Tae. Thank you for this audience."

The Liskash beckoned with one skinny finger. "Come forward."

The first line of dinos formed a square around the Mrem, spears pointed in. Emoro wished again for his battle claws, or one little stabbing spear. The commander gestured them to move. Sherril glanced back imperiously and strode forward, following the double-line of Liskash into the throne room.

Once inside, the doors closed behind the Mrem with a hollow BOOM. Emoro glanced back to see two guards hefting a huge latch into place across a pair of brackets. Easily undone if necessary.

The lines of Liskash spread out again into a double border between the Mrem and Lord Tae. Sherril stepped off, Emoro close behind him. The Liskash shifted with them, keeping their beady eyes fixed on them. The closer they got to Tae, the more the headache he had felt coming on increased. The Dancers were aware of it, too. Both of them had been moving their hands and bodies in light, subtle motions as they walked. Those increased in intensity, and the pressure receded from Emoro's mind. It was still there, though.

Sherril halted at the prescribed limit and bowed again. Emoro followed suit, signing to his warriors to do the same. His knees felt as if they wanted to bend, too, to take him to the floor where he would prostrate himself. He fought the impulse. It was no doubt coming from the lordling on the throne. Tae was going to keep trying to control them.

"We came here of our own free will," Emoro growled, forcing the words out as he forced his back to straighten. "We do not bend to yours."

Sherril turned so the Liskash lord couldn't see him, and glared. He purred at the Liskash, offering a supplicating gesture.

"I apologize, Lord Tae. It was agreed that I would speak for the group."

"It was not," Cleotra snapped. Sherril's fighting ridge went up at the sound of her voice. "I speak for myself."

Lord Tae smiled. His face moved but his eyes bore no expression at all. "No offense is taken. All these reactions teach me more of your culture."

Sherril seemed relieved. "We are pleased to bring

you the fruits of our history and our arts," he said. "I have memorized the sagas of our people, from the cold days until now. There are many heroic poems that you will enjoy, translated into your own language by myself. The first one I would have you hear is of the first Clan Leader of the Lailah. In fact, Soroo was an ancestor of mine. He lived—"

"No." The refusal was dry but final. "I may wish to hear your poetry another time. Frankly, your voices hurt my ears. I am a student of your religion. I wish to see your dance."

Cleotra threw back her head proudly. "The hour is late and we were not given time to refresh ourselves," she said. "Our Dance is not a simple thing. My apprentice and I have been marching for two days. In our normal routine, we limber up and do exercises before beginning our rituals. They are sacred things, not mere entertainment!"

The ridge above Lord Tae's eyes went up. "I would see those exercises as well as your dance. You may begin."

"*We* begin with refreshments and repose upon comfortable seats," Cleotra said.

Lord Tae looked a little bored. "Oh, very well."

He did not move or speak, but very shortly, a rap sounded upon the door. Emoro and the other warriors tightened their muscles in preparation, but when the portal was unlatched, it was to admit an eight of gray-scaled servants. They bore huge pillows in a mismatch of colors and hammered metal trays with enameled pitchers and bowls upon them.

Petru took charge. He ordered the servants, who were as dull as their skins, to place the pillows on the shining floor to one side of the area they had been allotted. Once they were placed to his liking, he escorted the Dancers there and assisted them to sit down. Cleotra settled gracefully upon the ugly cushions. Ysella plumped down beside her.

Sherril swaggered after them. A low argument ensued between Petru and the counselor. Her green eyes blazing, Cleotra stood up between them. Effortlessly, she lifted her left foot and kicked each of them in the head. Emoro rumbled in his own throat. What a warrior she would have made!

Lord Tae rolled back on his padded throne, laughing. "Fantastic! So limber!"

She stood glaring as they both staggered backward. They didn't look at one another or at the Dancer, but Petru pulled a drab purple cushion along the floor a short way from the Dancers, and Sherril sat down on it, waiting patiently for Petru to serve refreshments to Cleotra and Ysella before bringing him a selection of dainties.

Lord Tae watched with curiosity as the Dancers lapped the pale white liquid from the wide goblets and sampled the savory brownish nuggets of food. Some looked chewy, others crunchy. Emoro licked his chops. It had been hours since he had had a decent meal, out on the road, though he had eaten the nuts and dried fruits that served as field rations, but he was a warrior. He could wait until the lizard had finished toying with them and they were safely back in their fish-trap. Cleotra set down her goblet.

"Are you satisfied?" Lord Tae asked. Cleotra rose in one smooth motion. Behind her, Ysella was as awkward as a frog.

"I thank you, our host," Cleotra Mreem said.

"Then dance for me."

Scaro Ullenh made sure that his guards were well deployed, keeping watch on the Liskash. He stood as close to the Dancers as he could manage without getting in their way. He didn't want to miss a moment. As a warrior, he saw Dances performed during sacred feasts and other occasions, such as the circle to protect them here in Ckotliss. He had never beheld the warming-up sessions. He had fantasized about the females throwing themselves about in their exercises, lithely and energetically in wild abandon. He had mated with many a Dancer after they had finished their rituals for the day, but it would add spice to see what made them so hot and ready. Now he would. And perhaps he could approach Cleotra later on to help her burn off that excess energy. He grinned to himself.

The valet settled himself on a pile of cushions with the dombek drum between his knees. He rattled off a quick roll, then began a slow, syncopated rhythm. One, two-three, one, two-three, one, two-three.

Cleotra and Ysella touched fingertips and paced off a circle about two Mrem-lengths in diameter. Scaro fancied he could feel the power of the gods sealing it, so intent were the Dancers' expressions. Ysella, for all her adolescent awkwardness, once she began to focus, moved almost as smoothly as her mentor. A pity she was too young for mating. He couldn't blame her for fixing on *him*. He was handsome, well groomed, and possessed of enviable style that attracted the eye of many a Mrem female. Still, until she matured, he wasn't going anywhere near her!

Once they had created their sacred space, Cleotra led Ysella through a series of exercises. They began with simple steps and stretches, and moving into thrusts, kicks and claw swipes, shifting sideways, jumping backwards, leaping and pirouetting. The steps swiftly became more complicated and rapid. In fact, if he did not know they were Dancing, he might have thought they were fighting one another. The drum beats sped up until they were moving so fast he could hardly follow. Ysella was open-mouthed and wide-eyed, but Cleotra looked serene, as though she was Dancing with the gods themselves. No wonder she was to be Cassa's chosen successor.

Scaro found himself breathing hard. His resolution deserting him, he wished to mate with both of them right there in the middle of the throne room.

They stopped. The drum ceased. Cleotra strode magnificently to face Lord Tae. She was not even breathing hard. Ysella was.

"Our exercises are complete," Cleotra said. "Now we will perform for you the Coming of the First Dawn."

"I would rather see the Wooing of Assirra by Aedonniss," Lord Tae said. "It is a story I have heard of, and have long been curious about."

Cleotra's eyes flashed. "That is a sacred Dance, not suitable for outsiders."

Lord Tae's brows drew down. "If you do not want my help, you may leave."

The Liskash guards behind them lifted the latch from the door.

Cleotra looked as if she might storm out. Scaro speculated on whether any of them would make it out of there alive. His task, should all things go awry, was to see to the Dancers' safety. He stood on the balls of his feet, ready to spring to their defense. Liskash took a long time to die, but they were slow moving. He could probably kill six or seven of them before getting the Dancers out of the room.

Cleotra lifted her chin. She was still angry.

"For the sake of my people, then, I break my vows. Ysella!"

The girl ran to her side. Cleotra assumed a pose with her hands outstretched, palms down. Her fingers moved gracefully as if each was a bird flying through the air. Ysella moved at once to a distance of two Mrem-lengths and composed herself, her eyes cast modestly down, shoulders turned inward. She must be playing Assirra to Cleotra's Aedonniss.

Cleotra leaped into the air. Her hands and feet kicked out, and her tail lashed. She was a storm, she was a cataract, she was a whirlwind! The mighty powers of nature were all contained in one slender, lithe body. Scaro could not take his eyes off her. She kicked high and twirled in midair, coming down on her toes. Then, staying poised on the ball of one foot, she crouched low, watchful and wary. The world was created, but Aedonniss was alone and lonely.

Ysella moved then, wafting her arms in gentle waves. As the dombek thrummed, she moved sinuously around the circle, exploring the domain that had been made. She stopped, withdrawing into herself, as she saw the hulking figure of Aedonniss. He was powerful and fierce, but she was clearly attracted to him. She held back, not knowing what she should do. She was alluring in her grace. She seemed to rub affectionately against the air, seeking someone to share that caress. Scaro yearned to be the one that she sought. He could give her the love she craved.

Then he gave himself a mental kick. That was Ysella up there! An immature girl! But she had a mastery of the art that he would not have dreamed. What she would be when she was older! Scaro glanced at the throne to see what Lord Tae thought of their performance.

The Liskash noble wasn't even looking at them! He had his eyes closed. And so they remained throughout the rest of the magnificent dance.

Scaro shrugged. If he wanted to miss what he had asked to see, that was his problem. As long as no threat was imminent, he was going to enjoy the command performance. It must be good to be the lord of a whole domain.

Petru soothed and fussed over Cleotra all the way back to the guest quarters. He had wrapped her in a light cloak against the cool air. Night, thankfully, covered most of the horrors of Liskash architecture, artwork and décor. Nothing, sadly, could be done about the ugliness of their escort. It was even larger than the contingent that had brought them to the high keep.

"You channeled your anger at Lord Tae magnificently, Your Sinuousness. It was most impressive," he said.

"It was odd to Dance without my sisters," Cleotra said thoughtfully. "That ugly little worm did not show much appreciation."

"He had his eyes closed, my lady," Emoro repeated.

"The whole time?" Cleotra asked, outraged, as if she could not believe it.

"The whole time," Sherril said glumly. "And he did not want to hear any of my poems."

"No surprise there," Scaro commented, from the ranks. "The Liskash already hate us." Sherril shot an annoyed look over his shoulder. There would be ear-biting and rolling on the floor if they were safely at home.

"What I fear," Sherril said, "is why."

Petru massaged Cleotra's hand. The tension in it was extreme enough that she would need a thorough rubdown once he got her settled in her chamber. Once the performance was over, he had collared one of the less dazed-looking servants and gotten her to agree to bring food to their quarters. He could have eaten an entire arosh by himself, but the Dancers had to have meat too after their exertion. Lord Tae had a lot to answer for, not letting them prepare properly and asking for a forbidden Dance. Petru did not like him. His attire, and how ridiculously heavily Liskash dressed, was an eyesore, as was the entire stronghold. A waste of craftsmanship and materials. If he had been in charge, and perhaps he could offer some guidance when they were permitted to cross Ckotliss to the west, he would correct their color sense at least. It pained him that his personal adornments clashed with his surroundings no matter how he arranged himself. He had a headache that made his temper short, but his duty was to Cleotra. He cosseted and soothed her.

"Why do you think?" she asked Sherril.

The counselor looked around them. Too many of the dinos were close enough to hear. Petru knew that what they heard, Lord Tae heard. He shot a warning look at Sherril, who waved it away impatiently.

"I think he was enjoying the drumming," Sherril said.

Petru preened. He had been very good.

"How did our Dance look?" Ysella asked, sidling up to Scaro.

"Good," the lieutenant grunted.

"I thought you were wonderful," Gilas said, from behind her. "You move like leaves on the trees, or grain waving. I have never seen anything so graceful."

Ysella startled, her tail fluffing.

"Thank you," she said, pleased. Gilas beamed at her.

Petru chuckled to himself. *Ah, young love.* But that lad had many years ahead of him before he could settle down with a wife, let alone win a Dancer.

Up the wretched ladders and down into their deep, dank box again. Petru took both of his ladies into the room prepared for them. He was pleased to see that none of their possessions had been tampered with by Lord Tae's servants. Cleotra was exhausted, but restless. He brushed her entire body over and over again until she dozed on the clean bedding. She would have been better for fresh food. Where was that servant girl with the food he had ordered? All that was available was the stores they had brought with them from the camp. Dried fish would be too hard to chew. Petru resolved to simmer some in water to make a nourishing soup as soon as he had settled both Dancers.

Ysella had fallen asleep in a corner. He lifted her into her own nest of bedding. What a little, light thing she was. He felt very protective of his Dancers. Petru went through his various cases until he found a vial of calming oils and dabbed a little on her throat at the pulse points. She let out a happy buzz in her sleep. Petru patted her and went about his other tasks. Their jewelry had to be put away, as did his own. He rubbed an unguent into his hands. They became so dry after a night of drumming. But he had been good, hadn't he?

How irritating of Lord Tae to keep his eyes closed through the performance. He didn't understand the meaning of what he had seen, or not seen. The Dance spoke of the very essence of Mrem, the savagery in their souls that they channeled into beauty and grace.

A thin crescent moon was just hanging on the western lip of the roof in a lapis-blue sky. Morning was not that far away.

He had a chamber of his own, but he was reluctant to make use of it. Instead, he sat on the stone seat along the fountain and watched the water trickle by torchlight. Something troubled him. It lurked at the corners of his mind like the warriors lurking in the corners of the courtyard. He had faith in the Dance that protected them, but the power of the Liskash was undeniable. The pain in his head increased. He had powders and herbs to soothe ills, but this was an intense hurt.

Lord Tae could help him, he mused. If he obeyed the Liskash lord, he would never feel pain again. Peace awaited him. He must go to his god.

Petru wrinkled his nose. A terrible smell filled the courtyard, distracting him from his thoughts. He sniffed, trying to determine the source of it, and realized it was not in the air, but in his head.

He had to go to Lord Tae.

No! Petru clutched at his forehead, as if trying to pull the thought out. Fury filled him, making his tail lash. That ugly worm was trying to take over his mind! The Dancers. He needed them to strengthen the Dance. Then he would scratch the Liskash's beady eyes out.

He slipped into the Dancers' chamber. They were both restless, sensing the intrusion. He must waste no time.

"Priestess," he whispered, touching Cleotra gently on the shoulder.

She came awake all at once, her claws at his throat. Petru took her by the arms and thrust her away.

"You feel it, don't you?" he asked.

"And smell it," Cleotra said, furiously. "Awaken the others. We must escape as soon as we can. Ysella!"

The girl sat up in her nest, chirping to herself fearfully.

Cleotra sprang up and grabbed her by the hand. "Come out into the courtyard. Lord Tae works against us. We must Dance to strengthen the bond with our sisters and the gods."

Petru strode out in their wake. The warriors on duty were less sensitive than he was, but they heard and saw what was happening. They had sent an emissary to wake Emoro before he could. The stocky clawmaster came out to meet him, wiping sleep out of his eyes. Together, the Dancers began to circle one another. Their hands moved in and out toward one another as if feigning blows. Petru recognized it as a ritual to raise energy quickly. He felt the pressure ease considerably, though it did not go away.

"What is going on?" Emoro demanded.

"Don't you feel it?" Petru asked. "Don't you *smell* it?"

"Lord Tae? From all the way over there?" Emoro asked.

"All the city is under his control," Sherril said, coming out of his chamber. "The city and most of the region."

"He seeks to take control of us now," Petru said.

Sherril eyed him haughtily. "What makes you think so?"

"Because I felt an urge to serve him, that's what." Petru crossed his huge arms. "My duty is to Priestess Cassa and the Dancers, no one else. I don't expect you to believe me, but what do you smell?"

"Besides your cloying perfumes?"

"Counselor, enough!" Cleotra said, stepping away from the circle. She closed her hands, sealing the energy she had raised within herself. "This is deadly serious. If we are under attack, we must defend."

Sherril scowled. He hated it when anyone knew something before him. Petru felt a moment of triumph for having been right first, but the tightening sensation around his brows increased again. He winced. So did Sherril.

"He is trying to pierce through the veil the Dancers put around us," the counselor said. "He didn't want an exchange of culture. He wanted to learn how the Dance protects us so he could learn how to combat our rituals."

"We could ask Lord Tae. I must go to him," young Gilas piped up, at Emoro's elbow. The warrior's eyes looked hazy. "He is calling me."

Ysella marched to him and slapped him, hard. He staggered backward a pace on the black and white tiles, his feet slipping. He looked at her in shock, but his wits were restored.

"We are doomed," Sherril said glumly.

"No," Emoro said. "We must fight free. Lord Tae is too treacherous. We were wrong to trust him."

"We had to try," Sherril reminded them. "The alternative is weeks more on the road without adequate supplies. The rest of the clan is behind us. The gates of the city will open at dawn. We must make our way there now."

"With every Liskash in the city under his control?" Petru said, horrified at the thought of being overwhelmed by lizards. He brushed at his fur frantically. "We would never make it."

"Then we must make him let us go," Emoro said, with a fearsome snarl.

"If he hasn't foreseen our response and moved to counter it," Sherril retorted.

Almost as he said it, Liskash in full uniform with knives and spears began to pour over the front wall, exactly where Emoro had told him he feared they would.

"Halt! Surrender in Lord Tae's name!"

"He has," Petru said. His heart quailed at the sight of dozens of lizards racing from the roof perch to all three ladders leading down to the first walkway. He did not want to be a slave in this place! "We're trapped!"

"To the rear wall," Emoro ordered them. "There are ladders there the servants use. They're thinner and can bear less weight, but they'll do. There is usually only one guard at the bottom. Go. We will halt them, or at least slow them down. Warriors, to me!" He glared at Petru. "Hurry! Run! Leave your luggage."

"I will not!" Petru said, outraged at the notion of abandoning his lovely jewelry, his perfumes, or his treasured cosmetics to the lizards.

"It may be your possessions or your life," Sherril said.

"Well . . ." Petru chewed on his lip, considering which was worse. Emoro smacked him in the ear like a kitten. His eyes glowed. That was out of character for him. He was usually submissive to Petru. "You'll pay for that."

Emoro looked unrepentant. "I will, if it's what it takes to save your life. Go! I will be right behind you."

"You had better." Petru reached out and stroked

his cheek. He grabbed a Dancer with each hand and hurried them across the courtyard. Sherril was already clambering upward. They heard wails of warning coming too late from the outside.

If Aedonniss didn't spare Emoro, He would be sorry when Petru reached his court!

The sky had just begun to glow at the horizon when Scaro heard scrabbling sounds. He woke from the light doze he had allowed himself, propped up against the cool, sweating wall next to the ladder. It was too much to hope that the Mrem girls he had flirted with the night before had come back for a quick assignation. No, this was a truly furtive sound.

Neer had heard it, too. He opened lamplike eyes toward Scaro, and signaled a question. Scaro nodded. It took only a moment for his sensitive ears to pinpoint where the sounds were coming from. His own eyes widened as he counted sounds. Sixty, seventy, over a hundred Liskash!

Treacherous worm, Scaro knew he couldn't trust him! He wanted slaves, not art! He threw back his head to sound the alarm, and felt that he couldn't draw a single breath. His abdomen hollowed out as he tried to drag in air, but it was as if his body would not obey. He dropped to his knees. So did Neer and the Mrem on his other side. The Liskash noble was strangling them all at once from afar. Scaro's vision darkened. He begged Aedonniss for delivery and heard a mocking presence in his mind. Scaro growled, and choked his blocked throat.

You do not control me, he told Lord Tae, fighting to stay conscious. *You are not my god. Let . . . me . . . go!*

He threw his body against the ladder, pushing it over. It clattered to the cobblestones.

Out of the alleyways and doorways opposite the residence, bulky, gray Liskash in leather tunics poured. Their pinched snouts peered out from leather caps. All of them had spears, shelds and knives. In the center of Scaro's darkened vision, a looming figure with a bronze badge on his cap stooped with a long knife. His throat was to be cut.

Then the grip on his mind loosened and melted away. His belly relaxed. Writhing on his back, Scaro gasped in breaths of air. A sensation of warmth surrounded him, like a mother embracing her kits. The Dancers had reestablished their protection of him and his warriors!

Taking no time for reflection, he saw the knife descend in an arc. He rolled to one side in plenty of time. Thanks be to Aedonniss that the insect-eating Liskash were so slow in their reactions! Scaro sprang up before the lizard officer could react and kicked the knife out of his hand. He leaped, rolled again, and came up with the dagger. The officer was reaching around him for his spear when Scaro stepped in, palmed his chin upward and cut his throat with his own knife. Scaro grabbed for the nearest cold body with dagger and claws out.

His vision brightened. Scaro took in the numbers streaming past him. The first hundred and a hundred more had righted the ladders and were climbing the walls. He signed to Neer and one other warrior to follow them. They kicked as many Liskash off the rungs as they could, fighting their way to the top. Scaro danced on his toes, avoiding thrusts by Liskash soldiers with incredible ease. Lord Tae was no general. He must want to capture the prize that no noble had ever possessed.

"Save the Dancers!" he bellowed.

Six of them could not turn back the tide. Emoro had given his orders once they had seen the quarters in which the Mrem would be housed. Scaro knew which way they would try to escape.

"Mrem, with me!" Scaro shouted. The other three kicked away from the onrush, leaving dead Liskash in their wake.

He had patrolled the perimeter of the cursed building over and over again in the dark. Within a handspan he knew exactly where the ladders at the rear were placed. They rounded the rear of the building.

"Scaro!" A voice echoed down to him from above. He moved out from the high wall looked up and saw Emoro racing along the narrow walkway at the top of the pylon. Scaro counted the warriors with him. Half were missing. They must be defending within. But the Dancers were safe. Ysella's golden eyes were wide and terrified. Cleotra only looked angry. That was good. "What's the matter with you, Drillmaster? There were only two hundred of them?"

"Thought you could use the wakeup," Scaro called.

"Thanks, boy! An eighthday of sleep would have been too much for me!"

"We'll guard your way," Scaro said. "I can lead you to the gates. I know several narrow ways where they will have trouble sending large forces after us."

"No!" Cleotra shouted, furiously. "We're going for the castle. Every hand will be turned against us unless we stop Lord Tae himself!"

"A Liskash noble?" Scaro asked. But those decisions were not his. "I will get you there safely, Your Sinuousness!"

Each of his warriors had a knife or a spear taken from Liskash they had slain at the front of the building. It wasn't going to be enough, Scaro knew, but he would die trying.

Cleotra scrambled down the ladder of the third stage, four or five Mrem-heights above him, and stepped aside on the walkway. Scaro realized she was going to jump. She would break her legs! He ran to catch her.

"No!" she shrieked. "Out of the way!" She threw herself into space as dozens of Liskash appeared around both sides of the building.

No Mrem could make that leap and live, but Scaro moved. To his endless admiration, she tucked herself in a ball in midair, and hit the ground rolling. She came up on her feet with a look of satisfaction. She was hardly even dusty.

"My lady," he croaked. He and Neer hastened to stand between her and the host of dinos now surrounding them. Cleotra moved her body, hands and tail in a hypnotic pattern. The closer he was to her, the stronger Scaro felt.

Less daring than she, Ysella slid down the ladder in

Sherril's wake. Petru and Emoro brought up the rear with the eight and half-eight of warriors. The big oaf of a valet was gasping for breath. He didn't matter. What did was obeying the bidding of the Dancer.

"Come with me," he said. He thrust out the dagger and prepared to fight his way through.

"No," Sherril said. He walked up to Scaro and took the knife away from him. Scaro nearly kicked him in the belly for that, but Emoro waved a hand.

Sherril held up his hands as the countless uniformed lizards crowded them against the wall.

"We surrender," he said. "Lord Tae wants us as his slaves. We give up. Take us to him."

"What are you doing?" Ysella gasped.

"Why, giving in to superior numbers, child," Sherril said, with a pitying expression. "We are overwhelmed. It is obvious that the noble has decided we are too great a prize to lose."

A spear nudged Scaro in the side.

"Give us the weapons," another brass-hat said to him.

Sherril passed over the dagger and signed to all the warriors to do the same. His innocent expression put Scaro on alert. He had to give credit to the wily elder. They wanted to get into the stronghold.

Surrounded by an endless field of ugly slate-colored faces, Scaro marched his warriors toward the keep. Above his head, he saw the flash of metal. More Liskash guards awaited them on the first level. His keen sight picked up not only spears, swords and blades, but chains. Lord Tae intended to bind them before he had them dragged into his sight.

"Clawmaster . . . ?"

"Drillmaster, I see," Emoro said mildly. "Don't let it happen."

"Yes, sir," Scaro said.

"Climb," the brass-hat said, as they reached the wall. Scaro put a foot on the rung. "The females first!"

"Sorry, I don't understand your accent," Scaro said. He swung up, signing to his men to follow him.

When they had all reached the first walkway, lizard guards reached out to seize him.

"Lord Tae wants only the females," their commander said to the brass-hat. "Chain them and kill the rest."

Scaro waited just long enough for one of the lumbering fools to come toward him with the chain in its hands. He stepped forward, grabbed the hanging links, and elbowed the guard in the face.

Momentarily stunned, it let go of the hank of chain and clapped its hands to its face. Scaro came around with a roundhouse kick and knocked the guard off the wall. It wailed as it fell. The guards took so long to react that he had time to whip another with the armful of chain. It dropped its pike. Neer seized it and stuck it between the guard's feet. It, too, screamed in its death fall.

"Go, Dancers," Scaro gritted, swinging the chain back and forth in a deadly figure-eight. He backed up toward them, keeping the dinos at bay. The enemy tried to pass, but he smacked down one after another. Blood lust rose in him as white bones pierced through gray skin and green blood spattered the walls.

"We can't get to the ladders!" Ysella cried.

"Put your foot in my hand, child," Emoro said. He boosted her upward. She scrambled over the edge of the next level and disappeared. Gilas followed her, finding clawholds invisible to the naked eye. Cleotra shinned up as easily as if it was a level floor. Scaro admired her. He hoped he would get to tell her one day. "Stay alive if you can, Drillmaster. I'd hate to lose you."

Easier said than done, Scaro mused. But the others had gone, climbing the walls like spiders. It didn't matter now what happened to him. He hissed at the onslaught of Liskash guards.

"Get me if you can, worms!"

Ysella sprang to her feet on the stone walkway and spat out a mouthful of dust. Gilas pulled her up by the elbow.

"Are you all right, my lady?" he asked.

"I'm fine," she said. She wanted to glance over the edge, but the roiling masses of Liskash at the base of the building terrified her. She felt the pounding in her head. Lord Tae was calling them. She would not submit! "Will he die?"

Gilas twisted his mouth and his ears lowered. "I don't know, but he's good, Dancer. I have to protect you."

"Run, Ysella," Cleotra said. Her eyes glowed with anger, Ysella hoped not at her. "We must reach the throne room." She sped fleetly toward the next ladder. Two guards panted in her wake. Ysella and Gilas ran to catch up with them.

Their goal was all the way at the corner of the

building. Ysella concentrated on reaching it, and not
hearing the screams and the clashing of metal. Scaro
must live!

A cry came, not from the walkway, but from behind
her. Ysella spun. Gilas lay at her feet. Looming down
on her was a gigantic Liskash with a metal helmet
and a tunic covered with plates. More of his kind
were coming up behind him.

He reached for her. Ysella cowered.

"Cleotra!" she cried.

Her mentor was almost to the ladder.

"You are a Dancer, Ysella!" she shrieked. "Act like
one! You have the skills! I must reach Lord Tae!"

With that, she leaped for the ladder and swarmed
up it. Petru and Sherril stayed close behind her. A
claw of warriors went with them.

Emoro ran back with the rest of the Mrem. He
wielded a bronze-hafted spear. "Behind me, Priestess!"

"No," Ysella cried. "Cleotra is right! I can do it!"

She began to weave back and forth before the
enormous Liskash. It watched her in fascination as
she bounded in past his guard. The ritual of the
Destruction of the Great Mountain would serve here.
Ysella felt deep inside herself for the connection to
the infinite. The power of Aedonniss was with her,
as were her distant sisters. She felt the power growing inside her.

Emoro charged past her and struck the Liskash
with the polearm. The point caught between the
plates on the creature's chest. It grabbed for the
shaft and twisted. Emoro staggered within a hand of

falling over the side. His warriors swarmed over the huge guards. They screamed out war cries that stirred Ysella's blood. She Danced faster.

The guards began to look confused. The throbbing in her head subsided. Lord Tae's presence was driven not only away from her, but from the Liskash as well!

"That's it, girl," Emoro said, encouragingly. He took swift advantage of the first guard's wavering, and plunged the spear into its open mouth. Green blood spurted out. It splashed on Ysella. She gasped, looking down at the green liquid running through her fur. It was *hot*.

The shock made her lose her place in the dance. The constricted feeling came back in force. Lord Tae wanted her to surrender, to kneel on the ground. She felt her knees go weak. The hot sun beat down on her head, making it ache more. She trembled with fear. Emoro glanced away from the guard he had just smashed in the teeth.

"Help us, Priestess!" he shouted. "Do it for the sake of that boy, if nothing else! He worships your very feet! If you don't Dance us out of here, I can't see how we can retrieve him and heal his wounds."

"Gilas?" she asked, shakily. "Not Scaro?"

"Yes, Gilas! He's a good youngster. I want him to grow up and be a mighty warrior. Help us! Help him."

Ysella put her soul into her Dance, more deeply than she had ever done in her life. Gilas was in love with her. She should not have ignored that. When a heart was given, it was a precious gift!

She flung herself at the enemy. Energy poured

through her from the heavens and the earth. She was the volcano, she was the tree, she was the lightning! She Danced under the noses of guards, leading the warriors behind her. They took advantage of the spell she created, breaking Lord Tae's hold on his slaves' minds.

Then she made the mistake of looking back, just as Emoro speared one of the guards in the eye. The bursting of the black orb into dark green goo made her stomach heave. Her rhythm faltered. She hummed to herself to get it back, and found she was chirping instead. She should be angry. They had been tricked into the city to become slaves! She didn't want to die here.

Ysella began the Dance again, but her momentum was broken. The guards' eyes lost their haze, and they pressed forward, stepping over the bodies of their own dead.

"Retreat!" Emoro shouted, yanking his spear out of a guard's belly. "Come on, girl, you've done well."

Priestess, she wanted to say. But she hardly felt she deserved the accolade. The warriors closed around her and hurried her toward the next ladder. The lizards feinted toward them. Ysella tried to restore her link to the other Dancers. They saw the same sun she did. They were together in mind and intention. She twirled, trying to gain power.

"Dancer!" Emoro shouted, moving to shield her, but it was in vain. A wall of armored Liskash overwhelmed them. Ysella was knocked off her feet by a heavy weight striking her in the back. Her head hit the stone. Color exploded in her vision, followed by blackness.

"This way, to the north side," Sherril said, pointing over the lead warrior's shoulder as they came off the ladder. He heard the war cries behind him but did not look back. "We'll come down right over the throne room."

"Yes, sir," the warrior said. He and the two claws who had sheared off from Emoro's contingent to escort Cleotra had one Liskash weapon apiece in their grip. Not enough, Sherril feared. Their greatest defenses were the Dancer's protection against the Liskash noble—and his own brain. He had memorized all the ins and outs of the keep when he had been there. He had flattered Lord Tae mightily to get a tour of the building and its environs, and carefully memorized all that he could about it. The noble knew where they were, but not necessarily where they were going or how they would get there. It was a game of The King Dies, with both sides truly fighting for their lives. Sherril intended to win.

The long stone walkway on the north was deserted except for a frightened female Liskash who leaped back into her doorway as the Mrem raced by.

"Curse it," Sherril said. "Tae will see through her eyes. We will be interrupted."

"I will get you through, sir," the lead warrior of the first claw promised him. He was a big, rangy male with black and gray stripes and a jagged scar where his left ear ought to be.

The sounds of panting behind them caused the warriors to spin in place.

"As you were!" Emoro growled, racing towards them. The Mrem were streaked with blood, both red and green. One male was limping on a badly wounded foot. Others bore bleeding gashes. Emoro himself had a cut on his upper arm that missed his shoulder joint. Cleotra's eyes widened with dismay.

"Where is Ysella?"

"Down," Emoro said, his voice tight with pain. "I set her in an empty chamber and closed the door. With luck no one will notice her until this is over. If any of us live."

"One of us must," Sherril said, with determination, pointing to the ladder. It had been painted to blend in with the wall, but it cast a shadow he could see. "There's our way up. Lord Tae hasn't ordered his soldiers to draw the ladders up. He could trap us, but he hasn't."

He pushed past the warriors to be the first on the rungs. Behind him, Emoro let out an exclamation of irritation. Sherril turned to glare, then realized another shadow was looming over him. An enormous Liskash guard with a metal helmet peered over the edge of the level at him. Many more figures were behind him.

"Greetings," Sherril said, as if he was glad to see them. "Lord Tae called for us. We were frightened by the battle at the front, so we came this way. Will you take us to his presence?"

He hadn't believed it when it worked the first time, nor could he believe that it worked again. Lord Tae was much too confident in his powers. The big-jawed lizard seemed to chew over this information for a while, then stood back.

"All right. Come ahead." He beckoned Sherril up.

The counselor ascended, and straightened out his coat with dignity. The others scrambled upward. Sherril noted with dismay that there was only a single eight of warriors left behind Clawmaster Emoro. The Liskash took the hard-won weapons away from the Mrem.

"Escort us. We must abase ourselves in his presence." *That ought to please the wretched worm's ego,* Sherril thought.

Each of the Mrem was flanked by two Liskash guards. Sherril regarded the creatures marching beside him as nonentities, of no importance except as messengers to Lord Tae.

With spears pointed at their backs, the Mrem ascended to the top of the building and made their way along the hammered-metal of the walkway. It was slippery in the dew of dawn. Sherril looked down. He was not afraid of heights, but a misstep would be fatal. Below, in the courtyard, a square formation of guards waited. They all wore the same metal helmets and leather tunics, but Sherril saw that some were the elite guards that had flanked them the night before, and some were Mrem.

Automatically, he turned to the right, making for the ladder on the inside of the west wall. The officer halted the line and put a hand into Sherril's chest.

"Do you truly wish to serve the god Lord Tae Shanissi?" he asked.

"Of course," Sherril said, opening his eyes wide with feigned sincerity. "That is my dearest wish."

The guard grinned. "Then it is the god's wish that you fling yourself off the building and sacrifice yourself in his honor."

Sherril sighed. "Oh, very well," he said. "But I prefer that the god himself watch me perform my sacrifice."

The guard pointed down. Sherril followed his finger to a shining figure seated on a raised, royal blue dais, surrounded by dull-colored guards.

"Lord Tae is there. Now, jump!"

Sherril moved to the edge, and the guards stayed with him.

"What are you doing?" Cleotra demanded.

"Sacrificing to Lord Tae, of course," Sherril said. He spread out his arms. Then he dropped onto his back and braced himself. With his long, strong feet, he kicked both guards under their tails. They bellowed surprise as they plummeted to the first walkway below. The first struck the edge with the back of his head and went limp. The second clawed at the edge, then fell helplessly down, bounced, and down again. Sherril grinned.

"Is that enough of a sacrifice?" he called down to Lord Tae.

The commander bellowed and charged at him. Sherril dodged out of his way, avoiding the point of the spear. Emoro signed to his warriors to defend. Petru took Cleotra's arm and towed her toward the ladder.

Sherril dodged and dodged again. The walkway was a Mrem-height wide, but that wasn't much room. The lizards had the advantage of numbers. They charged at him. He took to his heels and ran, his slower foes in pursuit.

In the courtyard, Lord Tae shrieked his displeasure. Guards made for the ladders on all sides and began the long climb up to intercept them.

Sherril raced to find a way down that was not filling up with angry Liskash. For once, he had not completely thought out his exit strategy. *That is not like me*, he chided himself. *But at least I buy time for the Dancer*. Emoro had her fully surrounded, on the opposite side of the building, heading for the way down. Lord Tae danced and shook his fists in anger. Sherril felt the pressure of his mind, pulling at his muscles to make him slow down. He felt as if he was crawling through mud.

The noise was deafening. Sherril had to concentrate to think. If Cleotra could break his hold over those Mrem below, they would have allies. Perhaps enough to overwhelm the Liskash noble. If not, enough to get the Lailah to the gates of the city would do. They had to survive. He had to survive. He looked for a hiding place. Yes, there was a door standing ajar just past the corner ahead. He threw himself down the ladder, raced in, slammed the door closed, and flung himself against it. The room was full of rolled tapestries and wooden chests stacked to the ceiling. They were too tightly packed for him to hide among.

BAM! The door jerked against his back. BAM! Sherril dug in his heels on the stone floor. BAM!

He was flung forward against the chests, striking his jaw. Sherril lay dazed for a moment, thinking how much his mouth hurt. The door opened and Liskash poured into the room.

Sherril had not always been a pampered counselor to the clan leader. Once he had been the second-youngest kit in a large family. As the Liskash made for him, he sprang up and bared his claws and teeth. He threw himself on the nearest lizard and bit into his neck. He spat out bitter-tasting blood and kicked the still-flailing body away. His claws lashed out at the next guard. The Liskash screamed as his eyes were gouged out. Sherril wasted no more time on him, but flung himself down and kicked upward with his powerful legs. He raked bellies and buttholes with his toe-claws, driving the wounded out of the room.

But there were always more Liskash. Sherril fought as hard as he could, but he began to tire. The walls of the small room seemed to loom up and strike him on the shoulders, the back, the head. Hands grabbed him and pummeled him. He was a mass of bruises, but he could not stop fighting.

He spun and leaped for another Liskash that tried to get behind him, biting his throat and tearing it like one of his feral ancestors.

Suddenly, he felt his head jerked backwards. He found himself looking into the eyes of the commander who had ordered him to jump. He knew Lord Tae was looking out of the creature's eyes.

"How do you like this sacrifice, slave?" the guard captain asked. He raised his fist, and brought it smashing into Sherril's temple. The counselor collapsed, disappointed in himself.

Emoro watched the guards pouring upward, but they were pursuing Sherril. Good. Lord Tae was ruled by his ego. Sherril had insulted him, so he must be punished first.

"I hope that leaves us enough time to get down," he said.

"That way, Clawmaster," said his lead warrior, Nemru Ssar. He pointed to a ladder that had just been vacated by a contingent, all of which was intent on pursuing Sherril. The counselor led the Liskash down the west wall and down a level on the south. Eights of lizards scrabbled at the door behind which he had barricaded himself.

The mental pressure he had been feeling since they came over the wall eased ever so slightly. Lord Tae had fixed his attention on Sherril. That meant Emoro had a brief gap of time in which he must try and get the Dancer as close to the evil bastard as he could.

"Four of you ahead," Emoro said. "Lady, Petru, you stay close to them. The other four, follow. I'll be at the back. Nemru, I'll trust you to find us a way down."

"Yes, sir," Nemru said. He set off running. At the ladder, he stopped to let two warriors proceed the Dancer downward. Petru slid along the rails like a kitten and thumped onto the floor. Nemru went afterwards, with his remaining warrior. Emoro kept one eye on them and the next on the Liskash noble. Petru kept throwing him anxious looks. There was no time to respond. All Emoro's thoughts must be on helping the Dancer to her goal. She kept her arms and body moving in the rhythm that brought the gods' protection. As long as she was alive, they had a chance.

Two more levels to the courtyard. The next ladder was to the east. The levels got progressively larger as they descended, so it was a longer and hence riskier run. Emoro watched out for the guards.

Nemru bore grimly down toward a set of steps propped in the southeast corner. It was leagues from where they wanted to be. Emoro almost ordered him to turn back. What they were doing was in full view of Lord Tae. There were no secrets now. It would be a full battle.

Emoro felt the pressure on his mind return. He turned a wary eye to Lord Tae and discovered the noble was watching them. Though there were Liskash on the same level, they did not approach. Tae was letting them come down, into the midst of his elite guards. Arrogant bastard. He was sure he couldn't lose.

He was about to get a surprise.

"Take the easy way down, Nemru," Emoro said suddenly.

"But, sir...?"

Emoro cut him off. "It's a war game now. We need to live as long as we can."

Nemru led them to a ladder above the eastern wall, facing the entrance to the throne room. The lizards actually let them descend, making room for them at the bottom.

"Your power is impressive," Lord Tae said, peering at Cleotra. "But I see the weakness in it. Even in a group, you are not as strong as I am."

"Strong enough," Cleotra said, her eyes flashing like emeralds. She wove a pattern in the air with her hands and threw them forward as if casting handfuls of sand. "Strong enough to set your slaves free."

"What?" Lord Tae demanded.

The Mrem who were in the square of fighters fell out of their perfect formation. Confusion was on their thin faces. But not only Mrem; Liskash soldiers wavered. Lord Tae shook his fists.

"You hairy mammals are weaklings! You cannot defeat my strength."

Emoro grinned. They were about to try. He made a gesture.

Before the noble could restore full control, the Mrem warriors leaped at the guards.

Five whole eights guarding the lizard noble faced only one eight of Mrem. In spite of the fights he had already fought, Emoro was ready for this one.

The floor under their feet had a sheen of water on it from overnight condensation. Emoro used the slick surface to glide around his enemy, an immense, slate-faced Liskash in jingling plated leather. The guard chopped at him, but he was too slow to hit the clawmaster. With the protection and interference created by the Dancer, Emoro almost felt at an advantage, even though he was unarmed. He ducked in under the lizard's guard and kneed him in the stomach. The guard's grip weakened momentarily, but long enough for Emoro to disarm him and stab him in the throat with his own weapon. The body began kicking and convulsing. Emoro leaped back, and fell on his tail because of the slippery floor.

"Careful!" Petru's voice reached him through the din of battle. Emoro glanced up at the valet. Petru stood with his hands on his hips, his broad body and thick fur concealing the Dancer. Only the tips of her fingers and tail were occasionally visible as she Danced behind Petru. She was fighting the battle none of the rest of them could see.

Two of the guards made for Emoro, chopping at him with their rectangular-bladed swords. He didn't bother to get up, but slashed at their legs with his captured weapon. He gashed one of them on the thigh badly enough that the soldier staggered back.

Lord Tae let out a high-pitched laugh. Emoro scanned the battle to see what had struck him as so funny. To his horror, a circle of Mrem in armor were beating a warrior. The Mrem had fallen to his knees and had his hands over his head.

He glided over the cold stone floor. With the sword in both hands, he swung. The blow severed the spine of the first Mrem. It fell dead at his feet. Emoro felt sorry for the creature, but at least it was a clean, fast death. The others turned toward him, clubs in hand.

Never in his life had Emoro thought he would have to battle fellow Mrem, but he had to see these as puppets, only the skins of good people. If they were lucky, when the battle was won they would have their minds restored, but they were the most dangerous beings in the field at the moment. They did not behave as true Mrem because they were being controlled by a lizard, but they were faster than the Liskash soldiers. Emoro had to dodge swiftly to avoid being bludgeoned.

The Mrem who had been beaten staggered to his feet. With a pang, Emoro recognized Nemru. One eye was swollen closed, and welts stood out under his fur.

Emoro did a quick surveillance of the battle around him. He was pleased to see that there were far fewer Liskash standing than when they had begun.

"We are winning, Nemru," he assured the warrior. "Keep fighting."

"I will, Clawmaster," the male said. He grinned, showing broken teeth in a bloodied mouth. He scooped up a dropped sword and stood tail to tail with Emoro.

Liskash hurried, at Lord Tae's orders, to supplement the Mrem surrounding Emoro and Nemru. Emoro fought like a savage, seeing only one victim after another. There was no time to oversee the rest of the battle. As long as his mind was clear and his arm was still attached to his body, he would fight. The two of them turned and turned again, shifting across the courtyard.

At last, he saw an opening toward Lord Tae. The only guards near him were a pair of small, spindly red-scales. The Liskash noble had his eyes closed, concentrating.

"With me, Nemru," Emoro said. He lunged toward them. Nemru followed.

The red-scaled guards saw them coming and shrieked out a warning. Lord Tae's eyes flew open. They met and captured Emoro's.

Pain overwhelmed him. Emoro felt as if his head would burst open. He clutched his sword, but he could not see to swing it. He felt his body being pummeled from more than one direction at a time. Nemru's voice roared hoarsely in his ears. He fought against Lord Tae's mind, begging the Dancer to intercede for him.

A pillar came hurtling toward Emoro, and struck him in the side of the head. Blessed unconsciousness followed.

"No!" Petru screamed. His voice echoed off the stone walls all the way to the metal lip of the pylon. He strode toward the puny red creatures, pointing a dangerous claw at them. "How dare you lay even a single scale upon my love!"

The Liskash bending over Emoro's fallen body looked up in astonishment. They got up, brandishing their swords. Hah! Swords! As if that would spare them.

Petru took each around the neck with one huge hand and slammed them into one another until they sagged in his grasp.

Emoro lay covered with blood, his eyes open and sightless. Petru threw the Liskash aside and went to pick him up. He felt pressure and scented the stink from the lizard god, but was in no mood to pay attention to it.

"Emoro, are you alive?" he asked. "If you are dead, I will never forgive you."

He was not the only thing that Lord Tae controlled. Gray-scaled soldiers in their appalling armor sprang up around him like weeds. One of them dared to reach for his arm.

Petru shook it off in horror, disgusted by its scaly fingers. "Don't you dare touch me!" Others moved in to grab him. Petru backed away. "I said, don't you dare. Touch. Me!"

The nearest Liskash chopped at him with a sword. As neatly as a Dancer, Petru swiped a leg upward under the creature's guard and knocked his head sideways. Before the slow lizard could recover, Petru ducked and grabbed him by the ankles. The Liskash's helmet flew off. His skull bounced against the floor. Green blood spattered his fur. It clashed with the golden dust he was wearing. Petru was revulsed and offended.

The other lizards rushed him. Petru picked up the Liskash by his feet and swung him like a bat, back and forth. Lizards went flying in all directions.

Slow, deliberate applause reached his ears. He turned to see Lord Tae watching him with amusement.

"Oh, you find me entertaining, do you?" Petru asked, angry beyond any time he could ever recall.

"Very diverting," the Liskash said. "Very."

All Petru could think to do was wipe the smile off the skinny lizard's face. He strode deliberately toward him, flexing and flexing his claws. Lord Tae watched him come, mild curiosity on his face. A Mrem grappling with a Liskash passed between them. Petru kept his eyes on the noble, but he should have looked down.

By the time his foot hit the patch of blood on the floor, it was too late. Petru slid forward his entire length and hit the ground with a thunderous BOOM! The view of the blue sky faded to black.

Petru's fall opened up the field between Cleotra and Lord Tae for the first time since the Lailah had descended into the courtyard. Her energetic leaps and whirls did not weaken her voice. Her ties to her distant sisters were far too strong, now. Their love and warmth bolstered her. Lord Tae's thrusts into her mind were mere pinpricks.

"You are not going to want to be here when he awakens," Cleotra said, in amusement, with a glance at the bulk of her beloved valet stretched at full length on his back.

"Why not?" Lord Tae asked. "A servant knocking himself out?"

"Because having him knock himself out won't have been his fault. It will be yours. He didn't just slip."

"You give me too much credit, Dancer," the Liskash said.

"Not credit, blame. But you will not be able to respond to his accusations. Because you will be dead."

Lord Tae's brow ridge went up. He felt for his servants, and discovered to his horror that the vast room was nearly empty. His Mrem slaves wavered, undecided which force ruled their minds. His control had been weakened by the presence of the Dancer. No matter; he still had Liskash soldiers.

Those still standing hobbled or staggered to range themselves between him and Cleotra. There were only seven. It would be enough. It must be enough.

"You are alone, Dancer," Lord Tae said. "You have nothing left."

"I have everything," Cleotra said, her eyes glittering like emeralds.

He opened his mind to her, commanding her to

spin. Her body swayed in a hypnotic pattern, her arms and legs moving in rhythm. She spun, a look of annoyance on her face. He smiled.

"Then dance for me," Lord Tae said, sitting back on his throne. "Power raising is so primitive. I will have no trouble conquering the rest of your people. I know how vulnerable you are. In the meantime, you will be my puppet and entertain me with your art."

Cleotra stopped. He attempted to make her begin again. She did not. Instead, she undulated toward him, cracking her knuckles and stretching her limbs as she came. Lord Tae watched her in growing horror.

"You should have watched me, Lord Tae Shanissi," she said. "What most outsiders don't know is that this art form, as you scornfully call it, is also a fighting form."

Cleotra enjoyed the look on the Liskash noble's gray face as she gathered herself and sprang, her claws reaching for his eyes.

The Dancer lounged in the cushions on the stone throne as Sherril kicked Lord Tae's head around the courtyard. The funny thing was that its expression had not changed from the horror it wore when he died. Sherril glanced up at Cleotra in annoyance. He should have been the one on the throne, but he could persuade no one else to this point of view. Still, his efforts had been acclaimed heroic, and his name would also go down in the sagas, along with that of his illustrious ancestor. He was reasonably satisfied.

Petru, his fur brushed to feathery perfection, was

dining daintily but heartily on a whole roast arosh brought to him by the grateful Mrem, the former servants of the noble.

"As soon as possible, we are going to redecorate this entire keep," Petru said. "Those tapestries are going on the fire tonight. I cannot stand them another moment."

Emoro lay on a heap of pillows nearby. Petru fussed over him and fed him soft tidbits, the best of the meat. It was difficult for Emoro to chew. His impact with the pillar had knocked out his lower right canine. The rest of the warriors were being cared for, their wounds cleaned and bound.

". . . Well, I know a way you can show your gratitude," Scaro was saying to a female Mrem with dusty orange fur. He fingered the corner of her jaw. To Sherril's amusement, the female looked interested in the offer. Ysella no longer looked jealous of his attentions to other Mrem. She sat on the bottom steps of the throne with Gilas, making adolescent small talk.

Word had spread swiftly among the Mrem of the city of Tae's death. They had been arriving in groups, casting themselves at Cleotra's feet, to beg to be taken in by the Lailah. Cleotra had accepted their homage as her due. To be fair, she had killed the Liskash noble. That did count for something, Sherril thought grudgingly.

"We will wait here for the rest of the Clan of the Claw," Sherril said, booting the Liskash's skull between two pillars and according himself a goal. "I will dispatch messengers to Bau Dibsea and Cassa

Fisook. They should send runners. The rest of the Clan should arrive within weeks. We can assemble here, gather the supplies that we need, and move on to the west as soon as we can."

"Why?" asked Cleotra, gesturing with a graceful hand. "This is a pleasant place. We need food. What we really need is a chance to catch up with *ourselves*. It is spring. The growing season is upon us. This god-hold now belongs to us. Why do we not stay here a season, raise food and fatten our animals? Scattered Mrem will hear of us and join. There will be time enough to set out."

Sherril, as usual, hated any idea that wasn't his, but it was a sound one. It all depended upon how he worded the message—without any mention that it came from the Dancer. It would please him to pick out a chamber in the horrible little noble's keep all for his own. It would remind him of better days, and better yet to come.

"It shall be so, Your Sinuousness," he said.

The following is an excerpt from:

Queen of Wands

John Ringo

Available from Baen Books
August 2012
hardcover

Chapter One

You okay?" Mark Everette asked as he came out of the bathroom. The executive was already dressed and had a suit-coat over his shoulder on a hanger. "You don't look so good."

"Thank you for your phrasing," Barbara Everette replied. Mark's thirty-four-year-old—one year his junior—wife was sitting on the edge of the bed with her head in her hands. She'd been in much the same position when he started his morning ablutions. Normally she'd have been dressed and getting breakfast ready by now. "I'm fine," Barb continued, looking up and wincing at the light from the bathroom. "Just a headache."

"Okay," Mark said, frowning. "You've been getting a lot of those, lately. Maybe you should see Dr. Barnett."

"I doubt that the good doctor could do much for me," Barbara replied. "You're going to be late. Allison can fix breakfast."

"I don't have time to take the kids to school," Mark pointed out.

"I've got it," Barb said. "Just . . . go. And let Lazarus in when you leave."

Barbara sighed in relief as Mark left the bedroom then felt a pang of regret. She really should be drawing strength from her husband, not feeling drained. But Mark had never been much of a nurturer. He expected to be supported and comforted, not the other way around. And explaining her current problem as anything other than 'a headache' would have the men in the white coats at the house faster than you could say: 'Mommy had to go away.' Because Barb was hearing voices.

A year ago this never would have happened. Just a year before she'd been a nice normal home-maker with, on the outside, the perfect life. Nice house in a nice neighborhood, steady husband with a good job who neither cheated on her nor abused her, three great kids and the respect of her friends and fellow home-makers. Need a hand with the bake-sale? Call Barb. Charity auction? Barb's your gal.

Oh, Barbara Everette had her oddities, anyone would admit. Most of her fellow home-makers did not pack a pistol in their purse. And when the rest of the gals were down at Curves going through a gentle work-out guaranteed to raise no more than a glisten, Barb was practicing and teaching a variety of Oriental martial arts and tossing around men twice her size. Both of those oddities were a legacy of an Air Force dad who'd dragged his family around to a multitude of Far East postings as were the occasional loan-words she'd slowly filtered out of her vocabulary. The church ladies of Algomo, Mississippi were unfamiliar with such pejoratives as 'kwei-lo' and 'gaijin.'

But a year ago she'd made either the greatest or the worst mistake of her life. Tired of the endless domestic routine she had insisted on 'just one weekend' alone. She just wanted two days to do whatever she wished, mainly find a nice hotel and sit around reading.

A series of chance happenings, or more likely God-driven choices, had left her marooned in a backwater Cajun town. One that had been taken over by a demon.

That was when Barbara Everette discovered that there was more inside her than she'd ever dreamed. She had been a committed Believer since she was quite young, it was just part of her make-up. She'd inherited the full measure of an Irish temper along with the slightly curly strawberry-blonde tresses, Faith kept that in check.

But in Thibideau she'd discovered there were times for that full-blown rage to manifest in the *service* of the Lord. Such as when a cult was killing women to feed their demon Master. And she discovered that true devotion, faith and service paid off when the Lord gave her the power to not only challenge the demon but blow it's lousy ass straight back to Hell.

She'd survived. Police had become involved. Then psychiatrists had become involved when she refused to admit to 'reality.' There were, of course, no such things as demons. Yes, a group had been committing serial crimes, but *demons* weren't involved, Mrs. Everette. Take the nice pills.

Fortunately, there were people to deal with the police. Barbara was recruited by a group that dealt with 'Special Circumstances.' That was the euphemism the FBI had coined, very quietly, for those rare cases where things got 'beyond normal activities.' When werewolves stalked the night, vampires drifted through open windows, when demons and their worshippers gathered their powers. When the supernatural intruded on their normal and customary doings.

To fight the supernatural required very special skills, ones that the majority of the populace, much less the police, did not develop. It required not only Belief but a firm commitment and connection to a god.

'A' god was the part that at first surprised Barbara. She was the *only* member of the Foundation for Love and Universal Faith that was a Protestant Christian. The rest were pagans of various flavors, Hindu, Wiccan, Asatru worshippers of the Norse Gods. The group was in contact with and occasionally drew on support from the Catholic Church and in some cases specific rabbis became involved when a Hebrew rite was of use. But she was the only Protestant for sure.

But she had, by then, become able to sense the power of others, its source and level. And the people she now associated with were, unquestionably, on the side of Light. Otherwise, she could not have fed power to her closest friend when a demon drained her soul. Given that Janea was a high-class call-girl, stripper and a High Priestess of Freya, the Norse goddess of fertility, joining FLUF had required some reevaluation of the details of her Belief. 'Suffer not a witch to live' simply did not compute.

The current problem was just a new development. She knew that, intellectually, and generally she could wrap her emotions around it. But it was a royal pain in the ass. It wasn't ESP; she couldn't read minds. She just heard voices. If she couldn't feel the similarity to her God channel she'd simply go to the shrinks and get the nice pills to make the voices go away.

The voices were generally simply unintelligible whispers but sometimes they got comprehensible. And generally when she could hear them, clearly, they were negative. 'You're no good.' 'You're not a good mother.' 'Everyone hates you.' Sometimes there were positive messages, but those were rare. She could ignore it, mostly. She knew she wasn't a bad mother, that she wasn't a bad person. But it was just so *constant*.

And then yesterday she'd seen something. She wasn't sure what it was, but it looked like a black snake wrapped around a woman's neck. The head, which was more humanoid looking, had its fangs sunk into the woman's shoulder.

Barb had almost asked the woman about it before she realized that nobody else was noticing the snake. And she'd received a serious 'death stare' from the woman, more like a girl, for no reason she could determine. As she passed the woman the thing had hissed at her quite clearly. Again, nobody in the grocery store noticed. The woman didn't even appear to notice.

But things were getting seriously weird in Barb-world these days.

Mark left the door to the bedroom open, his back set in disapproval, and a black cat oozed into the room and up onto her lap.

As soon as Lazarus curled into her lap, the voices didn't stop, but they were muted. She scratched the cat on the back of the head and pulled him in close.

"What's happening, Laz?" she whispered. "What in the *hell* is happening?"

"Mark, I'm going to have to go out of town," Barb said as she pulled the half-and-half out of the refrigerator. It had taken her nearly thirty minutes to put on a bit of make-up and a jogging suit. Something had to be done.

"Again?" her husband asked, surprised.

"It's been nearly two months since I went to a Foundation meeting," Barb said, trying to keep a combination of annoyance from the voices, annoyance at Mark and low-blood sugar from causing a blow-up. "It's beyond time."

The problem was, okay in honesty, she'd coddled Mark. She had, throughout their marriage, managed the household. It could, arguably, be other than coddling. Mark was a disaster in the kitchen when they were first married, to the point that she'd thrown him out. And, frankly, it was just easier to pick up after him than get him to do it. So she cleaned the house, she did the cooking and the dishes. Over the years, Mark had gotten to the point where he barely knew where the pots and pans were. So going away before Allison stepped into the breach was a serious problem; the entire household generally fell apart.

The *other* problem was, no one knew what Barbara did on the side. Mark was not someone she could sit down and calmly explain that she was now fighting demons. Demons didn't exist in the world of peanut processing. Besides, the Foundation was as secret as the best mystics in the world could make it. So she had to lie. Lying wasn't one of those things good Christian wives were supposed to do with their husbands, but there really wasn't another choice.

"Allison will manage the house," Barb said, looking over at her fifteen year-old daughter. A year ago she'd have said that was the greatest of trepidation, but since the night Barb had 'adopted' Lazarus, Allison had been an absolute model child. In fact, Barb was fairly sure that Allison knew damned well that Mommy's trips didn't have much to do with prayer meetings. Oh, there was quite a bit of praying but it was generally along the lines of *"Lord, please keep the demon from eating my soul."*

"I've got it, Dad," Allison said, looking up from the book she was reading. Normally, there was no reading at the table. Breakfast was generally an exception. "Jason and Brooke will help."

"Oh, yeah?" Jason asked, grumpily. The male twin had his father's dark looks as did Brooke. Allison seemed to draw almost entirely from her mother. "Who's gonna make me?"

"*I* will," Allison said, staring him down. "Or do you *really* want to take me on, little brother?"

"No," Jason admitted, bending his head back down to his plate. "Allison's got it. We'll help."

"Fine," Mark sighed, picking up his suit. He'd finished breakfast and was on his way out the door. "Whatever. Write when you get work."

"I love you, too," Barbara snapped as the door closed. "Lord, forgive me for that."

"He will," Allison said, handing a bit of bacon to Lazarus. The cat licked it for a moment then got it into his mouth and disappeared under the table purring.

"It was uncalled for," Barbara replied, pouring a cup of coffee. Her hand shook so badly that she slopped some of it on the counter and when she tried to pick up a spoon to stir the cream and sugar she dropped it back into the drawer.

"Mom, are you okay?" Allison asked.

"Everyone keeps asking that!" Barbara snapped

then sighed. "I'm sorry, Allison. No, I'm not okay. But I will be. I just need to go...see some people."

"It's not cancer, is it?" Brooke asked, worriedly. One of her friends had died juvenile leukemia when she was still in pre-school and it had left a scar. "You're not dying, are you, Mommy?"

"No, it's not cancer," Barbara said, getting the mess cleaned up and her coffee stirred. She could perform a full Swan Drifts Over Mountain Above Clouds maneuver, something that no more than ten people in the world could equal. She could damned well stir her coffee. "I'll be fine. I just need to go see some friends and get some advice."

"It's the Change, isn't it?" Jason said, not looking up from his plate. "Bobby Townsend's mom is doing the Change. That's what he calls it, anyway."

"It's not menopause, Jason," Barbara said, trying not to laugh. "I'm only thirty-four. That won't happen until I'm in my fifties. You'll be out of the house."

"Good," Jason said. "Because Bobby says his momma's going crazy."

Lazarus had finished his bacon and now oozed back out from under the table and rubbed against her leg. Whenever the familiar touched her, the voices became less. But she couldn't pet him and use both hands. She looked down at him then picked him up and set him on her shoulder. "You. Stay."

"That looks...really weird, Mom," Allison said as Barb pulled out the makings of breakfast. The cat had all four feet planted on her left shoulder and was swaying to keep in place. But he wasn't moving.

"Yeah," Barb admitted, preparing some instant oatmeal. It was about all her stomach was going to take this morning. "But it works." She glanced at the clock and shook her head. "Time for you guys to be done. Out the door in ten."

"Brooke, eat it or throw it away," Allison said. "Moving it around your plate doesn't count. Jason, three bites then head for the room."

"Yes, Mother," Jason said, sarcastically. She really had sounded like Barbara who had gotten *her* parenting skills from a military spouse and her officer husband.

"Mom, what's really wrong?" Allison asked as soon as the younger kids were gone.

"Not something I can explain, honey," Barb said, sitting down at the table.

"Mom, I *know*, okay?" Allison said, gesturing with her chin at the cat still perched on Barbara's shoulder.

"No, you don't 'know', Allison," Barbara replied, tartly. "You suspect some things and you think you know others. If the time ever comes, I'll explain as much as I can. But you do not 'know' anything."

"I know where that cat came from," Allison pointed out.

About six months ago, Allison had fallen into bad company. The bad company in this case being a softball coach with almost 'magical' abilities. Barb had at first feared that there was hanky-panky going on when the coach started taking the girls off for 'team-building exercises.' Then, after using her connections in the Foundation to get background information, her more paranoid side had starting ringing alarm bells. The coach had previously been associated with both Satanic and Santeria sects. And the change in the team had been . . . demonic. Metaphorically.

Barb had charged in in full demon-slayer mode: battle-gear, bell, book and cross, ready to take on demons or acolytes with mundane or magical weaponry.

In fact, the coach had been a poseur. He used the trappings of Satanic rites to convince the girls they had magical backing. When Barb burst out of the darkness he'd, literally, wet himself.

What had Barb charging in was a 'magic rite' involving the sacrifice of a young cat. She'd gotten there just a bit too late to save the black cat's life, but not too late to save the souls of some young girls. They got the immediate impression that playing Satanist was not in their best interest.

And then God had given her a greater gift than she had ever imagined; the ability to raise that cat from the grave. Lazarus came back not as some sort of zombie but as a fully functional cat, albeit one that could not be far from Barbara. Will she, nil she, Barb now had a familiar. Another thing the Bible was, unquestionably, dead set against. It got confusing.

And Allison had proof positive, every single day, that Mommy was something special. Barb had been in full-fig down to the balaklava, but there was no way that a daughter wasn't going to recognize her mother's voice. And when Mom had turned up at home, there was that same cat. Seeing God's power manifest tended to change a person and it had changed Allison immensely.

"I mean, Lazarus is a little *obvious*, isn't it, Mom?" Allison continued.

"It seemed appropriate," Barb said, realizing that she was for the first time admitting she had been the battle-armored figure in the night. "What on earth got you to bring that up *now* of all times?"

"I think it took me this long to work up the courage," Allison said.

"What I do on these trips is not open for discussion," Barbara said and then held up a hand to forestall a reply. "It's simply not. Among other things, there are aspects that are really and truly legally classified. And there are things I just don't want you to know. There are things *I* don't want to know. But the current problem is ... complicated. I'm not going to discuss it with you, but I am going to get help. Okay?"

"Okay," Allison said, biting her lip. "You *are* going to be okay, right?"

Barb stopped considering blouses and decided to get it over with. Digging into the back of the closet she finally found the Black Bag.

The bag had at first resided in the back of the Honda. But as she came to accept that her place was in Algomo not slaying demons, it had crept slowly through the house and eventually been covered by shoes in the back of the closet. Pulling it out was a wrench, the final statement that it was time to go be Other Barb.

She didn't like that side of her. It was more than the fear of pride, one of the deadliest sins. It was that that side of her awoke an anger she fought every day. She had tagged that side of her Bad Barb and, at first, she had mentally translated Bad as Evil.

Over time she had come to realize that the words were right, but the meaning wrong.

"Tho I walk through the valley of the shadow of death, I will fear no evil," Barb said, pulling the bag out and setting it by the bed.

"Because He comforts you?" Alison asked, tearing up. "Because that's not a comfort to *me*, Mom."

Barb reached down and slid open the zipper of the bag, throwing back the cover.

Only the top layer of the materials in the bag were revealed but that was enough. One side of the bag held a katana, a long, curved, Japanese sword that had already slain one demon. The other side held an AR-10 carbine that had helped slay another. Between the two were a cluster of stakes, knives, bottles of holy water and a King James Bible.

"No, sweety," Barbara said, kissing her on the head. "Because I am the baddest bitch in the valley."

—end excerpt—

from *Queen of Wands*
available in hardcover,
August 2011, from Baen Books